W9-BNR-003

THE LACEMAKER'S SECRET

"*The Lacemaker's Secret* allows the readers rare access to Wisconsin's old-country heritage in a very factual and picture-perfect manner ... [Ernst creates] authentic story lines based on real life ways and situations. My old log cabin makers hat goes off to her for bringing attention to many important stories and sites of pioneering and the people who risked everything to begin again in the New World." —Alan C. Pape, former restoration chief at Old World Wisconsin (1971–1983) and preservation editor for *Log Home Guide magazine*

MINING FOR JUSTICE

"The eighth in the series contrasts the difficult life of Wisconsin's Cornish miners with the heroine's burgeoning romance, highlighting both her researching skills and her unusual feel for the past."

—*Kirkus Reviews*

A MEMORY OF MUSKETS

"Veteran Ernst provides a new perspective on the Civil War woven together with a compelling mystery." —*Kirkus Reviews*

"Extremely well-written." —*Suspense Magazine*

"Kathleen Ernst knows how to spin a tale, weave an intricate plot, and hide clues in the embroidery. *A Memory of Muskets* takes two stories separated by more than a century and knits them together into one thoroughly satisfying read." —Kathy Lynn Emerson, Agatha Award–winning author of *How to Write Killer Historical Mysteries* and *Murder in the Merchant's Hall*

DEATH ON THE PRAIRIE

"Fans of Laura Ingalls Wilder will savor the facts … Ernst does an exceptional job of sharing the kinds of character details that cozy readers relish." —*Booklist*

"A real treat for Little House fans, a fine mystery supplemented by fascinating information on the life and times of Laura Ingalls Wilder." —*Kirkus Reviews*

"'Die hard fans of Laura Ingalls Wilder' takes on a whole new meaning when Chloe and her sister embark on a 'Laura pilgrimage,' visiting all of the Laura Ingalls Wilder sites, in search of proof that a quilt given to Chloe was indeed made by Laura herself… Fans of Laura and Chloe both will enjoy *Death on the Prairie*. … Ernst spins a delightful tale of intrigue that interweaves facts about Laura's life with fan folklore, and of course, murder. I give this book an enthusiastic two thumbs up!" —Linda Halpin, author of *Quilting with Laura: Patterns Inspired by the Little House on the Prairie Series*

"The sixth installment of this incredible series… is a super read that sparks the imagination." —*Suspense Magazine*

"As superbly pieced together as a blue-ribbon quilt, *Death on the Prairie* is deft and delightful, and you don't want to miss it!" —Molly MacRae, Lovey Award–winning author of the Haunted Yarn Shop mysteries

"Suspense, intrigue, trafficking in stolen artifacts, blackmail, murder: they're all here in this fast-paced mystery thriller. Chloe Ellefson sets off on a journey to visit all of the Laura Ingalls Wilder sites in search of the truth about a quilt Wilder may have made, and in the process of solving several crimes Chloe learns a lot about the beloved children's author and about herself."

—John E. Miller, author of *Becoming Laura Ingalls Wilder*
and *Laura Ingalls Wilder's Little Town*

TRADITION OF DECEIT

"Ernst keeps getting better with each entry in this fascinating series."
—*Library Journal*

"Everybody has secrets in this action-filled cozy."
—*Publishers Weekly*

"All in all, a very enjoyable reading experience."   —*Mystery Scene*

"A page-turner with a clever surprise ending."
—G.M. Malliet, Agatha Award–winning author
of the St. Just and Max Tudor mystery series

"[A] haunting tale of two murders … This is more than a mystery. It is a plush journey into cultural time and place."
—Jill Florence Lackey, PhD, author of *Milwaukee's Old South Side*
and *American Ethnic Practices in the Twenty-First Century*

HERITAGE OF DARKNESS

"Chloe's fourth … provides a little mystery, a little romance, and a little more information about Norwegian folk art and tales."
—*Kirkus Reviews*

THE LIGHT KEEPER'S LEGACY

"Kathleen Ernst wraps history with mystery in a fresh and compelling read. I ignored food so I could finish this third Chloe Ellefson mystery quickly. I marvel at Kathleen's ability to deepen her series characters while deftly introducing us to a new setting and unique people on an island off the Wisconsin coast. In the fashion of Barbara Kingsolver, Kathleen weaves contemporary conflicts of commercial fishing, environmentalists, sport fisherman, and law enforcement into a web of similar conflicts in the 1880s and the two women on neighboring islands still speaking to Chloe that their stories may be remembered. It takes a skilled writer to move back and forth 100 years apart, make us care for the characters in both centuries, give us particular details of lighthouse life and early Wisconsin, not forget Chloe's love interest, and have us cheering at the end. A rich and satisfying third novel that makes me ask what all avid readers will: When's the next one?! Well done, Kathleen!"

—Jane Kirkpatrick, *New York Times* bestselling author

"Chloe's third combines a good mystery with some interesting historical information on a niche subject."   —*Kirkus Reviews*

"A haunted island makes for fun escape reading. Ernst's third amateur sleuth cozy is just the ticket for lighthouse fans and genealogy buffs. Deftly flipping back and forth in time in alternating chapters, the author builds up two mystery cases and cleverly weaves them back together."   —*Library Journal*

"Framed by the history of lighthouses and their keepers and the story of fishery disputes through time, the multiple plots move easily across the intertwined past and present."   —*Booklist Online*

"While the mystery elements of this book are very good, what really elevates it are the historical tidbits of the real-life Pottawatomie Lighthouse and the surrounding fishing village."   —*Mystery Scene*

THE HEIRLOOM MURDERS

"Chloe is an appealing character, and Ernst's depiction of work at a living museum lends authenticity and a sense of place to the involving plot."   —*St. Paul Pioneer Press*

"Greed, passion, skill, and luck all figure in this surprise-filled outing."   —*Publishers Weekly*

"Interesting, well-drawn characters and a complicated plot make this a very satisfying read."   —*Mystery Reader*

"Entertainment and edification."   —*Mystery Scene*

OLD WORLD MURDER

"[S]trongest in its charming local color and genuine love for Wisconsin's rolling hills, pastures, and woodlands ... a delightful distraction for an evening or two."   —*New York Journal of Books*

"Clever plot twists and credible characters make this a far from humdrum cozy."   —*Publishers Weekly*

"This series debut by an author of children's mysteries rolls out nicely for readers who like a cozy with a dab of antique lore. Jeanne M. Dams fans will like the ethnic background."   —*Library Journal*

"Museum masterpiece."   —*Rosebud Book Reviews*

"A real find ... 5 stars."   —*Once Upon a Romance*

"Information on how to conduct historical research, background on Norwegian culture, and details about running an outdoor museum frame the engaging story of a woman devastated by a failed romantic relationship whose sleuthing helps her heal."   —*Booklist*

"A wonderfully woven tale that winds in and out of modern and historical Wisconsin with plenty of mysteries—both past and present. In curator Chloe Ellefson, Ernst has created a captivating character with humor, grit, and a tangled history of her own that needs unraveling. Enchanting!"   —Sandi Ault, author of the WILD mystery series and recipient of the Mary Higgins Clark Award

ALSO BY KATHLEEN ERNST

Nonfiction

Too Afraid to Cry:
Maryland Civilians in the Antietam Campaign
A Settler's Year: Pioneer Life Through the Seasons

Chloe Ellefson Mysteries

Old World Murder
The Heirloom Murders
The Light Keeper's Legacy
Heritage of Darkness
Tradition of Deceit
Death on the Prairie
A Memory of Muskets
Mining for Justice

American Girl Series

Captain of the Ship: A Caroline Classic
Facing the Enemy: A Caroline Classic
Traitor in the Shipyard: A Caroline Mystery
Catch the Wind: My Journey with Caroline
The Smuggler's Secrets: A Caroline Mystery
Gunpowder and Teacakes: My Journey with Felicity

American Girl Mysteries

Trouble at Fort La Pointe
Whistler in the Dark
Betrayal at Cross Creek
Danger at the Zoo: A Kit Mystery
Secrets in the Hills: A Josefina Mystery
Midnight in Lonesome Hollow: A Kit Mystery
The Runaway Friend: A Kirsten Mystery
Clues in the Shadows: A Molly Mystery

The Lace Maker's Secret

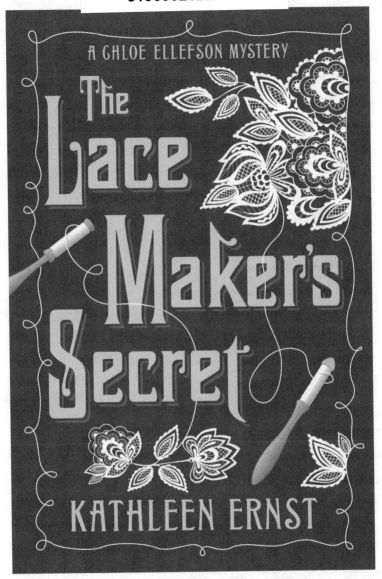

A CHLOE ELLEFSON MYSTERY

The Lace Maker's Secret

KATHLEEN ERNST

MIDNIGHT INK
WOODBURY, MINNESOTA

This is not an official publication. Some names and designations used in this story are the property of the trademark holder and are used for identification purposes only.

FIRST EDITION
First Printing, 2018

Cover design by Kevin R. Brown
Cover illustration by Charlie Griak
Editing by Nicole Nugent
Images on pages 387–392:
    #1, 3 from the University of Green Bay Archives
    #2, 4 photos by Kathleen Ernst
    #5, 6, 7 photos by Scott Meeker
    #8 from The Lace Museum, #2013-0412-001
    #9-10 photos by Beverly Wolov
    #11 by the Friends of Lace.

Midnight Ink, an imprint of Llewellyn Worldwide Ltd.

This is a work of fiction. Names, characters, places, and incidents are either the product of the author's imagination or are used fictitiously, and any resemblance to actual persons, living or dead, business establishments, events, or locales is entirely coincidental.

Library of Congress Cataloging-in-Publication Data
Names: Ernst, Kathleen, author.
Title: The lacemaker's secret : a Chloe Ellefson mystery / Kathleen Ernst.
Description: First Edition. | Woodbury, Minnesota : Midnight Ink, [2018] |
    Series: A Chloe Ellefson mystery ; #9.
Identifiers: LCCN 2018017807 (print) | LCCN 2018022735 (ebook) | ISBN
    9780738755533 (ebook) | ISBN 9780738753546 (alk. paper)
Subjects: LCSH: Murder—Investigation—Fiction. | GSAFD: Mystery fiction.
Classification: LCC PS3605.R77 (ebook) | LCC PS3605.R77 L33 2018 (print) |
    DDC 813/.6—dc23
LC record available at https://lccn.loc.gov/2018017807

Midnight Ink
Llewellyn Worldwide Ltd.
2143 Wooddale Drive
Woodbury, MN 55125-2989
www.midnightinkbooks.com

Printed in the United States of America

DEDICATION

For Bev Wolov, with thanks;

And in honor of all the Belgian immigrants—especially
the women—who endured so much to provide better lives
for their descendants.

The endurance of these Belgian women is incredible.
—Hjalmar Rued Holand,
"Wisconsin's Belgian Community," 1933

AUTHOR'S NOTE

No immigrant who arrived in Wisconsin in the middle of the nineteenth century had an easy time. Still, the trials faced by the Belgians who settled in Kewaunee, Brown, and southern Door Counties were especially daunting. Their stories are honored at the restored Belgian Farm at Heritage Hill State Historical Park in Green Bay, and through programs and exhibits at the Belgian Heritage Center in Namur.

Through my fictional characters I've tried to present an accurate picture of the Belgian immigrants' experiences, but as always, minor details have been changed to serve the plot. The Belgian Farm buildings were moved to Heritage Hill in the early 1980s, but the establishment of the Belgian Heritage Center in Namur is a more recent development. The Center is located in the former St. Mary of the Snows church, which was closed and decommissioned in 2001; preservation efforts began in 2010. Also, Green Bay's Gala Reception for the Belgian Delegation took place in 1917, not 1919.

To learn more about the featured locations:

Heritage Hill State Historical Park
 http://heritagehillgb.org

Belgian Heritage Center
 http://www.belgianheritagecenter.org

Neville Public Museum
 http://www.nevillepublicmuseum.org

The Shrine of Our Lady of Good Help
 https://www.shrineofourladyofgoodhelp.com

CAST OF CHARACTERS

Contemporary Timeline (1983), Green Bay and Southern Door County, Wisconsin

Chloe Ellefson—curator of collections, Old World Wisconsin

Kari—Chloe's sister

Deputy Knutson—Door County Deputy Sheriff

Sharon Bertrand—owner of Belgian Acres B&B, Lejeune Farm West

Toni Bertrand—Sharon's daughter

Hugh Lejeune—Sharon's cousin, Lejeune Farm East

Richard Lejeune—Hugh's son

Elise O'Rourke—lace scholar

Isaac Cuddy—registrar, Heritage Hill State Historical Park

Mrs. Delcroix—volunteer, Heritage Hill State Historical Park

Roy Galuska—restoration specialist, Heritage Hill State Historical Park

Jason Oberholtzer—graduate student studying Belgian-American architecture

Linda Gauthier Martin—descendant of early Belgian immigrants

Ethan Hendriks—Chloe's best friend

Max Compton—curator, Neville Public Museum

Nadine Lamotte—board member, Namur Belgian Heritage Foundation

Renilde Claes—descendant of early Belgian immigrants

John Tate—Chloe's former supervisor

Contemporary Timeline (1983), Villages of Eagle and Palmyra, Wisconsin

Roelke McKenna—officer, Village of Eagle Police Department

Libby—Roelke's cousin

Justin and Deirdre—Libby's kids

Chief Naborski—chief, Village of Eagle Police Department

Marie—clerk, Village of Eagle Police Department

Skeet Deardorff—officer, Village of Eagle Police Department

Father Dan Grinke—priest, St. Theresa Catholic Church

Kent & Ginny Bobolik—residents of Eagle

Historical Timeline, Belgium (1848–1853) and Door County, Wisconsin (1854–1871, 1881, 1914–1919)

Seraphine Moreau Lejeune—lacemaker and early immigrant

Octavie Moreau—Seraphine's twin sister

Jean-Paul Lejeune—Seraphine's husband, Lejeune Farm West

Octavie, Jules, Pierre, Cecilie, Joseph, Ermina—Seraphine and Jean-Paul's children

Etienne Lejeune—Jean Paul's older brother, Lejeune Farm East

Emelie Lejeune—Etienne's wife

François, three sisters—Etienne and Emelie's children

Sister Odile-Alphonse—nun at School of the Apostoline Sisters, Bruges

Dominique Anselme—early Belgian immigrant

*Adele Brise and her parents—early immigrants to Wisconsin

*Father Edouard Daems—Belgian priest who encouraged the first Walloon settlers to settle near Green Bay

*Antoine Ricard—a guide

*Michael Heynen—Consul for Belgium at Green Bay

*Mrs. Brand Whitlock—wife of the American Envoy to Belgium

* *Real people*

ONE

"SOMETHING IS BURDENING YOU," Libby told Roelke McKenna. "Spill it. Now."

"Nothing's wrong."

Libby's eyes narrowed. "I don't believe you."

Roelke turned to the kitchen counter where an old-fashioned percolator burbled with promise. Trust his cousin to just *know*. He'd had another rough night, but he didn't want to talk about it.

"It's more than Chloe spending the weekend in Stoughton," Libby insisted. "Something's been bothering you for weeks."

Roelke poured a mug of coffee and added cream. "No, it's the Chloe thing." That wasn't totally a lie, because he did miss Chloe.

"When are you two going to get engaged?"

Roelke choked on his coffee. "When ... what?"

Libby folded her arms. "Oh, come on. You two are great together. Can you honestly say you haven't thought about it?"

"I've thought about it," Roelke admitted. "And the topic has come up." Awkwardly. He didn't want to talk about that, either. "I'm

1

picking her up later, but she'll only be home long enough to pack again. She's going to Door County for the week."

"Sounds nice." Apparently diverted, Libby turned and cracked the oven door. A rich wave of banana, vanilla, and cinnamon swirled into the room.

"Please tell me that's Libby's Legendary Banana Bread Pudding." His favorite Sunday-morning treat at his cousin's house.

"It is, and it's just about ready." Libby began setting the table with practiced precision. "So, why don't you take a few days off and go with Chloe? Door County must be peaceful in late November. It could be a nice romantic getaway."

"She'll be working," Roelke reminded her. "She was asked to develop a furnishings plan for a Belgian farmhouse that's being restored at an outdoor museum in Green Bay. Heritage Hill, it's called. You know how she is." Nothing excited Chloe more than diving into a new aspect of immigrant history.

"Well, come eat supper with us sometimes." Libby turned off the heat beneath a small pot of maple syrup. "Pour some juice, will you? I'm going to check on the kids."

"Sure," Roelke said, but Libby was already gone. That was how his cousin moved through life—brisk, focused, straightforward. A single mother who supported herself by freelance writing, she didn't waste time on the superficial. Her dark hair, threaded with gray, was clipped no-fuss short. She usually wore whatever jeans and pullover happened to be handy, although today she'd upped her game to black trousers and a royal blue blouse.

He leaned against the counter, took a bracing sip of dark roast, and blew out a long sigh. He *had* to do a better job of hiding what was weighing on his conscience. Libby, who'd known him longer than anyone, picked up way too easily on signals he didn't even know he was sending. Something *was* burdening him ... but for the first time ever, Libby was the last person he could confide in.

He couldn't confide in Chloe, either. They were sharing his family's old farmhouse outside Palmyra, and doing pretty well. She was the curator of collections at Old World Wisconsin, a big historic site just outside the Village of Eagle where he worked as a cop. She had a tendency to fling herself into her history world with a passion he didn't always understand. She was four years older than him too. Still, despite their differences, he loved Ingrid Chloe Ellefson as he'd never loved another woman. He could talk with her about almost anything, and expect a fair hearing and a thoughtful response. But not this.

You have to try harder, he told himself. Figure out a way to live with—

"Roelke!" Libby's nine-year-old son, Justin, ran into the room. Roelke barely managed to get the glass he'd just filled onto the table before the boy barreled into him with a hug.

"Hey, buddy!" Roelke ruffled Justin's hair and turned to Deirdre, who'd followed more sedately. "And how's my girl?" Deirdre, who had just turned five, raised her cheek ingénue-like for his kiss. She wore a pink dress and tights. A sparkly headband held her curls away from her face. Libby, who hadn't worn a dress since her own wedding, was perpetually bemused by her daughter's love of all things princess.

"Breakfast is ready." Libby shooed her family toward the table. She got the casserole out of the oven and transferred bacon to a plate.

Roelke finished pouring pineapple juice before sliding into his chair. "What's your plan for the day?"

"We're going to mass," Justin announced.

"You're going to ... mass?" Roelke repeated blankly. To the best of his knowledge Libby hadn't been inside a church since her wedding, either.

She shrugged, spooning some of the steaming pudding onto Deirdre's plate. "No big deal."

"Mama says you have to sit still," Deirdre said.

"You could come with us," Justin added hopefully.

The thought of walking into God's house made Roelke's gut clench. "Um ... I can't today. I have to go pick up Chloe. She spent the weekend with her sister's family. Do you remember visiting the farm where Anja and Astrid live?" Chloe's nieces.

"Of course!" Justin scoffed, pushing his glasses to a more secure position on his nose.

Talk moved to other things, and Roelke was glad. Being in this kitchen, with these people, was good for everything that ailed him. The ranch house was tired and cluttered. A pile of research books on the counter waited for Libby. A plastic bin of toys stood in one corner. Magnets pinned the kids' vibrant artwork to the refrigerator. Before Roelke met Chloe, Libby and her children were the only family he had. Listening to the kids chatter, seeing Libby watch them without worry in her eyes, was good.

"Dishes!" Libby reminded the kids when the meal was over. They dutifully rinsed and stacked plates and glasses in the sink before racing off. "We'll leave for church in about twenty minutes," she called after them. "Don't get all mussed up."

Roelke leaned back in his chair. "So, mass. What brought that on?"

"I think I've waited too long, actually." Libby began clearing the other dishes. "I need to expose Justin and Deirdre to church, don't you think? They can't make their own choices one day if they've never experienced a church community."

"Makes sense," Roelke agreed. "What else?" He knew her pretty well too.

"Well, if you must know, I want to go. I'm feeling profoundly grateful these days. You know, about Dan."

Roelke had not seen that coming. "Oh."

"When I heard that the kids' father was in jail, I cried with relief."

"Once sentencing takes place, he'll be headed to prison."

"*Good.* When he got so angry at me last fall and started harassing us, I couldn't imagine any positive outcome." Libby leaned back and ran a hand through her hair. "This seems . . . like a miracle, almost."

"Yeah." Roelke toyed with his fork. Dan Raymo had gone all stalker after seeing Libby, his ex-wife, with another man. Roelke was also grateful that the asshole had ended up behind bars.

But thinking about that summoned bad memories. Roelke wiped a hand over his face, remembering the bleak moment he'd realized that Raymo was too smart to get caught; the sickening twist inside when he'd realized it was up to him to stop Raymo before someone ended up dead. Roelke remembered how numb he'd felt after planting a stash of cocaine in Raymo's car. All too soon a gnawing guilt had replaced that emptiness.

"Do you ever go?"

He blinked, interrupted from his gloomy reverie. "What?"

"To mass."

5

"Not in years."

"Well, I'll see how it feels." Libby began rinsing dishes. "You would be welcome to come with, you know."

"Chloe's expecting me," Roelke said, with an undeniable sense of escape. "You guys have fun. I gotta go."

"Sure. But Roelke..." She hesitated. "Take care of yourself, okay? And *please*, let me know if I can help with ... whatever."

After saying goodbye to the kids, he climbed into his truck and drove west. From the small town of Palmyra, where Libby lived, he had about an hour's drive to Stoughton, where Chloe had grown up. November had been cold, but they'd had only a dusting of snow. It was a scenic rural drive, mostly. But Roelke tapped an irritated rhythm on the steering wheel with his thumbs. He *had* to figure out how to live with what he'd done to Libby's ex-husband. If he didn't, Libby would pry and poke and prod until she figured it out.

He slowed to let an impatient driver pass, frowning at himself. It shouldn't be this difficult. No one knew what had happened. It was time—past time—to put the mess behind him and move on.

I'm a simple guy, he thought. All that really mattered to him was being a good cop and taking care of his family. When he started his law enforcement career, it had never occurred to him that one might get in the way of the other. But when Libby and the kids were being stalked last September, when fear turned his cousin into a stranger and the children's lives were threatened, he'd run into that conflict like a battering ram.

Roelke was profoundly ashamed of the choice he'd made. But if he could live that day over, he wouldn't change a thing.

———

Roelke's spirits lifted as he approached the outskirts of Stoughton. He and Chloe wouldn't have much time together today, but he'd take what he could get.

He reached for the slip of paper where he'd scribbled the address of the nursing home where Chloe was visiting her great-aunt Birgitta. Skaalen, that was it. Stoughton—like Chloe—had a strong Norwegian heritage.

He'd planned to park, but when he pulled into the lot he saw her sitting on a bench in front of the building. Only Chloe would wait outside in twenty-degree weather, he thought. Her parka was unzipped, and her long blond braid dangled over one shoulder. She must have been a little chilly, though. She'd pulled her feet to the bench and sat with arms wrapped around her legs.

Roelke pulled to the curb, leaned over, and opened the passenger door. "You could have waited inside," he called.

She didn't move.

"Chloe?"

No response.

Alarm bells rang in his brain. Had Birgitta died? He cut the engine and jumped out of the truck. *"Chloe!"*

She jumped. "Oh!"

"What's wrong?"

She raised both hands in a helpless gesture. "I have no idea who I am."

———

Chloe hadn't realized she was cold until she stepped inside the warm diner. She felt odd. Dazed, sort of. November 27, 1983, she thought. *The day I learned I'm not who I thought I was.*

A gray-haired waitress with a tired smile pointed them to a booth. Chloe tugged off her parka and slid onto the seat. *Pull it together,* she ordered herself. *This was a good idea. It would be easier to talk face-to-face than in the truck.*

Roelke reached across the table and took Chloe's hands in his. "Okay. Tell me again what Birgitta said."

Chloe sucked in a deep breath, blew it out again. "She said my mother was adopted."

"Start at the beginning, sweetie. Take your time."

Anchored by his warm strength, she nodded. "My maternal grandmother's name was Maria. She had two sisters, Birgitta and Elen. Birgitta is the only one left. Sometimes she gets confused. Today when I walked into her room she greeted me as Elen. It always seems easiest just to go with the flow." Chloe nibbled her lower lip. "Maybe I should have corrected her."

"Seems like that might have done nothing but upset her."

"That's it exactly," she said gratefully. "Besides, I've been a bit afraid of Birgitta since I was little. She could be quite impatient." Chloe's cheeks grew warm. "The truth is, I like hearing snippets of her memories."

"But today you heard more than you bargained for." Roelke gently disengaged his hands as the waitress returned with two steaming mugs.

Chloe stirred in a generous dollop of cream before cupping the stoneware. "Birgitta mumbled something about my mother. Then she said, 'We don't know who Marit really is, or where she came from. I *told* Maria not to adopt that girl.'" Chloe sagged against the booth.

"Did you ask Birgitta about that?"

"What popped out was 'Marit wasn't adopted!'" Chloe rubbed her temples. Her mother, Marit All-Things-Norwegian Kallerud, was an avid genealogist and extremely proud of her roots. She'd won a coveted Gold Medal in the Norwegian folk art of rosemaling. She'd served as secretary of the Norwegian Women's Club, president of Society Nora, and frequent volunteer with Stoughton's Sons of Norway lodge. *Nobody* celebrated Norwegian heritage with more fervor than Marit Kallerud.

"Maybe she wasn't really adopted," Roelke mused. "If Birgitta's mind is wandering, maybe she mixed your mom up with someone else."

"I don't think so." Chloe sipped her coffee. Her first instinct had been the same—to deny the accuracy of a senile woman's memory. But I can't pretend, she thought. "Birgitta was very specific. She talked about the day my grandmother brought her new baby to visit her parents and Birgitta at the family farm. The details ... it was a real memory. I'm sure of it."

Roelke nodded thoughtfully. "Well, hunh."

"My thoughts exactly," Chloe said. "Hey, if you see the waitress, could you flag her down? I could use a pastry or something." Comfort food.

He managed to catch the waitress's eye and beckoned her over. "Could we get a cinnamon roll for the lady, and toast for me? Thanks." When she'd shuffled away he turned back to Chloe. "I can certainly understand why this news came as a shock, but ... does it really matter? Marit is still your mom. You're still the same person I fell in love with."

9

Chloe had to gulp inelegantly a couple of times before she could speak. "Thank you, Roelke. And I know you're right. It's just that…" She tried to still the thoughts somersaulting through her brain. "My parents raised me and Kari as full Norwegian-Americans. They were so proud of that, especially my mother. You know how she is."

"I know how she is," Roelke agreed.

Chloe pondered her coffee for a long moment. "It's just so strange."

The waitress planted their plates on the table. Chloe eyed Roelke's toast dubiously before reaching for her pastry. "Do you think I should ask my mother about it?"

Roelke considered. "I don't know about that. Maybe she doesn't know she's adopted. Maybe she does but doesn't want *you* to know. Either way, you'd be inviting trouble."

"You could ask her," Chloe suggested, only half in jest. "She likes you."

"That most definitely is not going to happen."

"Kari and I have a right to understand where we came from. Who we are."

"Well, ask Kari what she thinks."

"I will." Kari had always gotten along with their mother better than Chloe had. Maybe she'd have some new insight.

Roelke glanced at his watch. "I don't want to cut this short, but we should get going. You still have to repack. Although…" He eyed her. "Maybe you should postpone your trip."

"Because of this?" Chloe blinked. "No. I'm expected at Heritage Hill tomorrow. Besides, Elise is flying in today. We're meeting at the bed-and-breakfast in Door County." Elise O'Rourke and Chloe had worked together one summer, years ago now, at a Virginia historic site. They hadn't been close, and had lost touch. Still, it had been a pleasant surprise to get Elise's call earlier that month and learn that she was traveling from her home in the nation's capitol to northeast Wisconsin.

Roelke was clearly unconvinced about the trip.

Chloe studied the man she loved. His face had become as familiar to her as her own—the strong jaw, the dark hair, the ever-watchful gaze. But his eyes were shadowed, as they so often were these days. Roelke was a wee bit uptight by nature, but something else was going on. She'd caught him brooding more than once—jaw tense, eyes troubled. Even at night, when he slept, he seemed withdrawn.

He'd put off her queries, claiming, "It's just work stuff." Still, Chloe felt guilty for being so focused on her own problem. "Are you okay?"

"Of course. I'm just not sure it's the best time for you to go away. This news from Birgitta is big."

She hesitated but decided against pressing harder. "I've got all kinds of appointments already scheduled. Staying home won't change anything. The distraction will be good for me."

Although Roelke looked disappointed, he didn't argue. "Let's go, then. I'll feel better if you get up to Door County before dark."

Once, Chloe would have assured Roelke that she was quite capable of driving after dark, thanks very much. But she had come to accept, even appreciate, his instinctive concern. Officer Roelke McKenna was a perpetual Boy Scout who tried always to anticipate potential disasters and protect the people he loved. She was lucky to be on that short list.

But he can't help me with this, Chloe thought as they left the diner. Great-Aunt Birgitta's revelation had turned half of Chloe's identity into a big black hole—one that likely would never be filled.

———

The sun, a pale smudge among gray clouds, was setting by the time Chloe had driven around the city of Green Bay and headed northeast toward the Door County peninsula, which extended into Lake Michigan. Traffic was light, for the fair-weather leaf-peepers had mostly left the popular tourist destination. Patches of ruby-black sumac and stands of birch trees punctuated the muted landscape of tawny gold, chestnut, and a hundred shades of brown. This was one of Chloe's favorite times of year.

But it was hard to soak in the scenery. At least it should be quiet at the inn, Chloe thought. The timing of this consulting gig couldn't be better. A week away would give her a chance to come to terms with the astonishing fact that she might not be one of the dwindling number of Wisconsinites of "pure" Norwegian heritage after all.

Birgitta's news bothered her more than she would have expected. Over the years she had often rolled her eyes at her mother's ardent interest in Norwegian heritage. Mom's zeal in urging Chloe and her sister Kari to audition for the beloved Stoughton Norwegian Dancers when they started high school (both were accepted), to bake *krumkakke* and *sandkake* (Chloe was more excited than Kari), and to learn the language (Kari was more excited than Chloe) had often been annoying. Chloe's reluctance to revel in all of Marit's cultural activities had caused friction.

A pretty brick farmhouse caught her eye. It was, based on her preliminary study, the style associated with Wisconsin's Belgian community concentrated in parts of Kewaunee, Brown, and Door Counties. Okay, she thought, time to stop fretting about genealogy and start concentrating on the job. She'd been delighted by the invitation to spend a week learning about the experience of Belgian immigrants.

Now alert, Chloe kept her eye on the countryside. Highway 57, the main route into Door County, bisected the Belgian-American community. When she took her exit, she passed more farms—most clearly prosperous. Fields lay dormant, but a few Holsteins watched with languid disinterest as her rusty Ford Pinto passed.

A little more of Chloe's inner agitation ebbed away. This week was going to be a major treat.

She paused to check the directions sent by the hostess of Belgian Acres B&B. *The farm is a bit south of Namur and Brussels, on Hickory Road*.... A mile later she spotted the sign and made the turn. She drove slowly now, peering at mailboxes. Almost there.

She hadn't driven far when an abandoned farm came into view—a brick house set back from the road and a smaller outbuilding closer to the verge. "Oh my God!" she exclaimed, stomping on the brake. "I think that's a bake oven!" She pulled over, cut the engine, grabbed her totebag, and scrambled from the car.

Hit the flashers! Roelke barked sternly in her head.

Chloe slid in, poked the appropriate button, and scrambled out again.

The farmhouse, once a beauty, looked forlorn with plywood nailed over the windows. An old metal windmill, missing a blade, clanged metallically in the wind. Beyond the house a weather-beaten timber-frame barn leaned precariously, on the way to collapse, although a large white wooden six-pointed star, affixed to the gable end of the barn, appeared to be freshly painted. Sadly, neither seemed safe to explore.

But the small stone outbuilding, with a brick chimney and decorative brick eyebrow over the window, was still in good shape. Chloe was pretty sure it was a summer kitchen because of its size and proximity to the house—and because of the smaller enclosure extending from one gable end, which almost certainly housed an old brick bake oven.

Chloe had experience with such ovens. Two had been restored at Old World Wisconsin, one of which was situated in a summer kitchen much like this one. But in all her back road rambles she'd never seen one still standing on its original site.

"This is awesome!" she said happily as she crossed the road. A light wind stung her cheeks, and every breath puffed out ghostlike. The sun had dipped below the trees behind the house. No lights pricked the blue-gray evening in any direction. Surely no one would mind if she took a look, right?

Then she spotted a faint trail of crushed grass and weeds leading from the road to the summer kitchen. Obviously she wasn't the first vernacular architecture junkie to want a closer look.

She trudged up the slight incline and slowly circled the building. The shed's small access door was secured with only an iron latch, and she peeked inside. Yes! The dome of a plaster-covered oven rested on the earthen base that some farmer had constructed a century or more ago.

If it could be viewed from above, the brick oven was shaped like a light bulb. The opening, which could only be accessed from inside the kitchen, was narrow. The oven itself curved a bit wider. Ovens had a flat bottom, constructed about waist-high for ease of use. A woman began baking day by building a fire on the oven's floor. When the bricks were hot enough, she raked the coals out and used a long wooden peel—essentially a big paddle—to put loaves of dough inside.

The shed created a horseshoe of open space around the oven, designed to provide a mason access to check the oven or make repairs. Chloe was tempted to crawl inside the shed to get a better look, but one stone wall was badly cracked.

Don't even think about it! Roelke yelped.

"Yeah, yeah." She circled back to the kitchen instead, which looked sound. To her delight, the door didn't appear to be locked. She pulled off one mitten, turned the icy knob, and stepped inside.

The fading light revealed an empty room. She dug out her penlight and swept the floor and walls with the narrow beam, taking in whatever might linger in this place. She perceived a strong sense of busyness in this room where women had once cranked meat grinders, churned butter, and sweated over kettles of apple butter. Among the cobwebs and dust Chloe imagined a sturdy worktable, shelves of canned beans and tomatoes, crocks of fermenting cabbage and pickling cukes. The room smelled stale now, but she *almost* caught the faint scent of herbs hung to dry.

And freshly baked bread—lots and lots of bread. Chloe wandered the length of the room to the wall shared with the oven shed. The bake oven's door was closed and latched; the slot below empty of ashes.

The ovens Chloe had studied were about two feet at the highest point, and five or six feet deep. Since only radiated heat baked the bread or pies placed inside, dimensions were critical. Bread burned in too-small ovens, and emerged with soggy centers in too-large ones. The two she'd used at Old World Wisconsin could hold a dozen or more loaves at once.

The door on this oven was larger than she was used to. Curious, Chloe held her flashlight in one hand and unlatched the door with the other. Bending down, she peered into the blackness.

Surprisingly, the oven wasn't empty. Had someone laid one last ceremonial fire before closing the door for the final time? She could make out logs...

Suddenly all thoughts of fragrant loaves and capable farmwives disappeared. The dark shapes were not logs.

The last person to open this oven door had not shoved inside fuel or bread pans ... but a body.

TWO

CHLOE STOOD PARALYZED, MOUTH open. She couldn't see the entire body, only legs in blue denim, wedged in one on top of the other, and leather boots.

Bile rose hot and sour in her throat. She stumbled backward, then whirled and fled the summer kitchen. She made it outside before her gut seized and she bent over, hands on knees, retching.

Finally she fished a tissue from her coat pocket, wiped her mouth, and straightened. She turned slowly, scanning the deserted yard. Shadows painted the farm in shades of deep gray and black. The sober palette felt menacing now. Her heart began thudding. Was someone there behind that clump of trees? Peeking around the corner of the house?

The flashers on her old Pinto were, thank God, still blinking. Chloe stumbled to the car, jerked the door open, slid inside. She slammed and locked the door. Leaning her forehead against the steering wheel, she tried to slow her breathing.

This was not, unfortunately, the first time she'd discovered a body. But seeing a body shoved grotesquely into a bake oven, being alone in this unfamiliar place in the dark … she'd never experienced anything like *this*.

"Pull it together," she muttered. "Go get help." But her hands shook so badly that she dropped the key when she tried to fumble it into the ignition.

Lights appeared in the distance. The car slowed as it approached, then stopped. The window rolled down, and a middle-aged woman's face appeared. She didn't look like a maniac, so Chloe cranked her window down too.

"Do you need help?" the older woman asked. "Did your car break down?"

"My car's fine." Chloe licked lips gone dry as parchment. "But can you please go somewhere and call the police?"

———

By the time the wail of an approaching siren reached Chloe, she'd managed to calm down. A vehicle with emergency lights flashing appeared in the rearview mirror. She waited until the Door County Sheriff's Department car stopped before getting out.

The deputy strode to meet her. "I'm Deputy Knutson."

Knutson was a woman. There was something comforting about that.

"And your name is … ?" Deputy Knutson said encouragingly.

"Chloe Ellefson. Um … my full name is Ingrid Chloe Ellefson." Chloe provided her home address and watched the deputy scribble the information into her ubiquitous little notebook. She wore tan pants and boots, and she'd traded the expected Smokey hat for a warm brown knitted one. A gold star showed in sharp relief on her brown coat. Deputy Knutson had a stocky build and calm demeanor that was most welcoming. *Knutson is a common Norwegian surname,* Chloe thought. *We could be distantly related. That would be nice.*

Then Chloe remembered that after what she'd learned that morning, she might be related to anyone in Door County. Anyone at all.

"Ms. Ellefson? Can you tell me what happened?" The deputy's slightly raised voice made it clear she was repeating the question.

"Sorry. Yes. I was driving along when I spotted the summer kitchen..." Chloe talked Deputy Knutson through recent events.

Deputy Knutson turned to consider the summer kitchen, bizarrely lit by her car's pulsing lights. "You stopped just to look at that old building?"

"I'm very interested in vernacular architecture," Chloe said, a tad defensively. "Ethnic folk styles. And the farm is clearly not occupied. It was a rare opportunity."

"You shouldn't have tresspassed, but we'll let that go. Did you see anyone else? Or a vehicle?"

"No."

"When you found the body, did you touch it? Try to move it?"

A shiver rippled over Chloe's skin. "It was shoved into the bake oven, so—no."

"Okay, you stay here." The deputy pulled a flashlight from her duty belt. "I'll go check."

Chloe watched the other woman cross the road. She paused and shone her light on the ground. The earth was frozen, so footprints were unlikely, but perhaps she'd spotted the crushed grass. Skirting the trail, Deputy Knutson trudged on and entered the summer kitchen.

Chloe retreated back inside her car. It's too cold to stand outside in the wind, she told herself as she locked the door again.

More responder vehicles arrived. Soon doors slammed, bright lights lit the clearing, and yellow crime scene tape was strung along the edge of the yard. Chloe wanted to leave but wasn't sure if she should.

Finally Deputy Knutson approached the Pinto, and Chloe rolled down the window. "Did you get the … the person out of the oven?"

"We did."

"And is he … or she … are they … "

"The victim is deceased. There was nothing you could have done." Deputy Knutson glanced away, then back. "You're free to go, Ms. Ellefson, but I will need to speak with you again. Where are you staying?"

"At the Belgian Acres B&B. I don't think it's too far." Chloe hoped it wasn't too far, anyway. She desperately needed to be somewhere warm and welcoming.

"It's right over the hill," the deputy assured her.

Chloe put the Pinto in gear and eased past the assembled vehicles. True to promise, her headlights soon hit a sign: BELGIAN ACRES B&B, with LEJEUNE WEST–1854 in smaller print underneath. Lights glowed invitingly from the curtained windows of a lovely brick farmhouse, and someone had left the porch light on for her too. Chloe turned into the drive.

The front door opened before she'd even climbed the steps. "Ms. Ellefson?" a woman called.

"That's me." Chloe thumped her suitcase down by the door.

"I'm Sharon Bertrand." Sharon held the door wide. "Please, come in before you catch your death of cold."

The phrase was unfortunate, but Chloe managed a weak smile. "Thank you."

She stepped directly into a parlor. The room was comfortably furnished with a mix of antiques—a heavy horsehair sofa, a marble-topped side table, several ornately framed photos of long-dead women and men—and more modern pieces, including a recliner and a small television set. Discreet PRIVATE signs had been taped to two closed doors in the back wall.

Perhaps fifty years old, Sharon had a heart-shaped face and two gray-streaked brown braids. The blue wool shawl draped over her shoulders was clearly hand-knit, and her jeans were faded almost white. Chloe felt better.

"You can hang your things there." Sharon gestured to an already burdened coat tree.

Chloe unwound her scarf and stuffed it into one parka sleeve. "Thanks." She toed off her boots and left them on a mat by the door.

"I was starting to worry. I expected you earlier."

"I apologize. I found ... " Chloe hesitated, but there was nothing to do but relate the tale.

Sharon listened to the terse retelling with a growing look of horror. In a nearby lamp's yellow glow her cheeks lost their color, and she put one hand against the wall as if to steady herself. "The next farm? Right up the hill?"

"That's the one."

"Could you see who—"

"No."

"Dear God." Sharon's eyes were wide. "My cousin Hugh owns that property."

"Oh *no*…" It hadn't occurred to Chloe that the victim might be related to her hostess. "I'm so sorry."

"I think…I need to go talk to the officers." Sharon grabbed her coat then turned back, looking agitated. "That is—do you mind if I leave?"

"Of course not," Chloe assured her.

"This is a wretched way to welcome a guest. Your room is upstairs, first door on the right." Sharon nodded toward the staircase. "Oh—I serve breakfast at eight, but if you're an early riser, the coffee's always on by six thirty."

"That's fine." Chloe nibbled her lower lip. "Listen, would you like me to come with you? Or is there someone I can call?"

"No." Sharon zipped her coat. "My daughter's at work, and there's no point in calling her until I know more. I'll be fine. I'm just not being a good hostess."

"You do whatever you need to do. All I want is a hot bath and a warm bed."

"Your friend Elise is already here." Sharon fumbled with a pair of gloves. "She was exhausted, though, and went up half an hour ago."

"I'll see her in the morning." Chloe was just as happy to have the night to settle her nerves.

When Sharon left, Chloe waited until she heard the key turn in the lock and the deadbolt slide home with a satisfying *click*. She leaned against the door for a moment, grateful to be in. But her heart ached for Sharon Bertrand, who at best would have to live with the knowledge that a horrid crime had taken place at the next farm, and at worst had lost a relative.

Chloe plodded up the steep staircase. Her bedroom looked comfortable, more like a family's guest room than a chamber designed for an inn, but welcoming. The chenille bedspread was homey, not chic, but a comforter folded at the foot looked delightfully warm. A bookshelf was crowded with paperbacks, a few jigsaw puzzles, and several modern photographs, presumably of Sharon's family.

Chloe felt ready to collapse. Blessedly alone, she sat on the bed and flopped back on the pillows. Geez, she thought. What a *day*. She could still hear Birgitta's thin autocratic voice assuring her that Marit Kallerud had been adopted. She could still see the legs she'd discovered in the bake oven. After a few moments she rose up on one elbow and picked up the receiver of the phone on the nightstand.

———

Roelke sat at the kitchen table. He held a knife and a partially chip-carved plate—a future gift for Chloe—but his hands had stilled. He was on edge but didn't seem to want to *do* anything. Part of him missed her. Part of him thought that maybe a few days alone would be good.

When the phone rang he jumped up and grabbed the wall-mounted extension. "Roelke McKenna."

"Collect call from Chloe Ellefson," came an operator's dispassionate voice. "Will you accept—"

"Yes!"

After a click, Chloe's voice came over the line. "Hey."

The syllable quavered. Roelke's heart seemed to skip a beat. "What's wrong?"

Chloe sighed audibly. "I'll tell you, but promise not to freak out."

There were few things he hated more than being told not to freak out. "*Chloe …*"

She told him what had happened.

He didn't freak out, but it took a monumental effort. "Why on *earth* would you go wandering around an isolated farm at dusk? What were you *thinking*?"

"I was thinking I'd found a rare example of vernacular architecture."

Roelke didn't even know what that meant. He was, however, quite confident that it didn't warrant the woman he loved putting herself in an unsafe situation. "You can't just—"

"I didn't call to get yelled at, Roelke. I called to share with you, and to get some sympathy, and to hear your voice before I go to sleep."

He realized he was pacing when he reached the end of the phone's coiling yellow tether. "*Please* don't visit any more deserted farms alone."

"I don't know if the death happened today or three months ago. I just got a glimpse of legs, so I have no idea what condition the body was in."

Roelke pressed one thumb against his forehead. This was so wrong. Chloe shouldn't be seeing bodies in bake ovens. He glanced at the clock over the sink. He could be up there in three hours. He opened his mouth to say so.

Then he closed it again. Chloe wouldn't welcome his gallantry.

"…nothing to do with me," she was saying. "Tomorrow morning I'm going to Heritage Hill to meet the people who hired me. What I discovered is a tragedy. It shook me up. But it has nothing to do with my project."

"Maybe you should—"

"Don't even think of telling me to come home."

He dropped into a chair. "You're already upset about Birgitta's news."

"I'm still wrestling with that," she admitted. "But coming home wouldn't change anything."

He knew that. When Chloe was involved in some history project, passion sometimes overcame good sense, which made him crazy. But the truth was, Chloe was a smart, capable, independent woman.

"Just promise me that you'll be careful," he said with a deep sigh he hoped she could hear across the miles. "*Promise* me that."

"I promise."

Roelke didn't feel any better.

"Let's talk about something else," Chloe said. "Anything new at home?"

"Libby took the kids to mass this morning," Roelke said. He had no idea why those particular words came out of his mouth.

A moment of surprised silence echoed through the line. "She took the kids to mass?"

"She did."

"I didn't know Libby ever went to church."

"She wants the kids to understand what it's all about so they can make their own choices one day."

"Well, that's a good idea."

"Chloe?" He watched Olympia nibbling kibbles at her kitty bowl in the corner. "You know I was raised Catholic, right?"

"Um … yes, Roelke." Chloe's voice sounded suddenly guarded. "I do know that. Why do you ask?"

That, he thought, is a very good question. "I don't really know," he mumbled. "Just making conversation."

———

After saying goodnight, Chloe lay still. What on earth was going on with Roelke? She'd believed that whatever was worrying him was work-related, some confidential case. But she was starting to wonder. Was he having doubts about *them*?

No. She knew him better than that.

Although … she didn't have the most stellar history of guessing what was going on in guys' heads.

"Oh, stop it," she scolded herself. She loved Roelke. Roelke loved her. End of story. Besides, brooding wouldn't accomplish anything. Right now she needed to dig out her toilet kit and go run that hot bath she'd promised herself.

She forced herself to her feet. But instead of opening her suitcase she drifted to the window, pushed aside a pair of heavy Wisconsin-winter curtains, and raised the blind. The front yard was dark.

Chloe lived on a farm even more isolated than this one. She never hesitated to go outside alone at night, even if Roelke was working. Sometimes, last summer, she'd lain in the grass beneath her favorite ancient oak watching the stars sprinkled like glitter overhead while great horned owls called. More recently she'd sometimes wandered across stubbled moonlit fields, savoring the cold solitude.

But this farm landscape, so similar, felt spooky. She gazed toward the wooded hill that separated Sharon's farm from her cousin's. Were the responders still busy in the summer kitchen, or would their detailed inspection wait for daylight? Was the victim Sharon's cousin, or a stranger?

Chloe shivered as an icy finger ghosted against the fine hairs on the back of her neck. I'll take a bath in the morning, she thought.

She quickly changed into sweatshirt and long johns, slid into bed, and pulled the covers up to her ears.

Then she tried to chase away the willies with more pleasant thoughts. She had a week to explore the lives of nineteenth-century Belgian immigrants. She'd done some preliminary reading, but she hoped that unique identities of some of the first arrivals would emerge. Who were you? she wondered, taking comfort in the questions that so often framed her work. What were your lives like?

THREE

SERAPHINE MOREAU TOOK ONE last look at the cottage where she'd spent her twelve years. Just one room, a smoke-stained hearth, two beds built into opposite corners. The air smelled of musty potatoes and stale sweat and the sour stink of vomit. Seraphine had scrubbed and scrubbed but couldn't rid the room of it. Now she sniffed, trying to find a faint trace of her papa's pipe tobacco lingering in the cold room. It was already gone.

Seraphine hadn't cried when Papa died of fever three days ago, sunken-eyed and puking and gray-skinned. She felt oddly hollow, as if she'd slipped into someone else's life instead of her own. Octavie and I, she thought numbly, are truly alone in the world.

As if summoned, her twin sister stepped back inside. "It's a hard thing," Octavie agreed—knowing, as she usually did, what Seraphine was thinking. "We must have faith."

"I know," Seraphine mumbled.

Octavie took her hand. "Come along. Uncle is waiting."

Seraphine followed Octavie outside to the horse cart. A fat man was huddled on the seat, hat pulled low and collar turned high. "Be quick," he called. "It's a long way to Bruges."

Only a watery light colored the dawn, and the November air felt damp and cold. In the row of cottages, thin plumes of smoke rose from a dozen chimneys.

She glanced toward Tante Lejeune's cottage. She wasn't really Seraphine's aunt, but she'd been her mother's best friend. After Mama died, when Seraphine and Octavie were three, Tante Lejeune had brought the sisters into her own cottage each day while Papa worked. Jean-Paul Lejeune was three as well, and Seraphine's earliest memories were of playing with him—gathering curling wood shavings to link into chains, searching for pretty feathers. When his older brother Etienne's teasing grew hurtful, Jean-Paul defended her.

As years passed, Jean-Paul sometimes caught her eye when heading off with Etienne and the other boys, as if to say, *I'd rather spend time with you.* When Papa fell ill, he'd been the first to come chop wood for the Moreaus.

Tante Lejeune had come to say goodbye the night before. "As long as you girls are together," she'd said, "you'll do well." Seraphine had thanked Tante Lejeune for her help and care, all the time looking over the plump woman's shoulder. Jean-Paul had not appeared.

Now Seraphine felt a dull pain beneath her ribs. She'd never been farther than the nearby village. Her father, like Jean-Paul's father, had been a cottar—working the landlord's fields in exchange for a cottage and a bit of the grain he planted, scythed, shocked, and threshed. The city of Bruges, in Belgium's northern region of Flanders, might have well been the moon.

"Put your things in back." Uncle sounded annoyed. Octavie put her small bundle of spare clothes into the cart, and those things that had belonged to their parents: a skillet, tin cups and plates, spoons, a carving knife. Then she nodded encouragingly to Seraphine.

Octavie was older by thirty minutes, and silly as it seemed, that made a difference. The night Papa died, it was Octavie who'd offered comfort. "God will provide for us," she'd whispered, even as tears streaked down her cheeks.

"What if He does not?" Seraphine asked.

"He will." Octavie's voice was certain. Her faith never wavered. Seraphine's faith wavered all the time, like the flame of a candle placed near a drafty window.

But God had provided for them, in His way. The landlord gave the orphaned girls three days to vacate the cottage. They'd found the name and address of an uncle tucked away, and Tante Lejeune took the girls to the local priest. "I know someone at a lace school in Flanders," he'd told them. "I'll ask your uncle to take you there. The school's in a convent, so they'll take you in, even if you aren't Flemish. Just be prepared to do as you're told, and to work hard."

Seraphine was used to working hard. We'll have food and a bed, she reminded herself as she swung her own bundle, knotted up in a sheet, into the straw behind the cart seat.

She was about to climb up in front when someone yelled, "Wait!" Jean-Paul Lejeune was running from his family's cottage, last in the row.

The morning, and her heart, felt a little less raw.

He stopped in front of her, breathless. "Seraphine." He was a sturdy boy with an unruly thatch of black hair and a few freckles on his cheeks. He'd started working with the other tenant cottars that year—plowing and harrowing, and planting, cutting, binding, hauling, threshing, and winnowing grain as the seasons passed.

He'd muscled into the work, done his fair share. "That boy was born to work the land," Papa had said, more than once.

She was glad to see Jean-Paul, but worried too. "Shouldn't you be in the barn?" The landowner was strict.

"I had to say goodbye."

"*Oh.* I'm glad."

"And I—I brought you something." Jean-Paul held out one closed hand.

She obediently presented one palm, and he pressed a rosary into her hand. She gasped with pleasure. "Oh, Jean-Paul. It's beautiful!" The beads, carved from a reddish-brown wood, had the gleam of age and much handling. The small cross dangling from one end was made of brass. "But—where did you get this?"

He shrugged, digging the toe of one wooden *sabot* into the ground. "My grandmother gave it to me before she died."

"Jean-Paul!" It was Etienne. Jean-Paul waved impatiently: *Go on without me.*

Seraphine tried to give back the rosary. "You must keep it!"

He finally met her gaze. "I want you to have it."

"Thank you, Jean-Paul." Tears stung her eyes. "I will treasure it."

"Seraphine!" Uncle definitely sounded annoyed now.

She glanced over her shoulder, then back. "I wish..." But Jean-Paul was already running toward the barn.

FOUR

WHEN CHLOE PADDED TO the window the next morning, the landscape no longer looked ominous. Now that sunrise had banished the dark, her anxiety eased.

Elise was either an early riser or still asleep, for there was no sign or sound of her upstairs. Chloe showered, dressed, and followed the aroma of fresh-brewed coffee to the dining room.

A woman in her late-twenties stood with a steaming mug in her hands, staring out the window. Elise O'Rourke was thinner than Chloe remembered. She looked forlorn.

Then Elise realized she wasn't alone, and the sadness or loneliness disappeared. "Chloe!"

"It's wonderful to see you again, Elise." After a quick hug Chloe stepped back, studying her friend. Elise had bright red hair, and looked a little like an adult Anne of Green Gables. If Anne had slicked her gorgeous hair into a stern bun at the nape of her neck. And put on black-rimmed glasses. And worn a gray suit with pink blouse.

Elise's smile seemed genuine. There were dark shadows beneath her green eyes, but that suggested only a poor night's sleep in a strange bed. Did I imagine that haunted look? Chloe wondered. Probably a vestige of the willies she'd felt the night before.

Sharon came from the kitchen. "Good, you're both here." She set a basket of what looked like gooseberry muffins on the table. "Chloe, help yourself to coffee or tea."

Chloe didn't need to be told twice.

"I was just telling Elise about what happened last night," Sharon added.

"Ah." No wonder Elise had looked sad. Chloe asked hesitantly, "Was the victim identified?"

"It was my cousin Hugh Lejeune." Sharon's face had a gray, drawn look. Her eyes were red, the lids puffy. But her voice was steady. "His son, Richard, drove up from Appleton and made the formal identification."

Chloe's shoulders slumped. "Oh, Sharon. I'm so sorry."

"Thank you. Richard spent the night here, actually. He should be out any time." Sharon disappeared back into the kitchen.

A gloomy silence mantled the room. We're intruding, Chloe thought, exchanging a stricken glance with Elise.

When Sharon returned Chloe caught her hostess's eye. "Perhaps Elise and I should find a hotel in Green Bay—"

"Absolutely not." Sharon put the platter of eggs and sausage, and a glass bowl of fruit salad, on the table. "You girls are a welcome distraction. Please, stay."

Chloe shot Elise a sideways look: *I think she means it.* Elise gave a tiny nod.

"The *trippe* is a local Belgian sausage made with cabbage," Sharon said. "Chloe, since you said you're a vegetarian, I assume you'll stick with the scrambled eggs."

"Can you join us?" Elise asked.

"I ate before milking this morning, but I'd be glad to sit for a bit." Sharon helped herself to coffee and settled at the table.

Chloe broke open a warm muffin with her thumbs, savoring the puff of steam and nutmeg. "Sharon, do you handle the farm and the B&B on your own?" She hoped it wasn't too personal a question, but jeez, that seemed like more than enough work for three people.

"Not quite." Sharon glanced toward the window. "My husband died three years ago, but I've still got eighty acres and two dozen cows. My daughter, Antoinette, recently moved back home to help. She works as a nurse in Green Bay, but she hasn't forgotten how to milk. I'm sure you'll meet her while you're here."

"That will be nice," Elise said.

"And I hire help as needed. I've had a grad student from UW-Green Bay for a couple of years. He's an urban kid, so I suspect it's all a novelty, but he works hard and I'm grateful. You'll meet Jason tomorrow." Sharon managed the shadow of a smile. "He's become the son I never had."

Thank goodness Sharon has support right now, Chloe thought as she scooped up some scrambled eggs. "How long has the farm been in your family?"

"Since 1854, on my mother's side," Sharon said. "My parents died young, and my grandparents took me in. My husband was the youngest of three boys, so when we married it made perfect sense that we live here and take over. This has been my home for almost fifty years, and—"

"Sharon? I'm heading out." A trim, balding, middle-aged man wearing corduroy trousers and a wool shirt leaned into the room. He had the look of an outdoor enthusiast—except for the sallow tinge to his skin, the tight set of his jaw, the flat look in his eyes. He was obviously startled to see Chloe and Elise. "Forgive me for intruding."

"Don't race off, Richard," Sharon protested. "Have some breakfast."

Richard, Chloe thought. Hugh Lejeune's son.

"Thanks, but I'm not hungry. And I need to get home to Appleton. I'll be in touch about funeral arrangements. Don't forget that the crew will be up the hill on Friday. The police said there was no point in canceling." Richard nodded politely at Elise and Chloe before backing out.

"He'd already scheduled someone to replace the walls around the bake oven," Sharon explained. "The barns are probably too far gone to save, but we convinced him that the summer kitchen is worth preserving."

Chloe wouldn't have been surprised if Richard had wanted to raze the building.

Sharon made an obvious effort to be hospitable. "So, tell me, how do you two know each other?"

"We were both interpreters at an outdoor museum in Virginia," Chloe explained. "That was … what, Elise, nine years ago?"

"Something like that."

"And you haven't seen each other since?" Sharon asked. "How nice that you could have a reunion here."

Elise nodded. "I'm in the middle of an internship with the Smithsonian. I'm working with the lace curator at the National Museum of American History, and have gotten particularly interested in Belgian bobbin lace. When the Northeast Wisconsin Lace Guild called to inquire about bringing in a speaker, I volunteered. I'm giving a public program about bobbin lace at Heritage Hill on Tuesday night, followed by a workshop for the lace club. What better place to visit than the largest concentration of rural Belgian-Americans in the country?"

"That's right here," Sharon affirmed.

Elise dabbed her mouth with her napkin. "I called Chloe to see if she had any suggestions for museum collections to see. She told me she was coming up for a week for a consulting job, so I scheduled my visit for the same time."

"I'm working on a furnishings plan for the Belgian-American farmhouse that was just moved to Heritage Hill," Chloe said, in case Sharon had forgotten.

But she nodded. "We're all thrilled about that project. I'm involved with the Belgian Heritage Foundation in Namur, and we're expecting a great turnout for the Heritage Day potluck on Wednesday." She turned to Elise and explained, "We invited all the old Belgian families to attend supper at an old church and bring any old photographs or family heirlooms they might have for documentation. People are excited."

"May I come too?" Elise asked. "Maybe someone will bring a piece of old bobbin lace."

"You're very welcome, but ... " Sharon looked dubious. "I remember some of the old ladies making beautiful quilts, and knitting and crocheting lace collars—even tablecloths. But I don't recall anyone making bobbin lace."

Chloe had wondered about that. Although she knew nothing of Belgian lace, bobbin or otherwise, she knew quite a lot about the rigors of establishing farms in nineteenth-century Wisconsin. At least in the early years, the Belgian women who settled the area had likely been too exhausted to do that kind of fancy work.

"But perhaps someone brought a special piece of lace with them." Elise's eyes sparked with animation. "Or perhaps someone sent a piece here as a gift and it's been tucked away for a century."

Chloe hoped that Elise made a spectacular find while visiting Wisconsin. "You never know," she agreed, chasing a final grape around her bowl before successfully stabbing it.

Sharon crossed her arms, looking thoughtful. "You know, I'd almost forgotten, but when I was a kid, I once heard my grandmother speak of a beautiful piece of lace that came down in the Lejeune family."

"Really?" Elise asked eagerly. "What did it look like?"

Sharon shook her head. "I never saw it."

"Oh." Elise deflated again. "Didn't you ask her about it?"

"And confess to eavesdropping?" Sharon raised one eyebrow. "My grandmother was quite reserved. She lost a son, my uncle Herman, during the First World War. People said grief changed her. We children knew to *never* mention the war." She paused, perhaps remembering that lingering sadness. "Anyway, I guess the lace disappeared somehow. Maybe it ended up in some other branch of the family."

Elise smiled. "Oh, well. At least that conversation proves my point about fine lace sometimes showing up when you least expect it."

A clock chimed in the living room, and Chloe pushed back her chair. "I'd love to linger, but I need to be going. Isaac Cuddy, the registrar, is expecting me at Heritage Hill."

"I'm meeting him this morning too," Elise said. "They have one piece of lace in storage I'm itching to see. Want to head in together?"

"Sure."

The doorbell rang as they were sorting out coats and hats in the living room. Sharon hurried from the kitchen, wiping her hands on an apron, and admitted Deputy Knutson.

"Good morning, Mrs. Bertrand, Ms. Ellefson," the deputy said politely. "I'm sorry to intrude so early." She glanced questioningly at Elise.

"This is Elise O'Rourke, my other guest," Sharon said. "Have you found out what happened to Hugh?"

"Not yet." Deputy Knutson pulled off her hat, revealing a short, stubby braid of honey-colored hair. "Mr. Lejeune's car was found abandoned on an old farm lane about a mile away. Officers have been dispatched to his apartment complex to speak with neighbors. We'll know more later."

Sharon looked disappointed but nodded.

"The investigator assigned to the case asked me to speak with you again, Mrs. Bertrand, if you're up to it. You said last night that Hugh Lejeune was your cousin."

"A distant cousin." Sharon twisted the apron in her fingers. "Two Lejeune brothers and their wives arrived together in 1854. Hugh descended from the older brother, and me from the younger. I grew up on this farm, and Hugh grew up there. I've known him my whole life. ... *Knew* him." She paused. "He was quite a bit older, so we weren't playmates, but his step-sister Karen was my best friend. She died maybe ten years back. Hugh's wife died young, and he moved to his senior apartment in Sturgeon Bay five or six years ago. He couldn't keep up with the farm."

"And the property has been vacant since then?"

Surely Richard Lejeune answered all these questions, Chloe thought. She understood that cops had to check and re-check, watchful for any inconsistency. Still, she felt sorry for Sharon.

"Hugh's son, Richard, hopes to move to the property one day. He's renting out the fields, but he's got four kids to put through college and was out of work for a while, and hasn't been able to make the transition. Karen's kids aren't interested." Sharon gave a tiny shrug. "All my generation wanted to do was take over our folks' farms. That's changed."

"When was the last time you saw Mr. Lejeune?" Deputy Knutson asked.

"It was … about three weeks ago, I guess. He came back to check on the place from time to time. I was driving by, saw his car, and stopped to say hello."

"Did anything seem unusual at that time? Did he seem upset or worried?"

"No."

"Have you thought of anyone who might have wanted to harm Mr. Lejeune?" Deputy Knutson asked.

Sharon raised both hands in a helpless gesture. "Hugh was always a—a prickly sort. He had asthma, and he was small in stature, so as a kid he probably couldn't keep up with the other boys. I remember him as something of a loner, especially after his wife died. But I can't think of anyone who'd want to do something like—like *that*."

The deputy turned to Chloe. "Have you thought of any additional details?"

All I've been trying to do is *forget* the details, Chloe thought. "No. I'm sorry."

"Ms. O'Rourke?" Deputy Knutson turned to Elise. "When did you arrive? Did you drive by the Lejeune farm yesterday?"

"I guess so." Elise smoothed a strand of hair back from her face. "I flew into Green Bay and rented a car."

"Did you notice anything?"

"Honestly, I don't recall," Elise said with regret. "I remember passing the abandoned farm, but I was just looking for the B&B sign."

Deputy Knutson produced three business cards. "Please call if you think of anything that might be helpful." She put her hat back on and let herself out.

"Excuse me," Sharon whispered, her eyes filling with tears. "I've got dishes waiting." She hurried from the room.

Elise looked shaken too. Chloe *felt* shaken, but locking themselves inside the farmhouse wasn't going to accomplish anything. "Come on," she said firmly. "Let's get going. I'll drive."

They left the B&B in Chloe's Pinto. As they crested the hill and approached the abandoned farm, Chloe realized she was strangling the steering wheel with white-knuckled fingers. Elise pressed a hand over her mouth. Chloe was grateful to ease past one county sherriff's car and a white van, and leave the abandoned farm behind.

By the time she paused at a stop sign a mile or so down the road, the shared silence felt heavy. "So, Elise. How did you get interested in lace?"

It took Elise a moment, but she rallied. "Last year I got my master's in American Material Culture from Winterthur and U-Delaware."

"I've heard that's a superb program," Chloe said. Curatorial work was probably a good fit for Elise. Chloe remembered the younger woman as a satisfactory interpreter, but a bit on the quiet side for a job that required talking for hours on end with hundreds or thousands of people.

"I gravitated toward textiles. I want to earn my Ph.D. And when I landed the internship at the Smithsonian and started working with the lace curator, everything clicked. I started taking bobbin lace classes so I could understand what I was studying. Have you ever tried it?"

"Bobbin lace? No. I'm looking forward to your program tomorrow night."

"You're welcome to attend my workshop too. We'll have a few starter pillows available." Elise rubbed her pantyhosed knees with gloved hands.

Chloe took the hint and turned up the heat. She was dressed in warm corduroy trousers, turtleneck, and toasty Norwegian cardigan. "Um … do you have any warmer clothes along?"

"It's a Virginia thing. I like to present a professional image." Elise flushed. "I mean … no offense."

"None taken," Chloe said truthfully. She'd been working at Old World Wisconsin for a year and a half, and the only dresses she'd worn had been nineteenth-century reproductions. Her kind of job.

"Anyway, the Smithsonian lace collection is *amazing*. As I learned more about how lace is made, how much work and care went into each piece … well, it's humbling. In the 1700s, a laceworker would have needed a year of fifteen-hour days to make a meter of Valenciennes lace for a sleeve ruffle."

"Yikes. What do you know about the lace at Heritage Hill?"

"Isaac Cuddy said they have only a small study collection, but he sent a copy of an accession form for one piece that he thought might be of interest. Are you familiar with the World War I lace project?"

"I am not."

"When Germany occupied Belgium in 1914, Great Britain established a blockade of the Belgian borders so supplies couldn't reach the Germans. Unfortunately, that also isolated seven million Belgian civilians—including fifty thousand lacemakers who needed

41

their meager income more than ever." Elise twisted in her seat as if eager to make Chloe understand. "A Commission for Relief in Belgium was established among Allied nations. They negotiated to get shipments of thread to the Belgians. Wealthy people placed orders for lace."

"What an awesome program!"

"Chloe, the surviving war lace is astonishing. Unique in the lace world, and rare. Collectors would pay a fortune for a piece, but of course the *real* value lies in the stories they represent."

"And you think one of those pieces of war lace is here in Wisconsin?"

"The accession form says 'Valenciennes style, World War I.' Perhaps a wealthy Green Bay patron purchased it during the war."

"It's certainly possible." Chloe craned her neck, trying to see a road sign before a moving truck in the next lane blocked it.

"Maybe a treasure is buried in the Heritage Hill collection. It happens all the time, you know."

Chloe did know. No curator was an expert in every area. If a family donated a handful of items to a museum, some rare and valuable piece might well get cataloged and stored away in oblivion.

Their exit appeared, and she pulled over. "You'll find out soon. We're almost there."

Heritage Hill was well named. The outdoor museum sprawled on a fifty-acre slope in Allouez, on the city of Green Bay's south side near the Fox River. Highway 172 formed one border, the racing traffic providing disconcerting contrast to the grounds. But that means the site is easily accessible, Chloe thought. Old World Wisconsin, where she worked, was more remote, which made finding adequate minimum-wage staff difficult, and coaxing school groups to make the drive from wherever an ongoing challenge.

"How did you get involved here?" Elise asked as they walked from the parking lot to the Education Center.

"Heritage Hill is a State Historical Park, owned by the Department of Natural Resources," Chloe told her. "I did a consultant gig last year when an old lighthouse on state land was being restored. Pottawatomie Lighthouse, in Rock Island State Park, off the tip of the Door County peninsula. The park manager recommended me to the folks here. They don't have a collections curator at the moment."

Inside the large, modern building, Chloe and Elise checked in with the person at the ticket desk. Two minutes later a tall, broad-shouldered young man hurried to greet them. He was a good-looking kid—he couldn't have been out of college for more than a year or so—with thick blond hair and wire-rimmed glasses. The only odd note for a guy predestined to turn female heads was his air of mild anxiety. "Chloe? Elise? I'm so sorry to have kept you waiting." He'd been clasping his hands but pulled them apart long enough to quickly press each woman's fingers. "I'm Isaac Cuddy."

Once everyone had been identified, Isaac looked from Chloe to Elise and back again. "I'm delighted that you're both here, but I'm not sure how to divide my time."

"We've got all week," Chloe said. "I'm interested in learning as much as I can, and I suspect Elise is as well—"

"Absolutely," Elise confirmed.

"—so for now, there's no need to split up," Chloe finished. "After hearing Elise talk about World War I lace, I'm almost as eager to see your piece as she is."

Isaac nodded. "We store our study collections in the basement of our 1851 Moravian Church. Let me grab my coat." He hurried away.

Elise's forehead furrowed. "In the basement of an old church?"

"Ha! You've gotten spoiled at the Smithsonian." Chloe grinned. "Welcome back to the historic sites world."

When Isaac returned he was well bundled and wearing a fur hat appropriate for the Russian front. "It's just a short walk," he told Elise, with a sympathetic glance at her inadequate attire.

They left the education building and started down the slope on a wide, paved path. The temperature was in the single digits and a light wind raced over the hill. "Oh my," Elise murmured, tugging at her coat collar.

"Isaac?" Chloe asked. "How did a living history site come to be owned by the DNR?"

"This property used to belong to the prison." He gestured toward the brooding gray hulk of a building, ringed with walls and razor wire, visible in the distance beyond Highway 172. "Inmates maintained orchards here. But construction of the new bridge across the Fox River sliced the property in two, and this portion went to the DNR."

"I'm a little surprised the DNR developed the park as an outdoor museum," Chloe said.

"Oh, the idea didn't come from the DNR," Isaac assured her. "It was the citizens of Green Bay and surrounding communities. Especially the ladies. They wanted to preserve and protect the heritage of northeastern Wisconsin. The DNR approved their plan."

"God bless caring citizens," Elise murmured.

"Especially the ladies," Chloe added. Such civic-minded souls were a godsend to perpetually overwhelmed civil servants.

They reached the Moravian Church, a simple white frame structure. "At Old World we use the basement of our church for artifact storage too," Chloe confided as Isaac led the way down the cellar stairs.

"We have over six thousand objects in our collection," Isaac told them. "Most of them are in the restored buildings, but a small subset is here." He worked a key. "This way."

The room was lined with industrial shelving units, most filled with gray archival boxes. A few larger items lived on shelves lined with acid-free paper. "I got the lace pieces out yesterday." Isaac gestured to a large box resting on a worktable. "The piece of Valenciennes war lace is there in the center."

Elise stepped eagerly to the table—and immediately shook her head. "No. This is not Valenciennes." She leaned closer, studying the cream-colored lace. "Valenciennes incorporates flowers or other natural motifs. The geometric pattern in this remnant is the Torchon style."

Isaac, open-mouthed with dismay, took a moment to respond. "But...but the accession form says..."

"Does the accession number on the artifact match the accession form?" Elise asked.

"It does," Isaac insisted. "I double-checked."

"Where is the number?"

"It's tucked into the tissue." Isaac pointed to a piece of tissue paper carefully set aside. "Our lace pieces were all labeled and packed before I came to work here. I imagine whoever did the work didn't want to attach labels because the lace itself is so fragile."

"Unfortunately," Elise said, "having the accession numbers loose means they can get separated from the artifacts. A tag with a thread loop passing through the lace is almost always a better way to go."

Isaac was literally wringing his hands. Chloe couldn't bear the young man's distress. "Mistakes happen, Isaac. Someone just got a couple of pieces mixed up. Let's go through the other lace items."

Isaac made a *you go ahead* gesture, so Elise traded her leather gloves for a pair of cotton ones and took charge. There were eleven other pieces of lace still packed in tissue paper shrouds in the storage box. Elise removed them one by one. Isaac fetched the accession records for those so they could check for accuracy. The tag bearing the accession number for each piece—two collars, five doilies, and four unidentified strips or scraps—matched the description on the accession form.

"That's it," Elise said finally. "All of those pieces are correctly identified."

Isaac held out a piece of paper. "And here's the accession form that refers to the Torchon remnant. So ... I guess somehow ... the Torchon lace and the Valenciennes war lace got matched with the wrong labels. And then the war lace ... disappeared."

The basement was so quiet that Chloe could hear a dehumidifier kick on with a low electronic hum. There was no way to sugarcoat the situation. The lace Elise had most wanted to see, by far the most significant piece in the collection, was missing.

FIVE

IT WAS A COLD two-day journey from the cottage in Grez-Doiceau, Brabant Province, to the School of the Apostoline Sisters in the city of Bruges. Seraphine felt brittle and insignificant, like a leaf skittering aimlessly over a field.

Beneath her cloak she fingered Jean-Paul's rosary, taking courage from the beads. She knew why he'd given her such a treasure. For many years Mama's rosary had hung in a place of honor by the door. Seraphine had liked it there, liked feeling as if the mother she barely remembered was blessing her each time she left the cottage. After Papa died, and Seraphine and Octavie were preparing to leave, Octavie had reverently taken it from the nail. "Who shall carry this?"

Seraphine wanted very much to have that rosary. She also knew that Octavie longed for it even more. "You," Seraphine had whispered. Later, she'd confessed her envy to Jean-Paul. He hadn't said much, but he'd listened. Jean-Paul was like that.

47

Although Seraphine felt guilty that her story had prompted him to give up his grandmother's gift, she couldn't bring herself to regret it. Now I have beads of my own, Seraphine thought, to remind me of home.

They jounced through towns and past brown farm fields only dreaming of spring. Seraphine wasn't sure when they left Wallonia and entered Flanders. Belgium, only eighteen years old, was home to different groups of people. She'd been born in the southern region and spoke Walloon. The convent was in the northern Flanders region, where people spoke Flemish.

On the second afternoon Seraphine dozed off. Some time later she woke with a start. Their uncle had stopped the cart. "Have we arrived?" Seraphine asked.

"I'm not sure," he admitted.

Seraphine pressed her shoulder against Octavie's as she got her first look at Bruges. Tall, steep-roofed houses were jammed together. Carts and wagons and coaches and riders filled the narrow streets. Several ragged boys raced by, shouting words she didn't understand. Octavie and I don't belong here, she thought. But they didn't belong back in Grez-Doiceau any more, either. They didn't belong anywhere.

"It may be up there," Uncle muttered, rubbing his chin. "Over the bridge." He pointed ahead toward a huge brick church with a red tile roof. He slapped the horse with the lines and they lurched beneath an arch and around a corner. They stopped in front of a big double door painted dark green.

Their uncle lumbered down from the cart. He pulled a long rope dangling beside the door and a bell rang somewhere beyond. A little door within the great door opened, and a woman's face appeared at the grille.

"I want to go home," Seraphine whispered, even though she knew they could not.

Octavie squeezed her sister's hand. "We must have faith."

"I'm *trying* to," Seraphine muttered.

After Uncle explained his business, the big door opened. The woman waiting behind it wore a black dress with wide sleeves. A white cap fit snugly around her face. It was a round face, and looked kind. "I am Sister Odile-Alphonse," she called in accented Walloon. "Come inside, girls. I think you need some warm milk." They silently climbed down from the cart and took their bundles from the back. Their uncle, without a word, clambered back to the seat and called to the horse.

Sister Odile-Alphonse led the girls through a courtyard bordered on three sides by buildings and on the fourth by a tall brick wall. It was a relief to be off the crowded streets. Inside, the convent was clean and quiet. Sister Odile-Alphonse had them wait in a dining room while she stepped into the kitchen. Seraphine had never seen such a big room, or such fine furniture.

The nun returned with two steaming mugs. Seraphine took a sip and felt the warm milk slide down her throat and pool in her belly. Milk was a treat, and this was rich and good, nudging aside the day's damp chill.

Sister Odile-Alphonse sat down across the table. "Now, girls. Tell me about yourselves."

They exchanged a glance. "Our papa just died," Octavie said.

"What of your mother?"

Seraphine licked her lips. "She died when we were three."

"You've had much sorrow in your lives." Sister Odile-Alphonse tipped her head, regarding the girls with sympathy. "But this will be your home now. Our holy rule is 'Obedience, prayer, and work.' Do you understand?"

"Yes, Sister," the girls murmured. Seraphine hoped she could satisfy the nuns.

"In addition to making lace, you will study the catechism, reading, and writing. And Flemish, of course. Most of our students live nearby. As boarders, you will also work in the garden and help clean. When you turn sixteen, you will devote most of your time to lacework. Do you have any experience making lace?"

"No, Sister." Seraphine's heart grew heavy. Was experience a requirement? She'd glimpsed some of the women in the tenant cottages sitting by their windows on sunny winter days, bent over their bobbins and lace cushions. Many farmwomen earned a bit of extra money making lace in the winter. But no one had taught the motherless Moreau girls how it was done.

The nun seemed to understand her distress. "You're twelve? We do like to start girls who are seven or eight, but no matter. I expect you'll progress nicely."

Seraphine nodded earnestly. If making lace meant porridge in her belly and a safe place to sleep, she would learn to make lace.

"Lace has been made in Bruges for almost three hundred years. Do you know how the tradition began?"

"No, Sister," Octavie said.

Sister Odile-Alphonse smiled. "Once there was a family here in Bruges, so poor they lived in a rude little hut. A daughter named Serena, who was skilled at spinning thread, was their only source of income. She worked hard but her meager earnings were never enough. Serena was in love with Arnold, the son of a wealthy merchant, and Arnold was in love with her. One melancholy day she sat beside a lake and vowed to the Virgin that she would not marry Arnold until her family could be rescued from their misery."

Seraphine thought of Jean-Paul, sweat-stained and grinning, as he came from the field.

"A light appeared!" Sister Odile-Alphonse's face glowed. "It was the Virgin, who dropped threads that sifted through the tree branches and fell onto Serena's lap. Serena believed that the beautiful patterns they made were the answer to her prayer. She began to reproduce the designs, and attached the threads to little lengths of wood to help keep them sorted. Her lace became famous for its beauty. Wealthy people traveled from far away to purchase it. Serena and Arnold married after all. And *that*," she concluded triumphantly, "was the beginning of bobbin lace in Bruges."

"What a lovely story," Octavie breathed.

Seraphine fingered the rosary still clutched in one hand. What would it feel like to be visited by the Virgin? And to earn so much money that she never had to worry about anything again?

"Come along." Sister Odile-Alphonse rose with a rustle. "I'll show you."

She led the girls down a cold, silent corridor—so much empty space! Seraphine marveled—to a workroom where a dozen women were seated in high-backed chairs. Each had a little wooden stand holding a cushion in front of her. A piece of paper was affixed to the cushion, pricked with pins. Threads unspooled from dozens of wooden bobbins. No one stopped working when the door opened. Fingers flew among the bobbins, and a soft wooden *click-click-click* filled the room.

Sister Odile-Alphonse touched Seraphine's shoulder. "Come." She led the girls to a table in the back of the room. "These are samples of our finest laces." ·

Seraphine leaned closer … and could find no words. Sister Odile-Alphonse was still talking, using words like *Guipure* and *Torchon* and *Valenciennes* to identify samples, but the words seemed muted, far away. Seraphine stretched one finger toward a length of particularly delicate lace about seven inches wide. One edge was straight, but the other was deeply scalloped. The lacemaker had created a handful of flowers in every scallop.

"Do you like that piece?" the nun asked softly.

Something quivered in Seraphine's chest. This was beautiful for its own sake, with no necessity, no function. She had never seen anything like it.

"If you study and work hard," Sister Odile-Alphonse said, "one day you will be a *dentellière*, a lacemaker, able to do such fine work too."

For the first time since Papa had died, hot tears brimmed in Seraphine's eyes. I *want* this, she thought, and sent up a quick prayer of thanks.

———

JANUARY 1849

"No, not that bobbin." The nun leaned over Seraphine's work. "Look to the pattern."

The gap-toothed little girl in the next chair snickered. Seraphine shot her a fierce look: *Be quiet!*

"None of that," the nun chided. "Take your time. You're too impatient, child."

Seraphine nodded obediently, but frustration simmered inside. She and Octavie were the oldest girls in the classroom. The others were little, just seven or eight. And all of them were more adept at manipulating the bobbins than she was.

After the nun moved on, Octavie leaned close. "Don't mind," she whispered.

Seraphine frowned. She would mind—until she knew how to produce the delicate work herself. Keep trying, she ordered herself, and bent over her pillow.

In their first weeks at the convent, the newness of everything had kept her occupied. There were routines to learn, names to remember, expectations to be met. In addition to learning lace, Octavie and Seraphine struggled to catch up with the school lessons. Seraphine fell asleep trying to memorize everything she needed to know: where to sit in the chapel, how thick Cook wanted carrots sliced for soup, which nuns didn't mind whispers in the classrooms and which did, where to empty the slop buckets.

But she'd been at the convent for over two months now. The strangeness was wearing away ... but homesickness had crept into the empty spaces. Sometimes Seraphine cried silently into her pillow at night. It was little things that hurt the most. The sound of a nun humming her father's favorite hymn transported her back to the farm where she'd been born. The smell of sausage sizzling in a skillet reminded her of butchering time at the farm, when everyone could eat meat. A drover's whistle from the street brought to mind Jean-Paul, amusing himself by calling to birds overhead.

Keeping busy is best, Seraphine reminded herself, as the nun clapped her hands to signal the end of work time. Seraphine folded her work away reluctantly.

The next day was Sunday, and after chapel Seraphine slipped away from the other boarders and returned to the empty classroom. She felt a welcome sense of calm steal inside as she studied the pattern—the paper pricked with pins that had originally confused her—on her pillow. It was easier to work without the little girls busily clicking their bobbins nearby. She liked being alone with her work.

But she'd no more than begun when an elderly nun entered the classroom. "Seraphine!" she exclaimed, her voice rough as a rusty hinge. "I've been searching for you. Come with me." The woman beckoned with one crabbed hand.

Had she done something wrong? Bewildered, Seraphine hastily covered her work and scurried after the nun. Along the corridor, down the stairs, out the door, across the courtyard ... "Oh!"

Jean-Paul Lejeune stood waiting by the gate.

Seraphine stopped moving. He didn't move either, but some tension seemed to ease from his shoulders, and his lips twitched toward a small smile. Finally she collected her wits and ran to greet him. "Jean-Paul! What are you doing here?"

He glanced toward the nun watching with arms folded across her chest, hands tucked into her voluminous black sleeves. "I came to visit."

"Is something wrong?" Seraphine couldn't imagine why else he might have come.

"No," he said patiently. His cheeks were red with cold, and he slid his hands into his armpits for warmth. But beneath the black hair peeking from his wool cap, his eyes glinted, as if pleased with his surprise. "I wanted to see you."

"But how ... "

"I left right after work yesterday," Jean-Paul explained. "I got a ride from a merchant, in exchange for me driving partway through the night so he could sleep." He shrugged, as if threshing grain all day and then setting out on the road was of no consequence.

"But how will you get back?"

"I can't stay long. No more than an hour or so before I meet the merchant." He shrugged again, as if driving through the night in order to get home in time to thresh grain all day was of no consequence, either.

"Oh, Jean-Paul." Seraphine studied the familiar face—the steady eyes, the thin scar on his chin, the strong nose—which she had expected to never see again. "I'm so glad you're here."

SIX

THE FORD FAIRLANE'S DRIVER rolled down his window as Roelke approached the car. "Good morning, Officer." He was a heavy-set guy, maybe twenty-five, wearing a suit. "Was I speeding?"

"Posted speed dropped to thirty when you entered the village," Roelke told him. "You were fourteen over."

"Sorry," the guy said sheepishly. "I shouldn't play 'Radar Love' when I'm driving."

"Radar Love?" That was an extenuating circumstance. Roelke let the guy off with a warning and watched him drive away.

He wished he could jump into his truck, pop a cassette into the tape deck, and head off himself. Things had been quiet in Eagle lately, which was good in the obvious way, but he felt restless. He was bored. He missed Chloe. He was worried about her too.

Okay, enough with the speed trap. He got in the squad, noted the pullover on his duty sheet, and drove back to the Eagle Police Department.

Marie, the EPD clerk, was on the phone in the small main room. Chief Naborski's door was closed. Roelke settled at the officers' desk and spent an hour catching up on paperwork, the eternal bane of his professional life, before getting bored again.

He pulled out a folder of unsolved crimes he'd created for just such times. Not petty stuff like missing bicycles but real cold cases, dating back a decade or so. Eagle didn't have many, and for the most part they weren't sensational. A house fire that might have been arson. A runaway teen who was never found. Only one murder, the Bobolik case.

Roelke opened the Bobolik file. Five years earlier, when he was still working for the Milwaukee PD, Hattie Bobolik was shot in the back and left to die on the kitchen floor of her Eagle home. Investigators suspected her husband, Kent Bobolik, had done the killing, but they'd never been able to prove it.

In the past year the Eagle PD had fielded three domestic violence calls from the Bobolik residence. Roelke didn't know if Kent had killed his first wife. He *did* know that Kent had a habit of knocking his second wife around.

Drumming the desk with a pen, Roelke read slowly through the records again. He did this every once in a while. He liked feeling that Hattie Bobolik had not been forgotten. He liked imagining that one day he might find a tiny detail that everyone else had overlooked, something that provided a new avenue of pursuit, something that would give Kent enough prison time to contemplate his transgressions.

But that is not going to happen today, he decided some time later, and slapped the file closed. Why did he think he might find a clue that the experienced detectives had missed? I might as well go back out on patrol, he thought. Seeing and Being Seen. Taxpayers liked that.

He was washing his mug when Skeet Deardorff arrived. Skeet, a ginger-haired officer in his late twenties, lifted a hand in greeting. "Hey, Roelke. How's the morning been?"

"Too quiet," Roelke grumbled. "Pulled over one speeder. That was it."

"Well, one ticket's better than nothing." Skeet opened his locker.

"I let him off with a warning," Roelke admitted. "He was playing 'Radar Love.'"

"Extenuating circumstance." Skeet grinned. "I let a guy off once for a Lynryd Skynyrd song."

"'They Call Me The Breeze'?"

"Yeah. I love that one."

Marie swiveled from her typewriter. "I do not understand you two," she said pertly, and turned on her radio. Olivia Newton John was wondering if they'd ever been mellow. Skeet and Roelke shared a pained glance.

The phone rang before Marie could add further commentary. "Eagle Police Department ... " She listened, then nodded. "I'll send an officer over." After hanging up, she fixed Roelke with a stern look. "That was Father Dan Grinke at the Catholic church, calling to report some vandalism. If you're in the mood to do something productive, go check it out."

"On my way." Roelke grabbed the car keys and headed out the door. It didn't pay to get on Marie's bad side.

St. Theresa Catholic Church stood on the north side of town, across the street from the back of Sasso's tavern. It was an old building constructed of the pale brick Chloe called "Cream City," made from clay found near Milwaukee. The parking lot angled behind the sanctuary, and Roelke often pulled in when on patrol, especially on second shift. He hadn't been inside the church since attending the funeral of Bonnie Burke Sabatola, who'd been murdered just outside of Eagle over a year ago.

The man waiting for him was not the stout, elderly priest he remembered. Instead, a guy about his own age—Roelke was almost thirty—came bounding down the church steps. He was thin, with chestnut hair swept back from a high forehead, intelligent eyes, and a gentle smile. "I'm Father Dan." He extended a hand. "Thanks for coming, Officer ... " He squinted at Roelke's name badge.

"It's Rell-kee," Roelke said helpfully. He was used to people stumbling over his name. "Roelke McKenna. I understand you've had some vandalism?"

"Come into the sanctuary." Father Dan led the way.

Once inside, Roelke pulled off his hat and instinctively paused to bless himself. The church had a high, soaring roof. Stained glass windows glowed in the winter sun, bathing the sanctuary in soft light. It was silent. Peaceful. Roelke felt a long-forgotten sense of comfort.

Then that comfort wriggled away, replaced with a heaviness that pressed on his chest and weighted his shoulders. He put a hand on a pew to steady himself. He had no business feeling comfort inside a church.

"Officer McKenna? Are you all right?"

"Yes, I—I'm fine." Roelke restored his imperturbable cop face. "Where is the problem?"

"Up here." The other man strode up the right-side aisle, stopping by the window closest to the chancel. The design featured shades of blue, but the symmetry at the bottom was marred by a piece of cardboard taped over the glass. He eased it free and an icy

59

breeze shot through a jagged hole. He picked up a palm-sized rock that had been left on the windowsill. "This is the projectile. I found it on the floor."

Roelke eyed the stone, the hole. "That would do it. Do you have any idea who might have thrown the rock?"

The priest opened his hands. "No."

"No recent run-ins with surly teens? No one angry because their son wasn't chosen altar boy?"

"No." Father Dan's mouth twisted in a wry smile. "I haven't excommunicated anyone lately, either."

That surprised a snort of humor from Roelke.

Father Dan sobered again. "Any church community is full of conflicts, of course. The organist doesn't like the choir director's choice of anthem, or half the men in Knights of Columbus want to sponsor a turkey dinner and the other half want a corn boil. But there's been nothing truly rancorous."

Roelke pulled out his notebook and jotted down the basics.

"This must seem trivial," Father Dan added. "But replacing or even repairing stained glass is expensive."

"I'm glad you called it in," Roelke assured him. "It was probably just some kid acting up, but I'll be sure to let the other officers know. We'll keep an extra eye on the church for a while."

They walked back through the sanctuary. Father Dan paused at the front door. "I couldn't help noticing that you're Catholic."

"Raised that way," Roelke said cautiously, not sure where this was going.

"You're always welcome to attend mass here."

"I live near Palmyra. St. Mary's is closest." If he wanted to attend mass, that is. Which he did not.

Even though part of him, right this minute, wanted to slide onto one of the wooden pews. Maybe even sink down on the kneeler. But he hadn't prayed in years. At this point, he had no idea what to say to God.

"Of course." The priest smiled. "Let me also just say that if something is troubling you, I'm available to talk."

Roelke felt a spasm of something akin to panic. It was one thing for Libby, who'd known him his whole life, to make such observations. Quite another for *this* guy, who looked barely old enough to even be a priest. "I don't mean to be disrespectful, honestly I don't, but I lost most of my faith years ago. And recent events have been whacking away at whatever I had left."

The priest considered for a moment. " 'Consider it pure joy, my brothers and sisters, whenever you face trials of many kinds, because you know that the testing of your faith produces perseverance. Let perseverance finish its work so that you may be mature and complete, not lacking anything.' James, chapter one, verses two through eight."

Is he *kidding* me? Roelke thought. He nodded once, polite and professional, and turned toward the door. "Please let us know if you have any further problems."

———

"Oh my God." Isaac looked from Chloe to Elise. "Oh, my, *God*. The World War I lace is just—just gone!"

"Don't panic," Chloe began.

"I'm responsible for these artifacts!" Isaac was clearly panicked.

"The mix-up probably occurred a long time ago," Chloe pointed out, glancing at her watch. "And I'm due to meet your restoration expert at the Belgian Farm in about five minutes."

Isaac grimaced. "We haven't even had a chance to talk about your furnishings plan! I'm sorry."

Chloe wanted to grab Isaac's hand and say, *Stop apologizing!* Instead she said, "Can you point the way?"

He hesitated before nodding. "I'll show you. You don't want to keep Roy Galuska waiting."

They bundled up again and left the church. Isaac carefully secured the door behind them, tugging on the lock before he was satisfied.

"I'm going back to the Education Center," Elise said. "I'm not dressed for wandering around an unheated farmhouse."

Isaac watched her go. "She's upset with me."

"I don't think so. These things can happen."

He sighed, clearly unconvinced. "Well, let's go. It's just a short walk from here."

Chloe struggled to find a more upbeat topic. "I'm looking forward to coming back in the summer so I can see the site when it's open."

"The master plan divides the site into five heritage areas, which reflect major themes in our region's development." Isaac sounded more confident on this topic. "The fur trade and frontier life, small town development, the military era, the river and waterfront heritage, and ethnic and agricultural heritage. Bringing in the Belgian Farm establishes that theme." He pointed. "There."

Chloe, who'd been head-down into the wind, straightened to see a farmhouse made of red and cream brick. "Oh, that is lovely."

Then she noticed a smaller stone outbuilding to the right, and her gut clenched like a fist. She was an absolute idiot! She should have anticipated this. Should have somehow prepared herself to visit another summer kitchen.

A wiry man in a patched blue parka, wool trousers, and work boots appeared from a big log barn. Isaac made cursory introductions and scurried away.

Chloe smiled and stuck out one hand. "Thanks for taking the time to meet me. As I suspect you know, I'm here to work on a furnishings plan for the farmstead."

"Unhunh." Roy's grip was hard, and his blue eyes assessing. He had the look of a man who'd spent long years working outdoors in all kinds of weather. His face was lined, his cheeks stained a dull red from the cold. The bit of hair showing beneath a knitted cap was gunmetal gray. "What can you tell me about the house?"

Chloe gave the house more thoughtful consideration, wanting to rise to the unexpected challenge. "Well ... I'd say that the builder had an artistic eye. The alternating red and cream brick quoins at the corners are beautifully done. But he clearly was a practical man too. The color scheme isn't perfectly balanced, presumably because he was too thrifty to waste bricks."

"Hunh." Evidently she'd passed at least preliminary muster. "What is it you want to know?"

"It's too early for me to have specific questions," Chloe said carefully. "I understand you're in charge of building restoration? If you're willing, I'd love to have you give me an introductory tour."

He rubbed his chin, eyes narrowed. Chloe got the distinct impression that he was deciding if she was worth his time. Finally he waved a vague hand at the fledgling farm exhibit. "Well, the people who planned Heritage Hill always wanted a Belgian farm. A couple guys from the university had already done a lot of fieldwork. They were a big help, and the family was great to work with."

"Excellent." Chloe nodded.

"The Massart House came from Kewaunee County. It was built in 1872, 1873—somewhere in there. Architecturally distinct, with that two-toned brickwork, but still traditional. You know the bricks are a veneer, right?"

"I did not know that," Chloe confessed.

"The house was built of logs, then covered over." Roy placed one hand against the brick wall, and his face softened a little.

Chloe decided she'd been wrong about the reason he'd hesitated before starting the tour. He'd wanted to make sure she was worthy of the buildings, not his time. She felt herself warming up to Roy Galuska.

"We're a long way from done," he cautioned gruffly, gesturing toward a big pile of bricks near the house. "The back still needs to be re-bricked. Those are all original. Have you ever tried to remove old mortar from an old brick without doing damage?"

"I have not."

"It's a job. Easiest thing to do is leave 'em out over winter. The mortar takes in moisture, freezes, and pops off." He waved an arm toward the back lot. "And we'll be bringing in a couple more build-ings from other farms—a piggery, a chicken coop. Then we can start on getting appropriate crops planted, putting in fencing, get-ting some old-breed livestock … "

"And furnishing the interiors," Chloe put in.

"Right. Want to start inside the house?"

"Absolutely."

He led her inside. Chloe paused in the entry, pretending to study the space as she opened herself to any strong emotions that might linger in the house. Since childhood, she'd occasionally perceived some strong resonance in historic structures, left behind by someone long gone. More than once she'd been unable to stay inside some old building that quivered with malevolence or grief. This home held nothing distinct, just a faint jumble, and Chloe was grateful. She'd lose whatever respect she'd earned from Roy if she fled now.

Chloe wandered through the cold, empty rooms. She could hardly wait to see them furnished again, brought back to life by interpreters going about daily chores. "Room use is pretty clear. Bedrooms, parlor, pantry, kitchen."

"Winter kitchen," he corrected her. "Come on." He stomped outside.

Here we go, Chloe thought as she trudged after him.

Roy cocked his head toward the smaller stone building nearby. "The summer kitchen came from the same family."

You can do this, Chloe told herself.

"I numbered every stone before the building was dismantled for the move," Roy was saying. "One of the guys on the crew scoffed at that. Said I was wasting my time, and numbering the cornerstones and foundations would be enough." He snorted in disgust. "But these walls had stood exactly like this since 1902. Who was I to muck it up?" Roy patted the stones affectionately before opening the door.

Chloe took a deep breath and followed him inside.

"The structure's got double limestone walls," Roy said, "with about sixteen inches of rubble between them."

Chloe stared at the far wall. The bake oven door stood open, exposing a greedy black hole.

"The Massart family used that oven into the 1930s," Roy said. "Look at the size of this ash dump! When they raked the ashes out of the oven they fell through the slot and got shoved back through that lower passage. Then they could be shoveled into an ash barrel and used for soap or something…" He seemed to realize he didn't have her full attention and gave her a sharp look. "Something wrong?"

"Could you do me a favor and look inside the bake oven?" Chloe hugged her arms over her chest. She tried hard to avoid being a weenie, but in this case, so be it. "Make sure it's empty?"

"Make sure it's empty?" His expression suggested she'd sprouted a second head. Possibly a third. Then, "Oh, Christ. It was in the paper this morning that some tourist found… that was you?"

"That was me."

Roy glared at the floor. "What a horrible thing."

She wasn't sure if his anger was aimed at himself for questioning her motives, or at whatever sick person had stuffed a body into the bake oven. "It was horrible. And I guess I'm more freaked out than I realized. So if you could just…" She waved a hand toward the oven.

Roy grabbed a broom from one corner and used the handle to probe the dark baking chamber. "Nothing inside."

Chloe exhaled slowly. The summer kitchen was once more a place to imagine only sweating women at work; the bake oven not a tomb but only a rare relic of nineteenth-century architecture.

Roy hesitated. "What were you doing wandering around Hugh Lejeune's old place anyway?"

Why did people keep asking her that? "I was driving by, and I noticed that the farm was *obviously* abandoned, and—and I was pretty sure that the building near the road was a summer kitchen, so I just sorta pulled over to take a quick look, and…" She petered out.

"I might have done the same thing." Roy glanced at her then quickly looked away. "Let's go. That's all I've got time for today."

Chloe didn't mind aborting the summer kitchen tour. At least I broke through Roy's reserve, she thought. She hoped he recognized in her a worthy partner for the Belgian Farm project.

They walked back to the Education Building in silence, hands in pockets. "You've got the barn yet to see," Roy said. "I'm busy tomorrow, so meet me there on Wednesday. Ten o'clock."

"Um ... " Chloe began, trying to remember her schedule.

Roy stalked off.

"See ya," Chloe murmured. She wasn't annoyed, though. Roy was a crusty soul, but she liked him.

Inside, Chloe went in search of Elise. She finally found her friend upstairs, standing by one of the huge windows overlooking the site. She didn't hear or notice Chloe approaching, and her expression was once again ... sad. More than sad, really. Bereft.

Chloe hesitated. Surely this was more than reacting to Hugh Lejeune's death. Finally she spoke softly. "A penny for your thoughts."

"Oh!" Elise broke from her reverie. "You startled me."

"Is everything okay?"

"I was thinking about lacemakers, actually. Prepping for my program here tomorrow."

Chloe really didn't want to pry, but that seemed to be a disconnect. "You looked kind of ... sad."

"Did I?" Elise curved her lips into a smile. "I'm afraid I've gotten quite obsessed about my topic. I can speak knowledgeably about types of lace, but I wish I had more primary source material about the makers. Those women worked so hard to produce such beauty ... I can't help wondering about them. Did it bring them joy? Or did the long hours and delicate work make the process nothing more than a tedious chore?"

Chloe wasn't convinced that Elise's melancholy could solely be ascribed to her studies. However, Chloe was also easily distracted, and her friend's questions mirrored those she'd had many times when inspecting some anonymous piece of handwork: *Who made this? What was her life like?*

SEVEN

AUGUST 1853

"Are you staying?" Octavie asked. The other *dentellières* were covering their work to keep it clean overnight. Most lived nearby, and they chatted as they slipped their feet into the *sabots* left in a row near the door so no clots of mud could sully the workroom.

"Just a bit longer."

Octavie smiled. "I'm not surprised. I'm going to spend some time in the chapel."

"I'm not surprised," Seraphine echoed. She reached for a bobbin.

But Octavie didn't leave. "Seraphine, I have to tell you something."

Seraphine's hand stilled. She studied her sister's face ... and she knew. "You've decided. You're going to become a nun." Octavie had been thinking about becoming a novitiate for some time. When she was in the chapel, singing or praying, her serene face glowed in a way that Seraphine sometimes envied.

Octavie nodded. "I haven't done anything formal."

Seraphine heard Jean-Paul's mother in her memory: *"As long as you and Octavie are together, you'll do well."*

"Can you be happy for me?" Octavie whispered.

Seraphine stood and wrapped her arms around her sister. "Of *course.*"

"And you have Jean-Paul."

"Yes." He had not asked her to marry him. But Seraphine understood that he intended to do so. When the time was right.

When Octavie pulled away, her eyes shimmered with unshed tears—of gratitude for the blessing and, Seraphine knew, of regret that their paths were diverging.

After Octavie left, Seraphine let the peaceful stillness settle upon her. *Within* her. She touched one of her bobbins. I have the lace, she reminded herself. That's *my* vocation. Over the past five years, as she'd improved, she'd discovered a spiritual power in the lacework. The cloth-covered pillows before each high-backed chair suggested tiny altars. The mysteries of the designs revealed themselves in an almost mystical way. When Seraphine settled in the workroom with the glowing lamps and clicking bobbins, when the girls sang hymns in four-part harmony while they worked, she felt closer to God—and especially to the Virgin Mother who had long ago dropped threads into a poor girl's lap, and created lace. Seraphine was seventeen now, a skilled *dentellière*, and life had purpose.

Now she settled easily into a rhythm, hands guiding bobbins as she twisted and crossed threads to form the design. This pattern required four hundred wooden bobbins, heaped off to the sides and separated into groups by tall brass pins. When the sun set she positioned a lamp beside a water-filled globe so the concentrated light fell over her work.

The sky had faded from gray to black when someone opened the door. "Seraphine!" It was the plump girl who worked in the kitchen, grinning conspiratorially in the light cast by the candle she carried. "Your young man is downstairs."

"He is?" Seraphine felt a hitch of anticipation. Jean-Paul had come to see her.

In the kitchen, another girl was scrubbing the last pot with a handful of rushes. The dim room smelled of cabbage and fish. The man crouching on the tile floor by the hearth, warming his hands over dying embers, was shadowed. But he rose when Seraphine joined him, and wrapped her into an embrace. Seraphine nuzzled close, smelling the sweat and dust in his clothes, feeling his heart thumping and the warmth of his arms. Finally she pulled away and cupped his face in her hands. "I'm glad you're here."

Since leaving the farm and coming to Flanders, Seraphine had seen Jean-Paul only rarely. If he managed to make it to the convent, she had but an hour or two with him—usually under the always watchful, sometimes disapproving eye of one of the nuns. If they were lucky, the elderly nun would be their chaperone. On warm nights, she could be counted on to nod off in her wicker chair as swallows swooped overhead.

Still, their childhood friendship had only deepened and grown into something new and precious. And last year, when Seraphine had dared ask for a bite of bread for him, she discovered that the cook's helpers were sympathetic. Since then, he'd come to the kitchen's delivery door. If Cook was gone, Seraphine and Jean-Paul could enjoy a bit of unsupervised time together.

And he was early this time. "It's only Saturday night! How did you get here so fast?"

71

"It's Fair Day at home." He kissed her. "So we worked only the morning. I thought you and I might go to mass together tomorrow before I need to start back. I can sleep in the stable down the alley."

"That would be lovely."

The dishwasher set her pot aside, upside down to dry, and dumped the tin basin out the back door. She tossed a smile over her shoulder as she untied her apron. "There's a bit of cheese on a dish there, and some bread." She pointed to a cloth-covered plate. "I don't expect Cook will notice a slice or two gone."

Once alone, Seraphine and Jean-Paul settled on a bench. He put an arm around her, and she leaned against him. She'd learned the shape of his strong shoulders through his thin shirt. She dared dream of what else there was to know of him.

"Tell me about home," she urged, for the tenant farm was still home. When she and Jean-Paul married, she'd return and move into a cottar's cottage again.

Jean-Paul told her about the ripening grain crops, worms plaguing the cabbage, runaway oxen, the landowner's worsening fits of temper. "One day," he whispered against her hair, "I will have a farm of my own. I will till my own land, and make decisions, and not be beholden to a stingy landlord."

"You will," she agreed.

He kissed the top of her head. "Tell me about life in Bruges."

Seraphine told him of Octavie's conviction to become a nun. And she spoke of her lacework. "I'm working now on a design of my own making," she told him shyly. "I so want to become a *piqueuse*."

"A *piqueuse*?"

"A person who understands lace design and execution so well that she can create a pattern. That means pricking holes in a piece of cardboard to indicate where the lacemaker should place the pins that hold the threads she will manipulate, bobbin by bobbin. The best *dentellières* say a *piqueuse* is born, and that the arts and skill must come from somewhere inside. They cannot be taught."

He was quiet for so long that Seraphine regretted her impulse to speak. Octavie's news had left her feeling needy, eager to prove a calling of her own. But did Jean-Paul understand that, or did he think she was taking on airs? She stared at a row of tightly covered crocks on a shelf as heat rose in her cheeks.

Finally Jean-Paul shifted so he could look her in the eye. "This is so important to you?"

She put one hand on his arm. "Jean-Paul, when I open my eyes in the morning, I'm thinking about lace. When I'm sweeping, or polishing the chapel pews with beeswax, all I see in my mind are patterns. I believe that with more study and practice..."

"I see." He regarded her intently, eyes slightly narrowed beneath the shock of black hair that fell over his forehead. "Are you saying you need to stay here, at the lace school? Stay here with Octavie?"

She struggled to find the right words. "No, that's not it. I can continue my work ... elsewhere." Her cheeks were flaming now. "But you need to understand this if we are going to—to be together."

"That's what I want," Jean-Paul said simply. "I've always known that. I thought you did too."

"I *do*."

"We'll make plans to wed, then." He stroked her cheek, and the gentle touch made her tingle. "If I get my own farm, you will have to help with the work. But you will have time for your lace, Seraphine. I promise you that."

EIGHT

"I'LL CATCH YOU LATER," Elise told Chloe. They'd just returned to Heritage Hill after lunch at a nearby deli. "I'm meeting with the events coordinator to finalize plans for the program tomorrow night."

"Sounds good. If we don't connect before five o'clock, let's meet in the lobby." Chloe approached the cheerful woman at the reception desk. "Can you point me to the conference room?" She was scheduled to discuss her project with key personnel.

Most key, it seemed, was the woman already sitting at the head of the table when Chloe slid into a vacant chair. "You must be Miss Ellefson," she said crisply. "Good afternoon. I am Mrs. Delcroix, a member of the Heritage Hill Foundation. As I'm sure you know, the Foundation exists for the charitable and educational purposes of encouraging, promoting, and assisting in the development of Heritage Hill State Historical Park."

"Yes ma'am." Chloe caught the note of subservience in her own tone, but honestly, Mrs. Delcroix might have stepped from some Masterpiece Theatre production. She was a stout woman, with what would once have been called an "ample bosom." She wore a plum-colored dress with a big lacey collar straight out of *Upstairs Down-stairs.* Her brown hair was professionally styled in regal waves. Her expression was serene, but Chloe suspected that Mrs. Delcroix could bend others to her will while sipping hot oolong from bone china.

"And you have met our registrar and restoration specialist." She gestured to Isaac Cuddy and Roy Galuska.

Chloe started to say "Yes ma'am" again, but managed to switch to "I have."

A young woman with an engaging smile was introduced as the education specialist. "Unfortunately the site director couldn't join us today, but we shall carry on." Mrs. Delcroix folded her hands on the table. "Miss Ellefson, I represent the Belgian Farm Committee here at Heritage Hill. Perhaps you can tell us how you plan to proceed with the furnishings plan for the Belgian farmhouse."

"Of course." Chloe pulled out a file. "I understand from our preliminary correspondence that you have chosen 1905 as the farm's restoration date. And that one of your primary goals is to share a typical experience for a farm family of that time, not limited to what is known about the Massart family."

Mrs. Delcroix inclined her head. "That is correct."

"I will include biographical information about the Massarts, out of respect for the building donors, and because some visitors will want to know who once walked the floors," Chloe said. "But the remainder of the document will take a broader look at life in the Belgian-American communites. It will cover how each space in the house and outbuildings was used, and recommend appropriate furnishings. Some potential acquisitions may turn up as I do fieldwork this week, and if so, I will provide the particulars for your consideration."

Mrs. Delcroix did the single-nod thing again. Isaac nodded more nervously. Roy was looking out the window.

"I know from the materials you provided that a good deal of information about Belgian-American architecture and culture has already been collected," Chloe continued. "Has thought already been given to interpreting the farm exhibit?"

"It has." The education specialist passed some papers around.

The Belgian Farm—Interpretive Themes

People and Communities
> *Walloons and Flemish*
> *Family immigration and gender roles*
> *Aux Premiers Belges; communities in Door, Brown, and*
> > *Kewaunee Counties*
> *Rural Catholicism—prayer chapels, shrines, and*
> > *processions*

Creating Social Institutions
> *Father Daems and religious leadership*
> *Importance of education as part of the Catholic missions*
> *Growth of parishes in the Belgian community*
> *Visions and mission of Adele Brise—Shrine of Our Lady*
> > *of Good Help*

Expressing Aspects of Culture
> *Clothing and foodways*
> *Architectural styles typical of Belgian farming*
> > *community*
> *Leisure and cultural activities—the maypole, the Kermiss,*
> > *taverns, music*

Chloe read the outline twice before looking up. "This is terrific, and extremely helpful."

"What else do you need from us?" Mrs. Delcroix asked.

"I appreciate Roy's knowledge of the buildings that have been moved here." Chloe gave him a pleasant smile, trying to draw him into the conversation. "Roy, I hope you don't mind if I come to you with questions. And I'm sure that Isaac's knowledge of collections here will—"

"Isaac is a registrar, not a curator." Mrs. Delcroix's voice was clipped. "His function is clerical."

Red blotches stained the young man's cheeks. He stared at the interpretive themes as if committing them to memory.

Chloe's eyebrows lifted. What did Mrs. Delcroix have against Isaac? "I expect that Isaac's knowledge of site procedural issues will prove most helpful," she said firmly.

Mrs. Delcroix pinched her lips into a tight line. A phone rang somewhere nearby. Roy tapped a pen against the table.

Okay, Chloe thought. Time to move on. "I've got a driving tour scheduled for tomorrow morning with someone from the university. As you know, I expect to make connections with descendants living in the area at the Heritage Day potluck at the Belgian Heritage Center on Wednesday. I also plan to visit the Neville Museum, the Catholic shrine in Champion, and the Area Research Center at the UW-Green Bay, which has established a Belgian-American collection. My main goal for the week is to get as much local research done as possible. I can provide a preliminary report before I leave, but I'll need a few weeks after getting home to complete the final."

"Very well," Mrs. Delcroix said. "Meeting adjourned." Chloe started to rise with the others, but Mrs. Delcroix waved her back down.

"Just another moment, Miss Ellefson. I have a key to the Belgian Farm buildings for you."

Chloe signed the appropriate form and pocketed the key. "Thanks."

"Just one more thing. Heritage Hill is hosting a reception on Friday afternoon to honor donors. We'll celebrate St. Nicholas Day too, a few days early. I hope you can attend."

"Sounds like fun!" Chloe said cheerfully. "I'll be there."

———

Chloe spent the rest of the afternoon working in the staff library, which was tucked away in a warren of space above the hospital, part of the 1830s Fort Howard area. The education specialist stopped in, and at Chloe's request, recommended a restaurant for dinner. "Lorenzo's has the best pizza in Green Bay," she promised.

Elise was amenable, so Chloe navigated her way to Lorenzo's, which was crowded and smelled delicious—both good signs.

"So, Mrs. Delcroix was a trip," Chloe told Elise, once the waitress delivered their dinner—a thin crust with green peppers, fresh mushrooms, and extra cheese. "Formidable. I imagine she gets stuff done, though."

"Sometimes that's what it takes."

"I just wish she hadn't been so hard on Isaac. I wa—"

"What?" Elise leaned across the table. The couple in the booth behind her was enjoying an animated conversation. All Chloe could see of the man was a bright-blue knit cap. The woman wore a heavy sweater over hosptal scrubs.

Chloe raised her voice. "I was embarrassed for the poor kid." She pulled free a slice of pizza, breaking strings of cheese with her fingers. "Watch out, it's very hot."

"Maybe Mrs. Delcroix was embarrassed that the first artifact we attempted to see was missing," Elise suggested. "Not good."

"No." Chloe sighed. "Not good."

Elise opted for silverware and began cutting into her pizza. "Did you find anything interesting in the library?"

"Yes and no." Chloe licked a bit of tomato sauce from one finger. "Quite a bit of work has already been done by local scholars and Heritage Hill staff. Lots of good information—history of the Belgian settlement, architectural studies, food traditions. But women's voices are largely absent."

"As usually happens."

"Oh, I know." Chloe made a gesture of agreement. "But what I wouldn't give for a glimpse of an early Belgian woman's life after she arrived in Wisconsin. I'm not asking for a diary. Just a glimpse."

"Maybe something will turn up."

"I wish I had two months for fieldwork, instead of a week," Chloe admitted. "But writing the furnishings plan will mostly involve translating social history into objects. The farm is being restored to its 1905 appearance. It helps that mail order catalogs were common by then. I can document period styles."

"As my schedule permits, do you mind if I tag along this week?" Elise asked. "I'm interested in the early Belgian settlers too. Besides, this Virginia girl is leery of Wisconsin roads in winter."

"Sure." Chloe shrugged. "With the exception of religious artifacts, I don't think we'll find much that's particularly 'Belgian.'" She hooked two fingers in the air. "Most of the Belgian immigrants were Catholic, and by all accounts, quite devout."

That observation reminded her of Roelke's unexpected comment on the phone the night before: *"You know I was raised Catholic, right?"* She felt a familiar stab of worry.

Oh, Roelke, Chloe thought. What is going on with you?

———

Libby called the station toward the end of Roelke's shift. "Come to dinner tonight."

"Is that an invitation or a command?" he asked, but smiled. This was the Libby he knew and loved.

"Both."

"Dinner would be good. I'll be there in half an hour."

It was snowing lightly when he left the station, so he took his time driving the six miles from Eagle to Palmyra. Upbeat, he counseled himself. Keep it upbeat.

He arrived in time to play two games of Chutes and Ladders with Deirdre and Justin before supper. Libby served a homemade chicken pot pie, perfect for a cold evening. Then Justin settled down with his math workbook, and Deirdre with a Sleeping Beauty coloring book.

Roelke began filling the sink with hot water and squeezed in some soap. "So," he said, as Libby piled dirty plates on the sideboard, "how was mass?"

"It was ... I don't know ... a little strange to be back. But nice in a way too."

"Yeah?"

"I think it's the ritual, you know? You grow up with something, and then you grow away from it and don't even realize that you've lost anything." She reached for a dish towel. "Then you go back and it all seems a little ... I don't know. Comforting, maybe."

"Well, hunh." Although that was the same thought he'd had at St. Theresa in Eagle, the idea of Libby needing comfort was startling. But maybe it shouldn't be. She was strong, but she'd been through a lot. If Libby found comfort in going to mass, that was fine by him.

———

"Thanks for driving," Elise told Chloe as they arrived back at Belgian Acres. "It's been a long day. I'll see you in the morning."

So much for settling in for a nice catch-up chat, Chloe thought. The conversation on their drives, and over meals, had stayed focused on impersonal topics—work, research. Was that by accident or design? Chloe watched Elise go inside, wishing she knew what was on her friend's mind, hoping she was okay.

Then movement in the periphery, illuminated by an outdoor light, caught Chloe's attention. Sharon had just emerged from the barn. She turned toward the house but stopped suddenly, leaning against the barn wall, head bent.

That didn't look good. Chloe hurried to meet the older woman. "Sharon, are you all right?"

"Oh!" Sharon straightened at once. "Chloe, I didn't see you there. I'm fine. Just a bit tired today."

"I don't doubt it," Chloe said sympathetically. "Losing your cousin must have been such a shock."

"It was," Sharon admitted. "For you to find him the way you did ... *Why*? Why would someone do that?" She bleakly lifted her hands, let them drop. "Hugh could be irascible, cranky even, but everyone took him in stride."

Someone didn't, Chloe thought. But focusing on the crude internment wouldn't help either of them. "Was Hugh a wealthy man?"

"No. He was hanging on to the land in hopes that his son, who also is not a wealthy man, will be able to take it on one day ... *oh*."

"What?"

Sharon looked uncomfortable. "Nothing, really. It just occurred to me that Richard, Hugh's son, has a better chance of keeping the land now. Hugh might have lived for many more years. Whatever savings he had left would have gone to rent and medical care. In that case, Richard would have needed to sell the farm."

Which in theory places suspicion on Richard, Chloe thought— and immediately scolded herself. Living with a cop was affecting her. Richard couldn't have faked the haggard expression or the shadows in his eyes on Monday morning.

Time to change the subject. "Sharon, did your family have a summer kitchen with a bake oven too?"

"Oh, yes." Sharon nodded. "My grandmother used it well into the thirties. She could stick her hand in the oven and know instantly if it was hot enough to bake properly. I never understood how she knew when to open the door and take her bread or pies out, but she always got it just right."

Chloe looked over the farm compound. "Is the building still standing?"

"No. Once it started crumbling, my husband decided to just take it down. It was right beside the house—where we park now."

Bummer, Chloe thought, glancing at the row of vehicles: her Pinto, Elise's rental, a blue pickup truck.

Sharon paused as they reached the back door, her expression distant. "I've been thinking all day about happier times. When Karen and I were kids, we ran back and forth between the two farms all the time. In those days nobody thought twice about letting children disappear into the woods."

"Sounds like a great way to grow up."

"It was. Hugh was too old to play with us, but I remember one night when we all caught fireflies in mason jars. I couldn't tell you why, but that's as vivid as if it happened yesterday."

"My sister and I did that too," Chloe told her. "With cheesecloth over the jar so the fireflies wouldn't die before we let them go."

"That's how we did it too." A small, sad smile tugged at Sharon's mouth. "Hugh could be trouble, though, even then. He told Karen and me once that there was a treasure hidden on their farm. He swore that he'd overheard his parents talking about it. Karen and I looked for that treasure all summer that year."

"Find anything?"

"No. I'm sure Hugh made the whole thing up, but it kept us busy." Sharon shook her head. "Well. Enough reminiscing. I still have things to do this evening, and I expect you do too."

Inside, Chloe went straight to her room. She had one more challenge before she could relax and call Roelke. She gently eased the receiver from the phone, checking to see if anyone else was on the line, but heard only a dial tone. She called an operator and provided her sister Kari's number.

"Hey, it's me," she said, when the connection was made.

"Aren't you doing some work thing?"

Chloe eased down on the bed and stretched out. "Yes, but we need to talk."

"Is something wrong?"

"*Wrong* isn't the right word. But when I visited Birgitta yesterday morning, I learned something that you should know." She took a deep breath. "Birgitta told me that mom was adopted."

Pause. "No way."

"Seriously."

A longer pause. "And you believed her? Her mind wasn't wandering or something?"

"Well, she did think she was talking to her sister Elen," Chloe admitted. "But that said, I believe she was speaking truthfully about Mom. She had specific memories about the day Grandma brought her home."

"Good Lord," Kari said slowly. "I had no idea."

"Do you think Mom knows?"

"She's certainly never said anything to me about it."

"Maybe she does know, and that's why she's so into the whole Norwegian heritage thing. She's spent her whole life trying to fit in."

"Or maybe no one ever told her," Kari countered, "and she's into the whole heritage thing because she believes she's a good, pure Stoughton Norwegian. Which she might be, in any case."

"Should I tell her what Birgitta said? If she doesn't know, she has a right to." Chloe closed her eyes and crooked one elbow over her face. "We should do it together. She'd take it better coming from you."

Kari thought that over. "I don't see the point. If Mom does know, she clearly doesn't want *us* to know. And if she doesn't know, it could be ugly."

"But … if she *does* know she was adopted, she might have information about her birth parents." If so, Chloe wanted it.

"Let it go, Chloe."

"Doesn't it make you feel kind of weird?" Chloe sat up again. "We may not be all Norwegian, Kari. We could have Romanian blood, or Scottish, or Egyptian, or—or anything."

"I'm guessing grandma didn't go to Egypt to adopt a child," Kari said dryly, "but it is intriguing."

This conversation wasn't helping. "I gotta go," Chloe said.

"I'm glad you called. Let's talk more after you come home. Don't make any quick decisions."

Chloe tried calling Roelke at home but got no answer. She'd try again later. For now, the best thing to do was get ready for bed and then read some of her research files while getting toasty under the covers.

After slipping off her shoes Chloe grabbed her toilet kit and headed to the bathroom. But as she passed Elise's room she heard a soft sound from beyond the door, muffled but unmistakable. Elise was crying.

I *knew* something was wrong, Chloe thought. She raised her hand to knock.

Then she hesitated. She hadn't seen Elise in years. They'd never been close, and Elise had done nothing since arriving to encourage intimacy. Would she welcome a concerned query, or would it be an intrusion?

Chloe let her hand drop. Tomorrow, she thought, I will look for an opportunity to ask Elise what is troubling her.

She brushed her teeth and retreated to bed with a fat file, but she didn't look at the material. It had been quite the couple of days. Birgitta's news. Finding the body of Hugh Lejeune in the bake oven. The missing piece of war lace. The diverse assortment of personalities at Heritage Hill—Isaac, Roy, Mrs. Delcroix. Now Elise.

What Chloe most wanted to do was hear Roelke's voice. This time she let the phone ring twenty times, hoping he might be coming in the door, before hanging up.

Don't be such a baby, she scolded herself. Your problems are nothing compared to, say, Sharon's. Remembering how Sharon had sagged against the barn wall earlier, Chloe wondered if the demands of keeping up the farm and the B&B were taking a toll on her health. And of course now she had her cousin's bizarre death and entombment weighing on her. Thank goodness her nurse daughter had moved home.

And I hope Sharon revels in her childhood memories, Chloe thought, remembering how the older woman's face had relaxed when she was talking about catching lightning bugs and searching for long-lost treasure with the faithful determination of children. She wondered if Hugh had hinted at what might comprise that supposed treasure. Did he scare the girls with tales of ghosts protecting some long-lost cache of jewels? Describe gold doubloons as if errant pirates had once wandered Door County's wooded hills? The image made her smile ...

Until it occurred to her to wonder if anyone else had heard the tale of, supposedly, some lost treasure on Lejeune Farm East. Had Hugh stopped by his abandoned property and discovered someone chasing an old legend?

Chloe considered that possibility for about seven seconds before rolling her eyes. "Ludicrous," she muttered aloud. It was a good thing she was a fledgling fiction writer, because her overactive imagination definitely needed a safe outlet. Setting aside such fancies, she reached for an article she'd photocopied. Focus on the work.

It was a good strategy, for soon she was immersed in the 1850s, when the earliest Belgian immigrants came in search of farmland. The farmhouse that had been relocated to Heritage Hill dated to the 1870s. It was beautiful, and clearly reflected how much the Belgians had accomplished. But the story of Belgian emigration from Wallonia to Wisconsin had started twenty years earlier.

NINE

"SERAPHINE?" SISTER ODILE-ALPHONSE STOOD in the workroom doorway, hands tucked into her wide sleeves. "I thought I'd find you here. Shouldn't you be preparing for evening prayers?"

"I just wanted to finish this section. I won't be late, I promise."

Sister Odile-Alphonse came inside and studied the work on Seraphine's cushion. "This is your own design?"

"Yes, Sister."

The nun tipped her head. "I knew from the day you arrived that you would one day make fine lace. I saw it in your eyes. I would not want you to take pride from my words, but you have surpassed my expectations." She rested a hand on Seraphine's shoulder. "And you've been here only ... six years, is it?"

"Not quite that."

"But you're not going to stay with us."

Seraphine kept her gaze on her work, but she nodded. "I'm promised to be married. Next year."

"What is your young man's name?"

"Jean-Paul Lejeune. I've known him since I was a child. He's … " Seraphine's voice trailed away. How could she explain Jean-Paul to someone who had chosen God over any man?

"This Jean-Paul must be special. Still, I will be sad to see you go. You will leave behind your work … ?"

"Oh, no, Sister." Seraphine clasped the older woman's fingers, trying to make her understand. "I will keep working. I recently finished my wedding lace. It's *Duchesse de Bruges* style, and the design is my own." Seraphine tried hard not to sound prideful, but the lace was the finest thing she'd ever created. She had worked on it for over a year, staying late and alone in the silent room. "Jean-Paul knows how important my lace is."

"I'm glad to hear it." Sister Odile-Alphonse squeezed Seraphine's hand lightly before leaving her alone.

Seraphine turned back to her pillow. Just a bit more, she decided.

She was hurrying to chapel when one of the other boarders found her. "Seraphine!" she hissed. "Your friend is at the gate asking for you."

Seraphine felt a flower bloom beneath her ribs, but—why hadn't he waited a bit longer, and gone to the kitchen? "Jean-Paul is here?"

"Yes, but it's too late for a visit. He's arguing with the nun through the grille."

Seraphine slipped outside and crossed the dark courtyard. "I beg you," Jean-Paul was saying from beyond the door. "I *must* see—"

"I'm here," Seraphine called. "Please, Sister, may we have a few minutes? My intended would not have called at this hour without good reason."

"Oh, very well," the woman grumbled. She worked her heavy key in the lock. When the gate cracked open, Jean-Paul slipped inside. "No farther," she warned.

"Speak in Walloon," Seraphine told Jean-Paul. Whatever news was coming, it must be bad. "Tell me quickly—what's happened?"

"We must leave." Jean-Paul's voice was husky. "Tomorrow, first light."

Seraphine felt her world teeter. "What are you talking about?"

Jean-Paul stepped closer. "It was the Kermiss two days ago."

"That's good," Seraphine said, still bewildered. Kermiss was the annual harvest festival, when farm laborers like Jean-Paul received their meager share of grain bundles from the landowner.

"The landlord cheated us," Jean-Paul muttered angrily. "The harvest this year was better, and he *still* shorted our allotment. Etienne and I decided it was one too many times."

Seraphine's hands fisted in the folds of her skirt. She remembered her father complaining about the same thing. But her father had never done more than mutter behind closed doors. "What did you and Etienne do?"

"The oat crop was not fully harvested, and we ... " Jean-Paul tapped one foot in its wooden *sabot* lightly against the flagstone. *"Klompen."*

"No!" Seraphine gasped. It was an old trick, settling a dispute with the landowner by trampling his crops.

"Someone saw us. I'm in trouble, Seraphine. That's why we have to leave. Etienne and I have been talking about emigrating, going to America—"

"What?"

"You've heard that a small group went last year?"

Seraphine shook her head. "No." Little news of the outside world filtered into the convent.

"They've settled in a place called Wisconsin. It's the answer to our prayers! There is nothing for me in Belgium."

"But that's not true for me! I have Octavie. And my lacework."

"I know." Jean-Paul took both of her hands in his. "I am asking a great deal. But Seraphine, farmland can be purchased from the American government for almost nothing. I've been pinching and saving for years, and the best I'd hoped for was the chance to buy a hectare of land. But we can get one hundred times more land in Wisconsin for the same price! And every single shock of grain I raise will belong to me. To *us*."

She pictured a fertile, sunlit meadow, untouched, waiting for Jean-Paul. But—that meadow was in America. The other side of the world!

"You've told me that the factors pay only a pittance when buying from lacemakers, but sell to dealers at an enormous profit. In America there is no factor system. You can make lace and set your own price."

Seraphine bit her lip. Could that really be true?

"We must go quickly. We're to meet Etienne and his wife tomorrow evening in Antwerp. He's making the arrangements now."

The nun cleared her throat. Seraphine flapped a hand at her, too upset to care. "Jean-Paul, I can't travel with you."

"We'll marry, of course," he said quickly. "I know we'd planned for next year, but … it can't be helped."

"But … "

"I am going to America, Seraphine. I want you to come with me. But one way or another, I am going."

91

Seraphine pulled her hands free and rubbed her temples. She had dreaded leaving Octavie, even when only moving back to Grez-Doiceau! The thought of traveling to this unknown America brought a weight to her chest, made it hard to breath.

"Will you come?" Jean-Paul begged. "Will you meet me here tomorrow at first light?"

Seraphine took a few steps away from him, fretting her lower lip with her teeth. This was all too new and strange and sudden. She did not want to go to America.

But... she hadn't wanted to come to Bruges either, and if she had not, she would never have become a lacemaker.

And Octavie was going to become a bride of Christ. Seraphine wanted to be Jean-Paul's wife. The thought of losing him was more than she could bear.

She turned back to her intended. "Yes, Jean-Paul," she breathed. "I will go with you to America."

———

Seraphine waited for Octavie just outside the chapel. "Where were you?" Octavie asked anxiously. "Is something wrong?"

"Come away." Seraphine took her sister's hand and pulled her down the corridor. "I'll tell you upstairs."

The girls shared an attic bedroom with four other orphan girls. Now Seraphine lit a candle and sat on the floor between her cot and the wall, and gestured for Octavie to join her. Whispering, she told her sister what Jean-Paul had done, what he had asked, what she had told him.

"To America!" Octavie's eyes were wide. "You mustn't!"

Seraphine's throat grew thick and salty. "I don't want to. But it seems there is no other way. Jean-Paul is afraid to stay here, and … " She swiped away a tear. "We are promised to each other."

"*America.*" Octavie sounded stunned.

Seraphine fought rising panic. "I'll visit. Farming is much better in America, Jean-Paul says. We won't have to struggle for every morsel there."

Octavie didn't answer. Seraphine felt as if her heart might burst. The girls at the far end of the room began giggling over some jest. I will miss this place, as well as Octavie, she thought. The daily rhythms of life at the convent had become familiar and dear.

"But … I won't be there when you get married!" Octavie looked stricken. "I always thought … "

"And I won't be here when you take your vows." Seraphine scrabbled under her cot for a wooden box that had once held dried cod. Inside she found the cloth-covered packet she wanted. She slowly unwrapped a length of scalloped lace, wider than her hand and three meters long.

Octavie's eyes welled over. "Your wedding lace. Will you even have time to make a veil?"

"No." There would be no extra coins to buy the veil she'd planned to trim with the lace, not now. Seraphine pulled her little sewing bag from her box and removed scissors, a needle, and thread. She folded the lace trim in half. When she'd found the center, she took the scissors and carefully cut the trim into two pieces, quickly rolling and pinning the edges.

Octavie gasped. "What are you *doing*?"

"I'm leaving half of this for you. I'll hem the cut ends to prevent raveling. Perhaps you can use it when you take your vows. A bit of me will be there with you."

Octavie let the snowy length cascade over her hand. "But I have no gift for you!"

"All I want from you now is letters." Seraphine leaned closer. "Write to me about lace. Write and tell me that you are happy, and I will do the same." But she was crying now, and her nose was running too, because everything was changing.

———

Seraphine was up before dawn. She said goodbye to her startled roommates. Then she and Octavie picked up her wooden box, which held her spare dress, stockings, sewing bag, and the few tools and utensils they'd saved from the cottage. She'd tucked her half of the wedding lace at the bottom of her rag bag.

Then she and her sister walked the convent's silent corridors together for the last time.

The grumpy nun must have gotten the gist of last evening's conversation, for to Seraphine's surprise, Sister Odile-Alphonse was waiting in the courtyard. Beneath the white cap her face was placid, but her eyes were sad. "So, child. I understand plans have changed."

"Yes." Seraphine put her box down and wrapped her arms around the older woman.

"I shall picture you in America, content," Sister Odile-Alphonse murmured, stroking Seraphine's hair. "Perhaps opening up a small lace shop. Go with God, child."

Seraphine pulled away. "Thank you. For everything." Then she looked at Octavie, and words failed her. They clung together for a long moment, shuddering with sobs.

Octavie found the strength to pull away first. "I believe that we will meet again on this earth."

Seraphine clutched her sister's hand. "But what if we do not?"

"Have faith, Seraphine."

My faith is not that strong, Seraphine thought.

And as always, Octavie understood. "If you falter," she said, "I will have faith for both of us."

Sister Odile-Alphonse produced the key and unlocked the gate. Seraphine wiped her eyes and hefted her box. Then she set her shoulders, lifted her chin, and went to meet Jean-Paul.

TEN

THE NEXT MORNING, CHLOE found only a single place setting on the table. "Where's Elise?" she asked when Sharon brought in a plate of pancakes.

"Elise left early this morning. She said she'd see you this evening at her workshop."

"Oh." Chloe wrinkled her forehead. Elise hadn't mentioned an errand or appointment. And ... wasn't it just yesterday that Elise had expressed trepidation about driving on Wisconsin's wintry roads? Not to mention, Chloe thought, that I'd hoped to have a good talk with her today. Lovely.

"You're heading out for a driving tour with Jason Oberholtzer this morning?" Sharon asked.

Chloe tried to put Elise's mercurial disposition out of her mind. "I am." She poured maple syrup on her pancakes. Best to fortify herself.

Sharon looked pleased. "He's the grad student I mentioned—the one who helps out here on the farm."

"How did you meet?"

"He's doing a field study on Belgian architectural history, and he's gotten very involved with our preservation efforts. He came to a meeting here at the farm once, and it went from there." Sharon smiled. "I've got an errand to run, so give him my best."

While finishing her breakfast Chloe reviewed her questions for Jason Oberholtzer. Then she grabbed her totebag, bundled up, and left the house. She didn't feel like waiting inside on a sunny morning.

A Chevy Cavalier had joined her own Pinto in the lot. Chloe wandered on to get a better look at the outbuildings. To her left sat the beautiful old log barn, similar to the one at Heritage Hill. A century of wear and weather had bowed the ridgeline, but otherwise the structure appeared to be in good repair. Nearby stood a corncrib and what might have once been a hog barn or chicken coop. Beyond those, near the edge of the road, stood a small building—an old outhouse or tool shed, maybe.

Curious Holsteins watched from a pen by the barn. Chloe moseyed over and leaned against the fence, thinking about the people who'd milked cows right here for over a century. There's such power in *place* when thinking about the past, she thought. In walking the ground where—

"Good morning."

Chloe whirled to face a stocky woman wearing stained brown coveralls and manure-caked boots. "Hello!"

"Sorry! Didn't mean to startle you. You're one of the guests, I assume?"

"I'm Chloe. And you must be Antoinette." Sharon's daughter was in her mid- to late twenties. Her round cheeks were red from the cold. There was something familiar about her, although Chloe couldn't think why.

"Call me Toni, please." She grinned. "Either you were daydreaming or you have a particular interest in Holsteins."

"Daydreaming," Chloe admitted. "It's one of my talents. I was trying to imagine what this farm looked like a century ago. Is the original cabin still standing?" Often small cabins were repurposed when a second, larger home was built.

"I'm afraid not." Toni folded her arms, looking over the farm. "The big barn is over a century old. That chicken coop is original log construction too." She pointed. "When I was a kid we had a flock of Rhode Island Reds, but after my dad died Mom needed to pare back."

"Between the B&B and the dairy, it's a lot for one person," Chloe said. "I'm sure she's glad to have your help."

"The plus side of getting divorced, I guess. Back to the homeplace." Toni's voice held an unhappy edge.

Chloe wished she hadn't brought the family issue up.

"The timing is good, actually," Toni said, as if sensing Chloe's remorse. "Mom needed help." She shrugged ruefully. "Besides, this place is important to me. Family, you know? I mean, it's who I am."

It's who I am. Something I don't know anymore, Chloe thought.

But before she could swan dive into that particular pity pool, an old banana-yellow AMC Gremlin came down the drive. A young man was at the wheel. "I think that's my ride."

Jason Oberholtzer had a friendly smile and dark curls. He cranked down his window. "Hey, Toni. And you must be Chloe. Good to meet you. Hop in."

She slid into the car. "Thank you for sharing your time with me."

"My friends are tired of hearing me talk about Belgian architecture," Jason admitted. "I'm always happy for a new audience." He executed a tidy three-point turn. "And don't worry about my car. It's in better shape than it looks, and drives like a tank."

Chloe pointed at her old Pinto as they passed. "That's my ride. It does not drive like a tank."

"Museum curators and grad students do not drive high-end vehicles."

As she fished out her notebook, Chloe noticed the bright blue cap on the seat. "Say, did you eat at Lorenzo's last night? With Toni?"

He looked startled. "That's right. Best pizza in Green Bay. Were you there?"

"I was." That was why Toni had looked familiar. She'd been half of the noisy pair sitting behind Elise.

Jason turned onto the main road and, to Chloe's relief, headed away from Hugh Lejeune's place. "Is there something in particular you want to see?" he asked.

"I'm trying to soak up as much about Belgian cultural heritage as I can. And you're working on a field study, I understand … ?"

"I'm a cultural geographer, working with a professor at the university. We're surveying the vernacular architecture in the area around Namur, which is sort of the epicenter of Belgian-ness in Door County." Jason sounded excited. "After a hundred and thirty years, the Belgian-American settlement area retains its distinct identity. It's one of Wisconsin's largest ethnic enclaves. And, both culturally and architecturally, I believe it is *the* most intact."

"Very cool," Chloe said happily.

Over the next hour they pulled over at several farms. Jason proved himself well versed in local architecture. "Belgians didn't have particular woodworking skills like some of the Scandinavians, so you won't find distinctive notching, but the workmanship is generally quite good... What's really cool about all these log barns is that most are still being used... My professor says you'd be hard put to name an area with a greater density of log structures anywhere in North America... We're going to prepare a nomination for a Namur Belgian-American District for the Wisconsin Register of Historic Places, and then for the National Register..."

Chloe alternated between taking notes and staring out the window, soaking in the landscape. "Are you of Walloon descent?" she asked as they pulled away from one of the farms.

"No," he said, with obvious regret. "My family symbolizes the great melting pot. I'm also an army brat. We lived all over. People ask me where I'm from, and I have no idea what to say."

No wonder studying this deep-rooted community intrigues him, Chloe thought. Her own upbringing had nothing in common with Jason's. Stoughton, where her parents still lived, had a strong Norwegian identity—

Which you no longer have, Chloe reminded herself. Maybe no more than half, anyway.

Then what Jason had just said niggled at something she'd pushed to the back of her mind. Hadn't Sharon said—

"Have you noticed the white stars?" Jason pointed at a barn displaying a large wooden star on the gable end.

She twisted around for a better look. "I've seen a handful of them." Including the one on Hugh Lejeune's old farm. "What's the significance?"

"No one's really sure," Jason admitted. "Could be a builder's mark, could be patriotic. Want my theory? I think the religious Belgian immigrants wanted a symbol of Stella Maris on their farms—"

"Stella Maris?"

He braked as a school bus in front of them began flashing red lights. "Latin for 'Star of the Sea.' It's an ancient reference to the Virgin Mary, especially in Catholic countries with a history of seafaring and fishing. There are half a dozen Catholic churches in Door County alone named Stella Maris."

"Interesting." Chloe imagined devout Walloon settlers glancing at the stars as they went about their chores. "It looks as if land-use patterns haven't changed much."

"Eighty percent of the farmland in our study area is still in the hands of Belgians," Jason told her. "Now that you've got a sense of farm layout, there are two specific outbuildings you need to know about. The first is the summer kitchen with attached bake oven."

Something seized in Chloe's belly. Not *again*. "Actually, I'm somewhat familiar with summer kitchens and bake ovens. Perhaps visiting more wouldn't be the best use of your time today."

He looked disappointed, but only briefly. "You're right. I'm trying to fit a two-day tour into two hours. What do you know about the roadside chapels?"

"Not a darn thing," Chloe said gratefully.

After another mile or so, Jason pulled over. The farmhouse and outbuildings were visible some distance away. Only a small building with white siding stood near the berm. "That's a chapel?" Chloe asked doubtfully.

"Let's get out."

She was glad to stretch her legs. She followed Jason, but hesitated when he opened the door. "Shouldn't we tell the property owners we're here?"

"Not necessary." He ushered her inside.

"Oh!" Chloe said softly. The light from the open door revealed a small but lovely chapel, perhaps eight feet long. Directly opposite the door was a three-tiered altar carefully arrayed with religious statues, candelabra, and artificial flowers in painted vases. Two kneelers were positioned before the altar. Ornately framed certificates covered the side walls, and she studied them. Everything older than 1920 was written in French; more recent notices of baptisms, first communions, marriages, and deaths in English. "I feel like I'm looking at someone's family Bible."

"It's special, isn't it? This chapel is over a century old. Original log construction, sided over."

The perception of peaceful reverence was palpable. This was clearly a sacred place.

"Most of the Walloon immigrants were Catholic," Jason said. "Roadside chapels like this were very common. Not because people lived too far from a church, but because their faith was so strong that they wanted a convenient place to pray. Some chapels were dedicated with gratitude for blessings received. Others were built to consecrate a particular saint, or in honor of a loved one. They were built near roads, away from the main farm buildings, because neighbors and passersby were welcome to stop as well."

Chloe imagined weary farmers kneeling here to give thanks at harvest time, a terrified mother begging help for her sick child, a devout traveler slipping inside to pray.

"Unfortunately, quite a few were lost when the old farm lanes were widened. But a couple dozen still exist, and a few people have constructed newer chapels." Jason turned to leave. "I would never wander anywhere else on someone's farm without asking permission, but no one will mind if you visit a chapel."

———

In Eagle, Roelke pulled into St. Theresa's empty parking lot and studied the church. He didn't see anything amiss. The rock through the window was probably a one-time thing. Still, he got out and circled the building. He walked up the front steps, tried the door— and was surprised to find it unlocked. Frowning, he stamped slush from his shoes and stepped inside. "Father Dan?" he called. No answer. The sanctuary was empty.

Sun streaming through the tall windows created jeweled mosaics on the floor and gave the illusion of warmth. Roelke slipped into a pew. The sanctuary felt familiar. Memories summoned his childhood, when everything religious made sense. When he accepted anything a priest said as … well, as gospel. His grandparents had been devout. His mother had attended church regularly as well, taking her two sons with her. Looking back, Roelke hoped his mom had found solace there, a respite from her alcoholic husband. For him the routines had all been comfortable. Normal. It had never occurred to him, back then, to question anything.

Well, that wasn't quite true, he reminded himself. The congregation had included too many overzealous matrons who weren't content with a polite handshake after mass, but instead chose to suffocate him in perfumey embraces while he mumbled "Hello" into their chests.

Roelke smiled, but it quickly faded. When had he started to question his faith? When his dad broke his mother's arm in a fit of rage? Or had the questions come from within when he started taking a hard look at the world? He remembered visiting the magnificent Basilica of St. Josaphat in Milwaukee last winter. His best friend Rick had just been killed on the job, and the official story of his death didn't ring true. At Roelke's lowest ebb, he'd found himself in the Basilica, just sitting, craving faith and hope and solace. He remembered thinking that somewhere between altar boy and cop, his faith had faded.

Now, to his surprise, Roelke realized that part of him missed those old days. Not being an altar boy specifically, but hearing familiar prayers, watching familiar rituals, feeling a part of something so monumentally bigger than him. Maybe there's still something here for me, Roelke thought. A priest had helped him at the Basilica that horrible day. Maybe—

A side door opened, and Father Dan entered the church. "Officer McKenna? May I help you?"

Roelke got to his feet so hastily he banged one knee against the hymnal rack. He tried not to wince. "No, Father. I stopped by to make sure there hadn't been any more trouble. I did a quick security check and was surprised to find the front door unlocked."

"I'm meeting an engaged couple in a few minutes to discuss their wedding ceremony. I give couples a chance to see the church on their own, so I unlocked about fifteen minutes ago. But I came back early because I couldn't remember if I'd edged up the heat."

"It's not a good idea to leave the front door unlocked, even for a short time."

Father Dan merely smiled. "This church belongs to the people of Eagle, Officer McKenna. If it were up to me, it would be unlocked all the time."

"Father, I understand that this is a sacred place, but today's criminals won't respect that. Do you have any kind of security or emergency plan in place?"

The other man gestured toward the altar. "I trust in God to care for us. I can't do anything that might suggest doubt to my parishioners."

Before Roelke could think of a reply, the door opened behind him. A man and woman came inside with a blast of cold air. "Good afternoon, Father," the woman called cheerfully.

Roelke nodded to the priest, nodded to the soon-to-be-married, and made his exit.

———

Jason returned Chloe to Belgian Acres at one o'clock. Before getting out of the car she paused, hand on the door. "Are you coming to the Heritage Day potluck?"

"I wouldn't miss it!"

"I'll see you tomorrow, then. Thanks again for the tour."

Sharon stepped outside and waved as Jason drove away. "How was the tour?"

"Fascinating! I'll have a much better idea what I'm seeing when I drive by old Belgian farms now." Chloe considered the peaceful landscape. "I'm so glad this part of Door County is still rural."

"Oh, we've had overtures from developers from time to time," Sharon said wryly, "but we Belgians are just too darn stubborn to be courted. And the work being done by Jason and his professor is only highlighting how special our rural heritage is." She turned toward the house. "I'm sorry Jason couldn't stay and visit."

"He said he'll see you tomorrow for milking, but he needed to get to his other job now."

Sharon nodded. "He's got some work-study hours at the university archives. I was going to invite you both to join me for grilled cheese sandwiches."

She was under no obligation to provide lunch. But Chloe loved grilled cheese sandwiches, and welcomed the chance for a quiet conversation with the innkeeper. "That would be great, thanks."

They sat down to bowls of tomato soup and toasted cheddar sandwiches. "Toni can't join us?" Chloe asked, flapping open her napkin.

"She's gone in to work." Sharon stirred a few soda crackers into her soup. "Sometimes she meets friends for coffee before her shift. Which is fine with me, of course. Much better than joining them for drinks after work."

Chloe had no idea how to respond.

"Sorry." Sharon sighed. "That was inappropriate. It hasn't been easy for her, transitioning back to the farm after life in Chicago."

"I had a brief but very nice chat with her this morning," Chloe said. "She sounded happy to be back, actually. She told me a bit about the original outbuildings on the farm."

"You're welcome to visit the old barn and chicken coop, if you wish," Sharon assured her. "Just don't leave any gates open."

"Thanks," Chloe said. "I love old buildings." She took a bite, grabbing her napkin to capture an errant bit of cheese. "How much do you know about your family history, Sharon? You said two brothers immigrated together?"

"Etienne and Jean-Paul, with their wives, in 1854, just a year after the first Belgians arrived in Wisconsin. I'm descended from Seraphine and Jean-Paul Lejeune."

"Seraphine and Jean-Paul Lejeune," Chloe repeated slowly. She would think of them the next time she walked Sharon's property.

"I've always wanted to learn more, but I've never found time for the research." Sharon toyed with her spoon. "Don't you wish you could travel back in time, just to get a peek at your ancestors? There are some records in my family Bible that a distant cousin sent me, but it's all names and dates, just basic facts."

"Have any family artifacts survived?"

Sharon put down her spoon. "I do have a couple of things. I'll fetch them." She left the room, and her footsteps sounded on the stairs. She returned shortly with a pair of wooden shoes in one hand and a skirt draped over one arm.

Chloe clenched her hands in her lap to keep herself from touching. "They're beautiful." The skirt was brown with green and purple stripes near the hem. And the shoes ... oh, the shoes! Sturdy and worn, yes, but someone had taken the time to carve designs over the toe box.

"The *sabots*—that's what the Belgians called their wooden shoes—and the skirt belonged to Seraphine."

"They're *wonderful*."

"Seraphine must have had a hard life. All of the earliest arrivals did. I probably shouldn't admit this to a curator, but … sometimes when I'm facing a challenge I slip off my shoes and stand in Seraphine's *sabots*." Sharon's gaze flicked to Chloe, then away again as if afraid she'd see mockery.

But Chloe was anything but amused, or annoyed. "Standing in her shoes," she said softly, with complete understanding.

"Exactly." Sharon's shoulders relaxed. "Seraphine—all of the women who came in those early years—they were so courageous. Their faith was so strong. It's inspiring."

ELEVEN

SERAPHINE TRIPPED AS SHE stepped onto the gangway of the steamer that had brought them to Milwaukee, and one of her *sabots* almost flew into Lake Michigan. "Careful, *chère femme*," Jean-Paul whispered. "Lean on me, and take heart. We have reached Wisconsin."

The journey had been so long and wretched that Seraphine had despaired of hearing those words. Violent Atlantic storms had tossed their ship about like a child's toy. Dysentery had swept through the cramped quarters, and the thick stench of vomit and feces left her gasping. When Jean-Paul fell ill, Seraphine had almost dissolved with fear. When she wasn't cleaning and tending him, she knelt beside his bunk, praying the rosary. Octavie's absence was a hole inside of her. She couldn't lose her husband too.

Jean-Paul had survived, but sixty-two of the two hundred and four immigrants on board had not. The angry storms had blown them off course, prolonging the voyage. Insufficient food and water brought more misery. Sailors gave the passengers only thick bilge water, reddish and foul. Seraphine had spent the final weeks of the sea voyage on the bunk, weak from hunger and thirst, too wretched to pray for mercy. "I'm sorry," Jean-Paul whispered over and over, stroking her hair. "Things will be better soon."

Seraphine had wept with relief when they finally reached New York. She regained much of her strength as the journey continued west along canals and across great lakes. Those legs had not been as brutal, but they seemed interminable. When her *sabots* thumped from the wooden dock to Wisconsin soil, Seraphine squeezed her husband's hand.

The Milwaukee docks were busy with sailors carrying cargo from ships and drivers loading it into carts and wagons. The air smelled of tar and rotting cabbage. Gulls cried raucously overhead and drivers bellowed at their horses or oxen in languages she did not understand.

She edged closer to Jean-Paul. Belgium, the farm, the convent, Octavie … all she had known before seemed impossibly far away. Seraphine felt disoriented. Who was she to be here? Was she still Walloon? Still a Belgian?

"God brought us safely through the storms," Jean-Paul added. "Surely He intends us to thrive here in this new place."

Seraphine wasn't so confident. A bitter wind blew in from the water. How would they survive the winter? Autumn was waning. They were still far from their final destination. And—

"We're here!" Etienne clapped Jean-Paul on the shoulder as he and his wife, Emelie, joined them. Then he grinned at Seraphine and pecked her on one cold cheek.

Seraphine didn't know what to make of Etienne. Jean-Paul was steady; his older brother, impetuous. Jean-Paul had dark hair; his older brother's was the color of ripened wheat. Jean-Paul's features were fine and even; one missing tooth somehow made Etienne's ready smile only more jaunty. His high spirits had heartened the immigrants in dark hours during the journey, which was a blessing indeed. But she suspected that trampling the landowner's crops had been Etienne's idea, and she knew he had stolen two grub hoes before fleeing.

Etienne had also secured passports and passage for the four of them. "Did you give him the money?" she had asked Jean-Paul, bewildered. Jean-Paul had been saving what he could, but surely it wasn't enough.

"Etienne is taking care of it," her husband repeated, without meeting her gaze.

Emelie was a saucy, practical young woman already expecting her first child. She had startling blue eyes, and she could silence Etienne with a look.

Now Etienne announced that he'd made arrangements for a wagon ride as far as Green Bay, a city somewhere north of Milwaukee. "I only had to promise that we'd come back and help build a cowshed for the man," he told Jean-Paul.

And won't you be busy building our homes? Seraphine thought, but held her tongue. They had no money to purchase transport. She was chilled, weary, and too grateful for the ride to find fault.

———

NOVEMBER 1854

"Jean-Paul," Seraphine hissed. "This can't—" She stumbled, fell to one knee, clambered back to her feet. "This can't be right."

The uncertainty in her husband's eyes did nothing to stay her growing unease. "They said Ricard would know the way," he muttered. "They *said* so." He gave her a helpless shrug and kept walking.

"They" were the men at *Aux Premiers Belges,* where the first Belgian immigrants had settled the year before. Jean-Paul and Etienne had hoped to winter there, waiting until spring to search out the "forties" they'd been assigned at the land office. But every cabin was already crammed with recent arrivals, hungry and homesick.

"Now you must wait for Antoine Ricard to return," a man named Brise explained. "He's a mixed-blood Mexican who speaks a little French. He is away guiding another group to their land, and when he returns he can guide you too."

Seraphine eyed their dwindling food supplies, felt the winter bearing down.

The Lejeunes camped beside the Brise cabin. "At least you can rest for a few days," one of the Brise daughters, Adele, said consolingly. Adele, a few years older than Seraphine, was a kind, pious girl—a bit like Octavie. If the Brise family hadn't inexplicably started their farm in a dense forest, Seraphine would have wanted to settle nearby. But she did savor the respite, especially celebrating mass with a young Walloon priest, Father Edouard Daems.

Finally, in late November, Ricard had returned. *"Oui, oui,"* he said, nodding vigorously when Jean-Paul showed him his land claim papers. "Thirty miles American." The Lejeunes left *Aux Premiers Belges* before dawn, taking what they could carry. Etienne and Emelie's trunk, Seraphine's box, and the two sacks of potatoes they'd purchased in Green Bay would have to wait for another trip.

Now they were following Ricard through a forest, deeper and deeper, away from the bay of Green Bay which had, for a time, glimmered through the trees. There was no trail, just several inches of slushy snow to hide roots and rocks. They shoved through thickets and skidded down ravines and clambered over windfalls. The trees were so tall and thick that midday was gloomy as twilight. Every strange bird call startled Seraphine. Every cracking branch made her jump. The cold pressed into her bones, numbed her toes. She carried a bulky sack over one shoulder. The skillet dangling from one mittened hand slipped from her grasp over and over. Sometimes she didn't even notice until Etienne, coming along behind, picked it up and pressed it silently back into her hand. He had all he could manage helping Emelie, who was nearing her term and white with fatigue.

How could this Ricard possibly know where he was going? They'd been walking for hours. There were no landmarks. The endless forest had swallowed them. Their new friends at *Aux Premiers Belges* felt as far away as Octavie and the convent in Bruges.

Seraphine was plodding so numbly that when Jean-Paul stopped abruptly in front of her, she ran into him. "What?" She put the sack down stiffly.

Grinning, Ricard patted a huge tree and pointed at Jean-Paul. Then he grabbed a stick, kicked aside a thick layer of rotting leaves, and made quick marks in the earth: *NW*

Seraphine felt a prick of dread.

Jean-Paul wearily passed a hand over his face. "I think he's saying this is the northwest corner of our land."

"No." Her voice held a note of desperation. "It can't be. You said we'd find *farmland* here." She turned on her husband. "You told the man at the land office you wanted farmland, didn't you? Good farmland?"

"You saw the land at *Aux Premiers Belges*," Etienne said quietly, when Jean-Paul couldn't find the words. "They've had a year and a half to clear timber."

Seraphine had seen, of course. But she'd wanted to believe that somehow those first arrivals had made poor choices. She'd wanted to believe that their own tramp through forest primeval would end in that sunny, fertile meadow she'd held in her heart all these long weeks, and the guide would smile and say, "Yours."

Ricard gestured again, pointing at Jean-Paul, then his knife. Jean-Paul stepped forward and began carving his initials in the tree, claiming it as boundary of his land.

After nodding his approval the guide pointed at Etienne. "You, come now." Etienne's land was adjacent to theirs, and Ricard wanted to show Etienne his northwest corner.

"We'll be back," Etienne said. Seraphine squeezed Emelie's hand as she passed, and the two women shared a look of wordless understanding. Then Seraphine and Jean-Paul were alone, alone as they had never been in Belgium, or on the voyage, or at *Aux Premiers Belges*.

Jean-Paul turned from the tree, and she saw that he hadn't carved *JPL*, but *JP & S L*. "This is not what I expected," he said hoarsely. "Not what I promised."

No, it was not. Seraphine looked away. How could they farm here? How could she make lace when every waking moment would be spent struggling to defeat this dark forest? And if they didn't quickly find success, how would she save enough money to visit Octavie in Belgium?

"It will take more time than I knew to establish our farm. It will be difficult." Jean-Paul glanced at the towering trees and swallowed hard. "But I will not forget that you are a lacemaker, Seraphine."

Lace. Bobbins and thread, pins and pillows, light glowing through water-filled globes, quiet murmurs and sweet voices raised in song. The life she'd known at the convent felt so foreign that she couldn't grasp what Jean-Paul was saying.

But because she loved him, because she had married him with joy, she managed to nod. "Well," she said. "Here we are. Let's get to work."

Jean-Paul and Seraphine managed to erect a low shelter of branches tied into an inverted V shape. Jean-Paul went in search of water. Seraphine crawled into the windbreak and dragged her travel sack in after her. Tucked inside was the wedding veil lace she'd made in Bruges. She gently unfolded the protective cloth so she could see it. The fine threads. The flowers and scrolling vines. *I made this,* Seraphine thought in wonder, and had to blink against tears. This piece of lace bound her to Octavie. She closed her eyes and tried to imagine herself back to Bruges …

"Seraphine? What is that?"

She jumped as Jean-Paul crawled into the shelter. "It's just a piece of lace I made."

Jean-Paul had never seen it. Their wedding in Antwerp had been a hasty affair, nothing like the ceremony she'd imagined, performed quickly because Seraphine was working at an inn and Jean-Paul on the docks. She knew he was embarrassed by the necessity of marrying among strangers. She hadn't wanted to make him feel worse by showing him the lace she'd created in honor of their union.

"It is beautiful." The light was fading, and he leaned close, squinting. Then he sat back, regarding her with an expression she'd never seen before. "You told me about your work, but I didn't realize … " He shook his head. "Beautiful."

She folded her treasure back away. "Thank you," she whispered.

Dear Seraphine,

Please know I think of you every day. I am well, and aside from missing you, content. After discussing my vocation with the good sisters I have become a novitiate. I also continue to improve my lace skills, and have started teaching the youngest children. So many are very poor. Perhaps my calling will help me find a way to improve conditions for lacemakers.

Your loving sister,
Octavie

TWELVE

ROELKE WAS PATROLLING EAGLE'S mean streets that afternoon when Marie radioed his call sign, George 220. "It's a domestic," she reported. "A neighbor heard raised voices and breaking glass at 425 Everhardt Street."

Great, Roelke thought. Kent and Ginny Bobolik were at it again. "On my way. George 220 out."

When he reached the tiny rental home, Ginny's shrieks and a wordless bellow from Kent sounded through the closed door. Roelke tested the knob. Unlocked. Standing aside—in case Kent's rage got pointed at *him*—he opened the door. "Eagle Police!"

The Boboliks went silent. Roelke stepped inside, knees slightly flexed, every sense alert, scanning the room. But his arrival had, evidently, stolen the Boboliks' energy. Ginny, a skinny young woman at least twenty years Kent's junior, dropped weeping onto the sofa. Kent stood nearby, panting, scowling.

"So, what's going on?" Roelke asked, as conversationally as possible.

The brawl started, he soon learned, because Ginny put salt in the egg salad she'd made for their lunch. "I'm not supposed to eat salt," Kent said indignantly. "Doctor says so. That bitch is trying to kill me."

"I hardly put in any salt," Ginny insisted. "And he smacked me upside the head." Her right eye was already puffing up. She'd be sporting one hell of a shiner soon.

Through the window Roelke saw a deputy sheriff park at the curb.

"She hit me too," Kent grumbled. He might have been good-looking once, but his face had hardened into a perpetual scowl.

"Are you bruised?"

Kent, it seemed, was not.

Waukesha County Deputy Marge Bandacek walked through the open door, and Roelke shot her a grateful look: *Thanks for the backup.* He looked back to the Boboliks. "You two need some cooldown time. Kent, we're going to take you out to—"

"*No!*" Ginny launched from the sofa and clung to Kent like a limpet. "He didn't mean nothing. It was all my fault."

I *hate* domestics, Roelke thought.

With Marge's help, Roelke managed to detach Ginny from her husband. Marge cuffed Kent and walked him out to her car, where he could settle down. "I'm sorry, honey!" Kent called over his shoulder. "I love you!"

Roelke maneuvered Ginny back to the sofa. "I w-won't press ch-charges," she wept.

"Mrs. Bobolik." He squatted in front of her, trying to make eye contact. "We've had this conversation over and over. Why do you stay with a man who beats you?"

"He just has a temper is all," she snuffled.

Roelke considered banging his head against the end table a few times. Without Ginny agreeing to press charges, there was nothing he could do. One day the law would change, and officers would have the discretion to haul wife beaters to jail. That day couldn't come soon enough.

"He's always sorry," Ginny added. Her nose was running.

Roelke didn't see a tissue box so he went down the hallway to the bathroom, grabbed a handful of toilet paper, and gave Ginny that. She blotted her eyes, wincing, before noisily blowing her nose.

"I'm worried about you," Roelke said. "Do you feel safe in this house?"

She picked at a hole in the knee of her jeans.

"You deserve to feel safe."

"He's all I got."

Roelke opened his mouth, shut it again. He'd had this conversation with too many women, wealthy or struggling, young or not. He didn't know how to break through. How to convince a woman who'd been battered that there was a better life for her out there.

Sometimes, he thought wearily, I suck at being a cop.

———

Chloe spent the rest of the afternoon in her room at the B&B, organizing her notes. Her furnishings plan for Heritage Hill would include outbuildings as well as the house. Thanks to Jason Oberholtzer's tour, she had a much better sense of how they functioned.

At four thirty she heard footsteps, and Elise's door open and close. A little before five Chloe packed away her work. Time to go. Just as she stepped into the hall, Elise emerged from her room.

"Hey, Elise," Chloe said. "How was your day?"

Elise paused, hand on the doorknob. "Fine." She looked tired, but she took the effort to shape her mouth into a small smile.

"Is everything okay?"

Elise's shoulders stiffened. "Of course."

"I know we haven't seen each other for a long time, but I'm still your friend. If there's anything I can do—"

"There isn't," Elise said evenly. "How was your day?"

Chloe hesitated, wanting to say more. But she couldn't force Elise to confide in her, could she? "My day was good," she said finally. "I got a driving tour of the Namur Historic District, which was amazing. Then I spent the rest of the afternoon working here."

"Sounds good."

Chloe waited for Elise to say where she had been. Finally, when the silence became awkward, Chloe gave up. "Want to drive down to Green Bay together? We'll have plenty of time to grab something to eat before heading over to Heritage Hill for your program."

Elise hesitated.

"I'll drive," Chloe offered, to sweeten the pot.

"Thanks, but I think it might be best if we drove separately. I might need to stay later at the site than you want to."

Chloe didn't mind staying late. But Elise was already heading down the stairs.

Outside, the air was thick with moisture. "See you at the program, I guess," Chloe said.

"Great." Elise slid into her car.

Chloe watched Elise drive away. "I'll take that as a no on dinner." She sighed. Elise had chosen to plan her visit around Chloe's
stay here. What had happened to make her withdraw?

Twilight shrouded the old farm in deep shades of midnight blue
and turned the woods bordering the property into a black, shapeless
mass. Chloe wished she knew more about Seraphine Lejeune, who'd
once known this same landscape. Sharon gave what extra time and
energy she had to community projects. But I could do some digging,
Chloe thought. Anything she discovered would be a gift to Sharon
and Toni. That plan eased the sting of Elise's moodiness.

Chloe climbed into her Pinto and cranked up the heat. Once on
Hickory Road she drove carefully, testing the car's grip on the surface, well aware that the mist might freeze on the pavement in a
thin, treacherous layer of black ice. I do wish Elise had been willing
to ride with me, she thought.

At Lejeune Farm East, a Door County deputy's car was parked
by the side of the road. Deputy Knutson stood leaning against the
vehicle, arms crossed over her chest, staring at Hugh's old place.
Chloe braked and eased onto the shoulder behind the other car.

Deputy Knutson straightened as Chloe emerged. "Ms. Ellefson!
Is everything all right?"

"As far as I know. I was actually going to ask you the same
thing."

"Oh." Knutson kicked the heel of one boot against the toe of the
other. "I'll be honest. You finding Mr. Lejeune's body here ... I just
don't know what to make of it."

Chloe hesitated. She had no interest in setting foot on Hugh's
property again. *Ever.* Still ... there was a chance, just a chance, that
she might be able to sense something on the property that others

had missed. "Deputy Knutson? Would you be willing to look around a little bit with me? I thought … that is, if I just … maybe I might catch something helpful."

"Catch something helpful?" The deputy sounded doubtful. "I assure you, the crime scene team crawled over every inch of this place."

"I know the team was thorough," Chloe assured her. "But please, would you humor me? It won't take long."

The other woman made a gesture of acquiescence. "The scene's been cleared, so there's no harm in it. At this point we're looking for any help we can get. Let me grab my flashlight."

Chloe got hers as well. Her stomach knotted as they approached the summer kitchen, but she forced herself to step inside. She played the beam around the room to make sure no maniac was waiting to cram her into the bake oven. Since there was not, and the deputy had her back, she closed her eyes and tried to open herself, become receptive to whatever might linger in the room.

She sensed again the busyness of generations of Lejeune women bustling about with their never-ending labor. That sensation was reassuring, so Chloe tried to fine-tune her perception. Beneath the feminine energy there was a flash of something individual. A sense of security, of safety. Who had that come from? Had Etienne Lejeune's wife left that aura? Chloe took a slow breath, trying to go deeper into—

"Ms. Ellefson?" the deputy asked. "Do you see anything here?"

The moment was broken. Chloe opened her eyes. Whatever she'd just experienced had nothing to do with Hugh Lejeune's last horrid moments. "No. I don't see anything."

The deputy patiently followed as Chloe walked to the dejected house and paused, hand on one wall. Nothing. They followed the techs' trampled path through the weeds to the crumbling barn and poked their heads inside a smaller outbuilding or two. Nothing.

Chloe struggled to hide her frustration. She had a "gift" that she didn't understand and couldn't control. Maybe *homo sapiens* were slowly evolving, and a fluke of genetics had pushed her out front. But it was maddening to sometimes crack a door without really discovering what was inside.

Deputy Knutson coughed politely.

Okay, Chloe thought. All I accomplished here was give the deputy reason to suspect my sanity. But she didn't regret the brief foray. She'd only wanted to help. Nobody deserved what had happened to Hugh.

———

Roelke glanced up from the desk when Chief Naborski, who'd been at a meeting in Waukesha all day, walked into the Eagle PD at five thirty. "Hey, Chief."

Chief grabbed everything stuffed into his mailbox, riffled through, and jammed it back. "Why are you still here?"

"Busy afternoon." Roelke told his boss about the Bobolik call.

"Kent Bobolik?" Chief dropped into Marie's empty chair and rubbed his chin. "That guy's bad news. And the wife still won't press charges?"

"Nope."

Both men were quiet, contemplating the unhappy reality of Kent Bobolik's existence on planet Earth. "Well," Chief said finally. "All you can do is try."

"Do you think he killed his first wife?" Chief had been in Eagle when the murder took place. "I was looking at the case file the other day. It rankles me that no one was ever arrested."

"It rankles me too." Chief Naborski, apparently forgetting that he was sitting in Marie's modern chair instead of his own, tried to tip back on two legs and rolled halfway across the room before he could recover. "But was it Kent Bobolik who pulled the trigger? I didn't know then, and I don't know now."

Both men were still again, contemplating the unhappy reality of unsolved cases. Then Chief asked quietly, "What's on your mind, son?"

He *knows*, Roelke thought. His internal organs turned to ice. Chief knows what I did to keep Libby and the kids safe from her ex.

"I think it's more than Bobolik," the older man added.

Roelke said the first thing that came to mind. "I've been out to St. Theresa a couple of times this week. Somebody threw a stone through a stained glass window. I checked today and found the front doors unlocked. The priest seems unconcerned about security. It worries me."

"It should. What's your plan?"

He was supposed to have a plan? Dammit all. "Well, I need to help him understand why a security plan is important." He thought a moment. "I'll dig out some statistics about the rise in church-focused crime." He thought some more. "The priest believes that talking about safety acknowledges a lack of faith. I need to convince him to look at it another way. He surely wants people to feel safe in his church. A few security measures seems like a small price to pay."

"I like it." Chief Naborski got to his feet. "In fact, I think you should talk to the United Methodist minister too. Maybe even pull in some clergy from outside the village. If you can organize a meeting, it might help impress them that we take their safety very seriously."

"I'll get on it," Roelke promised. Chief wished him a good evening and headed out.

Time to am-scray, Roelke thought. He finished up the Bobolik paperwork and drove home.

At the farmhouse he stepped through the back door slowly. He hated walking into the kitchen when Chloe was away. Hated the silent emptiness that seized the room. Hated its *nothing* smell. Chloe liked to cook and loved to bake, and he'd grown accustomed to inhaling air scented with cardamom or homemade spaghetti sauce.

Every time she left town he promised himself he'd cook a steak, but he never did. Now he opened the refrigerator and grabbed a plastic container labeled *Eggplant-chickpea stew w/ wild rice*. Roelke dumped the contents into a small saucepan. By the time it began to simmer, the room smelled of curry. Much better. Roelke sat down to eat. Before getting together with Chloe he'd have sworn he hated eggplant, and he'd never tasted chickpeas. But the stew was delicious.

When the phone rang he bolted from his chair and assured the operator that he'd accept Chloe's collect call. "Is something wrong?" he asked. Usually she didn't call this early.

"No. I'm at Heritage Hill with a little time to fill. Elise is giving a program about Belgian lace tonight, followed by a workshop with a local lace club."

"There are such things as lace clubs?"

"Of course! I don't know how many members do bobbin lace, but I imagine we'll get knitters and crocheters. Maybe some people who do needle-manipulated styles, or ethnic, which would be fun. And I'd expect some tatters too."

"Well, hunh." Roelke had no idea what or who "tatters" were. But Chloe sounded good, enthused about this new element of her history world, and that put his mind at ease.

"So, how was your day?"

"One domestic call that wasn't any fun," he told her. "And I visited St. Theresa, following up after a vandalism incident." He leaned against the wall. "Father Grinke, the priest, seems unconcerned about security issues. Chief Naborski asked me to pull a meeting together. Bring in the Methodist minister too."

"That sounds like a good idea," Chloe said. "Speaking of churches, I learned about something special today." She told him about the little chapel she'd visited. "I could sense a century of devout people coming to pray. It was a privilege to be there."

Roelke liked the sound of that. Liked the image of having a place to reflect without having to worry about a priest showing up and asking questions. "Maybe you could show me one day."

"I'd love that."

"Chloe..." He paused on the edge of something he hadn't planned to bring up, hadn't figured out yet. "I've been thinking about... That is, I think I need to see if I can find my faith again."

"Okay," Chloe said cautiously.

126

"I love my job, but I spend too much time dealing with miserable people in miserable situations."

"I know you do. I worry about that."

Roelke crouched to pet Olympia, who'd wandered over to rub her head against his ankle. "Maybe I just need to believe there's something bigger out there."

"You have my complete support, Roelke."

"But you're not Catholic."

The caution crept back into her tone. "Does that matter?"

"No, it's just that . . . whenever we decide to get married—*if*, I mean—I don't know where we could have the ceremony. I don't think a priest would agree to marry us." Roelke closed his eyes. He was making a hash of this.

After a long pause Chloe said "I love you dearly, Roelke, but I'm not able to convert to Catholicism. Not even for you."

"Look, I'm not saying it's simple for me. I don't believe everything the church teaches. But I need *something*. I have to start somewhere I feel comfortable. And I think that's the Catholic church."

"Then that's where you need to be," she said. "I'll even come with you sometimes. I just can't convert."

"I don't expect you to." He'd known that all along, really, even if he'd let himself hope.

———

Chloe replaced the public phone receiver in its cradle slowly. Well, she thought, *that* was a conversation I did not expect to have tonight. She was truly glad that Roelke was thinking about filling a void in his life. Whatever burden he'd been carrying was taking a toll on him, and it was taking a toll on them.

Still, it had never occurred to her that spiritual differences would come between them.

For a long moment she let herself feel sad. Then she gave herself a mental shake. Faith is a big, complicated thing for anyone, she reminded herself, and doubly so for a couple. She and Roelke were not the first to confront that challenge.

THIRTEEN

ETIENNE AND EMELIE WERE bickering again. I can't bear this one more day, Seraphine thought. She was boiling potatoes in a kettle nestled in her cook fire, and fighting morning sickness. Unsuccessful, she ran outside and bent double, retching.

Finally she straightened and wiped her mouth on her sleeve, gulping in the cool, damp air. Things could be worse, she thought. At least her child would be born under a roof.

Emelie had not been so lucky the cold day last December when her pains began. Etienne and Jean-Paul were gone, off to Green Bay in search of work. Sleet pinged against the branches and sputtered into the low fire kept burning at one end of the brush shelter. Seraphine was terrified that the baby would die, or Emelie would die, or that the blood would attract a wolf or bear. Emelie screamed and groaned. Seraphine wept and prayed. Finally, *finally*, a tiny boy burst shrieking into the world.

"I would have died without you," Emelie whispered.

Seraphine put aside the rag she'd been using to clean her sister-in-law and leaned close. "I would have died long ago without having you to share with." In Belgium, Octavie had been her dearest friend. Emelie couldn't take Octavie's place, but she'd become dear too.

Emelie, infant François, and Seraphine huddled together under blankets until the men returned a few days later with a sack of bread and chunks of salt pork. "A fine son!" Etienne had exulted. "Seraphine, thank you."

By the new year the men had managed to build a more substantial shelter, with log walls and a roof made of cedar bark, for the five of them. Seraphine and Emelie gathered dead reeds from a nearby swamp to stuff into the gaps between logs. Still, that first Wisconsin winter was a frigid, hungry blur. Tempers sometimes flared. The men were gone for days or weeks at a time. The women struggled with homesickness, and with snow drifting against the path, and sometimes—despite their growing bond—with each other. When blizzards screamed around the cabin, or the temperature dropped far below zero, Seraphine tried to imagine herself back at the convent—warm and dry, full of soup and bread, settling down at her lace cushion—but she could not.

But finally, Seraphine thought now, the harsh winter is loosening its claws.

Jean-Paul appeared beside her, wrapping another shawl around her shoulders. "I'm sorry the unborn babe is making life more difficult," he said, rubbing her back.

"It's not so bad. At least this morning there was nothing in my belly to come back up." She'd meant the observation as a feeble jest.

But Jean-Paul did not smile. "Seraphine, we are almost out of potatoes." The last food they had. "Etienne and I have to leave again. We have all the shingles we can carry." The men had pegged together a shaving bench and learned to make cedar shingles, splitting and shaping and bundling them, hauling them to Green Bay on their backs. They earned $1.50 for each thousand delivered—after they'd paid off the price of the drawknife needed to shave them.

"If you sell every shingle you have, it won't be enough. Even if spring comes early, harvest is still months away."

Jean-Paul looked away, a muscle working in his jaw. "We'll ask the storekeeper for credit. He's Belgian. He knows how it is for us."

More debt, Seraphine thought dully. None of them wanted that.

Then the obvious answer came. She put one hand against her belly as her heart broke, but forced the words out. "Take my lace, and trade it for—"

"No."

"It's valuable. We need food, Jean-Paul. Emelie has François to care for. I need to eat for our little one. You and Etienne can't labor all day with empty bellies. Take the lace."

He closed his eyes, rubbing the back of his neck. "Very well, Seraphine." He blinked hard, as if a cold wind was stinging his eyes, although it was still beneath the trees today. "We'll leave right away."

Seraphine watched numbly as the brothers hoisted their bundles and disappeared into the woods. My lace, she thought dully. My lace is gone.

But when the men emerged from the woods days later, shouting hello, Seraphine saw they were carrying only more potatoes in sacks slung over their shoulders. She pulled Jean-Paul aside. "You sold my lace, and this is all you bring?"

He quickly pulled the bundle she'd given him from his coat pocket. "No, here it is. The storekeeper said he'd never find a buyer for something so fine. But he gave us extra potatoes, on loan."

"Perhaps we can sell it in a few years," she said slowly. She could no longer imagine the day when their farm produced such bounty that she could afford passage back to visit Octavie. "So I could visit my sister."

"That will be your decision," Jean-Paul said. "We've got enough food now to see us through, and soon we'll get seeds in the ground. Things will get better."

SEPTEMBER 1855

Seraphine ducked her head and stepped outside the cabin, her two-week-old daughter Octavie in her arms. Leaves were starting to turn yellow and red. "We've been here almost a year," she whispered. "Perhaps you were sent to save us." She kissed the infant, and Octavie waved a tiny fist. She'd arrived like a sunrise, easing the shadows away, giving her mother new purpose.

Seraphine adjusted the light muslin she'd draped over the baby to discourage biting insects and filter some of the smoke. The enormous trees had no market value. Every single one had to be hacked down and chopped into manageable lengths, which were rolled into piles and set alight. Burning green wood left an ever-present pall of smoke around the tiny cabin. Jean-Paul and Etienne had never worked with timber before, and went at it with only axes, necessity, and advice from the men at *Aux Premiers Belges*. At night the Lejeune men whimpered and groaned in their sleep. But each tree downed allowed more sunshine to sift through the canopy.

And life had gotten a little easier. Raspberries ripened in the woods. Seraphine had roamed for miles along the creek bed, collecting stones, and they now had a chimney. Jean-Paul trudged the thirty miles home from Green Bay carrying enough planks to make a door. The men built a second cabin on Etienne's land, and—although they quickly wore a path between the farms—the two couples finally had some privacy.

Seraphine had helped plant some of their old landlord's wheat kernels, spirited to Wisconsin in the hem of Emelie's skirt, and was too hungry to feel guilty. She was terrified that it wouldn't grow, planted here and there among the stumps, but by August they had a harvest. Once it was threshed, Jean-Paul went back to Green Bay to work and obtain supplies.

The next day Seraphine had trudged thirty miles to the nearest mill with a fifty-pound sack of grain. She'd twisted one corner of her sack into a cap of sorts, taking most of the weight on her neck and shoulders. She was terrified every moment—of going into labor, of being attacked by wolves, of getting lost with nothing but an occasional blaze gashed on a tree for guidance. But there was nothing to do but plod along, blinking back tears, clutching a heavy stick to help maintain balance and, if need be, to fend off wild animals. She managed to find the mill, and after sleeping on the floor overnight, she made the trip home with a sack full of flour. Octavie had been born three weeks later.

Today Jean-Paul was laboring for the second day at felling a tree four feet around. The sound of blade striking wood had been ringing through the clearing for hours. Seraphine had fashioned a cradle-basket from honeysuckle vines, and planned to put Octavie down to sleep in the shade. She sometimes took the axe and sliced through stump roots of a previously-felled tree, or skinned smaller branches from bigger ones and dragged them to the burn pile.

Jean-Paul paused and wiped sweat from his forehead when she approached. "How is—"

"Hello!" a man shouted. It was not Etienne.

Seraphine and Jean-Paul stared at each other. They'd had no guest since moving into the forest. She put a hand to her hair, considered her dirty apron. As starved as she was for new company, she wasn't sure if she remembered how to make conversation.

Then Father Daems appeared, carrying a leather pack over one shoulder. He raised a hand in greeting. "Good day!"

Jean-Paul whacked the axe into a tree, lodging it there. "Welcome!"

"Father, could you baptize our baby?" Seraphine asked eagerly. "And our nephew?"

"Of course," Father Daems assured her. "I was hoping I might celebrate mass too."

Seraphine served the men bread and jam. Then Father Daems and Jean-Paul went to fetch Emelie and Etienne from Lejeune Farm East. Seraphine put Octavie down in the cradle-basket and surveyed the room. Profound dismay replaced the sense of accomplishment she'd indulged in earlier. Their home was dark, and smelled of stale sweat and dirty diapers.

Seraphine hauled water from the stream half a mile away, tidied the room, and washed as best she could. She scoured the table, which would have to serve as a makeshift altar.

It wasn't enough. We may live in a wilderness, Seraphine thought, but we are not wild creatures. Her daughter was going to be baptized. She and Jean-Paul were going to celebrate their first mass in almost a year. She had to do better.

She pawed through her rag bag, found a piece of clean linen, and hastily hemmed the cloth into a tidy rectangle. Then, more slowly, she pulled out her wedding lace. *That lace was meant to help buy a ticket back to Belgium to visit Octavie*, a voice in her head reminded her.

I can spare just a bit for something so important, another voice said.

She cut a length of the lace to fit one long side of the cloth and stitched it in place. Once positioned on the table, the pale lace glowed against the wood.

When the others returned, Father Daems's face lit with astonished pleasure when he saw her surprise. Jean-Paul looked quizzical: *Weren't you saving that?* Seraphine moved one shoulder in a tiny shrug: *What else could I do?* He nodded, clearly pleased.

After mass, the priest drew Seraphine aside. "I haven't seen such an altar cloth since coming to Wisconsin."

"My sister and I learned to make lace at a convent in Bruges," she told him. "Please, take the cloth with you." She imagined him smoothing it out in distant cabins, an unexpected bit of grace for other homesick, heartsick immigrants.

"Thank you." He folded the cloth gently, tucking the lace edging inside, and placed it in his tabernacle.

Seraphine felt strange, as if she were waking from a long dream. For the first time since leaving Belgium, she felt happy. The worst was behind them. Another year of hard work, maybe two—well, maybe three—and she and Jean-Paul would seize their dreams.

———

Two weeks later more visitors arrived—three families this time, following Ricard with a familiar air of exhausted doubt. Two of the men carried a big trunk between them, and everyone was laden.

Jean-Paul strode to meet them. Seraphine slapped at a damp spot on her apron where Octavie's diaper had leaked before hurrying after him.

The Delforge, Rouer, and Anselme families had also come from Belgium's Brabant Province. The women wearily herded seven drooping children between them—two just babies. Tear stains were visible in the grime on young Dominique Anselme's cheeks. Two of the children were hers. "Come, sit," Seraphine offered. "I'll fetch water."

The men clustered around Jean-Paul—peppering him with questions, wanting his advice. Ricard finally interrupted, making shooing motions. "The sun, yes?" He pointed to the sky, then made a sinking gesture.

"Perhaps the women and children can rest here while the men go on," Seraphine suggested. Everyone seemed happy with that arrangement.

"I'll go with them," Jean-Paul told Seraphine. "There's so much they need to learn! And you can visit with the women. We'll return in a few days."

That evening the cabin was full of talk. Seraphine nursed Octavie and slapped mosquitoes and listened sympathetically. Her guests talked of their voyage—storms at sea, broken masts, shipboard fevers, rations cut to bits of black bread once a day. They spoke of their journey through Wisconsin—dishonest land agents, getting lost, wolves. "When we realized they were stalking us, we didn't know what to do," Dominique said, patting the baby over her shoulder. "Then my husband thought to throw our salt pork at them. That's what they were after. But now we have no meat."

"It will get better," Seraphine promised them. "It is terribly difficult … but it will get better."

The women spread blankets and settled their children for the night—whispering prayers, fretting over one little boy who didn't feel well, humming lullabies. Seraphine kissed Octavie's soft cheek, soaking in the scent of her, the warm weight in her arms. Then she settled down as well.

She woke in the night to anxious murmuring. "Can I help?" she asked.

"It's my Louis," Dominique whispered. "He is getting worse."

Tiptoeing carefully, Seraphine found the water bucket and a rag. She and Dominique spent hours wiping the skinny boy down, trying to ease the rising fever. "There, there," Seraphine whispered, trying not to think of the close quarters, of the other children who'd been traveling and playing and sleeping with Louis. When Dominique's strength wavered, Seraphine took her hand. "Let's pray."

Louis died just before dawn. By the time first light crept inside the cabin door, his skin was already turning black. Dominique began to sob.

"Holy mother protect us," Seraphine breathed. Louis had died of cholera. A sickening sense of dread seized her as Octavie began to whimper.

Four hours later, baby Octavie died of cholera too.

Three weeks passed before Father Daems returned. Jean-Paul, who'd come home to tragedy, was now engaged in brutal battle with a stubborn tree. Seraphine had watched him rage out his grief, sending chips flying with every axe blow. She was glad he had the work to save him, but she had no energy to attack her own chores. That morning she'd come outside blinking and sat on a log, missing her baby, missing her sister.

"I'm glad you've come," she told Father Daems. "Our baby…"

Jean-Paul joined them, breathing heavily, and put a comforting hand on her shoulder.

"I'm so sorry." There were shadows in the priest's eyes, and dark smudges beneath. His shoulders slumped with exhaustion. "The cholera has spread throughout the settlement. Many lives have been lost. Where is your baby now?"

Jean-Paul and Seraphine led him to the tiny cemetery they'd created in the woods. Wooden crosses marked the graves of their Octavie and the others who had died in their cabin, including both of Dominique Anselme's children.

"You didn't bury them here!" Father Daems exclaimed.

Seraphine exchanged a bewildered glance with her husband. "But—but what else could we do?" Jean-Paul stammered.

"Our dead must be buried in consecrated ground."

Seraphine stared at him. "But… the closest consecrated ground is thirty miles away. We did our best. If you could say a prayer for Octavie…"

"You must move her to *Aux Premiers Belges.*" The priest's voice was gentle, but firm. "She must rest there. And the others as well."

Seraphine watched the priest disappear back into the woods. Couldn't Father Daems understand that she and Jean-Paul had done all they could? While Jean-Paul dug the grave, she'd cut two inches of the wedding lace and stitched it into a flounce for Octavie's gown. They had buried her with love and prayers.

"I'll go fetch Etienne," Jean-Paul said dully. "We'll need to—"

"*No!*" The word exploded from her, low but fierce. "I want Octavie here. Here, with us."

"But Father Daems said—"

"Father Daems is wrong. If God would turn his back on Octavie for such a thing, I want nothing to do with—"

"*Seraphine!*"

"I won't have it, Jean-Paul!" Her knees trembled, and she sank to the ground. "I won't."

Silence stretched between them. Seraphine braced for one of Jean-Paul's rare bursts of anger. But he did not lash out. And I have nothing to apologize for, she thought, staring at the cross that marked her child's grave.

A woodpecker called from the trees. Jean-Paul bowed his head. "When I am able ... I will build a chapel in Octavie's honor, and in thanks to God for sparing us and my brother's family."

"Yes, Jean-Paul," Seraphine said, because he seemed to be waiting for a response. "That's a good idea."

———

Dear Seraphine,

Did you know there are over two hundred lace schools in Belgium? Sadly, I've learned that some young students work from 5:30 in the morning until 8:00 at night, with only brief opportunities to go outside. I don't believe a girl can provide healthy, happy service to either the lace factors or to God with such long hours! I hope to convene a meeting with a few others who wish to bring improvements to the lives of laceworkers.

We've had reports of illness in the settlement. I pray this finds all of you well.

Your loving sister,
Octavie

FOURTEEN

THE MEETING ROOM WAS filling by the time Chloe arrived for Elise's program. As she took a seat near the back she noticed Isaac Cuddy hesitating in the doorway, and waved him over. "Hey, Isaac. It's nice that you came."

"Is it okay, do you think?" He eyed the audience. "I'm like the only guy here."

"Who cares?"

"I don't want to make anyone uncomfortable. You know."

"No, I really don't," Chloe said mildly. "Isaac, I hope you don't mind me asking, but why are you so anxious?" It wasn't just this evening.

He leaned over, elbows on knees, and studied the floor tiles with apparent fascination. Chloe gave him space. A few stragglers scurried in, and the level of chatter rose. Finally Isaac muttered, "People think I'm a screwup, even when whatever goes wrong isn't my fault."

Chloe still didn't get it. "How could coming to a program be defined as screwing up?"

Isaac straightened, sighed, shrugged. "This isn't my first historic site job. Right out of college I went to work at a big historic house. Someone donated a patchwork quilt and asked that it be put on display. The quilt was in pretty good shape, but it had a few stains, and I ..."

I'm catching on, Chloe thought. "And you washed it?"

He nodded miserably. "I ruined it. Nobody told me I couldn't do that."

Chloe imagined the damage: running colors, weak spots in the old fabric tearing. Not pretty to contemplate, but not enough to ruin a career, either. "Isaac, most of us who go into museum work are passionate about what we do. That's a good thing, but sometimes we get too upset about problems. I'm sure you learned from the mistake. I hope you can put that episode behind you."

"I'll try." Isaac darted a tiny smile in her direction. "Do you know who my grandmother is?"

Chloe blinked. "Um ... no, I do not. Who's your grandmother?"

"Mrs. Delcroix."

"Mrs. Delcroix?" Chloe remembered the formidable woman who'd taken charge of the project planning meeting on Monday afternoon.

"She wanted me to major in history. She got me that first job. When I messed up there, she recommended me for the registrar position here."

"I see."

"When the curator left, I told Grandmother that I could do the furnishings plan for the Belgian Farm. I'm better at research and writing than taking care of artifacts. But she told me that I wasn't ready, and had to prove myself first."

142

And how does Isaac prove himself without being given a chance? Chloe wondered.

"I did talk to Roy Galuska about working with buildings," Isaac added. "They're not so fragile. But … it didn't work out so well. I think my grandmother talked to him, because he was against me from the start."

Chloe pictured Roy Galuska demanding that Isaac dissect the original builder's intention based on visual evidence. This kid wouldn't stand a chance with Roy, with or without Grandma D's commentary. But Chloe had no wish to entangle herself in this familial imbroglio. "Isaac, I've got a lot to do and a short time to do it. I'd welcome your help."

Clearly dumbfounded, Isaac actually made eye contact. "Seriously? That would be—"

A microphone crackled to life. "Welcome, everyone," Elise said from behind the podium. "I'm delighted to have you here … ."

Elise was a good presenter, and she'd brought slides. Chloe had already gotten a brief explanation of the extraordinary effort to keep Belgian lacemakers working during World War I. But seeing photographs of Belgian women making lace in front of bombed ruins brought the program's urgency alive.

"Many of the lacemakers created special designs to show their gratitude." Elise clicked the remote, the slide projector's carousel hitched forward, and a stunning lace panel appeared on the screen. "Lots of the pieces we've cataloged incorporate national symbols representing the Allies. They're unique in the lace world. This tablecloth features the coats-of-arms of the Allied nations. The oak leaf and acorn designs are symbols of endurance and strength."

"That is stunning," Chloe murmured. Isaac seemed transfixed as well.

The audience applauded heartily when Elise finished, and she was mobbed with attendees who had questions. Those who'd come only for the lecture, including Isaac, drifted out. Members of the Northeast Wisconsin Lace Guild bustled about to reorder the room for their workshop. Tables were hauled in, cushions and thread and bobbins unpacked. Chloe was delighted to see refreshments emerging from Tupperware containers, and as soon as it could politely be done, she made her way to that table. It seemed prudent to eat a brownie before trying to make lace.

After a brief business meeting, the lacemakers settled down to work. Elise was teaching some advanced technique. One of the experienced club members joined Chloe and two other newbie lacers in a corner for an introductory lesson.

Chloe settled with a dark blue cushion and a dozen bobbins. "There are two basic movements," the instructor counseled. "Cross, and twist. Combining them in different ways creates the stitches we'll learn tonight: half stitch, whole stitch, and whole stitch with a twist."

I'm already lost, Chloe thought, but was determined to keep up. She learned that bobbins were usually wound in pairs, and that there were worker pairs and passive pairs. She was shown the mysteries of the "pricking," a strip of paper with dots to indicate where the pins were to be placed, and dashes showing bobbin movement. She dutifully pricked holes with an awl as directed, pinned the pattern to the pillow, positioned the twelve bobbins she'd been provided. Much as she loved handwork, it all seemed very complicated.

Finally she was ready to actually make lace. She struggled to follow the pattern as bobbins crossed this way and that.

And then, abruptly, she *got* it. She forgot about the body in the bake oven and her worries about Roelke; the shock of Birgitta's announcement and her growing concern about Elise. I am making bobbin lace, Chloe thought, as women have done for centuries. Despite her absolute novice status, she felt a connection to the Belgian lacemakers who had worked so hard to feed their children.

"Oops—not that one." The instructor leaned over Chloe's shoulder. "Two crosses three." She touched the appropriate bobbins.

"Thanks." Chloe corrected her error. "Keeping twelve bobbins straight is tricky."

"Some historical patterns called for over a thousand bobbins," the instructor told her cheerfully. "I've never gone over three hundred, myself."

"Ah." Chloe bent back over the pillow. Okay, so she might not be quite ready to claim soulmate status with the women who'd created the amazing pieces now housed in the Smithsonian's climate-controlled, acid-free glory. It was still extremely cool.

She'd lost track of time when Elise called, "Sorry, everyone, but we need to pack up. I don't want to impose on Heritage Hill's kindness."

Chloe was astonished to see that it was almost ten o'clock. The instructor passed out business cards. "Call if you'd like another lesson," she said cheerfully. Lacemakers packed their supplies, pulled on coats, and called thanks to Elise and goodbye to friends. A maintenance man appeared and began breaking down the long tables.

One tall woman, perhaps in her fifties, approached Elise. "I brought something to show you," she said hesitantly when the last student had departed.

Chloe stopped stacking folding chairs and sidled close.

"My name is Linda Gauthier Martin. My great-grandmother's name was Dominique Anselme Gauthier. She came to Wisconsin in 1855, and this handkerchief belonged to her." The woman offered up a small, flat box.

Elise took off the lid and gently removed a piece of white linen fabric, trimmed on one side with lace. She unfolded it on the table and leaned close. *"Oh."*

"Oh!" Chloe echoed. This is what she'd come to see—an artifact documented to a specific Belgian immigrant. She quickly introduced herself to Mrs. Martin. "Thank you for letting us see the handkerchief. It's gorgeous."

"It's the work of a master," Elise agreed. "Did Dominique make the lace?"

"I doubt it," Mrs. Martin said. "Don't you? They settled up in Door County when the land was all virgin forest, and had quite a difficult time. It's hard to imagine her making bobbin lace. Her first two children died of cholera. Anyway, this style is Bruges, isn't it?"

"The official name is *Duchesse de Bruges*," Elise told them. "Named, they say, because the lace was considered worthy of royalty."

Chloe squinted. "The thread looks like linen, but it's incredibly fine." She had spun a lot of linen in her time, but nothing this delicate.

"Flemish spinners in northern Belgium were renowned for their linen thread," Elise explained. "Italian lace tends to look heavier, sturdier."

"And lace from Bruges is considered top-quality, right?" Mrs. Martin asked.

"Bruges is one of the great lace cities," Elise agreed. "Some historians believe that bobbin lace began there during the late 1500s. During the mid-1800s, when those first Belgian immigrants were leaving, there were dozens of lace schools in Bruges. One of the most famous was at the Convent of the Apostolines."

"Nuns made lace?" Chloe asked. She would have guessed that nuns focused more on practical skills.

"Oh, yes," Elise assured her. "They took in children and instructed them in catechism, some basic academic studies, and lacework. It started as a way to help the poor, but it supported the industry."

Chloe dumped the contents of her totebag on the table and extricated her notebook and the Polaroid camera. "Mrs. Martin, may I photograph the handkerchief? Even if we don't know who made the lace, we know who *owned* the handkerchief, and that's fantastic."

"Of course."

Elise dumped the contents of *her* briefcase on the table and extricated her own notebook and pencil. "And I'd like to document it as well. I'm intrigued by the scale."

"Oh?" Mrs. Martin looked perplexed.

"The design and execution of the lace is flawless," Elise explained, "but my guess is this particular piece of edging wasn't intended to border a handkerchief. A smaller design would have been more typical."

Chloe laid several Polaroid photos on the table to develop before leaning back over the handkerchief. "Maybe the lace was taken from a garment," she suggested. "Maybe the handkerchief was made for a wedding, and the only fancy decoration available came from a bonnet edging or—"

"Pardon me, ladies." The maintenance man jingled a key ring meaningfully.

"Sorry," Chloe said contritely. "We'll be out of here in five minutes."

Mrs. Martin and Elise quickly made plans to speak again. Then Elise packed her workshop supplies, and Chloe stuffed files, photos, notebooks, and other curatorial detritus into the appropriate briefcase and totebag. Four and a half minutes later they left the building. The maintenance man locked the door behind them.

"Wasn't that handkerchief amazing?" Chloe asked, as she and Elise gingerly made their way across the slick parking lot in a foggy drizzle.

"It was!" Elise agreed.

Chloe smiled as she unlocked the Pinto. Elise had seemed by turns sad, distracted, and aloof. It was wonderful to see her happy. I'll take this as a good omen for the rest of the week, Chloe decided. They could all use it.

The good vibe lasted as Chloe followed Elise's rental car around Green Bay and on north. They'd turned onto a smaller, rural road when Elise braked unexpectedly.

Then Chloe saw headlights where no headlights should be. Someone had slipped off the road.

Elise eased to the berm and rolled down her window. "I think that's Toni's car," she said as Chloe approached, and pointed to the white Chevy Cavalier crumpled against a tree.

"Oh, *no*." Chloe's heart sank. It did look like Toni's car. "Why don't you go find a phone and call for help." Elise, in her pumps and nylons and too-light coat, wouldn't be of any use here. "And tell Sharon what happened."

Elise nodded and pulled away. Chloe grabbed a flashlight and made her way to the Chevy. Through the window she saw Toni, looking dazed but very much alive. Thank you God, Chloe said silently.

The door opened easily. "Toni, are you okay?"

"I'm all right," Toni muttered. "Banged my head, though." She clawed at her seat belt. "Help me out."

"No! Don't move. I'll be right back."

Chloe scrambled back to her own car, popped the hatch, and propped it open with the tent pole dedicated to that job. Like most Wisconsinites, she always kept basic emergency supplies in the trunk. Roelke, bless his Boy Scout heart, had augmented her sleeping bag, ice scraper, and granola bars with a stash suggesting imminent roadside Armageddon. She set emergency flares to warn oncoming drivers, and draped a heavy-duty poncho over Toni.

Then she heard the faint hum of an approaching car. *That* reminded her that she was alone on a rural road not terribly far from Lejeune Farm East, where someone had stuffed Hugh Lejeune into a brick bake oven.

A shudder that had nothing to do with the clammy fog rippled down Chloe's spine. She slipped and slid back to the Pinto and grabbed the small snow shovel from the hatch, ready to swing like Robin Yount if necessary. The glow appeared at the curve. Chloe widened her stance. The other car slowed but kept driving.

The faint wail of a siren reached through the cold night. Thank God, Chloe thought again. Help was on the way.

Chloe got back to Belgian Acres an hour later, bone-weary. Toni was on her way to the hospital, and Sharon was too. Toni's car was being towed to a garage.

After plodding up the stairs, Chloe knocked on her friend's door. "Elise?"

"Yes?" Elise called. "Is Toni all right?" The door didn't open.

Okay, fine, Chloe thought, too tired to care. "She probably has a concussion, but it could have been worse."

"I'm so glad. Thanks for letting me know, Chloe. Good night."

Turning, Chloe found a note taped to her bedroom door. *Chloe, Ethan Hendricks called. He said it was nothing urgent, but to call back if you have a chance.*

Chloe's spirits rose at least a notch, maybe even two. She and Ethan had gone through forestry school at West Virginia University together, quizzing each other on strolls through the arboretum, sharing dendrology notes, backpacking in the Dolly Sods Wilderness or on the Appalachian Trail. After graduation Ethan had moved west and taken a job with the US Forest Service; Chloe had moved to Europe. But they'd stayed in touch and were still close.

She settled her nerves with a small bag of peanut M&Ms taken from Roelke's emergency cache. He really did think of everything.

Then she sat on the bed and called Ethan. "Hey, it's me," she said. "Is everything okay?"

"Yes," he assured her. "I called your house, and Roelke told me where you were. Chris and I have decided to go to Mexico for a few weeks. I worked so many fires last fall that I've got a lot of time coming."

"You deserve a vacation." Her sentiments were sincere, even if southern climes didn't particularly call to her. But Ethan isn't Scandinavian, she reminded herself.

Then she reminded herself that she might not be all Scandinavian either.

"Chloe?" Ethan had always been good at reading her moods, even over the phone. "Are you okay?"

"Sure." She twined the phone cord around one finger. "But I did get a little bombshell from my great-aunt Birgitta the other day." She shared Birgitta's revelation. "Kari thinks we should keep our mouths shut."

"What do you think?"

Chloe flopped back on the pillow and stretched out her legs. "I don't know. You know how my parents are. I was raised as Norwegian as an American can be. It's kind of overwhelming to discover that one-half of my identity is a complete mystery."

"If your grandparents wanted to adopt a child, don't you think they'd stay within the Norwegian-American community?"

"Maybe, but something made them keep the adoption a secret. Whatever that was might have forced them to look farther afield."

After a moment of silence Ethan mused, "I remember how happy you were in West Virginia. How much you loved the landscape. You said you felt at home there. Maybe there was a reason for that."

I can be remarkably dense, Chloe thought. That possibility, that she might have roots in Appalachia, had not occurred to her. If that was true, where had that particular line come from? Scotland? Ireland?

It was too much to absorb. "Maybe," she agreed. "But I'm too tired tonight to even speculate."

"How's your work project coming along?"

Chloe considered telling Ethan about the body in the bake oven but decided against it. Roelke had already scolded her for exploring. She didn't want Ethan to go all Neanderthal on her too. "I'm on the hunt for clues to early Belgian settlers' lives. It's been fascinating."

"I think Roelke misses you."

That was unexpected. "What did he say?"

"He didn't say anything. It was more … I don't know … his tone, I guess."

"I miss Roelke too," Chloe said. "Whatever you picked up on might have been work stuff, though. Something's been troubling him for weeks, but he's keeping it to himself." She plucked at the chenille bedspread. "He's considering going to mass, which is fine. But he's already worrying that if we get married, a priest won't agree to—"

"Married?" Ethan yelped. "Did you get engaged and not tell me?"

"No! I mean, it's come up a couple of times, awkwardly. Neither one of us has mustered up the—the *whatever* to actually propose. We had enough challenges before this whole religion thing came up."

"Do you belong to a church these days?"

"I haven't in a while." Chloe hesitated. "I still enjoy attending services with my parents sometimes. I feel at home there, but I don't really identify as a Lutheran anymore. I appreciate the writings of the Transcendentalists—Ralph Waldo Emerson, Henry David Thoreau—but Transcendentalism doesn't seem to be a viable alternative these days. I like Quaker philosophy, but the Quakers I know don't have music at their meetings. The Unitarian Universalist church in Madison has a phenomenal music program, and a message I like, but Madison is too far to drive on a regular basis—"

"So, no, in other words."

"I do believe in God, and consider myself a spiritual person. I just don't seem well suited for organized religion. Do you go to church?"

"I do. Every single day when I go to work, I'm surrounded by God's creation. That's my church."

No wonder Ethan and I are such good friends, Chloe thought. "I miss you. Come visit sometime, okay? You still need to meet Roelke."

"That would be great," Ethan agreed. "And speaking of Roelke, I suggest giving him a little more time. But don't wait too long. Otherwise a small problem could become a big one."

After hanging up, Chloe tried to get organized for the next day. In the frenzied rush of tidying up back at Heritage Hill, she'd jammed notes and files and index cards away in a jumble. If she didn't sort them out now, she'd regret it tomorrow.

She was almost finished when she found a sheet of paper she didn't recognize. Apparently she'd mixed a page from Elise's things in with her own. Several paragraphs had been typed on a typewriter sorely in need of a new ribbon. Chloe leaned toward the lamp to get a better look.

lives are so difficult here, yet their faith remains strong. I visited one cabin where three potatoes were to be cooked and divided among five people. Hardly a meal for a working family and yet when I arrived, unannounced, they gladfully insisted I share it. It was a dark and rude place, not fit to earn the appellation of "cabin." Yet when the man of the place described the scrap of a clearing as he believed it would become his eyes glowed and his voice grew vibrant.

I am recently returned from another tour, visiting newcomers some thirty miles and more beyond Aux Premiers Belges for the first time. At one, having promised earlier to celebrate holy communion, I went inside to lay out the sacrament on what I feared would be a filthy table. Instead I was astonished to find that not only had the gaunt, weary young wife scrubbed the table well, she had adorned it with a cloth trimmed with a strip of delicate lace, the likes of which I have not seen since coming to this place. She had, she told me, learned to make lace at a convent in Bruges. She gifted me the cloth, knowing it would serve well among

Chloe stared at the paper open-mouthed. This appeared to be part of a letter written by an early priest serving in the area, sent back to Belgium and—in the relatively recent past—transcribed. Where had Elise found the account?

And why hadn't she mentioned the letter's existence? Chloe's feelings were distinctly bruised. Elise knows how eager I am to find some primary source account of a woman's life in those early days, she thought. So ... why the secrecy?

Maybe it was no more than an academic's desire to withhold such a find until her project—in this case, presumably Elise's dissertation—was complete. Maybe she'd been sworn to secrecy by some collector or descendant who did not want to be deluged with requests for information, or for security reasons. Maybe it honestly hadn't occurred to Elise that Chloe would want to see even this passing reference to an unnamed young Belgian woman, although that stretched credulity.

Chloe slipped the page under Elise's door. In the morning, she'd ask her friend *ever* so nicely where it had come from.

She got ready for bed. But she was tired, not sleepy. Her brain pinged from the priest's letter to Elise's secrecy to the uncomfortable conversation she'd had with Roelke about religion.

Ethan's approach best reflected her own. She'd experienced the Divine when backpacking in the mountains of Appalachia and Switzerland. Now Wisconsin's prairies and forests prompted a response that was more quiet, but nonetheless real.

Maybe if Roelke went back to mass, revisited the rituals that had framed his childhood, he'd find a similar sense of peace. Or maybe, she thought, he's just trying to figure out who he is. He has every right to do that. People grow. People change. She would never get in the way of something that was important to him.

But … what if he decided he had to have a Catholic wedding? Would she be forced to make an impossible decision? Before meeting Roelke she'd survived one horrific breakup, but only barely. She didn't want to go through anything like that again …

Stop stewing, she ordered herself. For crying out loud, she and Roelke weren't even engaged. And at the rate they were going, they probably never would be.

Chloe made a conscious effort to put all worries aside. Think about something positive, she ordered herself. Like … like the gorgeous heirloom handkerchief Mrs. Martin had inherited. That the priest's letter and Mrs. Martin's handkerchief had presented themselves on the same day was a coincidence almost too great to be believed. Had there been one lacemaker in the early Belgian settlement, or two? What was the story?

FIFTEEN

"WHAT ARE YOU DOING, *chère femme?*" The toes of Jean-Paul's *sabots* appeared in Seraphine's vision.

"Oh!" Seraphine jumped, startled. "I was just ... making designs." She rubbed out the marks she'd scratched in the dirt with a stick.

Jean-Paul pulled a bobbin from his pocket. "I finished another one." But instead of handing it to her, his fingers clenched around it. "If you had known what it would be like here, would you have agreed to come?"

"Why, I—I don't know." She remembered blithely promising Octavie that she would, within a few years, return for a visit. And she'd promised Sister Odile-Alphonse that she would make lace in the New World. "I am a *dentellière*," she told herself at night when Jean-Paul was asleep. She tried to believe that she hadn't already lost her knowledge, her talent.

She realized Jean-Paul was waiting. "Probably not."

He blew out a long breath. "We should not have come."

"Jean-Paul!" Except for the weeks after their baby daughter's death, she'd never seen him so melancholy. Seraphine put one hand against his cheek. "I miss my sister. But we have much to be grateful for. Think of what we've gained in the past four years."

Two-year-old Jules was playing with chips at the woodpile, and Pierre—just six months old—was asleep in the cradle-basket. The farm was … if not prospering, at least improving. Their log cabin had a glass window. They had a real clearing now, and on fair days, an hour or two of sun. Their little wheat field had produced a bigger crop this year. Jean-Paul and Etienne shared a plow. That saved time, although using it to turn earth without an ox was brutal work.

When foraging for raspberries or morels she sometimes heard the ring of someone else's axe, the crack of a neighbor's musket. Narrow footpaths snaked through the settlements. The Lejeunes felt much less isolated, which was good, for emigration from Belgium had almost stopped. Anguished letters written by the first immigrants had dissuaded those who had been considering immigration.

Jean-Paul appeared unable to count blessings today. "I'm sorry, Seraphine."

She squeezed his hand to say, *We are in this together. We are making progress. Don't lose heart.*

He shouldered his axe. "Well. Back to it."

Seraphine watched him walk away. Why was Jean-Paul feeling so burdened?

And it wasn't just him. Etienne had stalked into their clearing the day before and announced, "Emelie told me to leave." When Seraphine went to make sure Emelie was all right, she found her sister-in-law digging turnips with tear-stained eyes. "The grain harvest is in, and all Etienne talks about is how many more trees he can cut before the snow comes," Emelie had flared.

I have known my share of despair, Seraphine thought now. And yet we *are* making progress. The harvest had been good ... *Oh.*

"Jean-Paul!" she cried. "Wait!"

Frowning, he came back.

"We need a Kermiss," she announced triumphantly. The annual harvest celebration was as much a part of life in Wallonia as Christmas or Easter. A special mass was celebrated to give thanks, followed by dancing and eating and fun.

"No one has time for a Kermiss."

Seraphine put a hand on his arm. "Please, let's speak with some of the others. There must be more to life than work and worry."

Her husband looked back at the towering basswood tree he'd been hacking all morning, six feet around. Then he took Seraphine's face between his rough, dirty hands and kissed her.

———

Everyone thought that celebrating Wisconsin's first Kermiss was a fine idea. The festival was scheduled to coincide with Father Daems's planned visit. The Macaux family, who lived in Rosiere, offered to host the celebration on their farm.

Seraphine washed and aired and pressed her best clothes, long untouched. She cleaned Jean-Paul's *saurot*—a loose-fitting shirt—and wide trousers as well, and oiled the stiffness of disuse from his good leather shoes. She baked in her Dutch oven half a dozen loaves of bread for the feast. And she made a special handkerchief to give as a prize.

And every bit of the extra work was worthwhile, Seraphine thought two weeks later, as they walked seven miles to Rosiere. She felt festive in her full brown skirt with green and purple stripes near the hem and the Sunday *sabots* Jean-Paul had carved with flowers for her. Etienne and Jean-Paul sang as they tramped along the forest trail, and sometimes Emelie joined in. Seraphine carried baby Pierre. Jules rode happily on Jean-Paul's shoulders.

Rosiere was little more than a wide spot in the trail, with a log church and several farms nearby. But the churchyard was filled with families wearing their finest, meeting neighbors with joyful shouts and thumps on the back. Then Father Daems called every-one together to celebrate mass.

After the service, a settler played his clarinet as everyone sang Belgium's national song, "La Brabançonne":

> *Worthy children of Low Countries*
> *Whom a fine passion has aroused,*
> *To your patriotic fervour*
> *Great successes lie in store.*

Seraphine's voice caught. When the song ended, the day was still. Men cleared their throats and mopped their eyes with ker-chiefs. Emelie sniffled and reached for Seraphine's hand.

Finally someone shouted, "It is time to dance!" and the hush was broken. Older women settled on benches nearby, and beneath their watchful gazes, mothers settled babies on quilts. Seraphine kissed Pierre and eased him down.

First came the Dance of the Dust, performed in thanks for the earth's bounty. Seraphine joined the circle hesitantly but the music reached inside her, buoyed her, and soon she felt giddy. Jean-Paul helped Jules, who was almost overwhelmed with excitement.

As the dance ended Jean-Paul caught Seraphine's arm. "Thank you," he whispered. "Thank you, my love."

The young people continued to dance while the married women busied themselves at the Macaux farm. A caldron of chicken *booyah* was already simmering over a fire. Seraphine helped set out baskets of bread and dozens of Belgian pies made with precious prunes or dried apples.

As a line formed at the table she noticed Emelie standing still, staring at the bounty. "Emelie? Are you all right?"

"I did not expect to survive that first winter. I truly thought we would freeze, or starve."

Seraphine put her arm around her sister-in-law's shoulders. "But here we are. The worst is behind us now."

After the Lejeune men filled their plates, Etienne cocked his head toward a group of men lounging against a fence with a keg of beer someone had hauled from Green Bay. "Come, Jean-Paul. We'll hear all the news."

Emelie planted her hands on her hips. "You have more than conversation in mind. Etienne, stay sober!"

Jean-Paul grinned. "I'll keep an eye on him."

"And no talk of politics," Seraphine added. Politics led to gloomy speculation about the possibility of a civil war in America. She didn't want their special day clouded.

"I'll keep an eye on him," Etienne promised. Laughing, the brothers wandered away.

Emelie excused herself too, so Seraphine filled plates for herself and Jules. They joined Adele Brise and her mother, who were picnicking in the shade. "It is wonderful to see you!" Seraphine exclaimed, remembering their kindness when the Lejeunes had arrived in *Aux Premiers Belges*.

"Organizing a Kermiss was a wonderful idea," Mrs. Brise said. "It reminds us all that we are still Belgians."

"It's a fine day, isn't it?" Seraphine scooped up some *booyah* and sighed with contentment. "Oh, this is delicious." The stew was thick with carrots and potatoes, and the long simmering had rendered the chicken pieces juicy and tender.

When Mrs. Brise went to check on the pies, Adele smiled. "I've missed you. And you now have two fine sons!"

"Perhaps you'll have a son of your own one day," Seraphine suggested.

"Perhaps. I ... I have believed for some time that God has some purpose for me. All I can do is wait and see."

Seraphine looked toward the dancers, laughing and whirling. "I thought God had a purpose for me as well," she dared confide. "I am a lacemaker, Adele. My sister, Octavie, and I lived in a convent in Bruges and learned at the school there. Octavie was called to become a nun." She paused to wipe a dribble of chicken stew from Jules's chin. "When I was making lace, I felt I had found *my* calling. But since coming here ... " Seraphine lifted her free hand, palm up. "Diapers to wash, trees to kill, potatoes to dig ... there is no time. Jean-Paul is carving bobbins, but we've no money to purchase thread."

"Don't despair." Adele's voice was quiet, but firm. "God will reveal his plan in his own good time. We must be patient, eh?"

"Mama!" Jules scrambled to his feet, pointing. "What are they doing?"

"It must be time for the races," Seraphine told him. "Shall we go watch?" She tucked their plates into her basket.

Belgian harvest festivals included horse races and greased pole climbs. No one here had horses or lard to spare, but the young men were eager to run. Seraphine and Jules cheered them. The traditional prize of a bridle had been replaced by a pair of red suspenders.

Then came the women's race, open to all. Over a dozen lined up, lifting their skirts lightly, leaning forward in anticipation. When the pistol fired they ran toward the far edge of the clearing.

"Dominique Anselme is the winner!" the man in charge bellowed.

"Oh my!" Seraphine stared with delight at the thin barefoot woman who'd crossed the finish line first. She'd only seen Dominique a few times since she'd lost both of her children in the cholera epidemic that had also taken baby Octavie.

"I believe Mrs. Jean-Paul Lejeune has donated the prize. Mrs. Lejeune?"

Holding Jules's hand, Seraphine stepped forward. "Congratulations!" She pulled the linen handkerchief she'd made from her apron pocket.

Dominique's triumphant grin faded. She looked from the lace-trimmed handkerchief to Seraphine, clearly dumbfounded. "I've never seen anything so beautiful! Is this truly mine to keep?"

"It is," Seraphine assured her. She leaned close and whispered, "In honor of your strength."

More women pressed close, wanting to see, exclaiming over the handkerchief. Seraphine backed away, smiling.

After hemming the handkerchief last week, she had hesitated. The occasion of the first American Kermiss called for a special prize. She *could* embroider the date in one corner. But she'd found herself unwrapping her precious wedding veil lace. A bit more gone won't hurt, she'd decided.

Now, looking at Dominique's glowing face, she knew she'd done the right thing.

———

Dear Seraphine,

Thank you for your good wishes. Since taking my vows, I have known only peace. I am known as Sister M. Octavie. No one could ever take your place, but it is good to be part of a community.

You will also be pleased to hear that I am learning more about how the factor system affects lacemakers. Lacemakers in Belgium are obliged to sell to these first buyers. The factors resell to dealers at enormous profit, and these dealers then resell the lace for another enormous profit. Yet young lacemakers at convents like ours, or those women who leave the lace schools and return home to work as farm or village chores permit, receive only a pittance. We must sweep this system away!

We shall meet again on this earth, my dearest sister. Do not lose hope.

Your loving sister,
Octavie

SIXTEEN

RAISED VOICES GREETED CHLOE the next morning when she came downstairs. "Mom, would you please just get off my back?"

"It was a fair question," Sharon snapped. "It's happened before."

Chloe stopped, unsure whether to tiptoe back upstairs as if oblivious, or sail through the door.

"I was *not* drinking last night!"

"Good to know."

A silence followed. Chloe felt safe announcing her presence. "Good morning," she called in a singsong that was most unlike her. She found Toni sitting alone, picking at a poached egg. "Toni! I'm so glad to see you. Are you all right?" A green and yellow bruise had blossomed on the other woman's left temple.

"I'll live." Toni tried to smile. "They kept me for observation for a while, then let me go. Nurses make terrible patients."

"It was treacherous last night." Chloe helped herself to a cup of coffee. "I'm sure you weren't the only one to slide off the road."

"I didn't slide off the road." Toni's voice was tight. "And despite what my mother wants to believe, I was sober. Someone ran me off the road."

Chloe put her cup back down. "You mean ... on purpose?"

"Right after I got off Highway 57, somebody comes up on my tail." Toni put down her fork. "Before I knew it, all I could see in the rearview mirror were headlights. Then I felt the car bump into mine. Next thing I know I'm skidding off the road. Maybe the driver was just going too fast, and skidded himself, but it sure seemed deliberate."

Chloe was horrified. If someone had bumped Toni deliberately, that meant that something menacing had happened to two members of the extended Lejeune family in a short period of time.

"As you know, the other driver didn't stick around." Toni's face settled into hard lines.

"A car drove by while we were waiting for the ambulance." She tried without success to recall what it looked like. "A dark sedan, I think? Maybe."

"A deputy talked to me at the hospital, but there wasn't much I could tell him. I have no idea what kind of car hit me, much less who was driving it."

Sharon came in from the kitchen and put a loaded plate down at Chloe's place. "Poached eggs this morning, and my rhubarb coffeecake. I always freeze a bunch. Rhubarb cheers me up."

"It smells delicious." Chloe picked up her fork, then put it down. "Is Elise ... "

"Elise left early again," Sharon told her. "Didn't even have breakfast. She said to tell you she'd see you at the Belgian Heritage Center later."

"Oh." Chloe felt a flash of annoyance. "Well, okey-dokey." So much for the bonding moment they'd experienced last night, the shared thrill of seeing Mrs. Martin's handkerchief. So much for getting an explanation about the transcription of the priest's letter.

She dug into Sharon's cheer-me-up coffee cake. It was warm, moist, redolent with cinnamon and ginger, and not too sweet. Perfect for a chilly morning filled with news that ranged from disappointing to alarming. "You two must be exhausted. Is there anything I can do?"

Sharon paused with one hand on the doorframe. "Not really. If you don't mind, just set your dirty dishes in the kitchen when you're done. I'm going to the mechanic's to see about the car." She fixed her daughter with a stern gaze. "And Antoinette is going back to bed. The doctor ordered rest and fluids."

"I'm not a child, mother," Toni said, but she pushed her plate away and stood. "Chloe, thanks for your help last night."

"No problem." When Toni's footsteps had faded up the stairs, Chloe turned to her hostess. "Shouldn't you be resting too?" Sharon's face had a gray cast. "You had a short night."

"It didn't help that Jason, who was scheduled to milk this morning, called at five a.m. and said he was sick."

"Oh no!"

"I managed." Sharon shrugged. "And I'll rest as soon as I know what's going on with Antoinette's car. I always feel better talking to repair people in person, don't you?"

"It helps."

Sharon rubbed one thumb over the knuckles of her other hand. "Chloe, I apologize for the awkward moment. I don't know how much you heard, but ... I do know that my daughter is a grown

167

woman. Still, it wasn't all that long ago that she was a wild teenager. Some memories don't fade."

Like a memory of hearing that your inebriated young daughter was in some kind of an accident? "I'm sorry."

"My daughter and I are very different people." Sharon smoothed a wrinkle from the tablecloth. "I'm passionate about this place and our heritage. All she ever wanted to do was move on."

Be careful what you wish for, Chloe told Toni silently. The things you take for granted might be the very things you miss one day.

"Into each life some rain must fall, eh?" Sharon summoned the ghost of a smile. "And the occasional monsoon." She paused, as if taking stock. "Well, I really should get going. I'll see you at the Heritage Center later."

Chloe lingered over a second piece of coffee cake, thinking about Toni and Sharon. God knew she and her own mother, Marit, had gone through rocky patches. None of which, Chloe thought morosely, will compare to the landslide to come if I broach the subject of her adoption.

To distract herself, Chloe ran through the day's itinerary. She was due to meet Roy Galuska at the Belgian Farmstead at Heritage Hill at ten to tour the big barn. After that she was free until three, when she was expected at the Belgian Heritage Center in Namur.

Chloe had finished washing the dishes when someone rang the doorbell. She squinted out the tiny peephole. Deputy Knutson stood on the step.

Chloe ushered the deputy inside. "Sharon isn't home, and her daughter's in bed," she explained. "Is there something I can help you with?"

The deputy removed her hat. "I figured Mrs. Bertrand would be eager to hear the autopsy results. Mr. Lejeune died of a severe asthma attack."

"Really?" Chloe wrinkled her nose in surprise. Sharon had mentioned the asthma, but Chloe hadn't expected that to be the cause of death.

"He'd been dead for at least a day before you found him. According to the victim's son, Mr. Lejeune used an inhaler. However, we did not find an inhaler in his pockets or anywhere at the scene. Mr. Lejeune had probably forgotten it and then got hit with a particularly bad attack when he was alone at the farm."

"But Mr. Lejeune didn't crawl into the bake oven before he died."

"No, and he most certainly did not latch the oven door," Deputy Knutson agreed grimly.

"Do you have any leads?"

"The investigator is doing everything possible to close the case."

Which probably means no, Chloe thought.

"I heard Mrs. Bertrand's daughter slid off the road last night. Was she hurt?"

"Toni's a bit banged up, nothing too serious. She believes someone deliberately bumped her into a skid. A car drove by after I got there, and slowed down, but ... I can't tell you more than that."

"Probably just someone gawking," the deputy said. "Or seeing if you needed help."

Chloe nibbled her lower lip. "Do you think it's possible that what happened to Toni had a connection to what happened to Mr. Lejeune?"

"I suspect it's just an unfortunate coincidence," the deputy said. "But we're keeping an extra eye on all the farms around here."

After the deputy departed, Chloe was heading for the stairs when she noticed that Sharon had placed Seraphine Lejeune's wooden shoes on a shelf. They were quite wonderful—sturdy and functional, yet delightfully decorated. She was tempted to try standing in Seraphine's shoes herself, as Sharon did when feeling troubled, but curatorial integrity and respect for her guest status kept her from it.

She did, however, pause in front of the huge family Bible resting on a marble-topped table nearby. Sharon had mentioned that the Bible held some family records, right? Any genealogical information would make it easier to dig out, she hoped, a story or two for Sharon and Toni. Chloe grabbed a tissue to shield the old leather from the oils in her skin.

The first thing she found tucked inside the front cover was a photograph of a young soldier from the World War I era, possibly the uncle Sharon mentioned. Beneath that she found a photocopy of a small certificate. The ink was fading, and the words were not in English, but Chloe could tell that it documented the 1854 wedding of Seraphine and Jean-Paul Lejeune in Antwerp.

Chloe copied the information on a pad she found by the telephone before exploring further. The next treasure was a *carte de visite*. This type of small photograph, mounted on cardboard, dated to the 1850s but had exploded in popularity during the American Civil War. The Lejeune CDV showed a dark-haired man wearing the uniform of a Union Army soldier.

Was this Jean-Paul Lejeune? Had he served in a Wisconsin regiment? Chloe carefully turned the CDV over, but no one had helpfully written the soldier's name on the back. Nor was it marked with a photographer's imprint. "Dagnabbit," she muttered.

None of the other records tucked away dated before the 1930s. She gingerly returned the World War I photograph, CDV, and wedding certificate to the Bible and eased the cover closed.

Ten minutes later she left the house. It was a beautiful blue-sky morning. The temperature had dropped, but the air was dry—a marked improvement over the previous night's freezing fog. Perhaps in their declining years Seraphine and Jean-Paul found time to look over this same landscape on cold mornings with, she hoped, a sense of pride.

Then Chloe noticed again the little outbuilding off by itself beyond the pasture, glowing in the sun. Jason Oberholtzer's tour yesterday had given her new insight. Could that be a roadside chapel?

She glanced at her watch. She *really* should get going, but... it wouldn't take long to check the structure out. If it was a chapel, and if it celebrated family lineage, maybe she'd even find some reference to Jean-Paul Lejeune serving in the Civil War.

Chloe made her way around the outbuildings and crunched rimed grass toward the small white frame structure. Narrow horizontal windows were placed high in the walls, admitting light without sacrificing privacy. As she came around the corner, she saw a cross fixed above the door. It *was* a chapel.

She pulled off one mitten, put her hand on the doorknob. It wouldn't turn. In quick succession she felt surprise, disappointment, and... and something else. A sense of grief emanated from the building. Chloe experienced it like an electric current running into her palm.

With a gasp she wrenched her hand away and stumbled down the lone step so fast she landed on her butt. What was *that?*

She scrambled to her feet and gathered enough courage to pick up the mitten she'd dropped in her hasty retreat. Then she retraced her steps. When she reached the yard she got into her car, started the engine, and took stock.

Jason had told her that people sometimes built roadside chapels to provide a convenient place to worship and pray. In other cases, gratitude for a favor granted—such as recovery from serious illness—prompted the construction.

It seemed clear that the Lejeune chapel had been built for another reason. Someone had spent a great deal of time in that chapel mourning a loss so great that his or her grief had permeated the space, persisted through time.

Had Seraphine or Jean-Paul built this chapel? Original log construction could have been covered with siding at a later date. If Seraphine had dedicated the chapel, what had broken her heart? Or did the grief come from one of her descendants?

Chloe wished she'd never approached the chapel. Finding it locked was a signal that, in this case, visitors were not welcome. Perhaps that was simply a sign of the times. Or perhaps it was because that building held a story so painful, so private, that it could not be shared.

Finally she put the car in gear. Time to get to Green Bay and do what she was supposed to be doing.

But approaching Lejeune Farm East three minutes later only ratcheted up her unease again. "Don't be ridiculous," she muttered. "You've been driving past this farm for three days. Nothing has happened."

Except . . . it had, maybe. Chloe nibbled her lower lip. The death of Hugh Lejeune had seemed like an isolated incident. Now, however, someone had run Toni off the road.

But for what purpose? Chloe couldn't imagine. She liked Sharon. She liked Toni. She probably would have liked Hugh Lejeune too, despite his reported crankiness. But she didn't know enough about the family to guess why someone would stuff a dead man into the oven and force Toni off the road. It was beyond improbable. It made no sense.

No wonder Roelke sometimes struggles, she thought. If she spent all of her professional hours trying to make sense of cruelty, of the myriad ways human beings inflicted suffering upon others, she'd struggle too.

———

Father Dan Grinke met Roelke at the door of the parish office building. "Thanks for coming," the priest said soberly. "I'll show you what I found."

He led Roelke across the yard to the church. Someone had spray-painted three black words on the wall: GO TO HELL.

"And this," the priest added, pointing to a statue in a garden bed. It was of Mother Mary. Had been, anyway, before decapitation. Now the painted plaster head lay beside the hem of Mary's blue robe.

Roelke stared in shocked silence. He'd been awake for much of the night. At three in the morning he'd given up and gone downstairs. He tried watching television but they had crappy reception at best, and there was nothing on anyway. In the end he finally dozed off on the sofa, with Olympia purring on his chest. He'd woken feeling bleary.

But you're on the clock now, he reminded himself. "You discovered the damage this morning?"

Father Dan's face was composed, but his eyes were dark with sadness. "It must have happened overnight."

"Let me document the scene," Roelke said. "Then we'll talk." He did what he needed to do. "Shall we go to your office?" He didn't want to go into the sanctuary again.

The priest's office was small, dominated by his desk and two guest chairs. Father Dan sat in one and waved Roelke into the other.

Roelke appreciated the courtesy. "Father, have you given any more thought to church security?"

"I will not make this church a fortress."

"I think we can find a middle ground." Roelke explained that he hoped to schedule a meeting with area clergy to discuss safety issues. "Today's incident only strengthens my belief that the conversation is needed."

Father Dan seemed to be listening with more courtesy than conviction.

"I'm concerned about that spray paint and the broken statue," Roelke persisted. "This wasn't some bored kid on a dare. I think that the person responsible was angry—maybe at the church in a broad sense, maybe at you. So I'll ask again: Can you think of anyone who might be holding a grudge against you?"

Something flashed in Father Dan's eyes, then disappeared. "I'm sorry. There's nothing I can tell you."

Roelke struggled to contain rising frustration. "I'm trying to keep you safe. If there's someone I should talk to—"

"Officer McKenna." The priest's tone suggested he was placating a silly child. "If someone is angry at me, surely sending a policeman after him is the worst way to go. I need to be open, nonjudgmental—"

"That's ridiculous!" Roelke exclaimed—and immediately regretted it. He drew a deep breath. "Forgive me."

"There's nothing to forgive. I'm grateful that the local police department is concerned about the welfare of Eagle's religious communities. But I'll leave the enforcement of civic laws to you. I must follow God's laws—"

"But how many times can you turn the other cheek?" Roelke demanded. "How many times can you watch someone harm people you love, and get away with it, without taking action?"

Father Dan didn't speak for a long moment. Roelke pressed a knuckle against his forehead. A heavy silence filled the room.

Finally the priest asked, "Officer McKenna, how can I help you?"

Roelke pushed to his feet. "You can attend the meeting about church safety. My clerk will give you a call."

———

When Chloe walked into the Heritage Hill Education Center, she saw Isaac Cuddy busy at a glass exhibit case in the main hall. "Good morning, Isaac!"

The young man whirled. "I was just cleaning out a couple of dead flies." He held out a crumpled tissue, evidently compelled to display the carcasses as proof.

"I'm glad I ran into you." She draped her coat over one arm.

"Oh?" Isaac blinked, as if unsure why anyone would be glad to run into him.

"We need to discuss how you can help with the Belgian Farm's furnishings plan," Chloe reminded him. "I do have a couple of ideas."

"Oh?" This time Isaac looked cautiously optimistic.

"First, the strong religious faith that helped the early Belgian immigrants face their challenges needs to be reflected in the house.

Could you check for any religious artifacts in storage? By 1905 the settlers would be able to have religious pictures in Victorian frames, for example. And it would be lovely to have something that even a poor immigrant could have carried."

"A rosary, maybe?" Isaac suggested.

"That sounds perfect." Chloe beamed her most encouraging beam. "I'm not Catholic, so I'll check with someone knowledgeable before getting too specific. But it will be helpful to know what you already have."

"I'll look into it."

"I also wondered if you could attend the gathering at the Belgian Heritage Center in Namur later today. It starts at five. Local people will be bringing family heirlooms to show us. Are you free?"

"Yeah, I can come." Isaac had perked up. "I'd be glad to help, and it'll be on my own time—oh. Gotta go." He locked the exhibit case and scurried away.

Chloe frowned after him. What on earth … ?

Then she saw restoration specialist Roy Galuska approaching from the other direction. Was that why Isaac had skedaddled so abruptly?

Well, no matter. "Good morning, Roy," she greeted him.

He grunted something unintelligible—Chloe chose to interpret it as a greeting—and scowled after Isaac. "You got to keep your eye on that boy. He's got no respect for what we're all about."

"Roy." Chloe couldn't let that statement pass. "He just needs more experience."

"Worthless." Roy slid both hands into pockets. His lined face was hard as slate.

Chloe was ready to change the subject. "Shall we head out? I really want to see the big barn through your eyes."

"Let's go then," he said gruffly.

He was already outside by the time Chloe caught up with him. For a moment she thought he was actually waiting for her. Then she noticed that he was gazing over the historic structures visible from this vantage point with a look of satisfaction. "This site? It wouldn't be here without the women. Women saved these buildings. They made it happen."

"I am in awe." It was no small thing to marshal enough support and enthusiasm to preserve and protect any old building, much less a park full of them.

The radio on Roy's belt crackled. "Roy? A man from the lumberyard is here."

"He's supposed to be here tomorrow!"

"Well, he's here today," came the patient voice.

"You go ahead," Chloe suggested. "I've got some work to do in the library anyway."

"All right. This won't take more than half an hour. I'll meet you at the barn." Roy stalked away.

Chloe hurried back to the staff library. Upstairs, she skipped the bookshelves and went straight to the metal cabinets tucked beneath the eaves. She found the *C-D-E* drawer and fingered her way through the labeled files. "Yes!" she said triumphantly as she pulled out the file she'd hoped to find: *Civil War, Belgian-Americans*. Then she settled into a nearby rocking chair and began to read.

SEVENTEEN

APRIL 1861

SERAPHINE WAS STANDING IN her cabin's open door when Emelie emerged into the clearing with her youngest daughter on her hip. Her son François, six, held the other girl's hand "You are waiting for us so eagerly?" Emelie teased. "You must be anxious to pick stones!"

"Just enjoying the sunshine." But Seraphine felt restless. A little uneasy.

"I hope Etienne and Jean-Paul get back from Green Bay today. There's much work to be done."

Seraphine hoped the men would return for all kinds of reasons. "Emelie, would you take Jules and Pierre out to the field? They're inside. I'll be along shortly."

Emelie shrugged. "Of course."

Seraphine took a well-worn path into the woods. A year earlier a log church had been built in nearby Namur, and they regularly attended mass there, but Jean-Paul had done as he'd vowed when baby Octavie died of cholera, and erected a small log chapel to honor her memory. He visited daily, and seemed to find peace there. Seraphine wished she had Jean-Paul's certainty. Sometimes she felt God was listening to her prayers. Sometimes she wasn't so sure.

Now she slipped inside and knelt in front of the altar. "Father, please keep my family from harm. Take care of my baby Octavie in heaven, and keep Jean-Paul and Etienne safe as they travel home to us. And please watch over my sister Octavie in Belgium." She paused before adding, "And please give my friend Adele Brise the strength to do what she was asked to do."

Her friend Adele had become a source of constant conversation. Two years earlier, in 1859, Adele had been carrying grain to a mill when she'd seen a blinding light that appeared between two trees. Adele dropped to her knees. The light took form as a woman dressed in white. The woman had appeared to Adele two more times. "I am the Queen of Heaven," the woman said, and instructed Adele to start a religious school for area children.

People who knew Adele—Seraphine included—believed her story. A neighbor donated land, and her father built a small wooden chapel at the site of the visions. But when Seraphine had recently visited with Adele's mother, she learned that the Catholic authorities had publicly rejected Adele. "They are calling her a liar." Mrs. Brise's voice had trembled with distress. "One priest said it was 'a myth.' The clergy of this diocese have declared she may no longer take Holy Communion."

Seraphine hated to imagine Adele being ridiculed and persecuted. "What is she going to do?"

Mrs. Brise had lifted her chin. "What the Virgin Queen asked her to do!"

Now Seraphine was about to rise when she remembered one more petition. "And please, let Jean-Paul come home with good news." The country was teetering on the edge of civil war. All of the arguments about states' rights and slavery had nothing to do with them, but the men were increasingly troubled.

She walked across the wheat field, where the others were heaving rocks onto the stone boat used to drag them away. "Every year a new crop," Emelie said dryly. "If only our other crops were so generous."

New rock piles dotted the field's edge by the time Jean-Paul and Etienne emerged from the forest trail. They cut across the field to meet their families. "Papa, I picked a lot of stones," Jules cried.

Jean-Paul let the sack of supplies fall to the ground and rolled his shoulders, wincing. "That's important work."

The words were right, but when Seraphine saw the stark look in his eyes she stepped backward. *"No."*

"I'm afraid so." He shook his head. "It's war."

Etienne offered a more colorful observation.

"Etienne!" Emelie snapped. Anxiety made her voice shrill. "I won't have that language."

Her husband picked up a stone and heaved it toward the forest.

"Come inside," Seraphine said. "We'll talk this through. Children, you keep working."

"François, mind the others," Emelie added. Among the cousins, he was oldest.

Inside the cabin, the men slumped at the table. Emelie sat by Etienne, her face tight. "I'll make coffee," Seraphine said. She blew embers in the hearth back to life and hung a pot of water over the flames. Then she fetched the little sack of coffee beans and her mortar and pestle, and sat down beside her husband. They all needed a treat today.

"We have made a decision," Etienne said.

Seraphine and Emelie exchanged a wary glance. "On your own?" Emelie demanded. "What of your wives?"

"Our wives aren't being asked to enlist," Etienne retorted. "This is men's business."

Emelie's brows lowered. "Not if it affects your families!"

Jean-Paul seemed intent on studying the plank table. Seraphine plied the mortar with unnecessary force. The aroma of coffee mingled with the lingering scents of wood smoke and fried fish.

"We have made a decision," Etienne repeated deliberately. "One of us will go."

Something tightened in Seraphine's chest. "Jean-Paul? This is true?"

"It is." He thumbed a knot in the wood grain. "We already have more than we ever could have had in Belgium. We owe a debt."

Etienne took off his cap and ran both hands through his hair. "One will go, and one will stay here to do the best he can with both farms."

We barely manage two farms with the four of us, Seraphine thought. "Who ... " She let the word trail away.

Jean-Paul lifted his hands. "That doesn't have to be decided today—"

"Yes, it *does*." Seraphine slammed the pestle down. "You think we don't need to know who is going to war?"

"Seraphine," Jean-Paul began.

"I am tired of not knowing!" Seraphine blinked hard against hot, angry tears. "I don't know if I will ever see my sister again. I don't know if God welcomed my baby Octavie into heaven because

181

she is not buried where Father Daems wanted. Emelie and I have been left alone over and *over*, not knowing if you are almost home or have been eaten by wolves!"

The others stared, clearly shocked. I don't care, Seraphine thought.

"We have to find a fair way to decide," Etienne said.

Seraphine went to the shelf near the hearth and lifted down a crock of dried beans. Most were a mottled cranberry red with black specks. Most, but not all.

She pawed through the crock until she found one of the stray black beans, and dropped it into the empty coffee sack. She added a small handful of the red beans. After pulling the drawstring tight, and giving the sack a few good shakes, she slapped the bag down between her husband and his brother.

"There is one black bean in this sack. You will take turns removing a bean until the black one is drawn. Whoever draws that one will go."

The men eyed each other uneasily across the table. Etienne hitched his shoulders in a tiny shrug: *This way is as good as any.*

Jean-Paul plunged his hand inside the sack and withdrew a red bean.

Etienne's turn. He also drew a red bean.

Back and forth. Back and forth. Back and forth.

This was a terrible idea, Seraphine thought, as Etienne passed the bag to her husband one more time. There couldn't be more than a few beans left. The ache in her chest grew painful, as if someone was pulling a string tighter, ever tighter. Emelie looked brittle, ready to snap in two.

Jean-Paul reached inside the sack, drew out his fist, slowly uncurled his fingers. The black bean lay on his palm.

Emelie closed her eyes, and some of the starch left her posture. For a long moment no one spoke. The boys' bickering voices drifted through the open door. "I've picked more stones than you," Jules insisted. François countered, "Have not!"

"So," Seraphine said finally. "Now we know who is going to war."

MAY 1861

Jean-Paul joined Company G of the 17th Wisconsin Volunteer Infantry Regiment, composed of Belgian farmers and French-speaking Canadians living in northeast Wisconsin. The morning he was to report at Fort Howard, in Green Bay, Seraphine woke before dawn. Reaching for him, she found herself alone. She threw back the quilts, grabbed a shawl to wrap around her shoulders, and slipped her feet into *sabots*.

In the darkness she could just make out the shapes of the table, the benches. The boys were asleep in the far corner, their breathing soft and steady. But the front door was ajar.

Outside, she made out Jean-Paul's shadow. He was sitting on the log by the front wall, elbows on knees, head low. She took a moment to calm herself before joining him.

For a long moment neither spoke. A fitful breeze passed through the clearing. A faint rustle suggested a mouse scurrying through the dead weeds by the cabin.

"I know you're angry with me," Jean-Paul said finally.

"No." She put one hand on his knee. "I am angry, but not at you." It was true. Her first burst of fury had subsided. She wished Jean-Paul had chosen to wait out the war, as so many other Belgian men were doing. But she understood why he felt that someone from the family should serve. "I'm angry at the men who started the war. And I might be angry at God."

"Seraphine!"

She leaned against him. She wouldn't be able to do so much longer. "Every time we make progress I think, *Now. Now we can catch our breaths.*" They had cleared sixteen acres, tree by enormous tree. Jean-Paul and Etienne had dug a shallow well. They'd built a little stable by planting cedar logs upright to form walls, and sectioned off one corner for the chickens they would one day acquire. Last fall they'd gone in together to buy an ox, and although Seraphine found the beast sulky and unpredictable, the task of hauling downed trees had become *much* easier.

"I know."

"And every time, something sets us back. The trees. The cholera. Now the war."

Jean-Paul sucked in a long breath, blew it out again. "You've had to work harder than I ever imagined—"

"I don't mind hard work."

"But I promised you time to make lace. Money enough for thread." His voice was low. "After the war it *will* happen, my love. I'll come home and work harder than ever—"

"Shh." Seraphine already regretted her complaints. He was the one facing battle. "I believe you, Jean-Paul. And I'm sorry that I've made this more difficult."

"I'm doing this for Jules and Pierre." His voice was husky. "I came here to make a good life for them. This country gave us forty acres at a cheap price. We didn't know it would be wooded land, but it's still *our* land. I couldn't let the country dissolve."

"You're a good man," she said, then stood. "Wait here." She went inside, and returned again with her gift. "This is for you." She handed him the new shirt she'd stitched in fits and starts when he was out of the house. "I expect a spare will prove useful."

"Oh, this is fine." Jean-Paul stroked the cotton. It was good quality, thick and soft, checkered with tiny red and white squares.

"And look here. Give me your hand." She guided his fingers into the pocket she'd added over the left breast. "It's a bit of my lace. No one but you will know it's there."

"You shouldn't have." He sounded horrified.

Seraphine struggled to shape her impulse into words. "I needed to send you off with something of me." It was her blessing. A prayer, even, and she wanted it close to his heart.

AUGUST 1862

For the sake of the farms, Seraphine thought, it would have been best if Jean-Paul had stayed behind.

She and Emelie and the children were slapping mosquitoes and digging the first new potatoes on a sticky-hot afternoon. Fifteen months had passed since her husband had walked away. Etienne had done his best. They all had—working together to plow, seed, scythe, rake, and bind their wheat. The women traipsed back and forth between the two farms daily with babies on hips. Seraphine cherished Emelie's company even more than her help.

Etienne, though, was clearly overwhelmed. Or perhaps just anxious for news, for he left the farms more and more often. Most times he took a short trip to other Belgian settlements, no more than a long day away. But Seraphine and Emelie were left alone with six children to manage along with cooking, laundry, planting onions, chopping firewood, and everything else. Seraphine had a baby, Cecilie, already seven months old. The little boys did their best, staggering under armloads of hay to the stable, struggling to chop weeds with grub hoes they could hardly lift. It was too much for all of them.

As if reading Seraphine's mind, Emelie said now, "I'd feel better if I knew Etienne truly went for news." She thrust her pitchfork into the ground between rows of the hilled plants and wiped her forehead with her sleeve. "Or if the news didn't come with a tankard of beer."

Seraphine squeezed her sister-in-law's hand. "It's been hard for him."

"Hard for us too," Emelie countered. "Especially you."

Seraphine crouched and gently separated the roots of the plant Emelie had just forked up. She felt weightless without Jean-Paul. He wrote letters about training in Madison, endless marches, a siege at Corinth, Tennessee. The experiences and places she couldn't imagine only emphasized how far away he was.

"He'll come home again," Emelie said. "I pray every night for—"

"Emelie!" Etienne shouted as he strode from the trees. His face was tight, his mouth compressed in a hard line.

Seraphine's muscles turned to jelly. She found herself sitting on the damp soil. "You have bad news."

Etienne held up both hands, palms out. "It's not Jean-Paul."

It's not Jean-Paul, Seraphine thought, limp with relief. It's not Jean-Paul.

"But I do have bad news. There's going to be a draft."

"A draft?" Emelie echoed blankly. "This country is free! There is no conscription in America!"

"There is now."

"But—but they can't draft you, can they?" Emelie's voice was rising. "You are Belgian!"

"When we arrived," Etienne said grimly, "Jean-Paul and I both signed a Declaration of Intent, promising to become American citizens. Only because of that, the government was willing to sell us land at a low price, with no need to pay everything at once. That Declaration makes me eligible for the draft."

Emelie was stunned into silence. Seraphine felt as if the ox had kicked her in the gut. They were barely managing now.

"The town assessor will create a list of every man aged eighteen to forty-five," Etienne explained. "The governor will appoint a draft commissioner. The best we can hope for is that my name is not selected."

Over the next few weeks, as the list was compiled, Seraphine clung to that hope. Etienne declared the wheat ready to harvest. He scythed first his field, then Jean-Paul's, and the women raked the stalks and tied them into bundles. She had carrots to dig and potato beetles to kill and filthy diapers to scrape and scour. Etienne can't be drafted, she thought. We can't cope without him.

But Etienne *was* drafted.

The Lejeunes did not attend the lottery, so a friend brought the news. Etienne was to report for military service in four weeks. "Some have already said they won't report for duty," the man said. "Forty men were drafted in the town of Brussels, and thirty-six of them are Belgians. Belgians are being drafted faster than Americans. We are being taken advantage of, I tell you."

Seraphine felt numb. What would she and Emelie do without Etienne?

After the man was gone, Emelie said, "This is not our fight, and you're needed at home."

"I know," Etienne said.

"Well?" She stood tapping one impatient foot, hands on her hips. "Will you go?"

Etienne looked away. "I have not decided."

Anger about the draft bubbled hot among the Belgian settlers all through autumn. When neighbors clumped in knots after mass, people spoke of Belgian men in Kewaunee and Brown Counties arming themselves with pitchforks and spades to march on Green Bay in protest. When Etienne walked into Brussels or Namur, he returned with tales of drafted men hiding in the woods.

"You should join them," Emelie prodded her husband.

"I may," he admitted. "I just may."

Then came word that a Belgian man had been killed by three men sent to arrest him for not reporting for duty. "He was trying to climb out a window when he was shot," Etienne reported. "He died in his wife's arms."

The next day, Seraphine and Emelie helped Etienne shock corn. When that was done Etienne stood sweat-stained, looking over the stubble. The look on his face made Seraphine's muscles tighten. It was October. Beyond the field maple trees blazed crimson and hickory trees gold. A skein of geese flew overhead, honking as they headed to Green Bay.

At last Etienne said, "I will leave in the morning."

Emelie stamped one foot. "No!" She struck him in the arm. Then she collapsed sobbing against his chest.

Etienne looked intently at Seraphine over his wife's shoulder, a clear question in his eyes: *Will you take care of Emelie while I am gone?* Seraphine nodded: *Of course I will.*

But who, she wondered bleakly, will take care of me?

———

MAY 1863

When Emelie fell, Seraphine leaned back from the plow handles, trying to let weight accomplish what her insufficient strength could not. "Whoa!" she hollered to the ox. "Brownie, *whoa!*" The perverse beast dragged her another few feet before stopping. Emelie slowly got to her feet.

"Are you all right?" Seraphine asked. "Perhaps we should wait until Jules and François can help us." They'd sent the boys to the creek to fish. They weren't strong enough to manage the ox or plow either, but sometimes having the boys walk beside the animal, switches in hand, helped.

"We can't waste a fair day." Emelie slapped at the dirt on her skirt. "But let's change places."

Seraphine walked up to grasp Brownie's halter, and Emelie settled herself behind the plow. "Get up!"

To help keep from tripping in the rutted field, Seraphine had pulled the back of her skirt between her knees and tucked it into the waistband in front. Still, it was impossible to do better than stumble along. Twice she went down on one knee, and once her left *sabot* flew from her foot.

Keep going, Seraphine ordered herself, as she had so many times in the two years since Jean-Paul had left. Just, keep, going.

They were making a turn when Emelie cried out in pain. Seraphine leaned back against the halter. "Whoa, Brownie. Whoa!"

Emelie was sitting on the ground, bent over, arms wrapped around her chest.

"Plow handle?" Seraphine asked sympathetically. The men could manage the plow when it bucked over a heavy clod. The women could not, and more times than not were whacked in the chest. "Let me see." There was always the fear of a cracked or broken rib.

"I-I'm alright," Emelie tried, but her voice shuddered. Then she began to cry.

Seraphine crouched and wrapped one arm around Emelie.

"I want Etienne to come home! And Jean-Paul as well!"

"I do too." Seraphine fought back her own tears. Etienne had left home as a member of the 34th Wisconsin Infantry Regiment, Company H—the Belgian Company. Jean-Paul was still slogging through Southern swamps.

Emelie raised her head. "I u-used to be p-pretty!" she quavered. "We used t-to have f-fun sometimes!"

Seraphine remembered Emelie as she had been back in Antwerp—shaking her saucy dark curls, pinching her cheeks to bring out the roses, laughing with Etienne. After leaving Antwerp, before the voyage got bad, she'd been the first to start dancing when someone brought out a fiddle or guitar on calm evenings. On stormy days, down in the hold, she told stories with such dramatic flair that uneasy travelers forgot their worries. Now her face was too thin, her mouth too tight. Hair straggled from its knot. Worry lines were etched deep beside her eyes. She wore a limp, patched dress that had faded from a rich chocolate brown to the color of dried mud.

"I know," Seraphine murmured, rocking Emelie back and forth, letting her cry. "I know."

When the tears subsided the women decided they'd done enough plowing for the day. They unhitched Brownie from the plow and managed to get her back into the stable. Then, arm in arm, they walked to Seraphine's cabin, where Emelie's oldest daughter had been watching the two little girls.

"Stay for supper," Seraphine urged. "Spend the night."

But Emelie shook her head. "No, I want to go home. I'm sorry, Seraphine."

After the others had gone, Seraphine gathered Cecilie into her arms and curled up on the bed, thinking about Emelie. When the little girl dozed off Seraphine eased her aside, got up, and scrubbed her hands.

Then she quietly pulled her old packing box from beneath the bed. Many things inside poked at tender places in her heart: Octavie's letters, the mound of unused bobbins Jean-Paul had whittled for her before enlisting, her wedding lace.

Jean-Paul had not asked where she'd gotten the money to purchase the cotton for his shirt. Seraphine had been able to talk the shopkeeper in Brussels into trading cloth for a short length of lace. She'd lost four inches of her lace to the shopkeeper, and one for Jean-Paul's shirt.

Now she snipped off another three.

The next morning, Emelie walked over to Lejeune Farm West with her children in tow. "Clouds are gathering," she said. "We'd best get right to it, see what we can get done before the rain moves in."

"Before we do ... " Seraphine handed her the lace she'd snipped and hemmed the night before, now pleated and stitched into a little flounce. "I thought you might pin it at your collar for mass, or fasten it in your hair."

"This is for *me?*" Emelie breathed. "But ... why?"

"Because you deserve it," Seraphine told her. "You truly do."

———

Dear Seraphine,

Our dear Sister Odile-Alphonse celebrated her Golden Jubilee. Fifty years as a member of this community! Her sight is failing, and she now spends most of her time at her spindle, winding thread on bobbins for the lacemakers. She remembers you fondly.

We get little news here, but do sometimes receive reports about the war in America. I grieve for your country and your family, and pray that your husband returns safe to you. I imagine that your own vocation as a lacemaker seems further away than ever. Yet when is the simple pleasure of a bit of lace more needed? Have faith.

Your loving sister,
Octavie

EIGHTEEN

In the staff library at Heritage Hill, Chloe gathered the articles she'd just read, slipped them back into the folder, and returned it to the file cabinet. She hated imagining the heartache for families who'd made the wrenching decision to start new lives in a free country—only to confront a vicious war.

And as always, Chloe thought as she left the library, the women left behind had to hold everything together.

At the Belgian farmstead, Roy was waiting beside the barn. "Hey, Roy."

Skipping the pleasantries, he put one gloved palm on the log wall. "What can you tell me about this barn?"

Really? Chloe thought. Again? But she played the game. Stepping back, she squinted at the wall. "Cedar logs, right?"

His eyes widened in grudging surprise. "Yeah."

"That spiral grain is indicative." She tried to sound off-hand. Sometimes her forestry degree came in handy. "And I imagine farmers appreciated the wood's ability to absorb moisture, which kept barns dryer."

The corners of Roy's mouth twitched.

"It insulates well too," Chloe mused. "Cedar barns were warmer and drier than most."

Roy barked out a laugh. "All right, missy. You'll do."

Chloe suspected that "You'll do" was high praise from Roy Galuska, and felt inordinately pleased. She added, "And ... I'd say the builder was in somewhat of a hurry. The structure looks sound, but the logs went up as they were—knotholes and all. Some of the wood is charred, which suggests that the builder took whatever wood was available."

Roy nodded. "Sometimes when forest fires burned through, certain stands of timber were left upright, scorched but still useable. Those burn marks could have come from the Great Fire. You know about that? Same day as the Peshtigo Fire across the bay, and the Chicago Fire."

Chloe stared at the blackened streaks visible in many of the logs. As most any Wisconsinite knew, the 1871 firestorm at Peshtigo was the most horrific in recorded history. The Chicago disaster attracted the greatest national attention. But Roy's comment was a good reminder that a tornado of fire had also raged on the southern Door County peninsula.

She was glad when Roy moved on, leading her inside the closest door. "This type of log barn was quite common on Belgian farms. Long and low. Double pen with a central drive-through."

Two areas with animal stalls, Chloe translated silently, separated by a big open space where farmers unloaded their hay wagons. "I see some items have already been collected ... ?" She gestured toward a heavy shovel leaning against one wall, a hand-cranked corn sheller, leather tack hanging from nails.

"The family gave us a few things. I'll give you a list." Roy continued through to the barn's center drive-through, open to the roof. Ladders provided access to the upper level on each side, used for hay or grain storage. "See that hay hauler? It came from the family. Before they got that, all the hay had to be pitched up from the wagon. The hauler made things a lot easier."

Chloe dutifully admired the two-pronged apparatus dangling from a pulley system that allowed farmers to hoist their crop to the haymows. "Cool."

"That's a double harpoon hauler. Lots of people preferred the Eagle fork, which did a better job, but the double harpoon is appropriate for this barn."

"Got it." Chloe made a mental note to not recommend the Eagle.

Roy talked at high speed. Chloe scrawled notes about wheelbarrows, manure hooks used to haul and spread the fertilizer, chains for the cow stalls, dummy wooden eggs placed in nesting boxes to encourage balky hens to lay their own. At one point she had to raise a palm, stopping the flow of information so she could catch up. "This is awesome," she said, scribbling frantically.

"I interviewed a lot of elderly Belgian farmers," Roy told her. "Asked each the same questions so I could see trends. Look here." He stepped to a manger and pulled out a big three-ring binder. "I keep this out here so it's handy." He opened the binder and flipped through his interview notes. "I talked to men and women both, if they were willing." He showed her a page of sketches. "This lady remembered her mother making fly chasers. She cut fringes from clothes and nailed them over doors to flutter in the breeze and scare away flies."

Chloe refrained from hugging him, but just barely. "Roy, this information is *gold*. That kind of detail adds authenticity and will really bring the farm alive."

He returned the notebook to the manger. "You can use this any time. But before you start making recommendations about tools and implements, you talk to me."

"Will do," Chloe promised. "In fact, if you're available, can we meet again tomorrow? I'll show you any relevant pictures I receive at the Heritage Day event in Namur this evening."

They agreed to meet at eleven thirty. "If we're gonna do this Belgian farmstead," Roy declared, "we're gonna get it right."

———

Roelke stopped for lunch at Sasso's tavern, a village institution. He generally didn't like spending personal time in the community where he worked. It was hard to relax while three guys he'd busted for drugs or drunk driving or whatever sent death-ray glares from their bar stools. But there weren't a lot of options for a quick meal in Eagle.

He was finishing his cheeseburger and fries at a corner table when Kent Bobolik stalked into the bar. When he noticed Roelke he stopped, hands clenching, face hard. Roelke could have stared him down, but decided to go with a grin and friendly wave, just to mess with him. Bobolik scowled and retreated to the bar.

And I am outta here, Roelke thought. He put enough cash on the table to cover the meal and a tip, and left. He didn't see Bobolik's truck parked out front, so he ambled around the building. Maybe he'd get lucky. Bobolik might just be stupid enough to drive with expired plates or something.

The truck was there, but alas, Roelke found no sign of even minor laws broken. He was about to head back to the squad car when he noticed a figure scurrying along the far side of Waukesha Road, engulfed in an oversized parka. When a gust of wind shoved the hood away, he recognized Ginny Bobolik. She jerked it forward again and passed St. Theresa church, then turned in at the parish house. Head down, shoulders hunched, she disappeared inside.

Roelke rubbed his chin thoughtfully. Well, hunh. He wouldn't have pegged Ginny Bobolik as a churchgoer. Maybe Kent's abuse was getting to her after all.

Or … maybe she was only going to ask for groceries at the food pantry parish volunteers ran in a back room.

Roelke watched for maybe twenty minutes, waiting to see if Ginny emerged with a food bag in her arms. She did not.

———

Chloe would have happily curled up someplace warm for the rest of the day, dividing her attention between a cup of peppermint cocoa and Roy's fat binder of interview notes. But the Heritage Day gathering in Namur could be extremely helpful as well, she reminded herself as she grabbed a late lunch at the local deli. Her professional cup was running over.

Namur was an unincorporated community, too small for hamlet status. Chloe spotted an old school and an older store that had both been converted to private use, evidence of consolidation and the lure of bigger markets. Several cars were already parked in the small lot in front of the former St. Mary of the Snows church, a pretty red brick building in the heart of the Belgian settlement.

After stepping inside Chloe opened herself for any powerful emotions that might still quiver here, but found—as she usually did in old churches—only a peaceful sense of faith and reflection. The soaring architecture featured tall arches. Stained glass windows depicted saints. Belgian flags and banners hung from the choir loft in the rear. Statues of Mary, Joseph, and a young Jesus still stood in the chancel, but a banner proclaimed that this was now the Belgian Heritage Center.

Mrs. Delcroix, the formidable volunteer raising money for Heritage Hill's Belgian Farm restoration project, was bustling about with the rest of the Heritage Day committee. "Miss Ellefson!" She waved Chloe over and introduced her to Nadine Lamotte, a sixty-something woman with frosted hair and a cheerful smile. "I'm on the board of directors," Nadine said. "Let me give you a tour."

They left the others preparing for the potluck. "A simple log church was built here in 1860. This building dates to 1893. It was recently slated for destruction, but at the very last minute, we managed to save it. Now we're raising money for exhibits here in the nave. What you see is only the first phase."

It may have been only the first phase, but the exhibits were beautifully designed to tell the story of the Belgian immigrants who gambled all on making new homes in Wisconsin's deep woods. Cases held photographs and artifacts. Chloe was particularly delighted with a section that gave guests the simulated chance to try pulling a plow, as men did before they could afford oxen, and carrying a sixty-pound sack of wheat, as women did when hauling grain to the nearest mill.

"We've gotten tremendous community support," Nadine told her. "Our heritage is special, and we're determined to preserve our food and customs and architecture. We're planning to interview our elders. Many of them still speak Walloon. It's similar to French, but linguists consider it a distinct language."

"The Heritage Center, and the working farms nearby, provide a lovely complement to the Belgian Farm exhibit being created at Heritage Hill," Chloe mused. It was a rare opportunity to see a collection of restored structures in a museum setting, traditional exhibits, *and* buildings still in use on their original location.

Chloe excused herself so she could get ready for the evening. Isaac Cuddy helped her set up two folding tables and drape them with clean sheets. "I'm really glad you're here," she told him. "A grad student was supposed to help, but he's sick and probably won't come. I've got an information sheet for every informant to fill out. If you could photograph each item, I'd be grateful. That way I'll be free to solicit stories and answer questions."

They had just settled down when Elise scooted into the church. "Hey!" she said, tugging on the fingers of one leather glove. "Need a hand?"

"We've got everything under control," Chloe said, not because she was mildly annoyed with Elise—although she was—but because it was true. "Feel free to pull up a chair, though."

Participants started arriving well before the advertised start time. Chloe couldn't have been happier in a European bakery. She forgot about Hugh Lejeune's demise, and she forgot about Elise's evasiveness and unexplained disappearances. Descendants of those first 1850s pioneers identified their lineage with quiet pride. Some brought photographs of their ancestors. Others brought treasured heirlooms with them: bonnets and hog scrapers, religious paintings and chipped crockery bowls, baby booties knit from homespun yarn and iron tools forged over coal fires.

"My grandmother knit these stockings while crossing the Atlantic," one woman said. "I've got two pairs, and I'd be honored to donate one set."

"That's generous," Chloe told her. "Today we're just gathering information. Someone from Heritage Hill or the Heritage Center will be in touch."

An elderly farmer wearing black-rimmed glasses that seemed too big for his face approached with a smile that was delightfully roguish. "I got something to show you," he said in slightly accented English, and plunked a wool shawl down on the table. "Don't ask me who made this, because I don't know. My grandmother found it on the ground during the Great Fire. Someone must have dropped it, trying to get away. My grandmother took the shawl down a well, and soaked it, and put it over her head while the fire raged all around."

"Wow," Isaac said reverently.

Chloe felt the way Isaac sounded. She pulled on her cotton gloves and gently unfolded the shawl for a better look. It was plain black, nothing fancy, ornamented only with a knotted fringe around the edges. But it told a powerful story.

"My grandmother was just fifteen, and she always said that shawl was the only thing that kept her alive that day." Behind his big glasses, the man's eyes had sobered. Then he shook off what he'd heard about the horrendous fire. "So you might say, young lady, that you wouldn't have had the pleasure of meeting me if that shawl didn't exist."

Chloe laughed. "That would have been a double loss, sir. Thanks so much for bringing this in."

The next lady brought two round crocheted pieces with beads added along the fringe. "Do you know what these are?"

"Doilies?" Chloe hazarded. "Maybe to put under a candlestick or vase?"

"No!" The old woman was clearly tickled to stump the curator. "My mother made these to keep insects out of beer mugs and water glasses."

"Ah!" Chloe imagined the pieces draped in place, stymieing inquisitive hornets. "Beautiful and practical."

It took over an hour for all of the informants to share their treasures. "That was awesome," Chloe said, leaning back in her chair. "Whether the items we saw tonight end up in exhibits here, on display at Heritage Hill, or remain with their owners, we got a rare show."

The background chatter had been rising steadily as more neighbors arrived with foil-wrapped plates, colorful Tupperware, cookie tins, and Crock-Pots. Nadine clapped for attention and welcomed everyone. "It's exciting to see so much interest in preserving our history and culture! This event is a collaboration between Heritage Hill, the university, and the Heritage Center. We're grateful for your continuing support as we develop new exhibits and programs right here in Namur."

Everyone applauded.

"Now, on to the *really* good part." Nadine waved Vanna-like toward the crowded food tables. "Please help yourselves. We've got *jutt*, gallons of *booyah*, and plenty of Belgian pies. And lots more. Eat hearty."

The people who'd been chatting in noisy clumps drifted toward the serving tables. Nadine made her way to Chloe. "How did it go?"

"Great!" Chloe said. "I'll make photocopies of everything for you. Say, what's *booyah*?"

"A chicken soup, but thicker. Almost stew. *Jutt* is cabbage cooked in pork drippings with salt, pepper, and nutmeg."

At moments like this, when she had to pass on traditional food, Chloe almost regretted being a long-time vegetarian. At least she could try the Belgian pie.

Isaac shoved Polaroid photographs and documentation sheets in her direction and beat feet for the supper line. Chloe gathered the pages and tapped their edges on the table as she turned to Elise. "So," Chloe asked in her best casual-friendly tone, "how was your day?"

"Fine, thanks." Elise smiled a bland smile.

Before Chloe could politely press for details, Sharon and her daughter Toni approached. "Hello, you two!" Sharon called.

"It's good to see you here," Chloe told them. "Toni, you're feeling okay?"

"I'm fine." Toni waved one hand in a *no big deal* gesture. "We did drive separately in case I run out of energy. But I swear, if I spend one more hour in bed, I'll go crazy."

"Come on," Sharon said. "Let's eat."

Even omitting the *booyah* and *jutt*, Chloe left the serving table with a loaded paper plate. In the interest of scholarship she sampled two kinds of Belgian pie, prune (traditional, she was told) and rice (a newer development) topped with a cottage cheese mixture. They were smaller than other pies, and absolutely delicious.

People lingered after the meal, as if reluctant to leave such warm fellowship on a cold night. One man had brought an accordion, and he sang and played many songs that were obviously local favorites, some in English and some in the local Walloon dialect. "Songs just sound better in Walloon," a man sitting nearby observed.

At some point a kitchen had been installed in what had once been, perhaps, a sacristy. Chloe slipped into the room during the musical interlude to thank the committee ladies. Her compliment to "whoever baked the pies" sparked a good-natured debate about whether it was acceptable to add applesauce to the prune filling, or to use cream cheese for the topping instead of cottage cheese. Chloe took notes and gratefully jotted down several Belgian pie recipes before returning to the main room. It was good to mingle at this kind of gathering—to make friends, establish connections, answer questions about the furnishings plan project.

Before she got far, a tall woman caught her arm. "Excuse me." She was elderly—mid-eighties, Chloe guessed—with white hair clipped short. She wore wool pants and a sweater that looked hand-knit with an embellished yoke. Her face was lined in a way that made her seem not old, but interesting—someone who had seen a lot of life and still relished new experiences. "I'm Renilde Claes. You're the lady who's studying Belgian heirlooms, right? I'm sorry I couldn't get here earlier, but I have something for you."

Chloe cocked her head toward her workstation, where she'd left the information and assessment forms. "Let's go over there." She led the way.

The woman pulled a sealed sandwich-sized plastic bag from a coat pocket. "Here. I want to donate this. It belonged to my grandmother."

"I'm afraid I'm not able to accept anything tonight—"

"It belongs in a museum." The woman was already turning away. "And my husband's waiting in the car."

"No, I need to get some information … " Chloe rummaged through her totebag until she found a blank documentation form. "Here we go. If you could just … " She glanced down at Renilde's offering and caught her breath.

Tucked into the plastic bag was a scrap of lace. The six-inch fragment was stained, and appeared to have been cut from a longer strip. But it was exquisite.

Did this piece of early bobbin lace represent what Elise so hoped to find?

"Mrs. Claes, if you could please wait one more moment—my colleague is around here somewhere. She studies lace, and will be thrilled to see this. I'll be right back, okay?"

Chloe hurried away, scanning the crowd. She saw people clapping friends on the shoulder, people reclaiming empty casserole dishes, people scrabbling among the coats on nearby racks. She saw babies napping on shoulders and children getting the *I'm too tired but won't admit it* grumps. She saw Nadine shaking an older man's hand, and Mrs. Delcroix staring down a hapless couple who'd probably just been hit up for a donation. Chloe did not see Elise.

Sharon joined her. "What a fun evening! I hope you got lots of good leads, Chloe."

"It was, and I did," Chloe assured her. "But speaking of good leads, have you seen Elise?"

"Not lately." Sharon looked around. "At dinner, she said she had a headache. I haven't seen her since. She might have decided to head back early."

Rats. "Well, I'll catch her at your place. Excuse me, but I left someone waiting." Chloe trotted back to the table.

The plastic bag holding the lace fragment remained. Renilde Claes was gone.

Chloe stifled a groan. Rule One of the Curatorial Code of Ethics: Never, *ever* take possession of any artifact without proper permission forms signed by all parties. She grabbed the plastic bag and darted outside with the vague hope of chasing down the elderly woman and pressing the artifact back into her fragile hand. A couple was walking away from the Center, but the woman was short and squat. Beyond the yard, a vehicle pulled onto the road, headlights puncturing the darkness. Chloe's shoulders slumped as she acknowledged defeat.

Back inside, Nadine made sure that Chloe had met all of the Heritage Center's board members. She was chatting with the farmer who'd brought the shawl when Sharon approached them. "Excuse me." Sharon towed Chloe a few steps away. "I can't find Elise."

Chloe frowned. "Didn't she go home?"

"I said she *might* have gone home. But her rental car is still parked in the lot."

"Then she must still be here." Chloe tried to sound soothing. "Did you check the ladies' room? The kitchen?"

"I've checked everywhere!" Two spots of color had appeared in Sharon's cheeks.

Toni joined them, a half-eaten chocolate chip cookie in one hand and a slow cooker under one arm. "What's going on?"

"Elise's car is in the lot," Sharon told her daughter. "But I can't find her."

"Her car's in the lot?" Toni repeated slowly. "I saw her coming out of the ladies' room about the time that the music started. She didn't look good, and I offered to drive her back to the farm, but she said no."

Chloe rubbed her arms with her palms. "This is weird."

"She has to be here somewhere," Toni said. "Maybe she went to see the chapel out back."

Sharon frowned skeptically. "In the dark?"

"Who knows," Chloe said. "But I'll go check." Elise might easily have slipped outside unnoticed through one of the side exits. "In the meantime, maybe you two should search the building again."

She pulled on her parka and zipped the bag holding the lace remnant into one pocket. After fetching her heavy-duty flashlight—thank you again, Roelke, she thought—she began surveying the yard. "Elise? Are you out here?" No answer.

Gravestones were clustered near the front door, and she splashed the beam over them. Nothing. In addition to the small lot by the road, a driveway led to more parking behind the building. Elise's rental car was parked, locked, and empty.

Chloe looped around the building, calling her friend's name, sending the strong beam of light this way and that. She also took the time to loop around a building to the east (BIRTHPLACE OF THE NORBERTINE FATHERS, according to a sign). She found the tiny chapel behind that structure, and stepped inside. There was no sign of Elise.

Back at the Center, Chloe scanned the yard one last time. The temperature was dropping. Leafless tree limbs bobbed in the wind. She nibbled her lip as a growing sense of unease pooled in her belly. The moon's faint glow revealed dormant farm fields stretching behind the Center. Chloe didn't know where else to look. Where on earth could Elise have gone?

Sharon and Toni came outside. "Any luck?" Toni called.

"I'm afraid not." Chloe trudged over to meet them.

"Elise is definitely not inside," Sharon declared. "We're going back to Belgian Acres to see if she's there. Maybe she accepted a ride back with someone."

Without mentioning that to anybody? Chloe thought. But there was no point in belaboring the obvious. "I'll come too."

She fetched her things from inside, said a final goodbye to Nadine and Mrs. Delcroix, and hurried back to the parking lot. Sharon and Toni had waited for her, their vehicles idling by the road, exhaust puffing ghostlike in the glow of Chloe's headlights.

They caravanned back to the B&B slowly. Chloe wondered if Sharon, leading the pack, was puttering because she hoped to glimpse her missing guest walking along the road. Not likely, Chloe thought, picturing Elise's heeled pumps. Besides, why on earth would Elise walk back to the inn when her car was at the Heritage Center? If the car wouldn't start or something, she would have asked for help from her friends, not light out on foot.

At Lejeune Farm West Chloe parked and followed the others inside. A lamp was lit in the living room, but the house was otherwise dark. And still, Chloe thought. It felt empty.

"Elise?" Sharon called, heading for the staircase. No answer.

"Elise!" Toni hollered. She followed her mother, with Chloe on her heels.

Upstairs, Sharon knocked on Elise's door. "Are you in there?" No answer. Sharon tried the knob, then pulled a key ring from her pocket and unlocked the door. Before stepping inside she felt for the wall switch and flicked on the overhead light.

Chloe felt a chilly sinking sensation in her gut as she surveyed the room. Elise's suitcase sat on its stand. A file folder and novel sat on the bedside table, a hairbrush and pair of earrings on the dresser. But there was no sign of Elise.

For a long moment no one spoke, as if collectively hoping that Elise would magically materialize. The ball in Chloe's gut froze solid.

Elise was simply ... gone.

NINETEEN

Finally Toni said, "There must be a logical explanation. Chloe, did Elise say anything about leaving early?"

"No." Chloe hugged her arms across her chest. "Something's been on Elise's mind this week, but I have no idea what."

Sharon dropped onto the bed, as if her knees had gone weak. "Perhaps this is my fault."

Chloe and Toni shared a startled glance: *Do you know what she's talking about? No? Me, either.*

"Mom," Toni demanded, "how could this be your fault?"

"Maybe Elise wasn't happy staying here, and someone offered her a ride to … well, I don't know where."

Toni frowned. "But—"

"The thing is, when Elise called to make her reservation last month, I did suggest that she might be more comfortable at one of the fancy B&Bs farther up Door County." Sharon rubbed her temples. "She's from out east. An old farmhouse in rural Wisconsin probably just wasn't her cup of tea."

"That's nonsense," Chloe protested. "Besides, even if Elise did decide to leave, she wouldn't have left her car and her luggage."

"Elise wasn't feeling well," Toni reminded them. "Maybe she had trouble in the parking lot, and someone drove her straight to an ER. We should check the hospitals in Sturgeon Bay and Green Bay."

Chloe nodded. "Good idea. And we need to call the police."

Sharon rubbed her temples again. Toni walked to the window and looked outside as if hoping to see Elise walking through the yard. Then she turned back to the others. "But... don't they make you wait a couple of days before reporting a missing adult?"

"Not when the circumstances are so odd," Chloe said stubbornly. "And coming right after Hugh's death, and your car crash—"

Toni winced. "I can't imagine how they'd be connected."

"I can't either, but Chloe's right," Sharon said grimly. "We have to let the authorities know."

Fifteen minutes later a county car arrived at Belgian Acres. Chloe felt relieved when Sharon ushered Deputy Knutson into the living room. A known entity.

The deputy listened to the story, taking notes. At her request, Sharon fetched her reservation book. "I always get full home addresses when guests make their reservation," she murmured, thumbing back a few pages. "Here it is."

No one could offer Elise's social security number, drivers' license number, or date or place of birth. "When we left, her rental car was still in the Heritage Center lot," Chloe said. "I don't have the plate number, but it had a Hertz sticker."

Toni looked puzzled. "Wasn't it Avis?"

"I could be wrong." Chloe tried to tamp down rising panic.

"I'll check on it," Deputy Knutson said, her tone modulated for calm. "The first thing to remember is this: In most cases, the missing person shows up on their own."

In most cases, Chloe thought. What if Elise's disappearance wasn't like most cases?

"If you're able, I suggest you also reach out to friends or coworkers as well," the deputy said. "How was Ms. O'Rourke's mood this evening?"

"I wasn't able to chat with her tonight," Chloe said, "but Elise has been distracted this week. I heard her crying in her room on Monday night."

Deputy Knutson looked up from her notebook. "Did you ask her why?"

"I didn't knock," Chloe confessed. "I figured I'd ask her in the morning, but I didn't get the chance until much later. She said everything was fine. I should have pressed the issue when I heard her crying." If I had, Chloe thought miserably, maybe Elise would still be here.

Sharon reached over and patted her hand.

"It was weird," Chloe said slowly, thinking back over the past few days. "On Monday, Elise asked if she could hang around with me this week. But something changed. Yesterday morning, and again today, Elise left the B&B early. I don't know where she went. Now I'm worried that she might have been depressed." Chloe knew what clinical depression felt like. How paralyzing, how dark it could be.

The deputy made another note. "Do you know who was the last person to see Ms. O'Rourke at the Heritage Center?"

Toni raised her hand. "It was probably me. She wasn't feeling well, and I offered to drive her back here, but she said she didn't

211

need a chauffeur." Toni's mouth twisted with regret. "I should have insisted."

We all missed opportunities, Chloe thought. But I am Elise's friend. I should have done better.

Sharon swallowed hard. "What if... what if someone took Elise against her will?"

Toni winced but made an effort to reassure. "At the Belgian Heritage Center in Namur? That hardly seems likely, Mom."

"We need to consider every possibility," Deputy Knutson said, tone neutral. "Who can provide a list of the people who were at the gathering tonight?"

"Nadine Lamotte." Sharon provided the phone number.

Deputy Knutson slid her notebook back into a pocket and stood. "Once I know who might have interacted with Ms. O'Rourke, I'll question them. Sometimes people remember relevant details that seemed of no consequence at the time. And I'll question people in Namur who live near the Heritage Center. If your friend needed help of some kind, she might have gone to a nearby house. Before I leave, Mrs. Lejeune, may I see Ms. O'Rourke's room?"

"Of course." Sharon gestured toward the stairs.

Toni, who stayed in the living room with Chloe, planted elbows on her knees and her face in her hands. "I didn't want to freak out Mom, but... I don't like this."

"I don't, either." Chloe pinched her lips into a tight line.

After the deputy left, the three women looked helplessly at each other. "We didn't see anything unexpected in Elise's room," Sharon said. "I'll leave the front light on."

"I'll make a couple of calls in the morning," Chloe said. "Other-wise... for the moment, I don't think there's anything else we can do." With subdued "good nights," they trudged off to their respective bedrooms.

Chloe called Roelke and shared the latest. "My mind keeps jumping to horrible conclusions."

"I don't like that this happened just a few days after you discovered a body next door," Roelke said.

"I can't imagine what might connect her disappearance to Hugh Lejeune's death. Elise has never been to Wisconsin before, and has only met a few people. Although ... she did leave the B&B by herself yesterday and today, and none of us know where she went."

"Hunh."

Chloe pictured him thinking things through, knee bouncing, eyes narrowed. "What?"

"A man died, and somebody hid the body, on the next property recently. Right about the time Elise arrived, right? Could she be mixed up in something—"

"No! That's ridiculous."

"I'm sorry, but you have to consider all possibilities. I'm sure the cops are."

"Well, I'll leave that theory to them." She nibbled her lower lip before reluctantly adding, "Although *something* has been troubling her. I wish I knew what."

"You haven't been in touch with her for years. Pushing her to talk probably wouldn't have helped the situation."

Chloe curled on her side, taking comfort from his familiar voice. She was sorry that she'd dumped yet another sad story on him. "How are you?"

"Me?" He sounded startled. "I'm fine."

"Really?" She hesitated, not wanting to push. But she hadn't wanted to push with Elise either, and now she regretted it. "Roelke,

213

something's been on your mind for a while. If it has to do with some work thing—"

"It does."

"—I will respect your need for privacy. But if it has anything to do with you and me—"

"It doesn't."

"—or if whatever it is might be pushing you to some bad place … well, then we need to talk about it."

He blew out a long breath. "Chloe, I'm sorry. There has been something on my mind. But it is absolutely not anything I'm able to discuss."

So it must be a work thing. Chloe got that—for a cop, some things had to be confidential. It didn't make her feel any better, though. "I'm worried about you, Roelke. Libby is too."

Silence. Then, "I'm fine, really."

Chloe didn't believe Roelke was fine. But a better discussion would have to wait until she got back.

"Listen," he said, "do you want me to come up? I'm good at moral support. Or do you want to head home? Now that you've seen the farm at Heritage Hill and met the people at the Belgian Heritage Center, couldn't you do the rest from here?"

Chloe felt strongly both ways about that idea. "It's an appealing thought," she admitted. "But I can't leave right now. Not without knowing what's going on with Elise. Give me a day or two to see what happens, okay?"

"I suppose." He sounded resigned.

"I love you," Chloe said, because sometimes that was the only thing left to say.

After hanging up the phone, Roelke ran a hand over his face. Damn. Chloe worrying about him—bad. Chloe's friend disappearing —worse.

He sank back against the sofa. Olympia was curled into a ball on the cushion beside him, snoring softly. Fatigue was sanding his eyes, tugging at his muscles, but Chloe's call had set off sirens in his brain.

Roelke suddenly missed Chloe so much his chest hurt. He wanted to drive to Door County and make sure she was safe. He wanted to wrap his arms around her, feel her silky hair against his cheek, inhale her Chloe scent.

And when she looked at him with those chicory-blue eyes and asked again what was troubling him, what would he say?

Nothing. No way was he ever, *ever* telling Chloe what he, Officer Roelke McKenna, had done to make sure that Libby's abusive ex went to prison before he could physically hurt Libby, Justin, and Deirdre. He had betrayed her trust.

He had also, he believed, saved the lives of his cousin and her children.

Okay, he told himself, focus on the problem at hand. What could an Eagle cop do to help find the missing woman? He didn't know Elise. Didn't know the area. Local law enforcement would not welcome interference from a stranger, no matter how well intended.

"Dammit," he growled, earning a startled look of disapproval from Olympia. He lightly scratched the cat between the ears in apology. Then he grabbed his duty belt and his truck keys, pulled on his black balaclava and Michelin Man coat, and left the house. He drove to Eagle and parked behind the PD, then walked quickly to St. Theresa Catholic Church.

In a street lamp's faint glow, the church property appeared empty and still. There were some trees just beyond the parking lot, and Roelke strode across the asphalt and pressed himself against one trunk, melting into the shadows. He was gambling that any nocturnal visitors would be approaching from the village to the east, not the road from the west.

Well, Roelke thought, I'm wide awake and have nothing better to do. He'd be ready if the jerk who'd been vandalizing the church showed tonight.

Three hours later, Roelke was feeling less committed to his stakeout. Other than a few late customers leaving Sasso's across the street, he hadn't seen a soul. His knees ached with the effort of standing still. His fingers were numb. Toes too. Despite the heavy parka, he was freezing his ass off. A sane cop would have watched from his nice warm truck, he thought, with a thermos of coffee. But he hadn't wanted to attract attention, and a vehicle with the engine running would have done just that.

He'd just discreetly checked his wristwatch—2:46 a.m., according to the lighted dial—when movement in his peripheral vision prickled every nerve to full alert. Someone was walking along the road toward the church. Roelke experienced a moment of déjà vu, for the person looked much like Ginny Bobolik had earlier—hands in pockets, hood up, head bent. But that's a guy, Roelke thought. The stride was longer, more masculine.

Roelke had thought that the vandal, if he returned, would most likely hit the east side of the church again. The parking lot was between the church and the nearest house, and a recently added vestibule built against a side door offered a bit of protection. This guy did turn into the parking lot. But instead of approaching the church, he cut through and turned left behind it. Roelke held his breath, but the man didn't so much as glance his way. That had to be the vandal. Who else would be walking back here at this hour?

The man crossed the back parking lot, passing the emergency outdoor stairway and two dumpsters. Instead of turning again, he continued straight to the rectory next door.

Not good, Roelke thought. There were no houses on the far side of the priest's house, just the church school. No way was this guy taking a shortcut home after tossing back one too many Buds at Sasso's.

Roelke wasn't well-positioned to follow, so he waited as long as he dared before moving from his hiding spot in the trees. The guy seemed confident, for he didn't pause, didn't glance over his shoulder. By the time Roelke had crept across the parking lot the man was huddled over the knob of the rectory's back door.

"Police!" Roelke bellowed. "Show me your hands!"

The man took off for the street. Roelke launched and brought him down with a flying tackle. The two hit the ground with a jarring thud. Roelke rolled to one knee and managed to snatch the guy's wrists. It took Roelke a moment to grab his handcuffs—stupid coat, he thought—but quickly enough he had the man restrained. Panting, Roelke stood and hauled the guy to his feet.

Kent Bobolik.

Roelke jerked Bobolik's coat open and began a pat-down. Almost at once he felt the handle of a knife in a leather sheath. *Jesus.* What had the SOB been planning?

Bobolik tried to jerk away, and Roelke gave him a shake. "What were you going to do with this?" he demanded, pulling the wicked hunting knife free and tossing it aside. Bobolik glowered.

A light came on over the stoop, and the door opened. Father Dan gaped at the unexpected tableau. He looked younger and more vulnerable than ever in leather slippers, striped pajamas, and a blue bathrobe. "What on earth is going on here?"

Roelke slid one hand down Bobolik's right leg, making sure there were no other pesky surprises. "Father Dan, go inside and lock the door."

Instead, the priest crouched and picked up something from the cement step. "What's this?" He held up a thin tool about eight inches long with a 90-degree bend at the end.

"A lock pick." Roelke glared at Bobolik. "Is there anything in your coat pockets that could hurt me?"

No answer but a sullen stare. Roelke checked the right pocket and found the rest of a basic set of stainless steel, plastic-handled picks: full hook, angle hook, straight. "Kent Bobolik," he began, "you are under arrest."

———

After hanging up, Chloe turned off the lamp and burrowed under the covers. Wind was rattling the windowpanes as if eager to get inside. She hated to think of Roelke alone in the farmhouse, burdened by whatever.

She also hated to think of her missing friend. "Elise," Chloe whispered, "where *are* you?"

The wind shrieked around the eaves.

Chloe sat up and turned the light back on. Her interaction with Elise at the Belgian Heritage Center that evening had been minimal, but she'd seemed fine. She had listened closely as informants shared their treasures with Chloe, ooh-ing and ah-ing over the heirlooms, sometimes asking questions. Her interest had certainly seemed sincere.

So, Chloe mused, was that all an act? When *she'd* been de-pressed, she'd managed to put on a good show—right up until she couldn't do it anymore. Was that what had happened with Elise? Had she snapped? Or did something happen while everyone was eating? Before then, Elise had seemed fine; by meal's end, she had a headache.

Chloe got up and padded across the room, floorboards cold against her feet even in wool socks. She grabbed some blank index cards and returned to bed to capture her thoughts. Roelke always made case notes on index cards. He wrote love notes on them too—how sweet was that? But for the moment she was focused on the practical.

What might make Elise disappear?

Chloe nibbled the end of her pen, thinking.

Someone harmed Elise

Just writing the words made every muscle clench. Chloe tended to agree with Toni on that score. Namur was tiny. Just about every-one at the gathering knew everyone else. It was possible that some pervert had happened to drive through the parking lot just as Elise was getting into her car, but ... it seemed unlikely.

Someone realized Elise was seriously ill, and rushed her to a
hospital

Except ... Toni had called the closest two hospitals, and neither had admitted Elise.

Someone said something that upset or frightened Elise enough
to flee

If Elise had felt threatened in some way, she might have fled without leaving a note or taking time to gather her things. Except … there was nowhere to go. Not on foot.

Elise didn't like B&B

Chloe almost didn't write that down. She suspected that Sharon had suggested that possibility to keep at bay the notion of a human predator grabbing Elise …

Wait a freaking minute. Chloe jerked upright, hearing Sharon's words again: *When Elise called to make her reservation last month, I did suggest that she might be more comfortable at one of the fancy B&Bs farther up Door County. She said she wanted to stay here …*

Elise couldn't have called to make her reservation "last month"—October. Chloe had deliberately waited to reserve until the first week in November because she didn't know how long it would take for Heritage Hill to reimburse her. If Sharon charged up front, as occasionally happened, Chloe wanted it to show up on her November bill.

And Elise didn't call me until *after* I'd made my reservation, Chloe thought. In that same conversation she'd suggested that Elise visit at the same time and stay at Belgian Acres too.

Chloe felt a creeping sense of betrayal. Okay, she told herself finally, don't overreact. Sharon probably misspoke, that was all. She was upset. She'd gotten confused.

Well, there was one way to find out. Chloe got up again, grabbed her penlight, eased open her door, and crept downstairs. She waited for a long while, listening to the wind, but heard nothing to suggest that Sharon or Toni had heard her.

Sharon's registration book was right where she'd left it, on an end table by the sofa. Chloe quickly flipped through the pages, squinting at Sharon's slanting cursive. There had been very few guests in the last several months, and it took only a moment to find an entry for Elise's call.

No ... *two* calls. Elise had called in mid-October and reserved a room for the first full week in December. Chloe had been the next to call, on November 4th, to book a stay from Sunday, November 27th, through Saturday, December 3rd. On November 9th Elise called again and changed her reservation to coincide with Chloe's.

Why? Chloe demanded silently, staring at the page. *Why?* She hated to speculate that Elise had come to Wisconsin for less than ethical reasons, but it was possible. It wouldn't be the first time that someone Chloe knew got involved in buying or selling artifacts through some less than open—or legal—channel. She remembered what Roelke had said earlier: *I'm sorry, but you have to consider all possibilities.*

Chloe closed the book and tiptoed back upstairs. She stopped at the bathroom, just in case someone had heard her moving about, then retreated back to her bedroom. Sitting cross-legged on the bed, covers pulled over her lap, she reluctantly picked up her first card, the one listing possible explanations for Elise's disappearance.

E did something wrong—left in a hurry because she got found out

Then she started a fresh index card.

Secrets

E had already booked at Belgian Acres when we talked about getting together, but she didn't say so

Something has been bothering E—distracted, weeping, disappearing Tues & Wed with no explanation

Chloe remembered the transcription page she'd found—the letter from the priest: *... not only had the gaunt, weary young wife scrubbed the table well, she had adorned it with a cloth trimmed with a strip of delicate lace, the likes of which I have not seen since coming to this place. She had, she told me, learned to make lace at a convent in Bruges...*

So, what was Elise truly after? Lace made in Belgium during the Great War? Or a rare piece actually made in Wisconsin's early Belgian settlement? Either or both, Chloe thought. Historians could get laser-focused when on the trail of, literally, a long-lost treasure. Especially if the hunter was desperate to gain tenure or a book contract or any other form of academic or professional acclaim. Elise was looking for a topic for her Ph.D. dissertation, and after that, one of the oh-so-rare curator of textiles positions.

The only comfort in that theory? That perhaps Elise hadn't been abducted, or walked into the night in a state of clinical depression. Maybe some element of a scheme had gone wrong, and Elise had phoned a colleague to pick her up.

But... Elise didn't know anyone in Wisconsin. Or did she? She'd lied about other things; she could have lied about that too. Was she working with Hugh's son Richard, who wanted control of the Lejeune property?

"Elise!" Chloe muttered. "What on *earth* was going on with you?" It seemed particularly wrong that Elise hadn't even gotten to see the scrap of lace Renilde Claes had left behind at the Heritage Center.

The bag containing the lace was still in Chloe's coat pocket. It can wait until morning, she told herself. She put her notes aside, scrunched under the covers, and turned out the light.

She lasted ten minutes before turning the light back on. The lace remnant sang like a siren from her parka. She'd never go to sleep if she didn't go get it.

After another tiptoed trip downstairs and back, she considered the lace through the clear plastic. Suddenly she sucked in a harsh breath. This design of flowers and swooping vines looked a lot like the edging on the handkerchief Mrs. Martin shared after the guild meeting. She dug out the Polaroids she'd taken of Dominique Anselme's handkerchief.

"It's the same lace," she breathed. She opened the resealable bag, let the spider web of old threads slide onto a clean index card, and leaned closer for a better look.

Her nose caught a faint whiff of smoke.

Was Renilde a chain smoker? Chloe frowned and sniffed again. No. This was not the stink of stale tobacco, but the tang of wood smoke.

TWENTY

OCTOBER 1871

SERAPHINE WOKE WITH A start in the night. "Jean-Paul?" she whispered. His side of the bed was empty. A familiar fear flared inside. She'd been left on her own too many times, spent too many sleepless nights worrying he wouldn't return.

He'd done his duty during the Civil War, and survived. In some ways he'd been luckier than Etienne, who'd been wounded by a Confederate bushwhacker in Kentucky, and returned with a painful limp. But Jean-Paul had come home with shadows in his eyes, whittled down to nothing but bone and sinew. He'd endured the siege of Vicksburg, Mississippi, fought in the bloody Atlanta Campaign, and been ordered to "scorch the earth" during Major General Sherman's March to the Sea.

His absence had been hard. His homecoming had been hard too.

Still, the family had accomplished a great deal since the war's end. Jules and Pierre had helped Jean-Paul enlarge their original cabin by adding an extra room and a loft. With each passing year they'd pushed the forest farther back, letting in more sunshine, making more room for crops. They raised a log barn and stable. They bought chickens, a fat Chester White sow, and—to Seraphine's joy—a brindled Guernsey cow. Jean-Paul purchased a hand-cranked fanning mill and Seraphine learned to cook on a small iron stove.

"Finally," Seraphine and Jean-Paul had told each other last spring. Finally they were getting established. Finally the struggles and heartaches seemed to be bearing fruit.

But 1871 had been the driest year in memory. Crops shriveled. Their well had gone dry. Seraphine and nine-year-old Cecilie had trudged from the ever-shrinking creek with buckets of water, dribbling it gingerly on the cracked earth along drooping rows of onions and potatoes and rutabagas. Fires had been smoldering in the woods for months—some started by lightning, more that escaped from piles where farmers burned their slashings. Every trip to church brought new tales of barns burned, hay crops destroyed, acres of timber reduced to ashes. Jean-Paul and the boys took to walking around their clearing, watching for flames.

Please, God, Seraphine prayed silently, send us rain.

She pushed aside the blanket, shoved her bare feet into *sabots*. Once her eyes adjusted to the gloom she tiptoed to the cradle, where baby Ermina was sleeping quietly. Then Seraphine draped her wool cloak over her nightdress and went out onto the porch, tasting smoke with every breath.

A murmur of male conversation drifted from beyond the garden—Jean-Paul and Jules, it sounded like, keeping watch. Their voices in the night made her feel protected, and frightened her too. Tugging her cloak more tightly, she picked her way toward her husband and oldest son. They emerged as shadows in the hazy darkness—Jules holding a shovel, Jean-Paul a spade. "How is it?" she asked quietly.

"Jules spotted a fire burning just underground," Jean-Paul muttered grimly. "Feeding on duff. There's centuries of dead leaves and such beneath these trees. We're watching for—"

"There." Jules pointed as a patch of earth glowed red, as if someone had blown on fireplace embers. He ran to the spot, flipped over the sod, and buried the sparks with soil.

Seraphine clutched her arms across her chest. How could they fight fires they couldn't even see?

"It's almost dawn," Jean-Paul said. "Jules, go get some sleep."

When they were alone, Seraphine stepped close to her husband. She could sense his fatigue, his tension. "You need rest too," she told him.

"I'll nap later."

She rested one cheek against his shoulder. "This is frightening."

Jean-Paul was silent for a long time. When he finally spoke, it wasn't of fire and drought. "After it rains, I will go to Green Bay."

She pulled away. "Why?" They could get most supplies now at Brussels or Namur.

"I am determined to bring you large quantities of pins and thread."

Seraphine caught her breath. If he'd wanted to distract her, he'd succeeded. "Pins? *Thread?* Do you mean … Can we afford to spend money on such things?"

"I believe we can. I've saved some of the lumber money." The towering trees they'd once burned as worthless had became a cash crop. Lumber mill owners sent out men with flat wagons and six-horse teams to haul logs from the forests.

Eighteen years, Seraphine thought. It had been eighteen years since she'd pricked a pattern and guided bobbins among the pins. "I don't know if I even remember how to—"

"You are a lacemaker. During the war, the lace you gave me felt like a talisman. It didn't survive the war, but I did." He put his hands, warm and strong, on her shoulders. "I've never forgotten the day back in Bruges when you told me about your dream. I promised you a chance. It's taken far, far longer than we ever imagined. But finally, *chère femme*, you shall make lace."

She flung her arms around him. "Oh Jean-Paul, *thank* you. If I can—" Over her shoulder she saw a line of flame zigzagging through the woods, shooting toward them like lightning. "Look!"

He whirled, then grabbed her arm and dragged her away. "Get back!"

The blaze hit a nearby tree, which exploded in flame with a crackling *whoosh*. Seraphine stumbled back as a wave of heat struck like a blow. Wide-eyed, she watched the giant torch writhe against the sky.

"The roots were likely already dead," Jean-Paul said grimly. "Go get Jules, and Pierre too. I need their help."

———

Jean-Paul and the boys managed to keep the fire from spreading, but by midmorning only Joseph, who'd just turned four, seemed carefree. He was a chubby-cheeked apple dumpling of a boy, with black hair as thick and unruly as his father's. Mina was teething, and the baby's whimpers winched nerves tight. Cecilie kept drifting to the window.

Seraphine pulled out her wooden box and took her lace from its wrappings. "Come see, Cecilie. In Belgium, girls start learning to make lace at about your age."

"It's so beautiful!"

"Would you like to learn how to make lace like this?"

Cecilie's thin face glowed. "Oh, yes!"

"Soon Papa is going to bring home lots of thread and pins." Seraphine paused, savoring the taste of those daring words. "Once I've practiced a bit, I'll teach you. But now, I'm going to snip a bit off for Adele Brise." Seraphine hoped that a bit of lace to mark a favorite Bible passage might cheer her friend, who was still denounced by the local priests. October 9th was the anniversary of one of her visions.

It was good to handle the lace again. Since leaving the convent Seraphine had often felt lost, adrift as a rudderless ship. Jean-Paul's unexpected promise made her feel more certain. She was Octavie's sister. She was Jean-Paul's wife. She was mother to five children. "And I am a lacemaker," she whispered. Perhaps one day, she thought, I really can visit Octavie. That dream had drifted further and further from reach, but today it felt more real.

If only it would rain. Please, God, she thought, glancing out the window. *Please.*

That afternoon Jean-Paul and the boys dug a large hole outside, right by the stone marking the northeast corner of the cabin. He put her lace, his grandmother's rosary, their money, sacks of rice and beans, and their best clothes in a small trunk, and buried it. "Just a precaution," he told Seraphine, but he didn't meet her gaze. He also dragged a barrel to the middle of the newly plowed oat field and filled it with water, and carried out a tin basin.

When Seraphine finished binding the edges of Adele's lace so they wouldn't unravel, she slipped the gift into her pocket and silently gathered several wool blankets from the beds and piled them, folded, by the door. Just a precaution, she repeated silently, but her nerves felt tight enough to snap.

At twilight, Jean-Paul and the older boys were still outside. Seraphine lit a lamp and settled Joseph and Cecilie in bed. A fierce gust of wind rattled the windowpane. "Where's Papa?" Joseph asked, rubbing his eyes with one plump fist.

"He's keeping us safe," Seraphine said. "He'll be here when you wake up in the morning."

Through the window she saw an eerie red glow that had nothing to do with the sunset growing above the trees. Something cold and hard formed in the pit of her stomach. Turning, she scooped Mina from the cradle. Then she sat at the table, not knowing what else to do. With the baby sleeping against her shoulder she closed her eyes and tried to pray.

The front door banged open. "Seraphine!" Jean-Paul bellowed. "Get the children! Where's the baby?"

Seraphine was already on her feet. "I've got her—get Joseph!"

Two more shadowed figures ran inside—Jules and Pierre. "I've got the blankets," Pierre yelled.

"Mama?" Cecilie cried. "What's happening?"

"Get up and put your shoes on." Seraphine frantically herded the girl toward the door as Jean-Paul scooped Joseph into his arms. "Jules, help your sister!"

They plunged outside, running and stumbling toward the oat field. A deafening roar sounded through the clearing. Mina's wails were hardly audible over the din.

Then the woods surrounding the farm erupted in flames.

Seraphine clutched Mina tighter. In the hellish wavering light she spotted the barrel Jean-Paul had left in the center of the field. "Cecilie! Boys! Get down—we've got to—where's Joseph?"

"Here, take him." Jean-Paul let Joseph slide to the ground. Seraphine could tell he was yelling, but she barely heard him. "I'm going to let the stock out."

"No!" Seraphine snatched at him. "You have to stay with us!"

"I'll go." That was Jules.

"Stay with your mother! I'll be right back." Then Jean-Paul was gone.

Seraphine's heart thudded like a mallet. "Lie down, all of you. Close together. Roll on your bellies." Pierre grabbed Joseph and yanked him down. Seraphine shoved Cecilie to the ground as well. "Jules, take the baby."

Her hands shook violently as she draped blankets over her children. She snatched the tin basin Jean-Paul had left by the barrel, scooped up some water, and poured it over the wriggling children's blankets. The night howled and crackled, whipped to a frenzied tornado of orange and yellow by the wind. Sparks and ashes drifted down like fiendish snowflakes. Several birds fell dead from the sky. Trees popped as they burned from the inside out. The earth was on fire. The woods were on fire. The sky was on fire.

And Jean-Paul hadn't come back.

But her children were right here. Steam rose from the wet wool as heat shuddered over the field. There was nothing to burn here, not even stubble, but the falling embers and blazing air could kill them. Seraphine dipped the basin over and over, splashing it on the blankets. Tears rolled down her cheeks. Smoke stung her eyes. Heat burned her lungs and bits of debris burned her skin.

When she'd emptied the barrel, sheets of fire still raged around the clearing. She kicked the barrel over and away before it could ignite. Then she dropped and wriggled under the edge of one blanket. The heat was unbearable but the children were quiet. She didn't know if they were too terrified to move, or dead.

TWENTY-ONE

CHLOE FELT DULL AND bleary-eyed as she plodded downstairs the next morning. She found Sharon at the dining room table, her hands wrapped around a mug of coffee. "Any news?" Chloe asked.

"Nothing helpful. Deputy Knutson called to say Elise's car is still at the Heritage Center, empty. No one in Namur has seen her or anything suspicious." Sharon slowly pushed back her chair. "Toni got called in to the hospital early. I'll get your breakfast."

After a silent meal, Chloe settled back on her bed beside the telephone. She first called the Helen Louise Allen Textile Collection at the University of Wisconsin–Madison and explained that she was trying to reach a friend, Elise O'Rourke, who had a pending appointment. The receptionist put her on hold for a few minutes, then returned. "I'm sorry, but no one by that name is in our appointment book."

"Are you sure? Maybe Elise made the appointment directly with someone else. Does someone on staff specialize in lace?"

"Yes. I've looked ahead a month in her schedule. There's no record that Elise O'Rourke scheduled an appointment with our lace expert or anyone else."

Lovely. Chloe sighed. "Okay. Thanks for checking."

Next, she pulled out the business card the lace instructor had provided at the guild meeting. When the other woman came on the line, Chloe explained the situation. "When you invited Elise to Wisconsin—"

"We didn't invite Elise."

"Um... you didn't?"

"No," the other woman affirmed. "I'm the program chair, so I know. She called me and asked if we'd like to have her come present about World War I lace, and offer a workshop. She didn't ask for an honorarium, or even travel expenses. It was such a generous offer, out of the blue, that I discreetly checked her credentials. I mean, you never know."

"No." Chloe rubbed her forehead. "You never know."

"Everything seemed legit, and members were thrilled with her visit on Tuesday. But as to her disappearance, I'm afraid I can't help you. I'm sure she didn't speak of anything but the details of her program."

Before making the next call Chloe had to dial Information for the number. It took longer to weave through the phone maze at the Smithsonian Institution's National Museum of American History, but finally she reached the curator of the lace collection. "Elise O'Rourke is a friend of mine," she began. "We were both visiting the area of Belgian settlement in northeast Wisconsin, and she's left the B&B without letting me or anyone else know. I was wondering if by chance she's checked in with you."

"I haven't heard from her." The curator sounded hesitant, as if unsure how much information to share. "But I can't say I expected to."

Chloe tapped her pen against her notebook. "I know she was hoping to find a piece of World War I lace, or perhaps a bit of lace made here in Wisconsin by an immigrant lacemaker. She's looked at the collection at Heritage Hill Historic Site, and she attended a gathering of Belgian-Americans who were invited to bring family heirlooms for inventory and study. Are you aware of any collections in the region with Belgian lace she might want to see?"

"I wouldn't limit your request to Belgian lace," the curator advised. "That's a fairly recent interest. Elise is a wonderful lacemaker, and she's been an excellent intern. When she came for her interview, however, she planned to study Ipswich lace for her dissertation."

Chloe's eyebrows rose. "Oh?" She'd never heard Elise mention Ipswich lace. Whatever that was.

"Ipswich, Massachusetts. The only documented handmade lace industry of any size in the United States. Evidence of lacemakers there dates back to the 1630s. Elise had already started analyzing known examples when she told me that after being exposed to our collection, she wanted to switch to Belgian lace."

"I see." Chloe couldn't think of any more questions. "Thank you. If you do hear from Elise, would you call me at this number?" She dictated. "I'm worried about her."

"Of course." The curator sounded worried now too. "I'm sorry I couldn't be more helpful."

Chloe's next call was to the historic site where she and Elise had met almost a decade earlier. She wasn't sure if John Tate, her supervisor in the way-back days, was even still employed there. The receptionist, however, cheerfully asked Chloe to wait while the call was transferred. The voice that boomed "Hello" was as robust as she remembered.

Chloe pictured the big man sitting in his closet-sized office, desk overflowing with staffing charts and time cards, reproduction drop spindles and boxes of square nails. "This is Chloe Ellefson," she began, and explained the reason for her call.

"I heard she landed an internship at the Smithsonian," John said slowly, "but I haven't seen or talked to Elise in several years."

Chloe sighed. "Well, I knew it was a long shot."

"Did you try calling her in-laws?"

"Her … her in-laws?" Chloe's eyebrows shot skyward again. "Elise is married?"

"Was married," John said sadly. "Her husband was in a moped accident while they were honeymooning in Bermuda. He died."

"Oh, no." Chloe closed her eyes as an ache bloomed beneath her ribs. "How long ago was this?"

"Maybe … three months? Word got around the museum world out here. Listen, I can ask a couple of the old-timers if they've heard from her."

Chloe provided contact information, disconnected, and dialed the county sheriff's office. "Deputy Knutson is out at the moment," the clerk said. "Would you like to speak with someone else?"

"No thank you. I'll try again later. Please just leave her a message saying that Elise O'Rourke was recently widowed, and so under a great deal of emotional strain."

Then Chloe sat motionless, staring blindly at the wall. No wonder Elise had seemed so sad. And if she hadn't wanted to talk about her grief, that was her call.

But another conclusion seemed clear as well. Elise had not been invited to Wisconsin, she had not set up an appointment with the textile curator in Madison, and Belgian lace was not a professional passion of long-standing. Elise had lied, over and over. Why?

———

By midmorning, a scowling Kent Bobolik had been processed at the Waukesha County Jail and Roelke was caught up on paperwork. Next stop: St. Theresa Catholic Church. He parked on the street in front of the rectory just as Father Dan emerged from the house.

"Officer McKenna!" The young priest waved.

Roelke cut across the yard. "Is there somewhere quiet where we can talk?"

"Of course. I was on my way to the sanctuary." He cocked his head toward the church. Roelke followed, and the two men settled into a pew near the back.

"I wanted you to know that Kent Bobolik is in custody in Waukesha," Roelke began. "I believe he was responsible for the recent acts of vandalism."

"I see."

"Ginny Bobolik swears she has no idea why her husband would try to break into the rectory." Roelke leaned forward. "Father, it would help a whole lot if you tell me why Kent Bobolik was angry enough to do what he did."

Father Dan's composure didn't waver. "I can't betray a confidence, Officer McKenna."

"Well, let me make a guess. I think Ginny Bobolik came to you because Kent was abusing her. I think he started the vandalism campaign when he found out she'd turned to you for help." Roelke paused, hoping for a confirmation.

None was forthcoming.

He forged ahead. "But something happened to wind Kent Bobolik up tighter. Something made him come to the church in the middle of the night with a lock pick and knife instead of a can of spray paint."

"I can't speculate as to Mr. Bobolik's motivation."

"Ginny had to pass the Methodist church to get here, so I figure she must be Catholic," Roelke mused. "You wouldn't have advised Ginny to divorce him, so … what did you say? Did you encourage her to ask him to get counseling?"

For a long moment no one spoke. Roelke felt the peaceful silence settle over him just as it had when he was a child, in awe of this sacred space. As a kid, fidgeting on the pew between his mother and his grandparents, he hadn't understood everything the church represented. He didn't now, either. Nonetheless he felt its tug.

Finally Father Dan spoke. "Something like that."

The knot of frustration inside Roelke eased slightly. "I want to help Ginny. Bobolik won't be in jail forever and I want to get her away from him. So far, even after her husband's arrest, she hasn't been willing to tell me anything I could use against him. Has she told you anything that might be helpful?"

"She has spoken to me about physical abuse. But I can't say more."

"Father, do you know that Kent Bobolik's first wife was murdered in her kitchen? The investigators believed he did it, but they couldn't make it stick." Roelke held the other man's gaze, desperate to make him understand. "Ginny could be next. I want to put Bobolik away, but I need your help!"

"I wish I could give it to you." Father Dan's words came haltingly, like the footsteps of a man trying to wade through treacherous water. "But after our first conversation, she insisted on speaking to me only in the confessional."

Roelke's knee began to bounce. Surely the priest wouldn't hide behind that. Not when Ginny's life was at risk.

"The confessional creates a bond of sacred trust that I have an absolute duty to respect. The Seal of the Confessional is inviolable—"

"There are times when it shouldn't be!" Roelke snapped. His knee bounced faster. He had Bobolik cold on trying to pick the rectory lock, but the man hadn't actually entered the structure. There was no way to prove that he was behind the vandalism, either. Roelke was very much afraid that Bobolik would end up skating on this one, just as he had before.

He opened his mouth, then closed it again. The priest had made his position clear. End of conversation.

Father Dan was contemplating the altar. "Officer McKenna," he said, not turning his head, "how long has it been since you unburdened yourself in confession?"

"A long time. Years." He'd made his first confession as expected at age seven, but only sporadically after that.

As if reading his thoughts, Father Dan smiled. "My first confession was uncomfortable. I had no idea what to say."

The priest's tone was so mild that Roelke regretted losing his patience. "Mine was like that too," he admitted. He'd mumbled something about calling his brother names before bolting from the dim confessional, confused and distinctly unrepentant. "Does confession count if you aren't totally sorry you did something wrong?"

"God doesn't expect perfection. Life is complicated. Those who are searching for answers, those who have lost their faith, are as welcome in this place as full believers."

Roelke stared at the hymnals in the rack affixed to the next pew. One had a water stain. He wondered if the roof needed repair.

"The same freedom to unburden that Mrs. Bobolik enjoyed can be yours as well. The Sacrament of Reconciliation exists to provide you with peace of mind and soul. The kind of peace that only comes when we know that we are right in God's eyes."

In his memory Roelke heard his grandma singing her favorite hymn, "Be Still My Soul."

"You can talk with me at any time. Or use the sanctuary as a place to think or meditate."

Roelke took a deep breath. "I—"

His radio squawked. "George 220. What's your ETA?" Estimated time of arrival.

Roelke thumbed the mic button. "George 220. I can be at the station in five minutes." He stood, avoiding the other man's gaze. "Pardon me, Father. I have to get back to work."

———

It seemed wrong to go about regular business with Elise missing, but Chloe didn't know what else to do. Sitting in Sharon's house, waiting for the phone to ring and picturing the worst, would be unendurable. She'd planned a busy day, including scheduled meetings with the collections curator at The Neville Public Museum in Green Bay to discuss Belgian artifacts, and with Roy Galuska at Heritage Hill to discuss information received from locals the night before. She also wanted to visit a shrine in the small community of Champion—once known as *Aux Premiers Belges*—fifteen miles northeast of Green Bay, where a young Belgian woman named Adele Brise had seen a vision of the Virgin Mary. It was an important place for

Catholics and was no doubt a good place to learn more about the early Belgian settlers' spiritual lives.

She drove into Green Bay with a list of directions taped to her dashboard, and managed to find the Neville Public Museum with minimal confusion. It was a new and attractive structure. Chloe checked in at the entrance desk.

Soon the curator, a plump man with a friendly smile, appeared to collect her. He wore a forest-green shirt, jeans, and wool socks with his sandals, attire that made Chloe feel at ease. He met her with hand outstretched. "Chloe? I'm Max. C'mon upstairs. Collections storage is on the fourth floor."

"I'll take that as a sign of respect," she said, following him into an elevator. "More often than not collections are buried in the windowless basement."

Max laughed. "We need all the space we can get. With over a million items in our permanent collections, we were bursting at the seams in our old location."

"You have a broad focus," Chloe observed. "History and science, right?"

"And art. We collect items of significance to northeast Wisconsin and the UP." Upper peninsula of Michigan, he meant. That makes sense, Chloe thought. Collections should be defined by cultural and regional boundaries, not political ones.

On the fourth floor, Max led Chloe through locked doors to a big room full of gray shelves lined with artifacts. Chloe was instantly distracted, but Max kept her on task. "I pulled all the items with known connections to the Belgian community. It's not a big group."

The pieces were laid out on a table covered with white paper: two steins, a gorgeous old shotgun, and two pairs of shoes. Chloe took photographs of the items, including the accompanying pink cards that recorded item descriptions, donor information, and estimated dates of manufacture. She couldn't help lingering over the shoes, hearing Sharon's voice. *Sometimes when I'm facing a challenge I slip off my shoes and stand in Seraphine's* sabots. Who wore you? Chloe asked the shoes silently. One pair was large, nothing fancy, all wood with tin bands attached to keep the wood from splitting. Some farmer, perhaps, had stumbled along rough fields in them, clutching plow handles, shouting to his ox. The second pair, with wooden soles and leather uppers, may have belonged to a woman. Had she danced in these at Kermiss festivals? Worn them to church? Had they survived the Great Fire? Chloe leaned closer, trying to sniff the leather without seeming obvious.

Max cleared his throat.

"Right." Chloe straightened. "Thanks so much for showing me these things. Just one more question. Do you by chance have any Belgian lace in your collection? Nineteenth century or earlier?"

Frown lines furrowed Max's forehead. "You're the second person to ask me that."

Chloe felt a quiver of energy, like a dog catching a scent. Had Elise learned something at the Neville that might help explain her disappearance? "Was the first Elise O'Rourke?"

Max looked even more taken aback. "Why, yes, it was."

"She's a friend of mine. A former colleague. Did you show her anything? Did she have any specific questions?"

He shook his head. "No to both. She made an appointment with me for yesterday morning, but she didn't show."

Chloe nibbled her lower lip. Elise had left Belgian Acres yesterday by eight a.m., but she hadn't kept a scheduled appointment here. One more scrap of information, Chloe thought, that does absolutely nothing to explain what's happened to her. "Did she happen to mention anything else when she called? She's gone missing."

"I'm sorry to hear that." Max thought for a moment. "Your friend did say one odd thing when we spoke."

Chloe felt a flash of hope. "What was that?"

"Well, I explained to her that despite the fact that this area is home to the nation's largest group of Belgian-Americans, we don't have many pre-1871 artifacts because of the Great Fire." He scratched his chin pensively. "And Ms. O'Rourke said, 'Forest fires aren't the only thing that can make important records hard to find.' Something like that."

Chloe's flash of hope faded. She didn't quite get the analogy, but it sounded as if Elise had been frustrated because whatever she was trying to research or document was proving elusive. Welcome to my world, Chloe thought.

"Sorry I can't be more helpful," Max said. "The only other Belgian piece we own, a spinning wheel, is on exhibit. Want to see it?"

The spinning wheel was quite lovely. Chloe photographed it as well. If the Heritage Hill staff wished, a skilled craftsman could reproduce the wheel for interpretive use.

"I'll take you back down," Max offered. Chloe almost declined; getting only this glimpse of the museum's enticing exhibits simply seemed wrong, and she wanted to wander. But you have an appointment with Roy at Heritage Hill, she reminded herself, with a quick glance at her watch. She was already cutting it close. In the lobby she thanked Max profusely, stuffed some cash in the donation box, and went on her way.

At Heritage Hill she jogged through the Education Center, on to the Belgian Farm, and into the barn. She opened the door to the first bay and stepped inside. A pigeon roosting in the rafters cooed in welcome. The barn was dim, musty, and still. "Roy?"

He was not there. Maybe he's running later than I was, Chloe thought. She left the door open, allowing a bit of gray light to penetrate the log structure, and grabbed the fat binder Roy had shown her earlier. Might as well get some reading done.

Roy had done an excellent job of documenting his conversations with the elderly Belgian-American farmers he'd interviewed in the course of his fieldwork. Chloe was reading about early farmers using horse urine to preserve wooden barn floors when her brain registered *Uncomfortably Cold!* She emerged from the interviews and discovered that almost thirty minutes had passed.

Okay, this was more than Roy running a bit late. Chloe returned his binder to the manger and walked back to the Education Center. "I was supposed to meet Roy at the Belgian Farm half an hour ago," she told the woman at the ticket counter. "Did he by chance leave any message for me?"

The woman shook her head. "No, and I haven't seen him. Did you try the Cotton House?"

"The Cotton House?"

"He lives there," the woman said patiently. "The lower floor is open to the public, but the second story provides on-site housing. It's good to have a staff member on site at night. It's a security thing. Go out that door"—she pointed—"and turn right. It's the big white structure. The Brown County Historical Society moved it here and opened it as a museum long before Heritage Hill was established."

"Awesome," Chloe said. "Thanks."

She had no trouble finding the Cotton House, a beautiful timber-framed Greek Revival structure, its white paint glowing in the wintry sun. Two graceful pillars adorned the front porch. The building reminded her of the Sanford House, now restored at her home site, Old World Wisconsin.

The front door was locked. Chloe knocked, waited, knocked again. Silence. Green shutters were closed for the off-season, so she couldn't peek inside. Maybe Roy had forgotten their appointment altogether and was working in the maintenance shop.

A discreet sign indicated that the public entrance was actually a door to the right of the narrow porch. For the sake of exploring all options, Chloe tried that door as well. To her surprise, the knob turned in her hand.

"Hello?" She stepped inside a room that evidently served to corral summer visitors waiting for the next tour to start. Interpretive panels mounted on the walls, and artifacts—silk bonnets, fine china—displayed behind glass on built-in shelving, would serve to occupy them in the interim.

But among these remnants of genteel 1840s life, Roy Galuska lay sprawled on the floor in a pool of blood.

TWENTY-TWO

THE POLICE OFFICERS WHO responded to the 911 call were finished with Chloe by noon. "Mr. Galuska may have surprised a burglar," a tall, silver-haired officer said.

"Were any of the display cases open?" Chloe couldn't remember.

"No. Evidently the guy didn't get that far." He slid his notebook away. "We may need to talk to you again."

She told him where she was staying, got in her car, and drove away. It was lunchtime, but the thought of food made her stomach threaten rebellion. She didn't know what to do except stick with her plan to visit the Shrine of Our Lady of Good Help in Champion. She'd driven out of the city before she realized she was crying. She couldn't reach a tissue, and she couldn't stop crying, and finally she just pulled over and let it all come out.

Chloe wasn't much of a crier—she tended to leapfrog grief and sink directly into depression or anger, depending on the situation. But everything that had happened this week was simply too much. She was upset about Hugh Lejeune. She was upset because she didn't know whether to be frantic about, or furious with, Elise. She was upset because Roy was dead. She was upset because Roelke seemed to think that their religious preferences might become problematic if they decided to marry. And she was upset because Birgitta's news had robbed her of her sense of self.

That's petty in the face of everything else, she told herself. Her pettiness was upsetting too.

Finally she cried herself out, mopped her eyes and nose, and drove on to Champion. She still felt sad and empty and dull. The shrine grounds were peaceful, though. That helped.

She first visited the small museum, where she learned more about Adele Brise, who had been visited by the Virgin Mary and spent the rest of her life providing religious instruction to children—with more hindrance than help from the local diocese, it seemed. The exhibits included photographs, Adele's prayer book, and other relics. Chloe took a few photographs, and made a note to speak with someone here about religious artifacts.

As she was leaving, an elderly man with a volunteer's badge gave her a friendly smile. "Is this your first visit?"

"It is."

"Then you'll want to visit the crypt," he assured her. "Go past the modern church and you'll see the entrance."

"I'm not Catholic," she said. This was a holy site for Catholics, and she didn't want to be insensitive.

But the man only smiled. "All are welcome. The crypt sits on the very spot where Adele had her visitations."

Past the main entrance, Chloe found stairs leading down to the crypt. The first thing she saw was an array of wooden crutches left behind by people who'd been healed after praying at the shrine.

Then she turned and caught her breath. Flickering candles and huge vases of roses flanked a statue of Mary. More candles burned on tiered shelves lining both side walls. The small, windowless chapel was beautiful.

Chloe slipped into one of the pews and contemplated the statue. Why did Catholics, who did not permit women priests, gave the mother of Jesus more attention than Protestants, who welcomed women pastors? Mary's posture and countenance welcomed all who understood that this was a place for reverence. Even for a raised-Lutheran, now Quaker-ish/Transcendentalist/Unitarian-Universalist-leaning non-churchgoer, there was a powerful sense of comfort in this place.

Maybe she was channeling Adele's intense emotions. Maybe the Virgin Mother was speaking to her. Or maybe she simply sensed the layers of faith and trust that had accumulated here as everyday people, Belgian pioneers and descendants and newcomers, gave thanks and prayed.

Chloe closed her eyes. It was too late to help Hugh Lejeune or Roy Galuska. Researching Lejeune genealogy could wait. There was nothing she could do right now to sort through things with Roelke, or to solve her unexpected identity crisis. The most important thing right now was finding Elise.

Please help me, she asked whoever might be listening. *I need to figure out what's happened to my friend.*

———

When Roelke got back to the EPD at lunchtime, Chief Naborski came out of his office. "Officer McKenna?" That usually was a bad sign but before Roelke could analyze his misdeeds, Chief grinned. "Every once in a great while, a cop's prayers are answered."

Roelke's boss was an affable man, but Roelke couldn't remember the chief grinning, or mentioning prayers, ever. "Sir?"

Chief Naborski leaned against the doorframe. "I got a letter this morning from the Green Bay Correctional Institution."

Green Bay. Where Chloe was working. Roelke felt a spasm of panic before realizing that his boss would not deliver bad news with a smile. "Um ... oh?"

"A convicted felon named Sylvester Mayhue was recently incarcerated in that facility."

GBCI was a maximum-security prison for adult male offenders. Roelke had never been inside, and he'd never heard of Sylvester Mayhue.

"Evidently life as a guest of the state is not agreeing with Mr. Mayhue," Chief continued. "Two months into a thirty-year sentence for molesting children, Mr. Mayhue has come forward with information about another crime."

"Oh?" Roelke said again. Everyone in prison hated child molesters, so he wasn't surprised that this Mayhue SOB was trying to cozy up to law enforcement in exchange for time away from the general prison population, or more TV hours or something. Roelke didn't like child molesters any better than anyone else, so he didn't give a rat's ass about Mayhue's general comfort. And Roelke still didn't understand what this had to do with him. He glanced at Marie, who was watching the exchange with a little smile.

Chief Naborski continued. "Mr. Mayhue is, it seems, an acquaintance of one Kent Bobolik."

Roelke's every cell quivered to full alert. Please, he thought. *Please* tell me—

"According to Mr. Mayhue, Kent Bobolik once bragged to him about—"

"About killing his first wife?" Roelke begged.

Chief Naborski's grin became predatory. "That's it exactly."

Roelke felt a fierce flush of vindication. A so-called jailhouse confession might, just might, provide what they needed to bring Bobolik to trial for Hattie's murder. "Who's going to talk to him?"

Chief spread his hands. "You've been looking at the case. You just arrested Bobolik. If you want to, you can—"

"I *do* want to." Roelke began to pace. If Mayhue's information seemed solid, it would go to the prosecutor. Roelke could dangle the possibility that *if* that information resulted in a conviction, it might affect Mayhue's sentence. Powerful motivator. "I'll drive up right now."

"You can wait till morning," Chief Naborski said. "They're expecting you at ten a.m. Review the files and prepare your questions. Mayhue will still be there tomorrow."

"Yes sir." He wanted to nail Bobolik so bad he could taste it.

But he wasn't waiting until morning to drive north. If he left now he'd get to see Chloe—and maybe help figure out what the hell was going on up there.

———

By the time Chloe got back to Belgian Acres that afternoon, a resolute anger was building inside. Good, she thought. Anger was better than feeling helpless.

She found a note taped to her bedroom door. *Chloe—No word about Elise. I'm going to be at a Parish Board meeting all afternoon, so please call me at the church if the police have any news.* Sharon had scribbled the phone number before signing her name.

Chloe dumped her totebag on the bed and crossed the hall to Elise's room. Deputy Knutson had checked the room without finding any clues. But maybe, Chloe thought, something that had no meaning for the deputy might have meaning for me.

Pawing through Elise's belongings made Chloe feel tawdry. You're trying to help, she reminded herself, and shoved her scruples aside. The suitcase and closet offered nothing illustrative. The top two dresser drawers were empty. The bottom one held a spare blanket. Chloe took it out to see if anything had been tucked underneath. Nope.

… Wait a minute. Chloe crossed her arms and frowned at the tidy room. Where was Elise's briefcase? No sign of it here, and according to the deputy's report, the rental car was empty. Had Elise carried the briefcase into the Heritage Center? Chloe tried to remember. She didn't think so.

She got down on hands and knees and looked under the bed. Not even a dust bunny. She crawled across the floor and looked under the dresser. Something was under there, shoved back against the wall. She couldn't reach it without flattening on her belly, which she could not imagine Elise doing. But her fingers met leather, and when she finally managed to fish the thing out, it was indeed the missing briefcase.

Chloe took it back to her own room. The case did not have a built-in locking mechanism. Perhaps Elise was new to keeping secrets.

The case held a stack of file folders, neatly labeled: *Lace Guild Program, Lace Guild Workshop, Green Bay Trip.* The first two held nothing but program notes. The third held receipts and confirmations,

250

including one from Hertz for Elise's rental car. I knew it was Hertz, Chloe thought, feeling mildly vindicated; Toni had thought it was Avis.

But the satisfaction faded quickly when she noticed something unexpected. Elise and Chloe had arrived at Belgian Acres on Sunday, and Elise told Deputy Knutson that she'd driven from the airport that day. But Elise had actually picked up her car two days earlier, on Friday. Another lie, another secret. What had Elise done on Saturday, and why didn't she want anyone to know?

Chloe turned back to the briefcase. A file labeled *World War I Lace, Belgium* included several articles about the program to assist lacemakers. The final file was labeled *Lace—Wisconsin*. The first item was a magazine article. The photocopy didn't show the publication's name, but someone had written *July 1919* in the upper right-hand corner of the first page. Chloe skimmed what seemed to be a travel writer's description of her trip to Door County. "The Lady Rambler" used most of the space to describe "the wild, ever-changing beauty of this little-known peninsula" and the "ardors of travel in this untamed land." Then the word *lace* popped from the page, and Chloe forced herself to slow down.

When the cheerful Belgian woman learned of my interest in her community she invited me to attend her granddaughter's wedding the following day. I was happy to accept, and was touched by the pious joy emanating from every guest. The bride was a sturdy girl of peasant stock, and I was surprised to see her wearing at her throat a bit of lace that far outpaced the rest of her best attire. I asked my new friend about it, and learned that an elderly lacemaker lives on a farm in Southern Door County. The next day I

251

endeavored to find the artistic soul who had created the lace, yet endured the worst privations and trials of pioneer life. After persisting through a rainstorm, find her I did, and it was well worth the effort. She told me stories of her girlhood at a convent in Bruges, learning to make lace. And as a final gift, she showed me the project she is working on now. It is a treasure indeed, gentle reader. But I won't say more, for you must come see it for yourself. I've been so charmed by Door County's residents, and so stirred by the beautiful landscape, that I do indeed plan to return.

So there *was* a lacemaker here in the 1800s! Chloe thought. Given the reference to "the project she is working on now," the woman was apparently still active. Elise must have been thrilled to find the article. Heck, I'm thrilled, Chloe thought, and before this week I didn't know a thing about bobbin lace.

The second item in the file was a full transcription of the letter from the priest—the one she'd seen an excerpt of on Tuesday night when one page got mixed in with her own papers. It was from Father Edouard Daems, written in September 1855. Chloe found the section that had caught her attention earlier:

I am recently returned from another tour, visiting newcomers some thirty miles and more beyond Aux Premiers Belges for the first time. At one, having promised earlier to celebrate holy communion, I went inside to lay out the sacrament on what I feared would be a filthy table. Instead I was astonished to find that not only had the gaunt, weary young wife scrubbed the table well, she had adorned it with a cloth trimmed

with a strip of delicate lace, the likes of which I have not
seen since coming to this place. She had, she told me,
learned to make lace at a convent in Bruges. She gifted me
the cloth, knowing it would serve well among

Chloe eagerly turned the page and continued reading.

all of the Walloon settlements as I travel to celebrate
mass. I thanked Madame Lejeune profusely and left filled
with gratitude for her generous nature.

"Lejeune!" Chloe whispered. "Seraphine was the lacemaker!"
Then common sense reined in her enthusiasm. "Maybe." Sera-
phine's sister-in-law was also named Madame Lejeune. And
Lejeune might be a common name in the Walloon settlements.

But … Sharon was the one who, as a young child, heard a rumor
of family lace. *When I was a kid, I once heard my grandmother
speak of a beautiful piece of lace that came down in the Lejeune family.* The family story wasn't proof of anything, but it was one more
piece of evidence.

Combined, the two accounts explained why Elise had come
here: she was on the hunt. She was likely the first lace scholar to
find and connect the priest's letter and the travel writer's article.
Perhaps she'd disappeared this week to dig into archival collections
in Green Bay or a county historical society. Perhaps she'd somehow
tracked down a private collector or another descendant.

The last thing in the file was a page torn from a notebook.
Someone, presumably Elise, had written *Seraphine Lejeune* at the
top of the page. It noted a few biographical details, including Seraphine's birth in Grez-Doiceau, Brabant Province, Belgium, 1836;
her marriage to Jean-Paul in 1853; her immigration in 1854. She'd

also scribbled several notes in the margin: *Bruges?* and *Etienne?* and, most bizarrely, *summer kitchen?*

"Elise," Chloe muttered, "what on earth did you find?" Seraphine was born in Brabant Province in Wallonia, so why was Bruges important? Wait—Elise had mentioned an important lace school in Bruges. Maybe she suspected that Seraphine had, somehow, learned the art there.

Etienne was Jean-Paul Lejeune's brother, although there might have been others in later generations. The phrase "summer kitchen" only conjured in vivid detail Chloe's discovery of Hugh Lejeune's body in the bake oven.

Elise arrived in Wisconsin earlier than she claimed, Chloe thought. Did some lace clue point Elise to the farm originally settled by Etienne Lejeune and his wife, last occupied by Hugh? Could Elise possibly have been involved with Hugh's death?

No. Absolutely not.

I'm sorry, Roelke's voice countered, *but you have to consider all possibilities.*

Chloe sighed. Like it or not, lace seemed to be at the heart of everything. A rare piece in the Heritage Hill collection had gone missing. Someone had, it seemed, broken into the exhibit room at Cotton House—in all of Heritage Hill, probably the most likely place where something genteel, such as a piece of antique lace, might be on display. Was Elise involved with those things too?

"Dammit," Chloe muttered. She needed more information. Maybe she should drive back to Green Bay and hit the university's Belgian-American archival collection ... but no, it was almost closing time.

Stymied, Chloe rubbed her forehead with her fingertips. She felt almost dizzy with frustration.

Not just frustration, idiot, she realized. She hadn't had anything to eat or drink since breakfast.

She headed to the kitchen, helped herself to a drink of water, and washed the glass. She was wiping it dry when she noticed the key ring hanging on a nail by the back door. One of the dangling keys, Chloe thought, might well open the chapel door. The chapel that just might have all kinds of family records on display.

But … Sharon had locked the chapel for a reason. Going inside would be a horrible breach of courtesy and trust. And the sense of grief emanating from the building, even through the walls, had been overwhelming.

But … Elise was still missing.

Chloe fetched her coat, plucked the ring from the nail, and let herself out the door. Hers was the only car in the lot, so if she was going to trespass, now was the time.

Shadows were stretching long and the temperature was dropping. Shoulders hunched against the wind, Chloe hurried around the main outbuildings and down the fence line to the chapel. As she approached the chapel an uncomfortable pressure grew in her chest. She clenched her teeth and forced herself to mount the step. She tried the first key—no luck. Trembling, she jabbed the second key against the slot. It wouldn't slide home. Her breath came in ragged bursts as she fumbled with the final key. "Thank God," she whispered as it turned in the lock.

Quickly she slid inside, pulling the door closed behind her. She clenched her fists against the sorrow quivering in the small room. Just do what you came to do, she ordered herself, so you can get out of here.

An altar against the far wall displayed statues and candles. Among the religious artwork on the two side walls were a dozen or

255

more certificates and other bits of family ephemera, beautifully framed. Chloe skimmed through them as the invisible iron band tightened over her ribs. She found on unexpected certificate written with calligraphy script: *Baby Bertrand, loved and lost August 16, 1955.* Had Sharon had a stillbirth? Chloe knew how much pain the loss of even an unknown child could cause.

A wedding photograph from the 1930s hung nearby. Death dates for the couple showed that the husband had died six years later while the wife lived into her nineties. Another photograph showed a man in a World War I–era military uniform. Someone had written *Our beloved Herman, The Battle of Château-Thierry, 1918* in one corner. This was Sharon's Uncle Herman, whose mother never recovered from his death.

Sharon's family had clearly experienced its share of blessings and tragedies. There was no way to know which loss had left such profound grief behind. And that's not why you're here anyway, Chloe reminded herself. She was interested in the pioneers.

She finally came to a rudimentary family tree, the type modern amateur genealogists used, with little white spaces provided on limbs and leaves where names could be entered. The Lejeune family, like most, did not neatly fit within the structure. Some leaves were empty; in other places names had been added in the margins near overflowing branches.

Chloe found *Sharon Lejeune Bertrand* and traced backward until she found Seraphine and Jean-Paul, the first of her branch to arrive in Wisconsin. Chloe followed their children's lines until— "Yes!" she murmured triumphantly when she found the name Renilde. At the Heritage Day gathering, elderly Renilde Claes had said her scrap of lace had belonged to her grandmother. According to the family tree, Renilde's grandmother was Cecilie, Seraphine's daughter. Awesome.

Chloe was quivering with the need to flee, but a branch nearby adding Etienne and Emelie caught her eye. Whoever had created the tree had drawn a line between Seraphine and Etienne. Chloe squinted at the notation in the dim light. Her mouth opened with surprise. Now she understood why the biographical notes about Seraphine included an underlined reference to Jean-Paul's brother.

TWENTY-THREE

ETIENNE APPEARED SOON AFTER dawn, staggering wraithlike from the clouds of ash and dust still swirling about what had once been Lejeune Farm West.

Seraphine, Jules, Pierre, and Cecilie were huddled under what was left of the blankets, shivering and coughing. I have three children left, Seraphine thought. Only three.

She had no idea how long the fire had raged. The heat had been so intense that she'd wondered if she was already dead. If they were all already dead. She'd called to the children but heard only the fire's crackling roar. All she could do was press her cheek against the dirt and wait.

Finally, *finally*, the inferno subsided. Seraphine struggled to identify a new sound. *Rain*. She shoved away the blanket, croaking her children's names. The three oldest were alive. Her little ones, sweet Joseph and precious Ermina, were not.

Seraphine felt numb and had no idea what to do. Jean-Paul will, she thought, and screamed his name—or tried to. The best she could produce was a hoarse whisper. He did not appear.

Finally Seraphine had shrouded her babies beneath a tattered blanket. Then she'd gathered Jules, Pierre, and Cecilie to her and rocked them like they were babies. The boys were wide-eyed with shock. Cecilie was wracked with violent shudders. "I'm here, Cecilie," Seraphine whispered. "I'm here."

Nothing seemed real. The sun had set on a familiar world. It had risen on something very different. *Everything* was gone: the house, the chapel dedicated to baby Octavie, the barn, fences, livestock, trees. Smoke twisted in the wind. Embers glowed among the ashes. The earth itself seemed charred. The air stank of smoke and worse.

Now Etienne surveyed them with bloodshot eyes, looking from the living to the dead and back again. His skin was streaked black with soot. His shirt was burned away, his arms were blistered. He started to speak, bent almost double with a racking cough, tried again. "Where is Jean-Paul?"

It seemed to take a long time for the words to reach Seraphine; even longer to produce a response. "He isn't here." She wet cracked lips with her tongue. It hurt to breathe.

Pierre began to cry. "Papa went to let the animals out of the barn. And then ... "

Etienne looked around, as if expecting the barn or Jean-Paul to materialize. His chin dropped to his chest for a long moment. Then he nodded.

Seraphine realized belatedly that he was alone. "Etienne, where is your family?"

He wiped one hand over his face. "We were going to the well. François and I had the girls. Emelie grabbed the baby. She was behind me." His eyes beseeched her to understand. "Right behind me! I got François and the girls into the well. Then I turned around. Emelie had the baby on her hip. She was running toward me." Tears tracked through the soot on his cheeks. "And then they were gone."

———

They didn't find Jean-Paul. Just a few bits of bone, and ash. Everywhere, ash.

Etienne led Seraphine and the others back to his property, where his three oldest children waited. Etienne's house was gone too. His barn. His crops. Everything.

"I'd go for help," Etienne rasped, "but I'm afraid I'd get lost. And God only knows how far I'd have to go."

Seraphine told him about the rice and beans buried in the trunk but they had no shovel, no kettle. They survived the next few days by digging root crops from the garden with throbbing fingers, choking down carrots and parsnips that were charred on the outside and raw on the inside. The food formed a sour lump in Seraphine's stomach.

Finally a neighbor from several miles away driving a horse-drawn wagon jolted into view. "My barn's still standing," he said. "A doctor's there. And a priest. I'll take you."

Etienne helped the children into the wagon, then turned to Seraphine.

"I can't." Panic pierced the numbness. "I have to wait for Jean-Paul."

His shoulders sagged wearily. "Jean-Paul is not coming, Seraphine."

"We don't know that! The bones might not be his! You don't know what it feels like to have someone just—just disappear, and to not understand what—how—"

"You are fortunate! It's better not to understand. Not to have seen." His dark eyes were haunted. "Now, get in the wagon."

———

Dear Seraphine,

We have heard of the devastating fire in Wisconsin's Belgian community. I am heartsick, and fearful for your safety. We are all praying for you. Please write as soon as possible.

Your loving sister,
Octavie

———

NOVEMBER 1871

They spent weeks in the barn, camping with over forty other refugees. Some were badly burned and panted with pain. Some sat stunned and staring. The priest and volunteers collected and buried the dead, including Joseph and Ermina, and Emelie and her infant. Seraphine wondered where the wind had taken the ashes of Jean-Paul. The ache in her chest was unbearable. She didn't know if scorched air had damaged her lungs or if the pain came from her broken heart.

It took many days for the first relief supplies to reach them. Wooden bridges had burned, and the corduroy roads made of logs had burned; even the paths marked with sawdust had burned. "Help *will* come," Seraphine promised Cecilie. The girl hadn't spoken since the Great Fire. She clung to her mother's skirt like a toddler. Her dark eyes had become huge, like bottomless pits.

Finally strangers, a man and a woman, found their way to the barn with a wagonload of blankets and quilts, coats and dresses, knives and kettles, barrels of potatoes and carrots and rutabagas. "People are donating everything they can," the man reported in English, speaking slowly to help them understand. "But Chicago burned the same night, and that news got out first. Then came word that hundreds or maybe thousands are dead north of Green Bay, where fire tore through the Peshtigo area. News of what happened here took longer to travel."

Women began to make soup. Seraphine roused herself and carried vegetables and knives back to her daughter. "Can you help?" she asked, brushing a strand of singed hair away from Cecilie's face. Cecilie took a knife. They chopped potatoes on a beam and swept them into Seraphine's skirt.

"I'll be right back," Seraphine promised. "No, you stay inside." She needed to face the flames alone before she could help Cecilie.

Men had kindled several cook fires outside the barn. For a moment Seraphine forgot how to breathe. When someone touched her arm she jumped.

"Pardon me," the American woman said softly. "I thought you might need one of these." She held out her arms, which were draped in shawls.

"Thank you," Seraphine whispered. She let the woman wrap a gray shawl over her shoulders. Fortified by the kindness, she approached the nearest crackling fire and dumped the chopped potatoes into the iron kettle.

Then she noticed Etienne standing a short distance away with his own children and her sons. What were they looking at? She found it disorienting to see open land and so much sky. Most of the thousands of oppressive trees were gone. Even their roots had burned, leaving odd holes in the earth.

She wandered closer. "...to rebuild," Etienne was saying.

The word struck like a club. How could she "rebuild" without Jean-Paul? She couldn't rebuild. She didn't even want to.

———

DECEMBER 1871

As it turned out, Etienne was right. There were pockets of trees still standing. Their foliage had burned away, and the trunks were charred. If these were chopped down quickly, before disease or rot set in, the trunks could be used for building. Men sent urgent requests for axes out with the aid workers, and they began work as soon as they could.

By December some of the refugees had left the barn. Every time Seraphine tried to consider how she'd care for her surviving children, her mind shied like a skittish mare. When they heard that citizens in Belgium had raised five thousand dollars to help those devastated by the fire, Seraphine felt a fierce, desperate longing. *I want to go back to*

Belgium, she thought. Back to Octavie. Back to the convent, and the sisters who had so kindly given her shelter once before.

That was, of course, impossible. The money still buried in the trunk wasn't enough for one passage back to Europe, much less four. And when she managed to recover the buried box, the precious coins it contained would go to food and tools and new shoes for her children. She had dreamed of selling her bridal lace when the time was right, and it was buried too, but no one in the community would be able to purchase such a luxury now. She had also dreamed of making simpler pieces that might sell—a collar, a pair of cuffs. But the wooden bobbins Jean-Paul had spent years carving for her had burned in the fire.

Stop remembering, she ordered herself, as she and Cecilie huddled together in one corner of the barn. But being burned out, surviving on charity, meant there was almost nothing to do. The simple communal meals were too quickly prepared, the dishes too soon tidied. None of the kind donors had thought to send needle and thread and torn trousers, or knitting needles and wool. Another load of relief supplies had arrived the day before, this time brought by a priest from Green Bay who'd tucked a supply of small Bibles in with the food. Cecilie had silently accepted a Bible, and if it provided the girl a whisper of comfort, Seraphine was glad. But she had avoided the priest.

Now she tightened her arm over Cecilie's shoulders. The girl held the Bible in one hand but hadn't opened it. Seraphine let her head rest against the wall. It was cold, and sleep was the best any of them could hope for. She let the desultory conversation flow by...

But she opened her eyes with a start when she heard a familiar name. " ... Adele Brise. I guess that will settle the question once and for all."

"What was that about Adele Brise?" Seraphine asked. Her breath puffed white in the air.

The woman who'd been speaking had a blanket pulled over her head, and spoke as if from a tunnel. "On the day of the fire, Adele and the sisters were at the church built where she was visited by the Virgin Mother. Some of the local families came too. They took up the statue of Mary and carried it in procession around the chapel."

"What happened?" Seraphine was almost afraid to ask.

"They say the fiery wind was so bad they almost suffocated. But Adele instructed everyone to turn in another direction and pray." The shrouded woman shook her head in wonder. "When the fire finally passed, everything in sight was burned ... *except* the church and school grounds. They say the outside of the fence was charred, but not the inside."

"If that doesn't convince the priests that Adele's visions were real, nothing ever will," another woman said tartly.

Seraphine was glad to hear that her friend Adele had survived the fire, and saved others as well. But she felt a flash of bitter envy. What would it take to have such faith? She'd seen it before—when her father died, and she and Octavie were homeless. *God will provide for us,* Octavie would say. *We must have faith.* Now Adele's faith had been proven in the face of the most ghastly disaster.

Pushing aside the shawls knotted over her bodice, Seraphine hooked a finger in her pocket and fished out the piece of lace she'd cut and hemmed right before the fire. She'd intended to give it to

Adele as a reminder that if the priests did not believe her miracles, friends did.

I don't think Adele needs this, Seraphine thought now. When the women began to speak of heating the evening's soup, Seraphine put a hand on Cecilie's arm. "We'll go help in a moment," she whispered. "I want to give you something first."

Cecilie looked up, a question in her eyes.

"You know I learned to make lace in Bruges. When your papa asked me to come to America with him, continuing my lacework was my dearest wish. Papa understood. That's why he whittled so many bobbins for me."

Cecilie nodded.

"After I had a family, I dreamed of teaching my beautiful daughters how to make lace." A lump formed in Seraphine's throat, and she swallowed hard. "I don't think I will ever be able to do that now. But I want you to have this." She pressed the strip of lace into her daughter's hand. "You can use it to mark a favorite verse in your Bible."

Cecilie studied the bit of lace in the fading light.

"It's my promise to you that life will get better," Seraphine added. "Everything is horrid and sad now. But I believe beautiful things are ahead for you. This lace survived the fire. Somehow, we will too."

Tears welled in Cecilie's eyes. After a long moment she whispered, "Thank you, Mama."

The next day, Seraphine was scrubbing an iron kettle with a handful of straw when she heard footsteps behind her. "Seraphine?" It was Etienne.

She rose from her crouch. "Yes?"

He stamped his feet against the cold. A blanket of snow had covered the landscape's worst scars, but here by the barn the ground was scuffed clear. "I've been thinking."

"I usually try *not* to think."

"We can't stay here forever."

"No. Of course not." Seraphine wondered how fast her wash water was cooling.

Etienne stared at the ground. "We should marry."

"We should ... *what?*" Seraphine's heart thumped a warning.

"We should marry. Jean-Paul is dead."

Thump. Thump. Thump. Seraphine tried to let Etienne's words in. "And Emelie is dead."

Thinking about Emelie rasped a new raw place inside Seraphine. Emelie had delivered her babies, and been her only companion. When the men were away she'd teased the children through their chores, making up nonsense rhymes and silly games. She could do a man's work in the field, and she could dance anyone down with a saucy smile on her face. Seraphine didn't want to picture the future without Emelie in it.

"I'm going to rebuild, Seraphine. What else can I do?" Etienne thrust his chapped hands into his armpits. "It's my responsibility to take care of you and your children. I can't do that in two places."

Thump! Thump! Thump!

"The priest who came to say mass is leaving tomorrow. We should talk with him tonight."

Seraphine pinched her mouth into a tight line and looked away. She didn't want to marry Etienne.

But … she had three children. Jules and Pierre were fine, capable young men, but too young to be on their own. Cecilie needed a home. Etienne had children that needed care as well. Jean-Paul was dead and most of her heart had died with him.

She hunched her shoulders as a wind burst around the barn. The world was a harsh, godless place. She couldn't manage on her own.

"Very well, Etienne," she said finally. "We will marry."

TWENTY-FOUR

CHLOE BOLTED FROM SHARON's chapel. After locking the door she ran a good fifty feet before stopping. Panting, hands on knees, she willed the sadness to seep away.

As she walked back to the house, she tried to make sense of what she'd seen on the rudimentary family tree. Jean-Paul and Emelie died in October 1871—the month the Great Fire had devastated the Belgian settlement. Seraphine and Etienne married in December 1871. That *might* explain why overwhelming grief emanated from the chapel. But after their marriage Etienne and Seraphine probably didn't live at Lejeune Farm West, the land claimed by Jean-Paul, now farmed by Sharon. Most likely Etienne started over on his own property, owned by Hugh Lejeune until his death. And Hugh had once told Sharon that he'd overheard his parents speak of a treasure hidden on their farm.

What if Hugh's treasure and the lost lace Sharon had heard her grandmother speak of were one and the same? Seraphine was the connecting link. What if Seraphine had taken some precious lace to

Etienne's farm? And ... what if Elise had somehow figured that out? Had she gone to look?

Chloe was so absorbed in her own thoughts that she had almost reached the back door before noticing Toni's car now parked beside her own. Damn. The key ring suddenly burned a metaphorical hole in Chloe's pocket.

Well, nothing to do now but try to brazen it out. She walked around the house and let herself in the front door. The living room and dining room were empty. She found Toni in the kitchen, finishing a sandwich. "Hey, Toni."

"Oh!" Toni jumped. "I assumed you were upstairs."

"Just out taking a walk." Not a total lie.

"Any word about Elise?"

"No." Chloe was not ready to broach the theories swirling in her brain.

"Before I forget, there was something in the paper I wanted to show you. Hold on ... " Toni got up and left the room.

Chloe quickly returned the key ring to its nail.

"Here." Toni returned, rustling through the pages. "There's a nice preview of the St. Nicholas party at Heritage Hill tomorrow. Sounds like a fun time. Are you going?" She glanced up, and her smile faded. "Hey, are you all right? You don't look so good."

"I'm okay, just ... It's been a bad day. One of my colleagues at Heritage Hill was killed last night or early this morning. I found him. The police think he surprised a burglar."

"Oh my God!" Toni's eyes went wide. "That's horrible! No wonder you look a bit ragged. Would you like a sandwich? We've got cheese or peanut butter."

The simple kindness made Chloe's eyes water. "Thanks, but no. Maybe a few crackers, if you've got them."

"Sure. And how about a hot drink?" Toni gestured at a percolator on the counter. "Mom left some coffee."

"That would be fantastic." Chloe sat. Toni delivered a short stack of saltines, a steaming mug, and a little cow-shaped pitcher. "Is there anything else I can get you?"

"No. You've been great." Chloe stirred cream into her coffee, sipped, and managed a smile. "This helps."

"If you're sure..." Toni took her plate to the sink. "I'm meeting some friends in Sturgeon Bay."

Alone again, Chloe finished her coffee slowly. The comfort she'd taken from her visit to the shrine had faded. Her excitement about discovering Seraphine's second marriage had faded too. Her brain seemed fuzzy. A heavy weariness pulled at her muscles. Perhaps that was the aftermath of finding Hugh, finding Roy, finding some insight about Elise's real objective in coming to Wisconsin. Perhaps it was because the kitchen was so cozy and warm.

So, she counseled herself, wash up and go take a nap. Putting palms on the table she started to push to her feet.

But the effort was so overwhelming that she dropped back into her chair. Too much, she thought. It's all been just too much.

———

Roelke hadn't planned to stop at St. Theresa church on the way home, but he did. The church doors were unlocked, the sanctuary empty. Roelke slipped into the back pew.

He didn't know how to meditate, as Father Dan had suggested, but it was good to sit and simply be. He thought about Libby and Justin and Deirdre—the people he'd been trying to protect when he set Dan Raymo up for a drug bust. He thought about what he'd learned about himself, and about the kind of man he wanted to be. And he thought about Chloe.

He didn't linger long. But even the brief respite was helpful.

At home he fed Olympia, called Chloe's friend and cat-sitter Dellyn, and packed for his trip. He tried calling Belgian Acres to let Chloe know he was coming but got no answer. Before hitting the highway he rummaged through his box of cassette tapes, looking for something upbeat that would power the drive to Door County. He grabbed Little Feat's *Let it Roll*, then put it back. If he got pulled over for speeding he couldn't count on the cop being as understanding as he and Skeet were. He popped a Charlie Parker Quintet tape into the player instead.

He managed the drive north without annoying the state highway patrol, perhaps because a misty rain developed in the Fox Valley corridor and slowed him down. The mist deepened into drizzly fog by the time he crossed into Door County. He got turned around twice while trying to find the B&B in the hazy darkness. "Finally," he muttered when he spotted the sign for Belgian Acres. He could hardly wait to see Chloe.

It was, therefore, quite anticlimactic to pull into the small lot beside the house and find no sign of her old Ford Pinto.

He emerged from his truck as a woman walked from the barn toward the house. They met in the glow cast by a light above the back door. She looked to be somewhere in her fifties and wore boots and jeans and an old wool coat that smelled faintly of manure. Her smile was polite but her face had a pinched, haggard look. "May I help you?" she asked. "I'm Sharon Bertrand, the innkeeper."

"I'm Roelke McKenna, a friend of Chloe's. I came up on business but hoped I'd get to visit her this evening." He pulled out his police ID.

272

The badge seemed to ease Sharon's mind. "I'm sorry," she said apologetically. "I'm not sure where she is. But please, come inside."

She led him into a kitchen that probably had changed little since the 1950s—linoleum floor, Formica-topped table, white curtains printed with little bunches of cherries over the windows. Sharon dropped her gloves into a basket by the door.

Then she picked up a notepad sitting by the phone on the counter. "Aha. Toni left a note. *Hey Mom, A county deputy called for you but said there was no news of Elise, she was just checking in. Chloe said she was going to see somebody in Namur. I'm meeting friends tonight, so don't wait up.*"

Namur, Roelke thought. Where Elise had disappeared. "Can you give me directions to the Heritage Center?" He wanted to see Chloe, right now.

"Why don't I show you. It's not far, but it might be tricky to find in the dark." Sharon sounded uneasy too.

They decided to drive separately. As Roelke followed Sharon's truck up the driveway, sleet rattled against his windshield. Great. The temperature had dropped below freezing. When he turned onto Hickory he felt his wheels spin before finding purchase on the asphalt. He made a conscious effort to relax the muscles in his shoulders, his jaw.

Namur was tiny. Roelke hadn't even realized they'd arrived before Sharon braked and pulled into a small parking lot. Her headlights lit a sign: BELGIAN HERITAGE CENTER, and in smaller font, *Namur Belgian Heritage Foundation.* Beyond the lot, a church was silhouetted black against the dark gray sky.

Roelke pulled up beside Sharon and rolled down his window. "I don't see Chloe's car."

"There's more parking behind the building." Sharon puttered around the church to a second small lot. The headlights hit the familiar green Pinto. Roelke's flush of relief lasted only a nanosecond. There was no other car in the lot.

Sharon got out of her truck. "I don't like this. There aren't any lights on."

Roelke didn't like this, either. He grabbed his big flashlight and strode to Chloe's car. It was empty.

"Let's check inside." Sharon's voice shook, and she cleared her throat. "I have a key."

They went through a side door, and she flipped on a bank of lights. "Chloe? Are you here?"

As they conducted a quick search—main room, kitchen, bathrooms—a beating sound built in Roelke's head, as if he could hear his heart. The building felt deserted. He knew Chloe wasn't here.

"Oh my God." Sharon stared up at him with panicked eyes. "Oh my God! Where is Chloe?"

Roelke barely heard her over his pounding pulse. He didn't know.

———

Chloe became aware of darkness and a painful chill in her bones. A damp, musty-earth smell filled her nostrils. The only sound was a distant metallic banging. What had *happened?* She struggled to remember. But she was too cold. Too tired. Nothing made sense. She let oblivion take her again.

The next time she surfaced, her head felt a little clearer. She curled into a ball, shuddering with cold, fingers digging convulsively into the wool of her sweater. The last thing she remembered was eating crackers and drinking coffee in Sharon's cozy kitchen. Why had she left the B&B without a coat or mittens?

I wouldn't have done that, Chloe thought. Someone had taken her from the B&B and dumped her here.

But—who? And *why?* She'd been alone in the house. Had Toni come back? Or had someone seen Toni drive away and let themselves in the back door? Chloe's breath quickened to ragged pants. Had that person left her to die?

All right, *stop*, she ordered herself. Freaking out wouldn't help anything. She forced herself to inhale and exhale slowly. She had to figure out where she was.

Tentatively she began exploring with her fingers. She lay on hardpacked earth that was littered with rough bits of rubble. When her hand inched to the right it met cold stone—a wall. Her left hand hit a different cold surface. Plaster maybe? In the darkness whatever she was touching was a shade lighter than anything else. Sliding her fingers higher, she felt the plaster curve away.

The banging sound returned, and understanding came in a flash. She was feeling the exterior of a bake oven. She pictured the small stone shed extending from the back of the summer kitchens on Hugh Lejeune's farm and at Heritage Hill. They'd been built to protect the bake oven itself from the elements, with a narrow horseshoe of open space providing cramped access for maintenance. She might be inside any bake oven shed, but the clanging sounded like Hugh's old windmill.

Hugh's farm. Bake oven. Chloe's panic revved up again.

At least you weren't shoved inside the oven itself, she reminded herself. And she could picture the small access hatch in the back wall. The door had been secured with a heavy iron latch, but maybe, just maybe, whoever had dumped her in here hadn't taken the time to secure it.

Shivering, Chloe crawled along the bake oven until she found the oven's back-end curve. Then she reached for the stone wall again. Where was the damn hatch? Her fumbling fingers finally met wood ... *there.*

Chloe put both hands against the door and shoved. Nothing happened. She shoved harder. The hatch creaked in protest but didn't move. She leaned back and gave the door a double flat-footed kick with everything she had.

The hatch didn't move, but the impact shoved her off balance. She fell sideways, yelping in pain as one hip landed on something sharp. A chunk of fallen mortar? She swiped away tears of angry frustration. This was not the time to give up or give in. There had to be some way out of here ...

Wait a minute. Sniffling, she thought back to the evening she'd arrived, when she'd stopped to see the abandoned farm. She'd been tempted to look inside the shed, wanting to get a look at the oven itself, but had been dissuaded because one wall was damaged.

Chloe oriented herself and, on her knees, began exploring the wall with her hands. She quickly found a gap where plaster had fallen from between two stones. Please, please, *please*, she thought, wedging her fingers into the crack. She pulled as hard as she could, leaning away from the wall. Her fingers throbbed in pain before a few crumbs of mortar came loose. That's okay, she told herself. Little by little, you can do this.

But when she poked one finger into the hole she'd made it encountered not open air, but more stone. "Dammit!" she muttered, remembering belatedly what Roy had said about the bake oven shed at Heritage Hill. *The structure's got double limestone walls. The original builder put about sixteen inches of rubble between them.* Apparently the Lejeune bake oven was constructed the same way.

Lovely. No way was she going to get through something like that. In desperation she yelled, "Hey! *Hey!* Somebody help me!"

An indistinct moan came from the other side of the oven.

Chloe scrambled back crablike. Prickles rose on her neck. It had never occurred to her that she might not be alone in here. "Um … hello?"

Silence.

She inched her way around the oven toward the far side of the open horseshoe. Almost immediately she felt something textured but smooth, and slightly yielding. She snatched her hand away, but quickly realized what she'd felt: a leg, encased in nylon pantyhose.

"Elise?" she dared. "Elise, is that you?" Chloe pawed the air until she made contact again. Leather pumps, shins in nylons, wool skirt, wool dress coat. *"Elise!"*

"Wh-what?" The word was barely formed but it was enough. "Geoffrey?"

Was Geoffrey her dead husband? Chloe shook the other woman's arm. "No, it's me, Chloe. Are you okay?"

"Mother," Elise mumbled.

Chloe felt for a pulse. For a long moment her bruised, cold fingers found nothing. Finally one finger felt a weak beat. Elise's skin felt icy. Her breathing was shallow.

And she's still, Chloe thought with new alarm. Elise had stopped shivering. That was bad. She'd been missing for … well, at least twenty-four hours. Twenty-four hours in the cold with inadequate clothing. No food. No water. She was experiencing hypothermia.

As I will soon enough, Chloe thought. Neither of them was adequately dressed for incarceration in a stone shed in Wisconsin, in

November. No, wait; it was the first day of December. That sounded even worse.

Chloe had to keep Elise as warm as possible. The litany of care she'd memorized for winter camping trips ran through her brain: wool clothing, down sleeping bags, high-energy food, warm fluids.

None of those things were available. But at least now there were two of them. Elise had curled into a fetal position before passing out. Chloe swept away bits of plaster debris and squeezed down against her friend. Her bones ached. Her fingers and toes were numb. But at least she was still shivering. Chloe willed herself to keep them both alive.

TWENTY-FIVE

"WHAT IS GOING ON?" Sharon's eyes glazed with tears. "First Elise, now Chloe!"

Chloe. Roelke's head cleared. Something inside went very still, and hot, and hard. "Is there a phone in here?"

"Yes, it's—"

"Call the county sheriff and tell them to get someone out here. I'm going to check with the neighbors, see if anyone saw anything." Roelke turned up his coat collar and went back outside.

The canvass didn't take long. Roelke went from house to house, banging on doors. No one had seen a blond woman. No one had seen a strange vehicle loitering near the Heritage Center. No one had seen a damn thing.

When he circled back to the church, a sheriff's vehicle was in the lot. Sharon and the deputy stood by the building, sheltering from the sleet. Roelke heard Sharon's voice rising. " ...and we can't find her!"

The deputy, a young woman with a round face and steady gaze, turned as he approached. "I'm Deputy Knutson. And you are ... ?"

"Roelke McKenna, Chloe's fiancé." That was a lie, but the word added weight to his involvement. "And a police officer, Village of Eagle in Waukesha County. Listen, nobody's seen a thing. We need to get a BOLO out, and we need a search team, and—"

"The Be On Lookout, I can do." Deputy Knutson interrupted him quietly, but in a firm *I'm in charge* tone. "For the moment, though, we're on our own. Twenty minutes ago a semi jackknifed just before the Michigan Street Bridge in Sturgeon Bay. We've got a multiple vehicle pileup, multiple injuries, and traffic backed up for miles. Most of the deputies are working the accident. It's a skating rink up there."

Roelke bit back a curse. "Chloe wouldn't have walked away from her car without good reason. Somebody must have forced her." His brain produced a movie of some sociopath dumping Chloe in the trunk of his car, and his hands clenched.

"I agree," the deputy said. "Sharon, can you think of any reason why the Heritage Center would attract trouble?"

"No! We've got a few artifacts on exhibit. They're precious to us, but nothing worth a lot of money. Even if someone did want to steal something, why would it involve Elise and Chloe? They're guests."

Roelke didn't get that, either. Someone with a grudge against the Heritage Center, or against a board member, had no reason to go after Elise *or* Chloe.

He stared out at the night. Okay, think. Elise was from out of state. Chloe from out of town. The only things they had in common was museum work and an interest in old Belgian lace. "Sharon, has anyone donated a piece of lace to the Center? Is there any lace on display?"

"No to both questions."

I've got bupkus, Roelke thought. "We've got to keep looking. It's possible Chloe went for a walk and twisted an ankle or something." It seemed unlikely, but if Chloe had gotten excited about some history thing, twilight and bad weather wouldn't have kept her from exploring.

"Sharon, why don't you go home," Deputy Knutson said, "in case Chloe calls." She turned to Roelke. "Officer McKenna, you and I can begin a search."

———

I don't want to die in a bake oven shed, Chloe thought. She wasn't ready to die anywhere, thanks very much. But the choice of the historic structure seemed particularly unfair. Her teeth were chattering. At least she was keeping hypothermia at bay.

Elise sometimes slept and sometimes muttered feverishly, calling for her mother or the man Chloe assumed was her dead husband. But she's hanging on, and I will too, Chloe thought. She was too pissed off at *whoever* to give up.

She tried to think who that *whoever* might be. I must have been drugged, she thought, outraged. Was it the coffee? Toni had served it. Sharon, according to Toni, had made it. Had one of them deliberately drugged her? Or had she bumbled her way into the middle of one more strike against the Lejeune-Bertrand family? The percolator of coffee had evidently been on the kitchen counter all day. Had the person who killed Hugh, and run Toni off the road, crept into the kitchen and tampered with it? If so, *why?*

Thinking was becoming a struggle. The cold dulled her wits. Her body ached with it. When she started getting sleepy she pressed one palm on a jagged chunk of plaster, willing herself to stay alert. The windmill's clank drifted into the shed. Hang on to that sound, she told herself. But the clanging seemed fainter now too.

Roelke, she thought, I'm sorry.

———

"Chloe!" Roelke bellowed. *"Chloe!"* He stopped on the berm, playing his flashlight beam left and right over the stubbled field, but he could only see a few feet. *Dammit.* The sleet hit the street with a tiny crystalline patter. Cold crept through his parka. Dear God, was Chloe out in this? Was she hurt, soaked, slowly freezing to death in a ditch?

A car appeared in the distance to the east, approaching slowly, stopping every few feet. Knutson, Roelke thought. He could see the faint arc of her searchlight scanning the sides of the road. When she drew close she cranked down the window. "Get in and warm up."

Roelke did as instructed. He pulled off his gloves and fanned his hands toward the heater vents.

"Anything?" Knutson asked.

"No."

"I drove out maybe three miles without seeing any sign of her."

"This is not working."

Knutson faced him, her face shadowed. "All we know is that Chloe's car was left at the Belgian Heritage Center. She might have fled someone on foot. If so, we might yet find her out here."

"This feels wrong."

"What do you want to do?"

Roelke was grateful that Knutson seemed to be taking him seriously, not trying to mollycoddle—or worse, patronize—the missing woman's frantic boyfriend. "I don't know," he admitted, angry at himself. "Maybe I should go back toward Belgian Acres. If Chloe was able to get away from—from whoever, that's the only place she'd know to go."

"Okay." Knutson nodded. "I'm going to try heading west. You go back toward the B&B and scan the road that way. If I don't find anything in the next hour, I'll meet you there."

Once back in his truck, Roelke started slowly toward the inn. He stopped often, getting out to scan the roadsides, shouting, listening. By the time he reached Belgian Acres his throat ached. Oh, Chloe, he thought. Where are you?

He didn't want to stop looking. Couldn't bear the idea of twiddling his thumbs inside until Deputy Knutson arrived. It made no sense to think that Chloe might have gotten this far and kept going, but he had no other ideas, so that's what he did.

Roelke's wipers slapped away sleet as he approached the hill, and he only made it partway up. He backed down and poured the clean cat litter he always carried in winter on the road before trying again. This time he made it.

The road flattened out again. Glancing right, a big white star— hovering close by, not in the heavens—caught his eye. In a world gone fuzzy and dark, it seemed to shimmer.

Roelke eased to the side of the road, hit his flashers, and grabbed his light for a closer look. The star was affixed high on the gable wall of an old barn, and appeared to be made of wood. Well, hunh. He had no idea what that was all about. The star seemed especially incongruous because the barn itself was in sad disrepair…

He sucked in a harsh breath. This is the place, he thought. The place where Chloe found the body in the bake oven. He'd driven past earlier, but he'd been so focused on finding Belgian Acres and seeing the woman he loved that it hadn't registered.

It registered now. All the trouble had started right *here*.

The barn door was open, and he trudged back and—hoping ice on the roof didn't send the structure crashing down around him—splashed his light around the interior, checking empty stalls. There was no ladder to the haymow. "Chloe!" he yelled. Nothing.

There were a couple of smaller outbuildings to explore, empty or falling down. Nothing.

He walked across the yard, crunching through dead weeds, shoulders hunched against the sleet. When he reached the house he saw boarded-over windows, shrubs growing wild. A metallic clang shuddered on the wind. An old windmill, most likely, although he couldn't see it.

He crossed the yard to the small structure closest to the road. This must be the summer kitchen. His heart banged like the windmill as he opened the door and stepped inside. Remembering Chloe's description, he played his light over the far wall. The bake oven yawned black and ominous, but at least the square door was standing open. He crossed the room with a sense of dread and checked inside the oven. Empty.

Roelke went back outside and stood motionless, straining to see through the dark fog, feeling cold mist against his cheeks, hearing the relentless patter of freezing rain. A dismal heaviness settled in his chest. *Something* had made him hope that he might find Chloe here. He didn't know where else to look.

He trudged back toward his truck, head bent. As he passed the bake oven shed he realized he hadn't inspected this end of the building. His flashlight caught a square wooden door.

Roelke jogged closer. An iron latch locked the door in place. He grabbed the handle, yanked it over, and wrenched the door open.

Someone made an inarticulate cry. He swung his beam to the right of the big central plastered mound. Two women were huddled together. He didn't recognize the still one.

But the other was his Chloe, supported by one elbow, shielding her eyes from the light. "Oh, damn," she said groggily. "I *do* have hypothermia."

———

As it turned out, Chloe did not have hypothermia.

"You're good to go," the ER nurse at Bellin Hospital in Green Bay told Chloe. The nurse seemed impossibly young, and her red scrubs top was printed with candy canes. "Your core temp was ninety-five when they brought you in, but normal now. All your vitals are where we want them."

Chloe glanced at Roelke, who sat in a plastic visitor's chair in one corner of the little curtained cubicle where she'd been resting. His face was impassive, but she caught the almost imperceptible easing of his jaw. "I'm all right, Roelke."

He nodded, but one knee was bouncing with suppressed tension and rage. "When will you get lab results back?" he asked the nurse. "If Chloe was given flunitrazepam—"

"That won't be confirmed for a day or so." The child-nurse patted Chloe's arm with a surprisingly competent air. "The bad news is that flunitrazepam has a short half-life. Our hospital lab's routine screening tests won't detect it."

Flunitrazepam, Chloe thought, committing the word to memory. Lulled by the luxury of warm blankets, she'd been half out of it when the doctor had mentioned his suspicions.

"The good news," the nurse continued, "is that the doctor's already ordered the specimens to be sent to a different lab. *And* that you got Chloe in here as quickly as you did."

"What about my friend?" Chloe asked the nurse. "Elise O'Rourke?"

"I believe she's been admitted. If you want to wait in the lounge, I'll see if there's an update."

Please let Elise be okay, Chloe thought in silent prayer. *Please, please, please.*

After Chloe dressed she and Roelke left the cubicle with release instructions in hand. In the waiting room, Roelke settled on a sofa and put one arm around her. Chloe closed her eyes, savoring his solid strength and warmth. A baby was crying down the hall, and a couple seated nearby argued in hushed tones, and the intercom blared a page.

All Chloe wanted to do was stay right here, safe. "Thank you for finding me," she murmured. "I was never so glad to see *anybody* as I was to see you."

He pulled back to regard her sardonically. "You didn't seem too glad. You announced that you had hypothermia."

"I thought I was hallucinating!" she protested. "You were the *last* person I expected to see. I assumed you were at home!"

"I'm just glad I got there when I did."

Chloe was too. Roelke had gotten Chloe and Elise, still barely conscious, out of the shed. In his truck, they'd slipped and slid back down the hill to Belgian Acres. Sharon had ensconced Elise on the sofa with a heating pad and layers of blankets to wait for the Green Bay ambulance to arrive. Chloe's memories of the trip to the ER, and her time there, were hazy. "I remember talking to the cop who came in after we got here. Sort of, anyway. Was I coherent?"

"Coherent enough. I'm sure he's already been in touch with the Door County Sheriff's Department. Deputy Knutson or an investigator will probably want to talk to you as well, but that can wait."

"Okay. Just one more thing. What is flunitrazepam?"

His fingers tightened on hers. "A tranquilizer, ten times more potent than Valium. Based on what you told us, *something* knocked you out long enough for someone to move you to the oven shed. Presumably he did the same thing to Elise."

"I keep trying to remember, but ... it's just not coming back." The fuzziness was scary and infuriating.

"That's the point." Roelke's voice was hard as ice. "It's sometimes used as a date-rape drug."

Chloe decided she didn't even want to think about that. "You said that you and Deputy Knutson were searching, but how on earth did you know to look at Hugh Lejeune's old place?"

"I didn't," Roelke admitted. "At first we were focused on your car being left at the Heritage Center, and we started the search there. I tried to hope that you'd set out on foot because somebody told you about an old chapel or something nearby."

"That could have happened," she admitted, trying to look remorseful.

"Deputy Knutson thought you might have tried to flee some threat on foot, but that just didn't feel right. I decided to search along the road back toward the B&B, but when I got there ... " He looked away, as if reassembling a sequence of events in his mind. "I had to keep going. When I got up the hill it was so dark and foggy that I didn't even see the summer kitchen and bake oven from the road." He rubbed one palm over his face. "But the star caught my eye."

"The one on the barn?"

He nodded. "Out of the dark and fog it almost … I don't know … glimmered. I got out for a closer look and realized I'd reached the abandoned farm where you found the body. Even though I couldn't see a connection, I had to look." He stroked her hair. "What is that star on the barn all about, anyway? Just decoration?"

Chloe straightened. *"Stella Maris."*

"What?"

Chloe reminded herself that Roelke had not been on Jason's landscape tour of Belgian-American vernacular architecture. "No one's sure, but a local Belgian architecture expert believes it's a religious symbol. *Stella Maris* is Latin for 'Star of the Sea.' It's an ancient reference to the Virgin Mary."

TWENTY-SIX

OCTOBER 1881

"Our Lady, Star of the Sea," the priest intoned, "pray for us. Amen."

Seraphine slipped back onto the bench at St. Mary of the Snows Church in Namur. Etienne remained on his knees, head bowed, shoulders shaking as he wept. Seraphine touched his arm, trying to offer comfort, then let her hand drop. Everyone grieves in their own way, she thought. Her grief smoldered deep inside. If she let herself cry, she might never stop.

"On this tenth anniversary of our Sad Day, our most terrible tragedy, let us remember the words of the Blessed Virgin. 'Sing as a group the Ave Maris Stella, and I will guard you from every danger.'"

But she did not guard us from every danger, Seraphine thought. If she had, Joseph and Ermina and Jean-Paul would still be alive. Emelie and her baby too.

"Let us rise." The priest raised both hands, and a rustle filled the church. He began to sing: *"Ave, Maris Stella, Dei Mater aima, Atque semper virgo, Felix coeli porta…"*

Seraphine listened respectfully. She didn't doubt the priest's sincerity. She didn't begrudge her neighbors who'd survived the Great Fire with their faith intact. Her friend Adele continued to work as the Virgin Mother had asked. But God and the Blessed Virgin had, apparently, found *her* lacking.

The service ended, and people solemnly filed outdoors. After another few minutes Etienne rose. His eyes glistened. He pulled a blue kerchief from one pocket and blew his nose. "I'm sorry."

"You have nothing to be sorry about," Seraphine said gently. She and Etienne had never developed the easy camaraderie that she and Jean-Paul had shared. The sense of partnership, the love. But she understood him.

The church was empty now, and still. "Come along, Etienne. The ladies will be laying the supper outside."

In the churchyard, women were indeed arranging bowls of chicken *booyah* and *jutt.* Although many of the younger women served some "convenience foods" at home, they knew better than to bring anything but traditional fare to a church supper. At the dessert table, Cecilie was putting out plates of Belgian pie and *gallettes*—waffles soaked in milk and sprinkled with sugar.

Cecilie has coped, Seraphine thought with some pride. Memories of the fire tormented her daughter, haunting her dreams, but she'd risen above the horror. She had recently married a farmer named Robert Claes.

"Etienne!" A group of men lounging in the shade beckoned.

"This is not a day for drinking," Seraphine cautioned.

He flapped one irritated hand at her and walked away.

Seraphine sighed. Only Emelie had been able to handle Etienne.

She wasn't hungry for food or company, so she found a quiet bench and gazed over the countryside. Even now, the landscape seemed dreamlike. Farm fields stretched toward the horizon behind the church. A herd of cows grazed contentedly in a pasture. The day had a tang in the air, but the sky was a vivid blue. It was difficult to remember the endless brooding woods. But the fire that had destroyed them … *that*, Seraphine would never forget.

"Mama?" It was Pierre. Her second-born son was twenty-three now, married with a son of his own. He and his bachelor brother Jules worked the land that Jean-Paul had started clearing twenty-six years earlier.

Seraphine scooted over. "Sit with me."

He hesitated, shook his head. "Mama … it's Uncle Etienne. He needs to go home."

"Already?" She sighed. Pierre meant that Etienne was drinking too much. She'd made sure he didn't bring a jug, but vigilance was useless when there was a tavern right next to the church.

"Jules is fetching your buggy." Pierre rubbed his chin. "Should I get François ? Do you need help?"

"Just getting Etienne in the buggy, perhaps. I can drive him home." She'd done it before. "Let François enjoy the picnic." Etienne's two daughters had married and moved away, but his son François had taken on more and more responsibility at Lejeune Farm East.

Pierre led her to the group of men drinking their memories away. "Time to go, Etienne," she called. To her relief, he came willingly enough.

With her sons' help she managed to get Etienne into the buggy. He slouched against the side and mumbled, "I'm sorry, Emelie."

Seraphine wondered how many times a heart could break.

Jules leaned close as she settled on the seat and took up the lines. "Mama, we were set to help Etienne work on your summer kitchen tomorrow, but he may not feel up to it."

"Perhaps, but the work needs to be done. François is worried about getting the roof on before the snow flies."

"We'll get it done," Pierre promised.

She smiled down at her sons. They were their own men, but also much like their father—steady, hard-working, good-hearted. "I don't doubt it."

———

Seraphine reined in the horse and paused in the drive when they reached Etienne's farm. My farm too, she reminded herself.

But in truth, she'd never felt truly at home here. She'd married Etienne because her heart was scorched with grief. She'd needed a helpmeet to care for her children, and she'd felt dead herself. With the three boys' assistance, Etienne had started over and done well enough. He'd built a log home, and after their first harvest, hired a mason to encase it in brick. "I won't have another house burn," he'd vowed grimly. Seraphine asked for round windows in the gable ends, just beneath the eaves. She sometimes climbed to the attic and looked out, searching for any hint of smoke or flame.

And for the first few years, she'd been busy. She'd cared for her sons and daughter, her nieces and nephew. She'd twisted the burned and tender loose ends of her life this way and that, trying to make something whole. She'd poured her heart out in letters to Octavie—*Dear sister, I must accept the fact that we will not see each other on this earth again*—and wept over the responses—*If that is so, may God keep you until we are reunited in Heaven.*

It wasn't enough. It never occurred to Etienne to ask if she had dreams. He drank too much, too often. She felt as brittle and soulless as a milkweed pod after all its seeds floated away. She'd been Jean-Paul's wife, but he was dead. She was married but had never felt so alone. She was a mother, but her children were now grown. She was a sister who would never see her beloved twin again. She'd been a lacemaker, but that dream had burned in the Great Fire. Yet what was there to do but keep going?

Octavie urged her to try lacework again, but it was too late. Her eyes were not as sharp as they'd once been. Her fingers often ached. She couldn't imagine handling bobbins made by someone other than Jean-Paul. Lace was something to keep with memories of Wallonia's low red brick farmhouses with steep tile or slate roofs, and blue flax fields in summer; of the clatter of the girls' *sabots* on stone walkways as they hurried to the convent each morning, and black-robed nuns sitting in the cloister; of pealing bells and doves cooing from the belfry.

"All a long time ago," Seraphine murmured. She picked up the lines and called to the horse.

When they reached the stable Etienne was snoring loudly, and she was unable to rouse him. She fetched blankets from the house, covered him gently, and left him to sleep it off.

———

Seraphine came awake in the night with a start, but fear kept her frozen. What had disturbed her? A whiff of smoke? A flicker in the darkness? No—someone was crouching beside her. Her fingers clenched the sheet.

Then, in the moonlight she recognized her husband. "Etienne? What are you doing?"

"I—nothing."

Something wooden scraped against the floor. He was sliding her old wooden box back under the bed! She threw aside the blankets and scrambled to her feet. "What are you doing with my box?"

He straightened. "Just looking."

"Looking for what?" she demanded, hands on her hips.

"I need money."

And why, Seraphine thought, does Etienne need money? The farm produced most of their food, and harvest profits covered other necessities. François, twenty-six now, was a hard worker; his cheerful wife was frugal. But Seraphine knew. Etienne couldn't count on his friends to always supply the liquor when they gathered.

She crossed her arms. "There is no money in that box, Etienne." Every coin Jean-Paul had saved before the fire had long been spent.

He shifted his weight from side to side like a petulant child. "There may be something we could sell."

"There is nothing to sell! The things in that box are mine!"

"All right!" He put up his hands, palms out in surrender. "All right, I'm sorry." He left their bedroom, closing the door behind him.

Seraphine listened to his footsteps fading away down the hall. What on earth had possessed him? She'd expected him to sleep off his drunk in the stable, not surfacing before first light.

I need money.

A fist closed around her heart. She lit a lamp, pulled the box back out, opened the lid. The rosary Jean-Paul had given her was tucked away, and the *sabots* he'd carved so beautifully for her, and the purple and green skirt she'd brought from Belgium. The skirt and *sabots* weren't worth anything. The rosary might fetch a little money. But her wedding lace was hidden beneath the skirt. Although she'd snipped pieces from it over and over, she still had about two feet of fine bobbin lace. *That* was worth something.

The thought of Etienne taking her lace in the night, stealing away to some buyer in Green Bay, made her feel sick. Her hands trembled as she unwrapped the lace, just to make sure it was still there. Then she tucked it under her pillow and tried to sleep.

Dawn spilling in the window woke her from uneasy dreams. After dressing she tiptoed down the hall, cracked the door to the spare room, and peeked inside. Etienne lay sprawled on top of the quilt in the clothes he'd worn to church the day before, once again snoring.

She thought about the lace while she gathered eggs from her flock of Leghorns and washed them in the kitchen. Etienne might not even remember stealing into her room last night. But sooner or later he would try again.

Finally, when François's wife was busy with the children, Seraphine took a tin with a tight-fitting lid from the pantry, transferred the sugar it held to another container, and quickly washed and dried it. She folded her lace in a protective cloth and waxed paper, tucked it into the container, and pressed on the lid. She had to be quick.

She slipped out the back door and, with a glance over her shoulder, hurried to the summer kitchen. She'd wanted one for years. The iron cookstove inside was functional for most things, but there were times when she still wanted or needed to do a large baking. The house, barn, stable, pigpen, chicken coop, corn crib, and granary had taken precedence, though, so Etienne had only recently started construction. The summer kitchen walls were finished, and a mason had constructed the bake oven. Now the shed walls were going up to protect that oven from the elements. Etienne had planned for sixteen inches of space between the building's inner and outer walls to help keep the structure cool in summer. The men had been dumping earth and rubble between the walls as they rose.

Seraphine walked along the chest-high wall. *There*—that triangular stone in the outside wall would serve as a marker. She removed several of the rubble stones the men had dumped between the walls, tucked the sugar tin into the hole, and covered it with stones. For good measure she scooped up some earth in her hands and poured it over the tin. She peeked at her handiwork and nodded. Good. The tin was buried, and today her sons and François would finish the shed.

———

Dear Seraphine,

You of all people will be overjoyed to learn that we are making progress in securing justice for the lacemakers. Queen Elizabeth has taken up our cause. She understands, I'm told, that the effort to protect the lacemakers will lift them from poverty at best and something like slavery at worst. It will also protect the lace industry so essential to Belgium's economy. Lacemakers today often favor the Guipures styles, which use a heavier thread and therefore are completed more quickly. The Queen fears, as I have long feared, that turning aside from delicate Valenciennes or the Malines or our beautiful Bruges could result in their complete disappearance. Already it has become

difficult to identify lacemakers able to execute a design without hav-
ing someone prick it for them. And the piqueuses are vanishing,
dying away with no one to replace them. There is talk of forming a
group called Amies de la Dentelle to organize support for our lace-
makers. May it be so!

A group called Friends of Lace, Seraphine marveled. What a
wonderful idea.

I do so wish you could find time to turn your hand to lacemaking
again. We must not let the old traditional patterns and styles vanish!
If you are able to work, but lack patterns, I will send you some.

Your loving sister,
Octavie

TWENTY-SEVEN

IN THE HOSPITAL LOUNGE Chloe yawned and stretched, trying to get comfortable on an uncomfortable couch. "What time is it?"

"Almost one a.m.," Roelke said.

The child-nurse entered the lounge. "Ms. Ellefson? I checked on your friend. Ms. O'Rourke needed more help getting warmed up, and the doctor wants to keep her under observation for a while. But she appears to be responding."

Tears of relief blurred Chloe's vision. "Thank you." The nurse nodded and hurried away.

"That's encouraging news," Roelke said. "Now, what you need most is sleep."

Chloe knew he was right, but she only wriggled closer, snuggling against him. "It was really scary, Roelke. I knew Elise was in bad shape. She was rambling—calling for her dead husband, I think. And sometimes she was crying for her mother, like a lost child . . . *oh*."

He shot her a quick glance. "What?"

"Give me a minute." Chloe squinched her eyes closed, trying to remember. Her clandestine trip to Sharon's roadside chapel seemed like ancient history now. But that certificate from 1955, written in careful calligraphy had suggested something interesting. Something she may have misinterpreted.

Roelke's patience didn't last a minute. "*What? Did you think of something helpful? The faster we can identify the SOB that did this to you and Elise, the better chance we have of—*"

"I don't know if this is helpful or not," Chloe said. "But here's what I'm thinking."

———

Roelke had been planning to find the closest hotel, but Chloe's speculation changed everything. "Stay here while I find a phone," he told her. "I need to call the Door County Sheriff."

It took some doing, but twenty minutes later he had the information he wanted. Back in the waiting room he found Chloe slumped on the sofa, sound asleep. Her long blond hair was loose. Beneath the harsh lights her skin looked even paler than usual. His heart tightened with gratitude and anger, and he needed to compose himself before waking her. "It's time to go," he said gently. "Are you sure you don't want to go to a hotel? I can go talk to Sharon by myself."

She shook her head. "No. I'm coming too."

Roelke drove slowly, for the roads were still slick. At Belgian Acres, Sharon's truck was the only vehicle in sight. Was that good or bad? He wasn't sure.

Sharon met them at the front door. "Oh, thank God," she cried, pulling Chloe into a hug. "You're okay? How do you feel? What about Elise?"

"I'm fine," Chloe assured her. "I slept most of the time we were at the hospital, so I'm probably in better shape than you are at this point." Sharon looked haggard. Her eyes were bloodshot and rimmed with dark, puffy circles. Hair had straggled from her braid.

"I couldn't sleep without knowing how you girls were doing."

"Elise needed more care and was admitted," Chloe explained. "But the nurse seemed optimistic."

"Thank God," Sharon said again. She dropped onto the sofa.

Roelke took a nearby chair and leaned forward, elbows on knees. "Sharon, is Toni here?"

Sharon shook her head. "No. It happens sometimes—she stays out late and sleeps at a friend's house. Especially since the roads got bad."

Or, Roelke thought, she might be miles and miles gone. He glanced at Chloe, who seriously did *not* look up for this conversation. But they'd made a plan, and she sat down beside her hostess. "Sharon ... I need to ask you something."

Sharon's forehead wrinkled. "What?"

"Actually, first I need to tell you something. I visited your chapel this afternoon."

The older woman looked stunned. "That chapel is private! And it's locked. How did you—"

"I borrowed your key ring." Chloe squirmed like a miserable child. "I'm truly sorry, but I was trying to learn more about your family history ... ." Her voice trailed away.

300

"You did *not* have permission to go there." Sharon's tone turned frosty. "Honestly, Chloe. You had no right to invade my privacy."

"No, I didn't," Chloe agreed, sounding as contrite as he'd ever heard her. "But here's the thing. It seems you lost a child in 1955."

Sharon flinched and scrambled to her feet. "That is none of your business!"

Roelke couldn't sit in silence any longer. "In a broad sense, that's true." He heard the edge in his voice but didn't try to temper it. "But we think that today it became Chloe's business."

Sharon looked from Roelke to Chloe and back again. "What on earth—"

"I saw the homemade certificate," Chloe said. "'Baby Bertrand, loved and lost August 16, 1955.'" She paused. "I imagined you grieving a baby who died during birth, or shortly after. But is that what happened? Or ... did you give your child up for adoption?"

Sharon's eyes widened.

"Please sit down." Chloe took Sharon's hand. Roelke admired her gentle tone. She'd been drugged and locked in a shed and left to die of exposure, and *he* felt ready to erupt like a volcano.

The older woman plopped back to the sofa. "But what ... why ... "

Chloe took a deep breath. "Sharon, when Elise and I were locked in that shed, she was semi-conscious. She rambled about a man named Geoffrey—"

"I don't know any Geoffrey," Sharon said stiffly.

Chloe raised a palm: *Give me a chance.* "I think Geoffrey was her husband. But she also called for her mother."

"And," Roelke added, "Elise was born on August 16, 1955." He'd been able to get that confirmed by the Door County Sheriff's Department.

Sharon's mouth opened but no words emerged. She pressed one hand against her heart.

"Here's what I know," Chloe continued. "Elise wasn't invited to Green Bay. She called the lace guild and invited herself. Her internship supervisor told me that she was studying lace made in Massachusetts, then suddenly switched to Belgian bobbin lace. When I told her about your B&B, she pretended it was new information, even though she'd already made a reservation. According to your guestbook, she switched dates *after* talking to me. She was already coming here. Right here, to your farm."

The only sound in the room was the soft skitter of sleet pelting the windowpanes. Roelke cleared his throat, ready to get to the real issue. "I know this is a lot to take in, Sharon. And it's always possible that Elise's birthdate, and the other discrepancies, are all coincidence." As unlikely as that seemed. "But I have to ask another question. Is it possible that Toni figured out that Elise might be her half sister?"

"I—I—the thing is … I did have a child." Sharon abruptly got to her feet again and walked to the window. Pushing aside the curtain, she stared at the night.

Chloe looked at Roelke: *Should I say something?* He shook his head. Sometimes the best thing to do was let silence become uncomfortable.

Sharon sighed. "My husband and I were both eighteen when we married. Too young. Just two years later we separated because he had an affair. I was so hurt, so angry, that I—I did something equally foolish." She waved a hand: *That's all to be said about that.* "I reconciled with my husband but quickly discovered that I was pregnant. We agreed that I'd have the child and give her up for adoption. It was the worst mistake of my life." She needed a moment to continue. "Toni was born three years later. But I never told her anything about it!"

In Roelke's experience, secrets were difficult to keep. "But could Toni have found out?"

"No, I—oh." Sharon's shoulders sagged, and she turned to face them again. "Three months ago I learned that I need a kidney transplant. Toni was tested, but wasn't donor-compatible." She licked her lips. "The adoption records had been locked in a cabinet since the day I gave my baby away. But one night I was just in despair, and I got the file out. I thought that maybe..."

Maybe the child you'd given up was compatible, Roelke thought. What a mess.

"The file was on my desk for maybe a day," Sharon said slowly. "No more. I gave up the idea of trying to contact my child almost immediately. I'd given her away! What right did I have to look for her now, much less ask for such a thing?" Her face was anguished.

Roelke needed her to focus. "We're not here to judge, Sharon. The issue at hand is whether Toni discovered that she had a half sister."

"Toni never gave me a *clue* that she'd seen the papers!"

"But it's possible that she did."

She hesitated, then seemed to deflate like a pin-pricked balloon. "Yes. It's possible."

"My understanding," Chloe said quietly, "is that it's difficult to find someone given up for adoption. Still, it's at least possible that if Toni saw your records, she could have somehow discovered Elise's identity. And the discovery that she had an older half sister might have made her feel threatened for some reason. Is it fair to conclude that, as your only child, she'd assumed that Belgian Acres would eventually come to her? If Elise *is* your daughter, and if Toni *did* figure that out, would she have been upset enough to—to lash out at Elise?"

Roelke saw a flash of denial in Sharon's eyes and spoke quickly, before she could muster her defenses. "Chloe said that Toni was the last person to see Elise before she disappeared at the Heritage Center."

"And she chose to drive alone that night, instead of coming with you," Chloe reminded her. "When I suggested calling the cops about Elise's disappearance, Toni said we should wait. She even quibbled about the company Elise rented the car from. Toni was the last person I remember seeing before I was drugged. She might have seen me coming back from the chapel and worried that I'd figured things out."

Roelke's knee began to bounce. "And Toni left us a note saying that Chloe was heading to the Heritage Center." That was irrefutable.

"Which I was not." Chloe's tone was firm.

"As a nurse, Toni also has access to drugs." Roelke got to his feet and prowled the small room. "The last thing Chloe remembers is drinking the coffee that Toni poured for her. If the coffee was drugged, Toni could have driven Chloe up the hill and locked her in the bake oven shed, assuming that she—and Elise—would never be found."

Chloe looked at Sharon. "The Heritage Center is only … what, two or three miles away? Toni could have left my car there, then cut back through on foot to pick up her own car." She twisted her fingers together in her lap. "Sharon, we're not in a position to accuse Toni outright. But surely you can see that she has to answer some questions."

Roelke studied Sharon. Toni's *mother*. That relationship trumped almost everything. He braced for an avalanche of angry denials, or a tearful order to get out.

But Sharon stood mute. After wiping away a tear, she didn't move for what felt like a very long time. Then she turned, walked woodenly to the phone, and picked up the receiver.

"What are you doing?" Roelke started toward her.

Sharon's voice was brittle as ice. "I'm calling the sheriff's department."

Once the call was made, they sat waiting in tense silence. Sharon clenched her hands in her lap and closed her eyes. Chloe stared miserably at the carpet. I hope to God we're right, Roelke thought, fingers drumming against his thigh.

Finally they saw the splash of lights in the driveway, heard a car door slam. Roelke strode across the room to open the door. "Thanks for—" he began.

A stocky woman stepped inside, frowning at him in confusion. Then she saw Chloe and froze.

Chloe stood up, arms crossed against her chest. "Surprised to see me?" she said acidly.

Roelke saw Toni's eyes go wide, heard the sharp intake of her breath, and *knew*. This bitch tried to kill Chloe, he thought. He shoved Toni into the room and slammed the door before she could bolt.

"I ... um ... " Toni fumbled with one leather glove, tugging each fingertip in turn. "I am surprised to find you up at this hour, Chloe. I figured everyone would be in bed."

"Is that what you figured?" Chloe snapped. "Or did you expect to hear a sad tale about me disappearing from the Heritage Center?"

Roelke saw Toni's defenses slide into place. Her shoulders went back, her chin went up, her eyes flashed with defiance. The moment of panicked surprise was already gone.

"*Why?*" Chloe demanded. She took a step forward. "What did I ever do to you?"

"I don't know what you're talking about."

"And what about Elise?" Chloe stepped closer, voice hissing with anger. "Why did learning you have a half sister threaten you? You didn't have to be friends! But why kidnap her and leave her to die?"

Toni tried to back up but bumped into Roelke. "I don't have to stand here in my own house and listen to you rave." She whirled and lunged for the doorknob.

Roelke grabbed her. "You're not going anywhere."

"I don't even know who you are." Toni tried to shake him off. Her breath smelled like booze. "Let go of me!"

"*Antoinette!*" Sharon's voice cracked like a whip. Toni stopped struggling. Chloe moved aside as Sharon confronted her daughter. "Did you see the adoption papers?"

"So what if I did?" Toni flared.

Gotcha, Roelke thought.

"Look me in the eye," Sharon demanded in a terrible voice. "Look me in the eye and swear you had nothing to do with what happened to Elise and Chloe."

"Mom, I …"

"You were the last person to see both of them before they disappeared. You have access to drugs. Between nursing and barn chores, you're physically strong. Swear to me, on all that's holy, that you were not involved."

The room went very still. Sharon waited a long moment, then turned away. In the silence Roelke heard another car coming down the drive. Flashing lights against the window confirmed the arrival of a deputy sheriff.

Thank God, he thought. He had no jurisdiction here. And if someone didn't take Toni Bertrand off his hands, he just might break her in two.

TWENTY-EIGHT

THE DEPUTY LOCKED TONI in the back of his car long enough to hear Chloe and Sharon out. Then he took her away for questioning.

Roelke spent the night on Sharon's sofa. Chloe didn't think she'd sleep—she missed Roelke, and her brain buzzed with wondering if Toni would confess or maintain her innocence. But after taking a hot shower and crawling under the covers, her limbs felt heavy and sleep came almost at once.

She woke with a start just after seven. After dressing quickly she trotted downstairs and found Roelke alone, sipping coffee and reviewing notes on a pad. "Hey," she said, and greeted him with a kiss.

He squeezed her hand. "How are you feeling?"

"Much better," she assured him, glad she didn't have to lie about that.

"Want some coffee? It's instant."

"Um, no." Her last cup of coffee in this house had led to very bad things. "What's going on? Any news about Toni?"

"Not that I'm aware of."

"Where's Sharon?" The house felt empty.

"Out. She took a phone call, then said that there was someplace she needed to be. And she apologized profusely for not fixing breakfast."

"As if that matters. Poor Sharon." Chloe rubbed her arms pensively.

Roelke hesitated. "I have to tell you, Chloe, that even if Toni is guilty, the cops may not be able to make anything stick. They may not even arrest her. Not without some kind of concrete evidence."

Damn. "Fingerprints in my car, maybe?"

"I assume she wore gloves or mittens."

Damn.

"Don't despair," Roelke added. "I'm not saying something won't turn up. The techs will go over your car inch by inch, and maybe they'll find something to show that Toni drove it to Namur. Or maybe they'll find some trace of the drug in the coffeepot." The percolator and mug had been scrubbed clean, but the deputy had taken them for analysis. "I'm sure there will be a thorough investigation. I just didn't want you to get your hopes up for a quick resolution."

"I won't," Chloe said, although that's exactly what she'd been hoping for. "Roelke, do you think Toni killed Hugh Lejeune too?"

He rubbed his chin. "It's certainly possible. Toni doesn't have the nerve to kill outright. I can see her snatching his inhaler and leaving him to die, then coming back later to hide the body."

"Yeah." That's what she'd figured too.

"Since you're without transportation, and I've got a meeting at the prison this morning, shall I drop you off at Heritage Hill?"

She shook her head. "Could you take me to the hospital instead? I want to see how Elise is doing."

Roelke was quiet on the drive south. "Are you up to this prison meeting?" she asked as they turned into the hospital entrance. "You must be exhausted. Maybe you could postpone."

"No way." His jaw set in the way she knew so well. "I have the chance to nail a killer."

"Okay." When he pulled up to the curb she leaned close for another kiss. "Good luck. I'll find a way to get back to Heritage Hill. Meet me there later? The St. Nicholas party is this afternoon. I'm sure you'd be welcome."

His gaze was ironic. "Are you up to a party today?"

"I am." She spoke with as much conviction as she could muster. "I've met lovely people here, Roelke. And the Belgian Farm is going to be an awesome addition to Heritage Hill. This gathering will be a chance for me to help honor Roy Galuska and everyone else who's worked so hard to make that happen."

Chloe fortified herself with a cup of coffee and a sticky bun at the hospital cafeteria, trying to decide what she wanted to say to Elise. Then she got the room number at the information desk and made her way to the appropriate floor. But when she reached the room, a low murmur of conversation drifted into the hall. Chloe peeked around the door and saw Sharon sitting in a chair pulled close to the bed, holding Elise's hand.

Chloe backed away. No way was she interrupting *that* conversation.

She found a seat in a nearby lounge. Twenty minutes later Sharon walked down the hall. Chloe waved her over. "How is Elise?" First things first.

"She's going to be fine." Sharon's eyes were red-rimmed, but she managed a tiny smile.

"Thank God." Chloe blew out a long, relieved sigh. "I know it's not my business, but ... is Elise your daughter?"

"She is." Sharon sounded dazed. "I never thought I'd learn what happened to my baby."

"How on earth did she find you?"

"It was a private adoption." Sharon gripped the arms of her chair. "I went to stay with a friend in Chicago. She hooked me up with a midwife who delivered the baby. I signed papers relinquishing my parental rights and she signed papers saying she would place the baby in a good home." She glanced at Chloe, then quickly looked away. "It sounds cold, but I was young and terrified."

"I'm sure you did the best you could."

Sharon shook her head. "I don't think so. Anyway, Elise said she's always known that she was adopted. When she asked, her parents gave her the agreement. There was no clause that demanded secrecy so she tracked down the midwife, who provided my name and address."

"Wow." Chloe sat back in her chair, thinking all that through.

"It's hard to take in." Sharon put a hand on Chloe's arm. "The hardest thing to accept is what Toni tried to do. I am so, so sorry."

"I'm sorry too, for your sake."

Sharon made a helpless gesture. "I feel as if I gained a daughter and lost a daughter, all in one day."

Chloe hesitated. "Have you heard if Toni has actually confessed to anything?"

"I don't know. Someone from the sheriff's department called this morning and asked me to go in for another interview later. I'll learn more then. I wish I could say that Toni's actions were beyond belief, but honestly…" Sharon pressed her fingertips to her forehead. "I can't. She admitted that she'd seen the adoption papers. I suspect she set out to discover Elise's identity. Toni worked in a Chicago hospital before her divorce. She had connections. I imagine she went to the midwife with a tale about wanting to find her long-lost sister, and the midwife provided the information."

"I suppose."

"But Toni did not contact Elise. Elise said she came to the B&B to get a glimpse of who I am. But Toni must have assumed that she had ulterior motives."

Chloe couldn't wrap her head around that. "What kind of ulterior motives?"

"I don't know. Antoinette has always seemed angry. Maybe she sensed that much as I loved her, my lost child was in my heart as well. As a teen, all she wanted to do was leave the farm and her parents behind her."

Chloe hated the pain in Sharon's voice. "Toni did come back to help you out."

"She came back because she had nowhere else to go." Sharon rubbed at a loose thread in her jeans. "I so wanted to believe that she'd changed. But in my heart, I never did."

———

Elise was sleeping, so Chloe decided to visit again later—and to accept Sharon's offer of a ride. "I'm not expected at Heritage Hill until this afternoon, for the St. Nicholas Day party," Chloe explained as they zipped up their coats near the main door, "so I thought I'd visit the archives at UW–Green Bay. With your permission, I'd like to see what I can dig up about your ancestors. Especially Seraphine. Her story intrigues me."

Sharon brightened. "That would be fantastic! Although I don't want to take time away from your project."

"That comes first," Chloe agreed. "I want to study their collection of historic photographs from the Belgian community, and photocopy any that document material culture of the appropriate era."

"Oh, it's a wonderful collection," Sharon assured her. "Jason helped identify the original photographs and worked with the families to obtain copies for the archives. You may see him there, actually. If you do, will you ask him to call me? I haven't heard from him since he called in sick on Wednesday morning. I'm getting concerned."

Like Sharon needs anything else to worry about, Chloe thought. "Of course."

After Sharon dropped her off at the university, Chloe spent several hours *not* thinking about Toni and happily poring over black-and-white photographs collected from Belgian-American families in northeast Wisconsin. She even had time to hastily dig out some materials about the immigrants' experiences compiled by early historians that might, she hoped, provide more insight into the Lejeunes' experiences. Those she photocopied to study when time permitted.

Before leaving, she asked the student working at the desk if Jason Oberholtzer was expected that day. The young man rolled his eyes. "Expected? Yeah, in half an hour. But he was supposed to work yesterday afternoon too, and didn't show. Guess who got called in at the last minute."

That didn't sound like Jason. "Well, I wish you better luck today," Chloe said. Perhaps Sharon was right to be concerned.

She found a pay phone in the lobby downstairs and was about to call a cab when she saw a flash of yellow through the window. Speak of the devil, she thought. Jason Oberholtzer had just driven his Gremlin into the parking lot.

He was locking the car by the time she caught up with him. "Hey, Jason."

"Oh!" Jason whirled. "I—um—hi! What a surprise. A nice one, of course."

The confident young man who'd given her the driving tour had faded to something resembling Isaac Cuddy's anxious self. Chloe studied him. "Are you feeling better?"

"Yes! Yes, I am." He abruptly sidled in front of the car.

If he hadn't done that, she might not have noticed the scratches on the bumper. They weren't deep, but they were long. "Jason," she said slowly, "what happened to your car?"

His expression suggested a deer in the headlights.

Chloe pulled up the *Jason Oberholtzer Facts* file in her brain. During his tour, he'd proved passionate about identifying and preserving Belgian-American structures. But she'd first seen him at Lorenzo's, engaged in an animated conversation with Toni Bertrand. But had it really been "animated?" Or... had it been an argument?

"Look, Chloe, it's nice to see you, but I need to get to work." Jason's words suggested urgency. His next move, leaning with all apparent casualness against the Gremlin, did not.

Chloe was in no mood to mince words. "Jason, did you run Toni off the road on Tuesday night?"

The color in his cheeks faded. "Did I... what?"

"It *was* you. Why?" Chloe's anger ratcheted up a notch or three. "Oh, my, God. Did you know what she had planned for Elise? Did you know and not tell anyone?"

His apprehension faded to blank confusion. "What did Toni do to Elise?"

"Are you telling me you don't know?"

"I don't! I swear it!"

Chloe studied him with narrowed eyes. "But you did run into Toni's car. I want to know why."

"I can't—"

"Oh yes, you can," she said grimly. She considered what else she knew about Jason. He'd been working part-time at Sharon's farm for several years. He also worked part-time at the archives, and as a grad assistant, so money must be very tight. Maybe he and Toni were *both* after the lace, and what she'd seen at the pizza place was a spat among thieves.

"Chloe, I—"

"You jerk!" she blazed. "Was it the lace? You're trying to find the lace?"

"What lace?" He sounded bewildered and looked ready to cry.

"I saw you with Toni on Monday night, Jason. I didn't hear specifics, but your voices were raised. The damage on your car seems consistent with the damage on Toni's. You didn't show up to milk on Wednesday morning, or to help me at the Heritage Center, and you missed work yesterday without even calling in. *Something* is up. Tell me, right now, or I call the cops."

Jason's chin dropped. Chloe folded her arms and widened her stance. She wasn't going anywhere.

Finally he straightened. "All right. I'll tell you." He drew a deep breath. "I don't know anything about lace. What I do know is that Toni is planning to sell Belgian Acres."

"What? Toni doesn't own Belgian Acres, does she?"

"No, but Sharon is very ill—that's supposed to be a secret—and Toni is her only child. Who else would the land go to?"

Chloe waited until two young women with neon daypacks walked by. "I suppose Toni is in line to inherit, but for God's sake, Sharon will hopefully be around for many years to come! I know she needs a kidney transplant. That's serious, but she might yet find a donor. Just because Toni has fantasies of selling the farm—"

"They aren't fantasies! Look, I've known Toni longer than you have. A few weeks ago I saw her in a tavern. She was pretty drunk, so I sat down to make sure she was okay. I was making small talk about the farm, saying what a special place it is, and Toni just—just *sneered* at me. She told me she's already got some real estate developer waiting to buy Sharon's farm. She also said that Hugh Lejeune's son Richard is struggling financially, and she thinks she could talk him into going in on the deal."

Chloe's sternum grew cold. That lent credence to the idea that Toni had been responsible for Hugh Lejeune's death.

"They want to build a resort on the property," Jason added. "And condos too. It made me sick to hear her talking about it. She was scornful of Sharon for trying to hang onto the farm after Mr. Bertrand died."

Chloe remembered the day she'd met Toni Bertrand: *Mom needed help. Besides, this place is important to me. Family, you know? I mean, it's who I am.* Chloe ground her teeth. That lying little—

"Toni has everything I ever wanted," Jason quavered. "A home. A place that's come down through generations. A family."

Another memory popped into Chloe's mind. Sharon had said Jason was an urban kid, but *he'd* said he was a military brat. "Where did you grow up?"

He looked away. "In foster care, okay? In Milwaukee. Twelve different placements over the years. Toni has everything I ever dreamed of, and all she wants to do was destroy it." Jason pulled off one glove and found a tissue in a coat pocket. "On Tuesday night I waited for her after her shift and tried to talk sense into her. But she just laughed."

"Why didn't you just talk to Sharon about it? Why keep her in the dark?"

"Because," Jason said in a small voice, "Toni said that if I did, she'd tell my academic advisor that she forged a letter of recommendation for me."

"Is that true?"

Jason twisted his hands together. "Yes. One day when I was a senior we were milking together—I think she'd come back for Christmas—and I said I was worried about getting into the graduate program. She offered to write me a letter, and sign it as a college professor in Chicago who'd worked with me on an independent study project. I know it was stupid, but I was so desperate to get in that I agreed." His shoulders drooped. "If that came out, I'd get kicked out of school for sure."

"Oh, Jason." Chloe regarded this desperately needy and rootless young man who'd found everything he craved at Belgian Acres—kindness, a sense of family stability, a mother figure. It wasn't that simple, of course. It never was. But when Chloe remembered the passion with which he had talked about family farms, and Sharon saying, *He's become the son I never had,* she understood.

"I couldn't tell Sharon. She'd be so disappointed in me. But when I tried to talk to Toni Tuesday night, she slammed the car door in my face and zoomed away. I was so angry that I followed her. I wasn't trying to hurt her, I swear! I just wanted to make her listen, and to understand how horrible her plan was. I was even ready to let her tattle to Sharon if it would mean stopping her. But as we drove and I thought about that I just got angrier, and angrier, and ... and then I was bumping her car. I *swear* I didn't plan to. It just sort of ... happened."

Jason's story rang true. But as much as Chloe might sympathize, she couldn't let him stay silent. His testimony about Toni's plans to sell the family farm—perhaps farms—to a developer could be vitally important.

"Are you going to tell on me?" Jason asked glumly.

She sighed. "Things have happened that you're not aware of, Jason. You need to talk to the police."

"The police!"

"After you've done that," she said firmly, "I suggest that you come clean to your advisor. He might be forgiving. I'll even write a recommendation for you, if you think it will help."

Afraid Jason might lose his nerve, Chloe insisted on calling the police herself. After an officer arrived, she provided a summary of recent events. Jason was clearly shocked to hear that Toni had likely been the one who'd drugged and kidnapped Elise, and done the same to Chloe. After that, he told the officer what he could add.

Back in the lobby, Chloe called for a cab. She felt sorry for Jason. She even understood, just a bit, his yearning for family. For a place to belong. Her own reaction to Birgitta's revelation had been telling.

To settle her thoughts, she pulled out the photocopies she'd made in the archives. Since the house at Heritage Hill was being restored to its 1905 appearance, her project research didn't need to go any further than that. But she'd learned enough about the Belgian community that she wanted to know more—for her own curiosity, and for Sharon's sake. Seraphine, a lacemaker of great ability, had survived harsh pioneer experiences: famine, cholera, the Civil War era, the Great Fire. Chloe really, *really* wanted to learn what might have come next.

TWENTY-NINE

AUGUST 1914

"Pierre's taking the motorcar to Green Bay next week, and asked if we wanted to go." Cecilie poured hot water into a dishpan. "We can do some shopping." She and Seraphine were cleaning the De Laval cream separator in the summer kitchen. The machine used centrifugal force to separate milk from cream with great efficiency. Disassembling, cleaning, and reassembling it again, however, was time-consuming.

Seraphine reached for the soft soap. "There's nothing I need."

"Mama, you're becoming a recluse."

Seraphine shrugged.

"A new dress would perk you up!" Cecilie unconsciously smoothed her dress, a cheerful blue gingham. "You don't need to wear black every day."

Seraphine was content with her black skirts and subdued blouses. The last time she'd gone shopping, the clerk had eagerly shown her dresses with machine-made lace collars. "The mechanization keeps improving!" she'd chirped. "Just the thing, and *so* economical."

Besides, Seraphine didn't like the city, and she didn't like the motorcar. Jules and Pierre had gone together to buy a Ford Model T Touring Car from a man who'd purchased it, broken an arm cranking it, and promptly offered it for sale. She liked seeing Jules and Pierre cooperate just as Etienne and Jean-Paul had long ago. She did not like the car's exhaust fumes, or the blaring horns as young men with more money than sense swerved through traffic.

"Thank you, dear," she said now, "but no."

Cecilie looked disappointed, but nodded. Cecilie had recently been widowed, and when her daughter had moved to Appleton to work as a stenographer, she'd returned to the farm Etienne had built after the Great Fire. Cecilie was quiet but spirited. Seraphine loved having her daughter at Lejeune Farm East, even if they didn't always agree.

The sound of hooves on the drive provided a welcome distraction. "François and Etienne must be back from the blacksmith," Seraphine said. She walked to the door as François strode across the lawn.

"Where's Etienne?" Seraphine asked, although she knew.

"In town." François wiped his forehead with a kerchief. "I'm sorry, Mama Seraphine. But I do have a letter from your sister!" He handed it over.

"Oh, *thank* you." She kissed his cheek and watched him head toward the barn.

She'd grown quite fond of her nephew-stepson, Etienne's and Emelie's first-born child. Although he's no child, she chided herself. At fifty-nine, François was already a widower with grandchildren of his own. After the grain boom, after the Great Fire, it had been François who'd managed the transition to dairy farming. They now had a herd of placid Holsteins, plus a few Guernseys, which were finicky but produced richer milk.

"I'll finish here, Mama," Cecilie offered. "You enjoy your letter."

Seraphine sat at the table. The summer kitchen was hot but peaceful, fragrant with the herbs hanging from the rafters. With four generations now sharing the house, Seraphine liked to think of this as her own space. Except for baking pies for Kermiss or making sausage on butchering days, the younger women preferred the fancy coal-fired range in the house, with its reservoir and warming oven and shiny nickel trim. Besides, she couldn't enter the building without thinking of the wedding lace she'd hidden from Etienne all those years ago, still undisturbed within the wall. Somehow, knowing it was there was a comfort.

But a letter from her twin sister was the best comfort of all. Seraphine opened it eagerly and was relieved to read Octavie's assurance that she was well. From there the news quickly moved on, as it usually did, to her work to improve the lives of lacemakers.

I am overjoyed to share the news that the Amies de la Dentelle, the Friends of Lace, are slowly making progress in our struggle to provide better education and wages. Women still earn less than a franc for a day's work, but we have brought several lace factors to our side, which can only improve the situation. The entire tradition will collapse if women leave their lace and take factory work for better wages. We are also working to raise standards of design and to restore old patterns.

I pray this finds you and your family well. Here in Europe we increasingly hear reports that the unrest caused by the June murder of Archduke

Franz Ferdinand, heir to the throne of the Austro-Hungarian Empire, might yet destroy all order. Belgium will remain neutral, so our work here will not be interrupted. But may God prevent any more violence.

    Your loving sister,
    Octavie

Seraphine put the letter down. Her sister's news was bittersweet. Etienne and François had spoken of the archduke's murder, but honestly, it all seemed very far away. Fortunately, Belgium and the United States had both declared neutrality. But as she folded the letter away, Seraphine felt a twinge of unease.

A blare from a motorcar's horn startled her, and she stepped outside. One of Etienne's friends had brought him home. "That was quick," she murmured. She hadn't expected her husband home from the tavern for hours.

He climbed out stiffly, slammed the door, and started toward the house. Then he saw Seraphine and changed direction, waving a newspaper over his head.

"Etienne? What's wrong?"

"It is war!" he cried hoarsely.

Seraphine put one hand against the doorframe, remembering the last time she'd been greeted with this news fifty years before. Etienne's expression frightened her. "In Austria? Or did Germany invade Russia?"

"No." Etienne angrily slapped the wall with his folded newspaper. "Germany invaded Belgium."

———

The arrival of the *Green Bay Gazette* had become each day's most important event. The adults lingered over their after-supper coffee, analyzing every report, trying to separate truth from propaganda, struggling to understand such distant events. German leaders had requested safe passage through Belgium so they could attack France. When King Albert refused, Germany violated Belgium's neutrality and crossed the border anyway. Early reports of Belgian defenders defeating their foes soon gave way to more sober reports of sieges and bloodshed.

Sprinkled among the stories of tactics and marches were horrific tales of a war waged on civilians. Some German officers responded to burned bridges, or stray shots fired from woodlot or roofline, by executing whoever they could round up. Reporters described the bodies of women and children and priests lying where they'd been shot. They wrote of homes burned, desperate refugees begging for bread in the streets, and zeppelin airships dropping bombs on Belgian cities. "That's barbaric!" François was aghast.

Seraphine always scoured the fine print for references to Bruges. By summer's end it had been listed among the occupied cities, sending five thousand refugees from their homes. When Seraphine closed her eyes at night, she saw Octavie and the other nuns stumbling along some roadside, dazed and hungry. She hadn't felt so helpless since the Great Fire.

"Mama," Cecilie said one morning as they fed the chickens, "I'm concerned about you."

"I'm sick with worry for your aunt Octavie," Seraphine admitted.

"There's a meeting this evening at the church, had you heard?" Cecilie asked. "To discuss ways to aid the Belgian people. Shall we go together?"

Seraphine tossed table scraps to the milling Leghorns. "You go and report back."

"You'll feel better if you find even a small way to help," Cecilie said firmly. "We'll take the buggy."

―――――

When they got to St. Mary of the Snows in Namur that evening, buggies and wagons and motorcars were parked up and down the street. Seraphine recognized most of the people crowding the pews inside, but the first speaker, a portly balding man, was a stranger. "I represent Green Bay's Belgian-American Club," he began. "We've established a fund to help relieve the misery and destitution caused by the German invasion." He paced, looking over the crowd. "As you know, our tiny home nation produces only about a quarter of the food needed for its citizens. German occupiers are demanding Belgian crops to feed their soldiers. Great Britain has established a blockade on Germany and occupied Belgium. Belgian people face starvation."

Seraphine looked out a church window, seeing only mothers with no food, children with no clothes. Even lacemakers with no thread.

"But international leaders are working to create an agreement that will permit aid to reach desperate Belgian citizens. In the meantime, our own Belgian consul is supervising efforts to raise money for supplies. Please give generously. Thank you."

Next, a woman spoke. "We're also collecting toys and clothes for the suffering children in Belgium. We especially need bicycles and velocipedes, but no donation is too small. I'm hosting a sewing circle at my home next Saturday…"

Cecilie nudged Seraphine: *Shall we go?*

Seraphine nodded. She was happy to sew or knit or donate money for food. But it still didn't feel like enough. Octavie, she thought, I want to help and don't know how. What do you need?

And perhaps Octavie answered, for when the portly man asked if anyone else would like to speak, Seraphine slowly stood.

Cecilie looked shocked. Seraphine felt shocked, actually, but it was too late to stop now. "My sister, a nun in Bruges, has been—"

"Louder!" someone called.

Seraphine cleared her throat and tried again. "My sister, a nun in Bruges, has been working to lift lacemakers from dire poverty. They rely on imported thread to make the famous Belgian lace, so at this worst possible moment, they are unable to earn even a pittance. I would like to collect money to buy thread. Once the obstacles are overcome, it can be shipped with the food."

The church was silent. People frowned in confusion. Finally the man from Green Bay said, "That's a noble goal. But it would be best if we focus on *essentials*."

Seraphine sat down abruptly, her cheeks burning. The meeting adjourned and noisy chatter filled the sanctuary. "I shouldn't have spoken."

"I disagree," Cecilie said pertly. "We should always speak up for those who can't."

Yes, Seraphine thought. But I shouldn't have spoken without thinking things through.

By the time they got home the men had finished milking. As Seraphine worked the cream separator with Cecilie, she thought about what she wanted to say. What she wanted to do.

"Mama," Cecilie said finally, "you have something on your mind."

"I do," Seraphine agreed. "I believe I know more about the plight of lacemakers than anyone else in Wisconsin."

Cecilie began stacking the small cones used to separate milk in thin layers. "I'm sure that's true, even if no one else knows that. You've never talked about your lace."

"Well, I want to help the lacemakers," Seraphine said. "It's time I start talking."

The next day, Seraphine found François alone in the barn. The cows were out to pasture. The barn smelled of musty hay. "I need your help."

He looked up from the harness he was oiling. "What can I do for you?"

She told him. His eyes grew wide. At one point he shook his head in disbelief. But he didn't interrupt. And when she finished, he nodded. "Of course."

"Thank you, François. This is something I can *do*."

THIRTY

"Here you go, miss." The taxi driver's tone suggested he'd spoken more than once.

"What?" Chloe jerked from the world described in the article she'd been reading, astonished to discover that they'd reached Heritage Hill. "Sorry." She fished out bills to cover the fare and a healthy tip. "Thanks so much."

It was no wonder she'd been lost in thought. What she'd learned about the German invasion of Belgium was shocking. The Belgian settlers must have been horrified by the ugly news. German forces had visited such agony upon the tiny country that the occupation was known as The Rape of Belgium. I'll read more later, Chloe promised herself.

Inside the Education Center she spotted Roelke at the lobby pay phone. She waved, and he held up one finger: *Be with you in a minute.* When his call ended, Chloe greeted him with a kiss. "I didn't mean to rush you. How did your prison visit go?"

"Pretty well." He smiled a satisfied smile. "With what I heard today, I think I can nail a man for murdering his wife. I just filled in Chief Naborski."

"That's *wonderful* news." She tucked her mittens and scarf into one coat sleeve. Guests were arriving for the St. Nicholas Day party, and the coat rack was already half full. A group of excited children hurried past, with two moms trailing behind.

Roelke smiled after them before turning back to Chloe. "How's your day been?"

She filled him in—what Sharon had said about Elise and Toni; what Jason had said too. "Last I saw, Jason was talking to a Green Bay cop."

Roelke looked even more pleased. "They'll liaise with the Door County guys."

"And gals."

"Of course. The point is, I think Antoinette Bertrand is going to have to pay for what she's done." He glanced at his watch. "I think the party has started."

Chloe smiled. "Let's go."

The party was getting underway in the lovely lounge overlooking the historic site. The museum director welcomed guests and asked for a moment of silence to remember Roy Galuska. Chloe reached for Roelke's hand as she heard Roy's voice in her mind: *You'll do, missy.* Thank you for so carefully restoring the Belgian Farm buildings, she said silently. I'll do the very best I can to meet your expectations.

Then the education specialist called young guests forward to hear the story of St. Nicholas, the kind bishop who'd devoted his life to helping those in need. "Belgian people know that he travels on his special day to leave little treats for good children. Did any of you put out shoes for him to fill with gifts, and offer hay or carrots for his horse?"

Young hands waved frantically.

"We have a special gift for everyone," the educator promised. "A *speculoos* cookie shaped like St. Nicholas himself." After dispensing the cookies, she herded the children away for crafts and games.

Mrs. Delcroix, head of the fundraising that made the Belgian Farm restoration possible, stepped to the microphone. "The importance of sharing is another aspect of St. Nicholas Day," she began. "Thanks to the many people who've shared their resources, buildings, artifacts, and knowledge, our dream of a Belgian Farm at Heritage Hill has come to life."

Chloe and Roelke watched from one side of the room as Mrs. Delcroix, resplendent in a ruby-red dress and pearls, acknowledged individually the cultural historians who'd preserved the history of Belgian immigrants, the architectural historians who'd documented the persistence of their structures, the families who'd donated buildings, the descendants who'd shared stories and photographs. Each received a small gift bag and a big round of applause.

"Finally, I'd like to acknowledge a newcomer as well." Mrs. Delcroix beckoned to Chloe.

"What?" Chloe hadn't expected recognition. Her contributions were minuscule compared to the years of work many people here had invested. Roelke gave her a gentle push, and she reluctantly joined the older woman.

"When we had a staff vacancy at a crucial stage in the process, Chloe Ellefson graciously stepped in to prepare a furnishings plan for the farmhouse. Miss Ellefson is not of Belgian descent, so we have a special gift for her."

Chloe accepted a small paper bag and a wrapped rectangular package from Mrs. Delcroix. She tore away the gift paper, removed the box lid, and grinned. *"Sabots!"* The reproduction wooden shoes were carved from a light wood—maybe poplar—and decorated with thin stripes of the red, gold, and black found in the Belgian flag.

Everyone applauded. "Thank you, Mrs. Delcroix." Chloe was so pleased she embraced the older woman. "And thanks to everyone who's been so helpful this week."

She rejoined Roelke. "You done good," he whispered.

Chloe toed off her shoes, nudged them under a chair, and tried on the *sabots*. In legacy of her hypothermia near miss she'd worn two pairs of wool socks that day. Thus padded, the clogs fit well. She was also delighted to find a six-inch *speculoos* in the small bag. It was, she discovered, a thin molded cookie, crunchy and well-spiced. "Ooh. So good. Try it."

Roelke did. "Reminds me of *springerle*." He was quite proud of his German heritage.

This is how museum work should be, Chloe thought. In some ways, her week in northeast Wisconsin had been simply awful. What she'd try to remember was the spirit of this gathering.

She also enjoyed introducing Roelke to some of the people she'd met—Mrs. Delcroix and a few of the Heritage Hill staff; Nadine La-motte and some of the elders who'd shared bits of their heritage at the gathering in Namur. Places like Heritage Hill and the Belgian Heritage Center were all about preserving traditions and honoring those who'd gone before. Chloe couldn't think of anyone more deserving of being remembered than the early Belgian immigrants—people like Jean-Paul and Seraphine Lejeune—who'd faced overwhelming trials and somehow managed to keep putting one *sabot* in front of the other.

Chloe and Roelke were helping themselves to cups of cranberry punch when Isaac Cuddy sidled into the room. Chloe waved him over. "Isaac manages the collection," she told Roelke. "He's been a great help."

He accepted Roelke's handshake and shrugged. "Not so much help, really. Chloe, is this your last day? I wish you could stay longer."

"Me too. But we'll stay in touch, okay?" Chloe almost felt guilty about leaving the nervous young man to his own devices—and the rebukes of his grandmother, Mrs. Delcroix. "It will take me a few weeks to finish the furnishings plan. I'll need a local contact."

That perked him up a bit. "That would be *really* great."

The education coordinator approached. "Sorry to interrupt. Isaac, did you have a chance to check for winter toys we can display during our Spirit of Christmas Past event?"

Isaac looked panicked. "Um … not yet."

Turning away to give them space, Chloe surveyed the room with a wave of emotion that was suddenly bittersweet. Roelke leaned close. "What's up?"

Trust him to sense her every mood. "These people have accomplished something very special," she said. "But I can't help noticing who isn't here." Sharon Bertrand and Jason Oberholtzer were, for all she knew, still speaking with the police. Toni Bertrand was, presumably, still in custody; Elise, as far as she knew, still in the hospital.

"I'm sorry, Chloe. I know you came hoping to forget some problems, not find new ones."

"I wish you could have met Roy Galuska. He was a crusty old soul, but totally dedicated to his work." She lifted the cup of punch in her hand. "To Roy. He knew and loved every log and brick and stone in the Belgian house and barn."

Roelke clinked his glass against hers.

As she sipped, something important popped into Chloe's brain. "Roy kept a binder of field notes in the Belgian barn. I wonder if anyone thought to retrieve it." Then another thought pinged in her gray matter. "And ... I wonder if he interviewed Hugh Lejeune."

"Hugh Lejeune?" Roelke looked puzzled. "What's the connection?"

"Roy talked to a lot of elderly Belgian farmers. Most were eager to tell their stories. If he interviewed Hugh, I'd like to make sure that Sharon and Hugh's son get copies. Let's go look, okay? It's not far, and I wanted to show you the buildings anyway."

They bundled up and started down the hill. Chloe slipped her hand into Roelke's. "I'm really glad you're here."

"Me too."

Twilight was descending, and wind jostled bare tree limbs. Chloe stopped in front of the house. "Isn't the two-toned brickwork pretty? It's not quite finished—that's why that brick pile is there— but the pattern will be exactly as it was on the original."

Roelke studied the house with the contemplative eye of someone who owned an old farm. "I like it."

"The barn is cool too. Let's go inside before we lose the light."

They entered the barn's north bay through a double door. Chloe hooked top and bottom open. Then she paused, letting her eyes adjust to the gloom.

Roelke came in behind her. "This is an excellent old barn."

"Isn't it? And look here." She stepped to one wall and ran her hand over a charred streak. "This scar is probably from the Great Fire. It burned here the same night as the Peshtigo Fire."

"Holy toboggans," Roelke said soberly.

Chloe retrieved Roy's big binder from the manger. "This is a real treasure." She put the notebook on a handy barrel, fished out her penlight, and began leafing through. No … no … no … She caught her breath. "Oh my God," she breathed, looking up at Roelke. "Look at this!" She pointed.

"'Interviews with Hugh Lejeune,'" he read aloud. "'Lejeune Farm East near Brussels and Namur, on Hickory Road, September 14th and September 21st, 1983.'"

Chloe took it from there. "'Mr. Lejeune met me on his property, which has not been farmed for some time. Buildings are falling into disrepair. Also present was—'"

Bang! Bang! They both jumped as the barn doors slammed closed. Chloe put one hand over her heart. "What on earth!"

"Probably just the wind," Roelke said. "Stay here. I'll check."

"Hook both pieces open," Chloe called after him. She'd become an extra-big fan of open doors, but evidently she had not done a good job.

Roelke disappeared outside. "Hey—" His exclamation ended abruptly. Too abruptly.

Then the doors slammed shut again.

Chloe's heartbeat zoomed to overdrive. Her skin dimpled with gooseflesh. "Roelke?" She waited for the door to open, for Roelke to burst back inside complaining about the wind and apologizing for scaring her.

The door stayed implacably closed and silent.

Part of her needed to race outside and find Roelke. The other part, the scared part, urged caution.

She took a step. Her foot landed on a chain once used to secure a cow in its stall. She nudged it aside with one new *sabot*.

What had Sharon said? *Sometimes when I'm facing a challenge I slip off my shoes and stand in Seraphine's* sabots. Chloe tried to channel the early Belgian women who'd faced everything life threw at them. She sucked in a deep breath, raised her chin, and marched toward the door.

She was reaching for the latch when it began to move, ever so slowly... as if someone was now trying to creep unheard into the barn.

Her courage fled. She did too, away from the door. She saw a corn knife hanging on the wall and grabbed it. Stumbling over the step into the barn's drive-through she almost fell, but managed to catch herself.

"Chlo-ee." The voice, an eerie falsetto, came from behind her. "There's nowhere to go."

Dammit. She cast frantically about for some haven. The south bay was a dead end. The hay piled on one corner of the drive-through floor was not enough to hide in.

But a wooden ladder led to the hayloft. Since her fingers had fused around the corn knife, she dropped the flashlight and began to climb.

Someone wearing a dark coat, with a wool cap pulled low, charged into the center bay with a pitchfork in one hand.

She scrambled up another rung. The ladder shook as he started after her. Please be strong enough, she begged the ladder. The wooden clogs were a godsend. Each rung caught in the hollow before the heel, giving her great traction. Her head cleared the loft.

A hand clamped around her ankle and yanked downward. Chloe kicked wildly. The intruder yelped, and she felt fingers slip from her leg. It sounded as if her pursuer fell down a rung or two. But before she could gain more height a fierce pain tore through her left leg.

"Ow!" Chloe lunged onto the loft floor. She dropped the corn knife and scrabbled for purchase with both hands. Then she rolled onto her back, intending to kick the ladder over. But when the ladder didn't move despite two kicks delivered with shuddering force, she realized it was attached to the wall.

The hand appeared, grasping the top rung. Male, she was almost sure of it. One more step up and he'd be on top of her.

Chloe raised her right knee and brought one wooden clog down on those fingers with every ounce of strength she had.

A shriek. An empty rung. A sickening thud from below.

She rolled onto hands and knees and crawled to the edge of the loft. In the shadows she made out her attacker, crumpled on the drive-through floor below. He'd fallen on his side, and it must have been one hell of a landing. But he slowly rolled onto his back and eased his legs and arms by turn, as if checking that each still worked.

Who *was* it down there? What had he done to Roelke? Unless Roelke was dead or unconscious, he would have taken the barn apart log by log by now.

Then the man's right hand curled around the stout pitchfork handle.

"Stop right there!" Chloe yelled, as if she had some power over him. "Do *not* move."

He bent one knee, pushed up on the other hand.

Chloe grabbed the corn knife. But—no way could she fight him off with that, no matter how sharp the blade. This guy was no doubt stronger than she was, and his weapon had a longer handle.

Then she spotted the double harpoon hay hauler Roy Galuska had pointed out, dangling over the drive-through floor. The rope controlling the hauler angled down to her side of the hay loft, anchored somewhere in the dark corners behind her.

Chloe shoved to her feet, swinging the corn knife in an arc—back, up, around, down. The blade didn't sever the rope so she slashed again, and again.

She heard the last strands pop. She heard the pulleys controlling the hay hauler whir as the rope whipped through. The hauler, with its two sharp down-pointing harpoons, dropped. Then she heard an unholy scream.

When she looked over again, the man was writhing. One of the harpoons had pierced his left shoulder.

Chloe's stomach soured. The pain she'd bundled away roared back, and she sat down hard on the loft floor. Her left calf was sticky with blood. Chloe knew she should make a bandage, rip up her shirt or something. But she had to find Roelke.

She crawled to the ladder, managed to get turned around, and started to descend. She looked over her shoulder to make sure Pitchfork Guy was still down, and whimpered every time her wounded leg had to bear her weight. But she made it.

She snatched the flashlight she'd dropped before approaching her attacker. Her shoulders slumped. *"Isaac?"*

Isaac Cuddy groaned in pain. "I need help!"

"Why? I was nice to you! *Why?*"

"I'm sorry, Chloe!" He began to blubber. "I didn't want to hurt you!"

A hot rage replaced the nausea. "Listen to me, you little prick," Chloe hissed. "If I find Roelke's dead body outside, I swear to God I will come back in here and finish the job."

She left him, limped back to the north door, and threw it open. Darkness had settled over the historic site. The St. Nicholas Day party's lights and laughter, just up the hill, seemed a hundred miles away. "Roelke?" All she heard was the wind.

She searched the ground near the door and spotted two lines where something had crushed the dead grasses. Drag marks? She followed them along the wall, around the corner, and—there. He lay unmoving.

"No-no-no-no-no." Chloe fell to her knees, gritting away the pain, and fumbled beneath his scarf for his carotid artery. Did he have a pulse? She didn't feel anything. Was that because he didn't have a pulse, or because her fingers were shaking? For the love of God, she'd taken lots of first-aid classes. She should know what to do.

"Roelke?" She gave up and put her hand against his cold cheek. "Please wake up. *Please*. You have to—"

"Chloe?" he mumbled.

Thank you, she thought, limp with relief. "Yes, it's me."

"Somebody clocked me." Roelke moved as if to rise. "I've got to—"

"Stay still."

"*Jesus*, my head hurts."

"You're going to be okay," she said, because he had to be. "I'm going for help."

THIRTY-ONE

ROELKE HATED HOSPITALS. HE especially hated being a hospital patient. And he *most* especially hated being a patient when Chloe was being treated somewhere else for God-knew-what injuries she'd sustained after he'd let some SOB get the jump on him. By the time she limped into his room that evening, Roelke had never been happier to see her.

She leaned over and kissed him softly. "Are you okay?"

"I've got a concussion, and one hell of a goose egg on the back of my skull. They're making me stay overnight for observation." He waved a hand in irritation. "But are *you* okay?"

She pulled a chair close and gingerly lowered herself. "Six stitches in the left calf and a tetanus shot. No permanent damage."

Thank God. "I told the cops what I know, but that's not much. What the hell happened? Who did this?"

Chloe exhaled slowly. "Isaac Cuddy. He must have heard us talking right before we left the party, and followed us down to the barn. After luring you outside, he went after me with a pitchfork."

That *bastard*. "He's in custody, right?" If not, Roelke thought, I am going after him myself. Right now.

Chloe put a hand over his. "He's in surgery, actually."

"Yeah?"

"Do you know what a double-harpoon hay hauler is? It lifts hay up into a barn loft?"

"Sure." He'd spent his teenage years helping out on the family farm.

"I sort of … dropped one on him."

Roelke took that in. "Holy toboggans."

"I climbed up to the loft, and he came after me, so I sliced the pulley rope with a corn knife. One harpoon caught him in the shoulder. I guess it did some real damage."

"Just what he deserved."

"I suppose." Chloe grimaced. "It's not something I'm proud of. But in the interest of full disclosure, I think I broke some of his fingers too. He was almost up the ladder and I stomped on them, really hard." She extended her good leg, displaying the wooden *sabot*.

Roelke reminded himself to never underestimate the woman he loved. "But why did he attack us?"

"Well, I have a theory." Chloe shifted as if trying to find a more comfortable position. "Remember what I started reading about Hugh Lejeune in the barn? I wanted to finish, so before they put me in the ambulance I grabbed Roy's notebook. The first time Roy interviewed Hugh, *Isaac* went with him. Hugh told this old family story about a treasure hidden on his farm."

Roelke was dubious. "Seriously?"

"Seriously. And although it's never been found, I think it was a piece of very old, very rare Belgian bobbin lace. Elise found some

341

leads about Seraphine, one of Sharon's ancestors, who made lace. It's a long story."

"And this involved Isaac … how?"

"I'll check the timing, but Elise had probably already talked with Isaac about the possibility of a valuable piece of lace turning up in Wisconsin. Hearing Hugh's tale after talking to Elise must have intrigued Isaac. When Roy went back the second time, Hugh told him that Isaac had called with a lot of questions about the treasure story. Roy was furious."

"How do you know?"

"He mentioned it in the field notes." She paused, clearly wanting to get it right, before quoting: "'Cuddy phoned Mr. Lejeune independently, was rude, will *not* be permitted to participate further. These old places are valuable for what they are, not for some monetary transaction!'"

"Well, hunh." Roelke rubbed his chin. "Where are these field notes now?"

"I gave the binder to the cops and explained that Isaac might have heard me mention Roy's notebook at the party, and was afraid I'd find notes linking him to Hugh Lejeune. If the whole story came to light, the piece of lace missing from the site's collection would become more suspicious."

Roelke remained unconvinced. All this for some old lace? But … it was possible, he had to admit. He'd been hanging around with Chloe long enough to know that antiques were no less alluring to some than diamonds or gold.

"I knew Roy had a problem with Isaac. Roy told me that Isaac didn't respect what we're all about." She twisted her mouth with regret. "Roy could be a curmudgeon, and Isaac was perpetually nervous. I assumed the two personalities didn't mix. But I should have asked Roy to explain."

"It's not your fault, Chloe."

She hitched her shoulders. "I'm just grateful that you're okay."

Roelke took her hand and concentrated on the warmth of her fingers. The hospital sounds—voices in the corridor, the occasional page, a squeaking wheel on an aide's cart—floated past. Finally Chloe said, "I think I'll spend the night here."

"No way. You need to get out of those clothes." He gestured toward her blood-stained jeans. "And you need a decent night's sleep."

"But I … " She hesitated, then nodded. "All right. I'll see you tomorrow. Early."

"Is that your definition of *early*, or mine?"

"Well … "

"Come whenever. I'll be waiting."

———

Chloe left the room reluctantly. She'd thought she knew how much Roelke McKenna meant to her. How much she loved him. But those eternal moments when she hadn't known if he was alive or dead had revealed something even greater. She never wanted to experience anything like that again.

She was passing the visitor lounge when someone called her name. "Chloe?"

"Mrs. Delcroix?" Chloe went to meet the older woman. "What are you doing here?"

"My grandson is still in surgery downstairs," Mrs. Delcroix said stiffly. "Are you willing to speak with me?"

"Of course." Chloe gestured toward a sofa.

Mrs. Delcroix perched on the edge and met Chloe's gaze without flinching. "I want to apologize for Isaac. I don't know everything, but I do know that he did something awful, and that you and your friend were both injured. I wish I could say I was shocked. But I'm not."

"I am," Chloe said honestly. "I never dreamed Isaac was capable of violence. He seemed shy. I was trying to help him gain some professional confidence. I thought he liked me."

"I don't doubt that he liked you." She pressed her lips together for a moment. "Chloe, when Isaac was in kindergarten he threw stones at a little girl who'd called him a name. He couldn't understand that his reaction was unacceptable. That was the beginning."

Chloe didn't know what to say.

"My daughter and her husband coddled him. Made excuses for his bad behavior. I thought Isaac just needed a firmer hand. But the boy seems to have been born with a big chip on his shoulder. He struggles in any social or professional situation. And when pushed, he blames everyone else for his inadequacies."

Isaac muttered in Chloe's memory: *People think I'm a screwup, even when whatever goes wrong isn't my fault.*

"Most of the time he muddles along." Mrs. Delcroix folded her hands in her lap. "But occasionally something seems to just—just snap. He lashes out. When caught, he freely admits what he's done, but he always has a list of excuses. What does one do with a child who is incapable of taking responsibility? Of working hard and learning from mistakes?"

"I honestly don't know," Chloe said helplessly.

"I encouraged Isaac into the history field. It's my passion, and I thought . . . well. Needless to say, I deeply regret urging him to apply for the registrar job at Heritage Hill."

"For whatever it's worth, I thought Isaac truly wanted a museum career." Had he conned her? Or had she seen glimpses of a true longing to fit in and do well?

"Perhaps. But he's gone way too far this time. His next stop will be a prison cell."

"I expect so." Chloe hesitated. "I'm sorry."

Mrs. Delcroix's eyes were bleak, but she didn't hesitate. "I am too. But I won't give up on him." She smoothed her skirt. "Now. Can I drive you back to Heritage Hill?"

"Thank you, but no. I can take a cab. That way you can stay here and wait for news."

"Isaac isn't going anywhere." Mrs. Delcroix stood and reached for her coat. "Come along, Chloe."

———

Heritage Hill's Education Center was locked and dark, but Mrs. Delcroix had a key. Chloe retrieved her shoes before climbing into Roelke's truck. She drove back to Belgian Acres slowly, thankful Isaac had hit her left leg instead of her right. And that the truck had an automatic transmission.

At the B&B she found Elise in the living room with an afghan and a cup of tea. "Hey!" Chloe said. "It's good to see you. Is Sharon around?"

"She went to bed already. I was hoping we could talk."

Chloe was exhausted. But this is important, she thought. "I'd like that."

"Want some tea? There's hot water." Elise got up and headed toward the kitchen. "How was the St. Nicholas party?" she called over her shoulder.

Where to begin? "Eventful." Chloe plopped into an easy chair. "I'll fill you in later."

Elise returned with a steaming cup and a coaster. "Fair enough." She settled back down. "Is your friend around? I understand I need to thank him for saving my life."

"I hope you can meet him tomorrow."

"Okay." Elise rearranged the afghan, then took a deep breath. "Chloe, I owe you a huge apology. As you know, there are some things going on that I didn't tell you about."

"Actually, you didn't just not tell me," Chloe observed as pleasantly as possible. "You lied to me. Several times."

Elise glanced away. "All I can say is I'm sorry."

Chloe felt her mild resentment fade. "I know you've had a horrible time. I heard about your husband."

Elise looked startled. "Geoffrey? You know he died on our honeymoon?"

"I do. I'm so sorry."

"I feel like I've been living in a nightmare," Elise said. "I tried throwing myself into my work, into the lace, but it wasn't nearly enough. And for the first time in my life, I started wondering who I was. Where I came from."

Chloe wrapped her fingers around the warm mug. I know the feeling, she thought. At least a little bit.

"I've always known I was adopted. I figured my birth mother had good reason to give me up, and I ended up in a wonderful family. But after my husband died, I started wondering. Maybe I was trying to fill a void. My parents got me in touch with the midwife they worked with. She gave me Sharon's name and contact information."

"But you didn't introduce yourself to Sharon."

"I didn't think I wanted to. I just wanted to meet her, see what kind of woman she was. My parents moved to the East Coast soon after the adoption, so there was no reason to think she'd suspect that I was her daughter."

"Is that why you hid your briefcase?"

Elise sighed. "When I found the page of Father Daems's letter you slipped under my door, and realized how careless I'd been with my files that night after the workshop, my instinctive response was to hide them." She rubbed her temples with her thumbs. "I just couldn't talk about it, even to a friend. I honestly believed that if I satisfied my curiosity, that would be that."

"But it didn't work out that way."

"No." Elise traced a knitted green zigzag with one finger. "Sharon's so nice! I started wondering what I'd missed out on. The fact that she gave me away suddenly felt hurtful. All these emotions came bubbling up and I didn't know what to do with them."

"That's why you got so distant?" This was starting to make sense. "Why you went off those mornings without explanation?"

Elise nodded. "I arrived earlier than I let on so I could drive around the Belgian settlements. But I got so overwhelmed that two days weren't enough. I needed to be by myself, to not have to talk to anyone. I kept trying to grasp the fact that the history here is actually my history. The surviving traditions are my traditions too."

Chloe thought about her own mother. If Marit knew she was adopted, had she been overwhelmed with wondering? Had she ever tried to find her own birth mother?

"And then there was the lace connection," Elise added. "Lace history is my passion, but it got all tangled up with family stuff. I started studying Belgian lace in particular when I learned about my biological heritage. I believe I was the first person to put the travel article and the priest's letter together. What are the odds that those snippets about an early Belgian immigrant lacemaker would lead to Sharon's family tree? To my own family tree?" She shook her head in wonder, or disbelief, or perhaps a measure of both. "I know this sounds weird, but... have you ever felt like someone who had died long ago was trying to send you a message?"

"Actually, I have," Chloe told her. "Maybe Seraphine wanted to bring you back to the homeplace. Maybe she wanted you to tell her story."

"That's a nice thought."

"Did you change your mind about telling Sharon who you were?"

"No. But I'm not sorry that it all came out. We've had a couple of really good talks."

"I'm glad."

"It doesn't take anything away from my real parents. The people who raised me."

"Of course not." Chloe hesitated. "It's just that—when you were growing up, didn't the not-knowing kind of... haunt you?"

"Not at all. Part of what knocked me for a loop after I got here was that all this new information hit me in a way I hadn't looked for, or expected."

"Oh."

"I know who I am, Chloe. A whole new layer has been added, and I've decided to see that as a gift. But it doesn't change *me*."

Elise's sense of self was admirable. Chloe chewed her lower lip pensively, wondering if she had as much grace. "Thank you for sharing."

Elise sat up straight. "Are we still friends?"

"Of course we're still friends." Chloe started over to hug her friend. But Elise pulled back. "Are you all right? You're limping!"

"Ah. Yes." Chloe sat back down.

By the time the tale was told, Elise's eyes were round with astonishment. "Isaac. I don't believe it."

"If I hadn't been there, I probably wouldn't, either."

"And he almost ... " Elise shuddered. "But you stopped him! I am in awe."

"I think it was the shoes." Chloe pointed at her new *sabots*. "Now, I'm off to bed. Thank you for talking with me." When she opened her arms to Elise this time, her friend hugged her back.

———

Chloe woke earlier than usual in the morning, but she came downstairs to find Sharon, Elise, and Jason Oberholtzer already sipping coffee in the living room. *Early* is relative on a dairy farm, she reminded herself, as well as in Roelke's world. Sharon's eyes looked red, but she had one affectionate arm around Jason's shoulders. Elise was leaning forward, clearly part of the conversation. Sharon won't be alone through the ugly mess of Toni's trial, Chloe thought. For that, she was truly thankful.

Sharon glanced up. "Chloe! Elise told us what happened to you at Heritage Hill! Are you—"

"I'm *fine*." Chloe headed for the coffeepot, trying not to limp. "I didn't mean to interrupt."

Jason got to his feet. "You didn't. I've got to get to work anyway." He held her gaze. "And ... thanks for your help yesterday, Chloe."

Sharon hugged him goodbye. As he left, a car came down the drive. "That's Deputy Knutson."

The deputy declined coffee but took a seat. "We're working closely with the Green Bay Police Department, and I thought you'd appreciate an update."

"Please." Chloe settled into a chair, mug in hand.

"According to the investigator who questioned him, Isaac Cuddy couldn't stop talking," Deputy Knutson said. "First, he admitted to stealing a piece of lace from Heritage Hill."

Chloe exchanged a disgusted glance with Elise. The "lost" World War I lace wasn't lost at all.

"He hadn't sold it already, had he?" Elise asked anxiously.

"No. It's in Evidence now." Deputy Knutson leaned forward, elbows on knees. "Ms. Ellefson, Cuddy also admitted to following you and Officer McKenna away from the party in hopes of finding Mr. Galuska's binder. He also admitted to letting himself into the ... " She paused, pulled a notebook from her pocket, flipped to the necessary page. "The Cotton House at Heritage Hill on Wednesday night. He thought it was empty at the time, but Mr. Galuska surprised him. They struggled. And Mr. Galuska ended up dead."

The terse summary was chilling. "Isaac easily could have killed Roelke too," Chloe said.

The deputy nodded. "The Green Bay cops found the brick Cuddy used to assault Officer McKenna at the scene."

"He hit Roelke with one of the old farmhouse bricks?" Dear God, Isaac Cuddy could have crushed Roelke's skull.

"And they've got the pitchfork he stabbed you with in evidence as well. But that's just the beginning." Deputy Knutson turned to Sharon. "Mrs. Bertrand, Isaac Cuddy was with Hugh Lejeune when he died."

Sharon blinked. "What?"

"It was Cuddy," Deputy Knutson repeated. "I know you wondered if your daughter was involved. She wasn't. She won't face murder charges."

"Oh." Sharon covered her mouth with her hands. "Of course that doesn't take away from what she did to Elise and Chloe, but still... I'm *so* glad."

"Cuddy returned to the property to investigate some old family story about hidden treasure." A note of skepticism crept into the deputy's voice. "As crazy as that sounds."

"That's just old family lore," Sharon said. "Hugh liked to tell that story, but I'm astonished Isaac took it seriously."

"Mr. Lejeune found Cuddy poking around, and he threatened to complain to Heritage Hill. When Mr. Lejeune had an asthma attack, Cuddy tried to coerce him into silence by grabbing the inhaler." The deputy's tone was hard. "He said he only intended to scare Mr. Lejeune. Obviously that's not what happened."

Chloe tried to purge from her mind the image of Isaac Cuddy watching an old man gasp for his final breath.

Elise looked stricken. "I told Isaac about the priest's letter that mentioned a lacemaker named Madame Lejeune who lived about thirty miles beyond *Aux Premiers Belges*," she said slowly. "I prattled on about what an amazing find a piece of her lace would be. He must have linked the priest's comment about a lacemaker named Lejeune, Hugh's story about a family treasure, and *my* comments about the value of old lace with known provenance. How stupid of me! I was just so excited it didn't occur to me to hold back."

"You can't blame yourself," Sharon said firmly.

Knutson nodded. "Anyway, when Mr. Lejeune died, Cuddy panicked and hid the body in the bake oven. It might not have been found for a long time if you hadn't gone looking, Ms. Ellefson."

"Glad to be of service," Chloe said weakly. "Did Isaac express any remorse for everything he's done?"

Deputy Knutson hesitated. "Evidently Mr. Cuddy readily confessed, but he had all kinds of excuses. He needed money to pay off student loans. He needed to find an antique of importance because no one took him seriously at work. That kind of thing."

Sometimes, Chloe thought, I can be a very poor judge of character.

After the deputy left, a pensive silence settled over the room. Chloe was glad Toni and Isaac were in custody and would answer for their actions. But it was a sad situation all around.

"Lace," Sharon said finally. "It breaks my heart to think that something so lovely could lead to tragedy." She looked at Elise. "Do you really think there might be a piece of Seraphine's lace hidden away somewhere?"

"It's possible," Elise said. "Let's lay it all out. In my preliminary research, the first thing I stumbled over was an article about Door County written in 1919 by a travel writer known as 'The Lady Rambler.' I can't quote it exactly—"

"I've got it." Chloe pulled her notebook from her totebag. "I found it in your briefcase after you disappeared," she added when Elise raised her eyebrows. "Here." She read aloud. "'An elderly lacemaker lives on a farm in Southern Door County. The next day I endeavored to find the artistic soul who had created the lace, yet endured the worst privations and trials of pioneer life. After persisting through a rainstorm, find her I did, and it was well worth the effort. She told me stories of her girlhood at a convent in Bruges, learning to make lace.'"

"That was Seraphine?" Sharon asked incredulously. "But she was born in Wallonia."

"The travel writer didn't give a name," Elise said. "And I have no idea how Seraphine ended up at a lace school in Bruges. But later on I found a priest's letter."

Chloe had copied that reference as well. "'I was astonished to find that not only had the gaunt, weary young wife scrubbed the table well, she had adorned it with a cloth trimmed with a strip of delicate lace, the likes of which I have not seen since coming to this place. She had, she told me, learned to make lace at a convent in Bruges. She gifted me the cloth, knowing it would serve well among all of the Walloon settlements as I travel to celebrate mass. I thanked Madame Lejeune profusely and left filled with gratitude for her generous nature.'"

"Oh my," Sharon said.

Chloe caught her breath as she remembered another piece of the puzzle. "I haven't had a chance to tell either of you about this, but a woman named Renilde Claes gave me—"

"Renilde?" Sharon interrupted. "We're distant cousins. We're both descendants of Seraphine and Jean-Paul, but Renilde's always lived in Sturgeon Bay, so I never got to know her well."

"Well, she came to the Heritage Center and gave me a piece of lace that belonged to her grandmother, who was Seraphine's daughter Cecilie," Chloe said. "It's in my room." She fetched the bag holding the strip of lace. "Elise, doesn't this match the piece Linda Gauthier Martin brought to your workshop at Heritage Hill?"

Elise studied the lace with awe. "Absolutely, yes. Linda said it belonged to her great-grandmother, Dominique Anselme Gauthier." She looked up. "Sharon, it seems almost certain that your ancestor Seraphine was a very talented lacemaker."

"I couldn't be more thrilled, but ..." Sharon lifted her hands, palms up. "As you know, I remember my grandmother speaking of a piece of beautiful lace, but I've never seen it. Maybe it ended up in some other branch of the family, like Renilde's piece. Maybe my grandmother was even referring to Renilde's piece."

Elise sighed. "I did fantasize about finding something here. I tried to imagine where Seraphine or somebody might have put it for safekeeping."

"Elise," Chloe said, "I also saw some biographical notes you'd compiled. Why did you scribble 'summer kitchen' in the margin?"

Elise looked chagrined. "I knew from census records that Seraphine had married Etienne. The summer kitchen would have been built *after* they married. I was just trying to think about places where nineteenth-century women spent the most time, that's all. Wishful thinking."

Chloe remembered the sense of feminine refuge lingering in the summer kitchen. And it was on Etienne's farm that the tale of hidden "treasure" had come down through the years.

"Sharon," Chloe said slowly, "when was it that Richard scheduled the workers to replace the bake oven shed walls?"

"Why, they started yesterday. You would have noticed if you'd gotten home before dark. Why do you ask?"

"Because," Chloe said, "I think Elise might be right."

———

The masons Hugh's son Richard had hired to rebuild the shed walls were already at work when the three women arrived at Lejeune Farm East. The roof had been removed, exposing the bake oven to the sunshine for the first time in a century. And most of the three freestanding walls were already dismantled. Chloe, who'd dreaded confronting what had become a cell for her and Elise, was relieved. All bad juju had been banished.

Sharon introduced herself to the man in charge. "You've gotten a lot done."

"Snow's moving in tonight." The mason, a big man with ruddy cheeks and scarred hands, shrugged philosophically. "Got to finish before then."

Elise was almost quivering with anticipation. "When you were taking down the walls, did you happen to find anything unusual?"

The man looked stymied. "Unusual?"

Chloe was already peering down between knee-high walls. "A package?" she said hopefully. "A box of some kind, buried in the rubble between the walls?"

The mason shook his head. "Nope. Haven't found anything except fill stones." His two companions looked equally perplexed.

"Mind if we help clear out the last of it?" Chloe reached for the closest stone and tossed it aside. It wouldn't take long.

The men quickly jumped to help. When the work was done, the big man shook his head. "That's it. Nothing there."

Chloe walked around the foundation, staring into the empty spaces, willing herself to see something that wasn't there. "I really thought we were on to something," she told Elise.

Elise lifted and dropped her palms in gesture of futility. "Obviously, we weren't."

"I don't know what you were looking for," the mason added. "The south wall was repaired some time back, but that's all I can tell you."

"Thank you," Sharon said. "I'm sorry we interrupted."

THIRTY-TWO

NOVEMBER 1914

FRANÇOIS WAITED UNTIL MOST of the family had gone to a neighbor's farm for an anniversary party to bring his friend the stonemason out to Lejeune Farm East. Seraphine took them to the summer kitchen and showed them the pale triangular stone marking the spot where she'd hidden her bridal lace so many years ago.

"I'll go through the inner wall," the mason said. He was an elderly man but clearly still capable. "That'll hide the patch."

Seraphine and François waited outside. "Thank you," Seraphine said. "I'm sure Etienne knows I hid the lace, but I don't want him to know I went to such lengths to keep it from him." She glanced away. "It probably seems silly, but I couldn't bear to have him sell it for liquor."

François regarded her. "Why do you stay with my father? Jules and Pierre would welcome you back to Lejeune Farm West."

In all these years, he'd never asked such a question. "Etienne is my husband, François."

"Not a very good husband."

"It has not always been easy." Seraphine watched the barn cat creep across the lawn, stalking a chipmunk. "But François, I know why your father drinks. So often he cries in the night. He dreams of his time in the war. He dreams of your mother."

"I lost her too," François said, low and fierce.

"Try to forgive your father," Seraphine said gently. "Everyone grieves in their own fashion."

Some time later the mason climbed from the shed with the sugar tin in his hands. It was covered with rust, and Seraphine almost lost her nerve. "I'm afraid to look inside." If the lace had disintegrated, her idea for helping Belgian lacemakers had disintegrated with it.

"We've come this far," François said firmly. He took the can and, with some effort, pried off the lid.

Seraphine looked inside. The waxed paper was brittle and the cloth wrapping looked dingy. Holding her breath, she slowly unwrapped her bridal lace. Seeing it was like contemplating a dear old friend. It had not survived unscathed. Yellow spots dotted the cream-colored thread. It could never be sold, now. But it would do.

François's eyebrows shot up, and his mouth opened with surprise. "You made that?"

"I did." Seraphine assured him. "A very long time ago." She felt a bit of the old pride and happiness stir inside.

By the time the family returned, the mason was gone and Seraphine was working in the summer kitchen. She stepped outside to wave as four generations of Lejeunes clambered from the buggy and farm wagon. Etienne lifted a hand in greeting before going into the barn, but François's youngest grandson raced over to greet her. He was a lively, mischievous boy, always in motion. One of his socks had slipped down, but he didn't seem to mind. "We had cake!" he announced. "You should have come. You didn't get to have fun!"

Seraphine laughed, caught his face between her hands, and kissed his forehead. "I had my own fun," she said. "I've been looking for long-lost treasure."

———

Two weeks later, Pierre drove Seraphine to Green Bay. "This is worse than I remember," Seraphine observed as traffic on Washington Street halted once again. She wrinkled her nose against the stink of exhaust and industrial coal fires. The din of factory whistles and car horns was unpleasant.

"There are almost as many motorcars as buggies these days, and the roads weren't designed for that," Pierre said. "The bicycles weaving through traffic don't help, either. But don't worry, Mama. I'll get you there on time." He tossed her a grin. "Are you nervous?"

Seraphine smoothed her new dress and adjusted her hat. "Yes. But I am also determined."

Pierre managed to reach the appropriate building without mishap. When a secretary ushered them into the office, Belgian Consul Michael Heynen came around his desk to meet them. He was well-dressed and sported an extravagant mustache. He smiled politely as he waved them into two leather chairs, but he looked harried. "What I can I do for you today?"

Pierre gave Seraphine a tiny encouraging nod. She sat straight and lifted her chin. "Before the war began, Belgium was the lace center of the world, and the United States purchased more Belgian lace than any other country. Today I am here to speak for the lacemakers. Most were quite poor before the war began. Now that the borders are closed, fifty thousand women have no way to get the thread they need, and no way to sell their work."

He tapped his fingers on the desk. "The German invasion has brought misery and destitution to Belgium, but I assure you, Mrs. Lejeune, that relief efforts are already underway."

"Yes, of course." Seraphine nodded. "But a special effort must be made to help the lacemakers."

Mr. Heynen crossed his arms. "What exactly are you asking me to do?"

"I would like your permission to raise funds that will be designated for the relief of lacemakers." Seraphine leaned forward, desperate to help him understand. "My sister in Bruges—"

"You're aware that Bruges is occupied?"

"Of course." Seraphine took a deep breath. "Before the war she was active in a group called *Amies de la Dentelle*. Because of her letters, I can speak quite knowledgeably about the situation."

"And how do you expect to raise these funds? The Belgian people in northeast Wisconsin are already working to get food and clothes into Belgium. I can't imagine that talking about a luxury item will spark much enthusiasm."

"I will speak to them as a lacemaker." She unwrapped her lace and placed it on his desk. She had done her best to clean what was left of her bridal lace by soaking it, then bleaching it in the sun. The spots were less obvious, and the lace was still crisp and beautiful. "This is an example of my work."

The consul leaned forward to study the lace, and his eyebrows rose in surprise. Pierre smiled.

"I am willing to speak at churches and to civic groups—any groups, not just Belgians. I'll take this lace as an example of what can be done. If people have the means, they may commission a piece of lace. If they are not able to do that, any money donated can purchase thread to send. With your help we might save not only the women and their families, but an art that has always made Belgium proud."

Mr. Heynen was staring at the wall now, his expression distant. Oh Octavie, Seraphine thought, I did my best.

Finally the consul nodded. "Mrs. Lejeune, I don't yet know enough about the situation to make any promises. But if you're willing to raise awareness and funds, I will see what can be done."

―――――

Dear Octavie,

The reports we read in the newspaper are terrifying. Please write and tell me where you are, and if you are safe. I am trying to carry on your good work of helping the lacemakers by raising funds.

Your loving sister,
Seraphine

THIRTY-THREE

AFTER THE DISAPPOINTING TRIP to the summer kitchen, Chloe dropped Elise and Sharon off at Belgian Acres. She was eager to spring Roelke from the hospital, but something about the lace enigma niggled at her brain. While the truck idled she closed her eyes, trying to think back over everything she'd discovered or sensed about Seraphine. Had she missed a clue?

… *Yes.* She had.

She jumped out of the truck and ran after the others. "Sharon! I need to use your phone."

Five minutes later Jason Oberholtzer came on the line. "I'm really sorry to bother you at work," Chloe began, "but I'm hoping you can do me a favor."

———

When Chloe got to Roelke's hospital room, he was dressed and prowling about like a caged cheetah. Her eyebrows rose. "Has the doctor cleared—"

"Half an hour ago."

Good thing she'd taken his truck, or he'd probably be long gone. "That's the best news I've heard all week." She kissed him lightly. "Let's get the heck out of Dodge."

"I thought you might get here a little earlier."

"I got up early, but—geez, Roelke. A lot has happened since I left last night."

As they went down to the lobby she told him what Mrs. Delcroix and Deputy Knutson had said about Isaac, and what she and Elise and Sharon had *not* discovered. "So I really thought we were at a dead end on the lace quest. But then I remembered something the travel writer said in her article: 'I've been so charmed by Door County's residents, and so stirred by the beautiful landscape, that I do indeed plan to return.' And I thought, did she? And if she did, did she visit Seraphine?"

"How could you ever know?"

"I asked Jason Oberholtzer, who works at the university archives, to see if Lady Rambler shows up in their card catalog. If you give me a minute, I'll call him and find out."

At the lobby payphone she fished a couple of coins from her wallet and made the call. "Any luck?" she asked when Jason came on the line.

"Oh, yeah." She could almost hear him grinning over the phone. "Lady Rambler did return to Door County, and she published a second article in 1919. We had a copy in the vertical files. Most of it is florid descriptions of the scenery, but let me read you one bit." He did.

"Oh," Chloe said. "Not what I expected, but I appreciate your help." She hung up.

"Not what you hoped to hear?" Roelke asked sympathetically.

She was still absorbing what she'd learned. "No, but interesting nonetheless. Do you mind if we detour back to Belgian Acres before going home? I want to tell Sharon in person. Besides, since you saved her life, Elise is eager to meet you."

"Fine by me," Roelke said. "Let's see this thing through."

Clouds were gathering by the time they reached the farm, but Roelke received a warm welcome and heartfelt thanks from Sharon and Elise. "I got lucky, that's all," he said. He was clearly uncomfortable with the praise, and Chloe loved him for it.

"I've got some news," she announced. "The Lady Rambler did return to Door County, she did visit Seraphine, and she did write about it. Jason will get us copies of the article, but here's the thing." They were sitting in the living room, and she looked from Sharon to Elise. "Remember the treasure she referred to in the first article?"

"Of course!" Elise was able to quote verbatim: "'And as a final gift, she showed me the project she is working on now. It is a treasure indeed, gentle reader.'"

"Well, the project Seraphine was working on was not a piece of lace. Lace wasn't even mentioned." Chloe looked at Sharon. "The treasure was your chapel."

"My ... chapel?" Sharon echoed blankly.

"The writer said that Seraphine had created at Lejeune Farm West the most beautiful chapel she'd seen. We know Seraphine married Etienne, but at some point she must have moved back here. Your chapel is old, right?"

"Oh, yes." Sharon nodded. "I never knew when it was built, just that it was after the Great Fire. To the best of my knowledge there never was a chapel built at Hugh's place."

Chloe flipped her long braid over her shoulder. "The writer also said Seraphine had created it in gratitude."

"Gratitude for what?" Sharon asked.

"She didn't explain." Chloe shrugged in frustration, wishing she had more to share. "Maybe the end of the war."

They all thought about that. Then Roelke said, "If I may, I'd love to see the chapel." He seemed to remember that Sharon's chapel was a sensitive topic, for he added, "Only if that's all right."

"Of course," Sharon said. "Let's go."

The four of them traipsed out to the little chapel. As Sharon unlocked the door, Chloe braced for the grief she'd sensed here before. It didn't come. "Sharon," she murmured, as Elise and Roelke took their first look around, "did you come here to grieve the daughter you gave up?"

"All the time." Sharon put a hand on Chloe's arm. "Everywhere else, my daughter's adoption didn't exist. My husband acted like it had never happened, and I carried on. This became my place to come and pray for her, even though it broke my heart."

Elise had found the simple but lovely certificate. "'Baby Bertrand, loved and lost August 16, 1955,'" she read softly.

"I'll have to update that," Sharon said. "My prayers have been answered."

Roelke was peering at the World War I soldier's photograph. "'Our beloved Herman, The Battle of Château-Thierry, 1918.'"

"My Uncle Herman," Sharon said. "My grandparents never spoke of him. Those were different times."

"I can imagine your grandmother coming here to remember him," Elise said.

But Sharon shook her head. "No. I was the one who hung Herman's photograph here, long after she died. My grandmother kept his bedroom exactly as it had been when he left. Sometimes she disappeared in there for hours, and we knew not to disturb her."

Chloe gazed at the photo of Herman, forever young. "Everyone grieves in their own way."

"She had a strong faith," Sharon said, "so perhaps she didn't want anything in the chapel to remind her of the war, and her loss. I hope she found a bit of peace here." She contemplated the small room. "I've kept this chapel locked for years, but I think it's time to respect tradition and keep the door open. Maybe others will find peace here too."

"Is the altar original, do you know?" Chloe asked. She liked thinking about Seraphine here, making decisions, arranging statuary and candles and memorials just so.

"As far as I know." Sharon walked to the altar, flush against the far wall. "I really should move it out and clean back there, and check for any structural damage. A neighbor had a woodchuck somehow get into their chapel, and it made quite a mess."

Chloe put her hand on the altar and sensed … something. Something good, but still distinct from the general sense of devotion that remained now that Sharon's grief had abated. She couldn't define it, but she needed to do something about it. "Let's move the altar out a bit while we're here," she suggested. "Roelke can help." Her fingers were still tender from her attempt to claw through the oven shed's stone wall.

He threw her a look: *Is this really the time?*

She held his gaze: *Please help me out.*

"Oh, that's not necessary," Sharon was saying. "Jason will help me sometime."

"Let's get it now," Roelke said cheerfully. "You'll feel better knowing."

The women carefully moved everything from the altar. Roelke wedged his fingers into the crack by the wall and pulled one end of the altar out a few inches. He got a better grip and slid it a few inches more. Then he frowned. "There's something back here."

Something tingled beneath Chloe's ribs.

With one more pull, the gap was large enough for Roelke to get through. He ducked, then straightened again. When he sidled back out he held an old red-and-white tin breadbox, dented and faded.

Sharon planted hands on hips. "What on earth is that?"

"I don't know, but it belongs to you." Roelke handed it over.

Sharon sat down, lifted the lid, and removed something flat wrapped in brown paper. She removed it and held what looked like a white pillowcase out to Elise.

Elise took it and drew out what was inside. Chloe craned her neck to see. "What? What is it?"

Elise's mouth made an O. Her eyes grew round too. "Oh, my, God," she said in a tremulous voice. "I don't believe it."

THIRTY-FOUR

MAY 1918

"So when the war began, people on both sides of the Atlantic knew the lacemakers needed assistance," Seraphine explained to the group of Episcopalian women in Sturgeon Bay. "At first we made no headway, even with Consul Heynen's assistance. Then Mr. Herbert Hoover established the Commission for Relief in Belgium, and in 1915 he was able to negotiate an agreement that permitted aid workers to bring thread into Belgium, and to take an equivalent weight in lace out of the country. As the war drags on, we continue to provide this vital assistance."

She warmed to her subject. Her eyesight was too poor to read notes, but she'd given similar talks so many times in the past three and a half years that they weren't needed.

"With your support," she concluded twenty minutes later, "we will continue to save lives." The ladies applauded.

A thin woman in the first row raised her hand. "But does the thread actually reach the women who need it most?"

Seraphine nodded. "Oh, yes. Relief workers in Belgium ensure that supplies reach even the remote lace centers." She answered a few more questions before inviting attendees to come forward and see the samples arranged on a dark tablecloth.

Cecilie, who was taking donations, smiled as the women exclaimed with pleasure over the lace. When Seraphine had begun speaking about lacemakers, she'd had only her own bridal lace as testimony. Then a wealthy donor in Green Bay received the table runner she'd commissioned, and promptly loaned it to help the cause. The beautiful cloth, made by orphaned girls at a convent in West Flanders, always commanded attention. The *Amies de la Dentelle* had also sent samples of various styles.

Pierre, who'd driven her to Sturgeon Bay, sidled through the crowd. "I think you should sit down, Mama."

"I'll rest in the car." She knew she'd be tired later, but speaking on behalf of Belgium's lacemakers always buoyed her. For the first time since Jean-Paul's death she felt a calling, a sense of purpose. The travels helped stave off her fear for Octavie and her dismay as anti-immigrant fever spread through Wisconsin. She'd gained new friends and reconnected with old ones. Dominique Anselme, who'd survived the loss of two children to cholera in Seraphine's cabin, brought the lace-edged handkerchief she'd won at the first Kermiss to one of the programs. "You helped me more than you will ever know," Dominique had said, pressing five dollars into Seraphine's hand. "It's a privilege to help you now."

Now the ladies' group president joined them. "Mrs. Lejeune? You have a telephone call."

Seraphine and Pierre exchanged an alarmed glance. "I'll take it," Pierre said. Seraphine had never become comfortable with telephones.

The woman led them to an office and gestured to the phone on the wall. "Hello?" Pierre shouted. "François? Is that you?" He listened, nodded. "All right. We'll be home as soon as we can."

Seraphine's spirits plunged. "Is it Herman?" When America had finally entered the war last month, Pierre's sweet grandson had promptly enlisted.

"No, Mama," Pierre said. "It's Etienne."

———

"I'm sorry," Etienne whispered. His breath rattled in his chest.

"Shh," Seraphine murmured. "It's all right." She wiped his flushed face with a damp cloth.

"It was … my idea … to come here." His good hand twitched on the quilt. "I didn't know … how it would be."

"We all did our best. And our children and grandchildren are flourishing." She took his hand in hers and kissed his forehead, feeling the fever on his scarred skin.

"Jean-Paul would be … so proud."

Her throat ached with regret. "Rest now, Etienne. I'll sit with you." His eyes drifted closed.

Etienne was eighty-four. He'd survived immigration and the cholera epidemic, the Civil War and the Great Fire, and too much alcohol. Seraphine didn't think he could survive pneumonia.

And she was right. François summoned the priest at sundown, and Etienne died that night.

The room was crowded with his family. Some of the girls started to cry. "Rest in peace," Seraphine whispered, dry-eyed. She had a sudden memory of Etienne and Emelie dancing on the deck of their ship one starlit night, soon after leaving Antwerp. Perhaps they were dancing again now, somewhere beyond the stars. She could not grieve.

They laid Etienne out in his gray Sunday suit. The next day, a steady procession of friends and neighbors streamed to the farm with pies and roasted chickens. When they offered condolences, she thanked them graciously. She and Etienne had been … partners. Survivors. But her real husband had died long ago.

When she couldn't bear the crush any longer she slipped outside, just as a shiny black touring car puttered up the driveway and parked on the lawn. Seraphine didn't recognize Mr. Heynen until he was close enough to take her hand. "Mrs. Lejeune. I'm so sorry for your loss."

Seraphine was astonished that the Belgian consul had made time for such a call. "It was kind of you to come."

"You have done so much for Belgium and the Belgian community these past few years … I wanted to pay my respects."

She smiled. She and Mr. Heynen had come a long way since that first impatient meeting when the war began. "Thank you, sir."

His face remained somber. "And … I'm sorry, Mrs. Lejeune, but I've been unable to find any trace of your sister."

That news was harder to accept than Etienne's death. Seraphine hadn't heard from Octavie since the Germans occupied Bruges in 1914.

"We should not assume the worst. The Germans control the post office and railway stations, so communication is difficult. With over a million refugees, record keeping is almost impossible. However … " Mr. Heynen adjusted his spectacles. "The situation in Belgium remains grim. For an elderly person … "

Seraphine knew what he was trying to say. "I'm grateful that you made inquiries on my behalf, Mr. Heynen."

After the consul left, Seraphine walked farther from the house. The fields beyond the barns would soon sprout green with wheat and corn and oats. What was springtime like in a country that had been under siege for so long?

Sometime later Jules and Pierre found her there. "Come inside, Mama," Jules said. "People are asking for you."

"I don't want to be rude to the guests," she agreed, and took his arm. "But boys, when the funeral is over…I want to go back to my own home."

———

MAY 1919

The harsh *aa-oo-gah* of Pierre's automobile car sounded from outside. "Time to go, Mama," Cecilie said, as she pinned a red, gold, and black rosette on Seraphine's blouse.

"I'm not sure why I need to go," Seraphine said. Her children were excited about the trip to Green Bay, but she'd have been happy to stay home. Since she'd moved back to Lejeune Farm West a year earlier, she'd felt more peaceful than she had for many years. Jules was an old bachelor, still working the land he'd worked with his father. Pierre's family had grown. They'd added on to the brick house built after the Great Fire. Jean-Paul's farm was prospering, and the house was full of children's voices. It was everything he'd dreamed of.

And blessedly, the war was ending. On November 11, 1918, an armistice had halted fighting on land, sea, and air between Germany—their last opponent—and the Allied nations. Peace negotiations were underway in France, and the Belgian government had just announced their intent to endorse the proposed treaty.

Seraphine was grateful that she'd had the opportunity to help during the war. But her knees often ached now, and she walked with a cane. The family was grieving the death of Pierre's grandson Herman, who'd been killed in battle in July 1918. More quietly, Seraphine grieved the loss of her sister. A year after Consul Heynen stopped looking, she'd still had no word of or from Octavie.

Cecilie gave her a stern look. "Mama, it's a huge honor to have a delegation from Belgium come all the way to Wisconsin! And you're a special guest. We are going."

Pierre and Jules sat in the front of the motorcar. Seraphine allowed herself to be squeezed in the back with Pierre's wife and Cecilie. They hadn't driven far before her worst fears were realized. Traffic clogged the narrow roads. Horses whinnied as motorcar drivers tried to squeeze past. Everyone in Door County was, it seemed, traveling to Green Bay.

"This is so exciting!" Cecilie exclaimed four hours later as they finally inched into the city. "I've never seen such a crowd, or so many Belgian flags!"

"All the factories and businesses are closing early," Pierre said. "This is a special day."

Ever since the consul learned that a delegation was coming to thank Belgian-Americans in northeast Wisconsin for their wartime support, a planning committee had worked feverishly to provide the warmest welcome possible. Fortunately, Seraphine's status as a special guest earned her family reserved seats for speeches and festivities.

After the delegation arrived at the train station, a parade complete with military escorts and marching bands led them to the city's Whitney Park. Seraphine's throat filled when the bands began the Belgian national anthem. She remembered hearing it played on a clarinet at their first brave American Kermiss. Who could have imagined a crowd of thirty thousand crushed into the city streets? When the music died the crowd roared, *"Vive les Belges! Vive les Belges!"*

If only all of the first settlers could have lived to see this, Seraphine thought. She was glad she'd come.

That evening Seraphine and her children attended a banquet at the Beaumont Hotel. After a fine meal the head of the delegation, Baron Moncheur, gave a stirring speech.

Then Consul Heynen approached the podium. "Before we adjourn after this marvelous day, I want to introduce two other special guests. Mrs. Brand Whitlock and Mrs. Etienne Lejeune, please come forward."

"What?" Seraphine gasped. "No."

"I'll go with you." Jules offered his arm. Seraphine reluctantly let herself be escorted from the table.

Mrs. Whitlock introduced herself as the wife of the American envoy to Belgium, and an active supporter of the *Amies de la Dentelle*, the Friends of Lace. "We began working to improve conditions for laceworkers, and to preserve the art itself, before the war began. When Belgium was invaded, we knew our efforts were in peril. Working with our allies—especially the United States—we were able to get desperately needed funds to thousands of homeless and destitute lacemakers. This program preserved our lace industry and raised morale during the brutal occupation. One of the largest streams of support came from northeast Wisconsin—thanks entirely, I understand, to the efforts of Mrs. Lejeune."

A wave of applause rose from the hall. "That's for you, Mama!" Jules murmured proudly.

Mrs. Whitlock held up a lace panel. "Mrs. Lejeune, in thanks for all your work to relieve suffering and preserve Belgium's proud lace heritage, I have the pleasure of presenting this piece of Valenciennes lace. The design includes an American Eagle and Belgium's coat of arms."

"Thank you." Seraphine couldn't find more words. She was pleased but overwhelmed by the gift.

"But we have another surprise for Mrs. Lejeune as well." Mrs. Whitlock made a beckoning motion. Heads turned. A low, questioning murmur rippled through the room as someone slowly walked through the tables toward the front.

Squinting, Seraphine's forehead furrowed as she made out the black and white of a habit. The nun was stooped with age. But as she drew close, her face glowed with joy.

Seraphine tightened her grip on her son's arm. Her heart skittered in her chest. Time seemed to stop as the two women gazed at each other. The room grew silent.

Finally Seraphine quavered, "Octavie?"

"My dear sister," Octavie said, and opened her arms.

———

After the tears and chatter, after the drive back to Lejeune Farm West, Octavie and Seraphine finally had a quiet moment. They walked slowly over the lawn, arm in arm. Tulips bloomed in flower beds and robins searched for worms. "So," Octavie said. "This is your American farm. It's lovelier than I imagined."

"It didn't always look like this," Seraphine reminded her. "I hated this place when Jean-Paul and I arrived. We had to battle the trees, and then after the fire … there were hardly any trees, and I hated this place even more."

"But you don't today?"

"No. I don't think I fully realized it until Etienne died, but it helps to know that Jean-Paul's dream has come true. I imagine him smiling down. Sometimes, when I walk over the lawn, I can almost feel him beside me. He and I fought to establish a farm on this very land … and somehow, we did." Seraphine adjusted her wide-brimmed hat. "That's been a comfort. Especially during these years when I didn't know if you were dead or alive."

"I'm sorry my letters didn't get through," Octavie said. "I did try. But conditions in Belgium … " She didn't finish the thought.

There would be time for stories later, but Seraphine did have one question. "Couldn't you have let me know you were coming? The delegation was communicating with the consul."

"The lace committee began planning this trip months ago. I asked if they would carry a letter for me. Instead they invited me to come along, at the committee's expense. But they suggested I keep my participation a secret." She smiled. "I think they were afraid I wouldn't live long enough to get here. But here I am."

"Here you are." Still dazed, Seraphine reached out and squeezed her twin's hand. "I can't imagine what you endured over there."

"And I can't imagine what you've endured over here. Yet here *you* are. What is your secret?"

"Gracious! Nothing clever." Seraphine considered. "So often all I could do was keep putting one foot in front of the other." She paused again, watching Pierre's wife snipping herbs in the kitchen garden. "Octavie, after Jean-Paul died, I lost my way. It was more than the crushing grief of missing him. He'd believed in me. I didn't know who I was anymore. I had my heart so set on making lace. I thought it was my calling."

Octavie tipped her head thoughtfully. "But you did, in the end, help thousands of other women ply their bobbins and survive the atrocities of war."

"Yes, but … "

"Because of you, Belgian lace flourished instead of becoming a casualty of the conflict. In that way, Seraphine, you *are* a lacemaker. Perhaps that was God's plan all along."

Seraphine thought about that, and about the people she'd gifted with bits of her lace since arriving in Wisconsin: Father Daems, Dominique Anselme, Jean-Paul, Emelie, Cecilie. Perhaps, she thought, I did do something good after all.

She savored the miracle of this moment, feeling as she had as a girl when Octavie helped her understand something. "I've missed you so terribly, Octavie. How long can you be with us?"

"I have permission to stay, so … as long as you'll have me."

Seraphine felt tears sting her eyes. "You will always have a home here."

"Thank you," Octavie said. "Remember what Tante Lejeune used to say? As long as we were together, everything would be well."

Seraphine struggled to retain her composure. Then a new idea made her smile. "I'm going to build a chapel in gratitude of your arrival. I'll put my new lace runner on the altar."

"I brought the wedding lace you gave me that night in the convent." Octavie was smiling too. "Perhaps we could add it as a border."

"Some of mine is left as well. I'll stitch the pieces back together." Seraphine wiped her eyes. "Oh, Octavie. I could not have imagined this day."

Octavie handed her a clean handkerchief. "I always believed we'd see each other again."

"I *wanted* to believe." Another tear trickled ran down Seraphine's cheek. "But my faith wavered."

"That's all right." Octavie's gentle smile seemed unchanged since their childhood. "I had faith enough for both of us."

THIRTY-FIVE

In the chapel, Roelke felt Chloe almost twitching with excitement. "What is it?" she demanded. He couldn't see, either.

"This is *war* lace!" Elise held up the panel. "See the American eagle? Belgium's coat of arms? And here's the date, 1917."

Roelke knew nothing about lace, but even he could tell this was something special. "Holy toboggans."

"It's gorgeous." Sharon tipped her head. "But that bit at the bottom doesn't seem to match." She pointed to one section of the edging that showed a few faint stains.

"It does look like a repair was made," Elise agreed. "But Sharon, although I don't know who made the war lace, this edging is the same pattern we've identified this week, made by Seraphine! To discover an unknown piece of World War I lace, trimmed with lace made by a known maker ... it's an unbelievable discovery."

"Why do you suppose it got hidden away in a bread box?" Roelke asked.

"I'm guessing Seraphine combined these two pieces of lace for the altar when she had the chapel built," Sharon mused. "After she died, my grandmother probably removed the runner because the war motifs reminded her of Herman. It's probably been in that bread box ever since."

"I'm not an appraiser," Elise cautioned, "but this is worth a *lot* of money."

Sharon looked horrified. "I would never sell it!"

"I don't mean on the open market," Elise added hastily. "But how about if a museum purchased it?"

"Oh." Sharon considered. "I'll give that some thought. Actually, I need to give a lot of things a lot of thought." She smiled. "Thought and prayer."

———

They said their goodbyes back at the house. "Please come again," Sharon said, and Roelke could tell she meant it. Elise hugged him too.

Chloe started for the left side of his truck. "You know I'm driving home, right?"

"I'm not an invalid," he began, but that only earned him a laser-eyed look. "All *right*. You may drive home."

They left the farm behind. "We'll have to come back and get my car when the police are finished with it," Chloe said, "but I'm glad we can make the drive today together."

"I am too." He put a hand on her leg, savoring the connection. "I haven't even had a chance to ask about the family thing. How are you doing?"

She braked to avoid a raccoon waddling across the road. "I'm still sorting things out. I had an interesting talk with Elise, who grew up just fine with the fact that she didn't know her birth parents."

"Hunh."

"Kari isn't bothered by Birgitta's news, and she doesn't want to ask my mom about it."

"And you feel differently?"

"I respect Kari's viewpoint. I haven't decided about telling my mom. But Roelke, *I* need to know. All of a sudden I'm not who I'd always believed myself to be. Kari and maybe even my mom made the choices that were right for them. *My* choice is to try and find out who my mom's birth parents were."

Roelke had no idea where to go from there. "Um … have any ideas about how to go about that?"

"Not yet." She made a turn. "I may not succeed, but I have to try."

"I'll help in any way I can," he said, and her smile was all the thanks he needed.

"Why don't you take a nap?" she suggested.

He wasn't a nap kind of guy, but truth was, he'd barely slept the night before. Nurses had come in every ten minutes to check vitals or something. He'd spent the long hours thinking about what had happened at the barn. He'd let the little SOB take him by surprise, and Roelke knew it would be a long time before he got over that. Like, never.

He'd also thought about Kent Bobolik. And Ginny Bobolik. And Father Dan Grinke. And he'd thought more about Chloe. What she'd come to mean to him. What would, and would not, be fair to her.

"Okay," he said now. "If you're sure you don't need company."

"I'll put in a tape." She rattled through the case on the front seat, holding up options one at a time. "Blues, no … Jazz, *definitely* no … Ah." She extricated a cassette and popped it into the player. "This'll do it."

Little Feat's *Let it Roll* rang from the speakers. I do love this woman, Roelke thought, before drifting off.

When he woke they were driving through the Kettle Moraine State Forest, maybe half an hour from home. He rubbed his eyes and sat up straight. "I'd like to make a stop in Eagle."

"Roelke, I am not stopping at the police department! You need to be taking care of yourself, not going to work."

"I don't want to stop at the PD. I want to stop at St. Theresa church."

She threw him a questioning look. He wasn't ready to say more. "Okay," she conceded. Ten minutes later she pulled into the parking lot.

"I may be a little while," he warned her. "Keep the engine running so you don't get cold."

The church was empty so he walked over to the parish house. The priest was in his office, and he looked up with a questioning expression when Roelke appeared in the doorway.

"Father Dan," Roelke said, "can we talk?" He explained what he wanted.

They walked across the lawn in silence. The sanctuary was cool and dim. Roelke hadn't stepped inside a confessional for years. He half expected himself to bolt. But he did not.

———

Snow began falling while Chloe waited. She watched big, soft flakes drift past the windshield and wondered why Roelke wanted to stop here. Maybe he wanted to update the priest about the Bobolik case.

Or was this more of the "work stuff" that had been bothering him? It was frustrating to not know.

I love the guy, she thought. I should be able to help him through the tough times. But if Roelke didn't want to talk to her, what could she do?

The answer came. "I could propose to him," she whispered. If their different approaches to religious faith were truly upsetting him, he might say no. But they loved each other. She wanted to get married, and she was pretty sure he did too. Offering Roelke that commitment was the only way she could think of to demonstrate that she'd *always* be there for him, no matter what. I'm going to do it, she vowed, and smiled.

Half an hour later, Roelke emerged from the church. He didn't meet her gaze when he climbed silently back into the cab. Okay, I'm not going to do it right this minute, she clarified silently, and put the truck in drive. But soon.

Fifteen minutes later she parked in their very own driveway. "Home at last."

"It's good to be home with you," Roelke said, and finally smiled in a way that made her heart happy.

Inside she made a fuss over feline Olympia, carried laundry to the basement, and pulled some potato soup from the freezer. Back upstairs she found Roelke making tea. "Can we just sit for a bit?" he asked.

"That would be quite lovely." She settled on the living room sofa, and he brought the steaming mugs. Chloe tucked her feet up and snuggled against him. She could feel his warmth through his flannel shirt, and hear his heartbeat. Tea was steeping and Olympia was purring and snowflakes floated past the windows. My life, Chloe thought, is darn near perfect.

After a while, though, something almost indiscernible poked through. Roelke was … different. She could feel it in his muscles, hear it in his breathing. She straightened so she could look him in the eye. "Something's going on. You seem … I don't know … peaceful, sort of."

He drew in a long breath. "I just went to confession."

That had not occurred to her.

"For the first time in a very long time," Roelke added. "And I'm glad I did."

She wasn't sure where this was going. "That's good."

"There's something I need to tell you. I should have done it a while ago, but … well, something happened that I didn't know how to handle."

Chloe nestled her head back on his shoulder, hoping it might make this easier for him.

"I did something I'm profoundly ashamed of, Chloe. But I believed—and still believe—I had no other choice."

"What did you do?"

"I'm not going to tell you. Not because I want to keep it secret, but because hearing it would create a burden for you. I'm trying to protect you. You have to trust me on that."

It took a moment to take that in, to absorb what he was trying to say. When she did, the answer was easy. "I do trust you, Roelke. I won't ask you to say more. So … that's what you talked to the priest about?"

"Yes." He tightened his arm around her. "I haven't known how to live with myself. I discovered I'm not the cop I thought I was. Not the man I thought I was. Not the partner you deserve."

There was a stillness in him, acceptance, but now she sensed pain too. "All I know for sure, Roelke, is that you are the man for me."

"I'll always regret what I had to do, but I've decided not to let that take over. I don't want to waste any more time with regrets. I've got to live with this new me."

"That sounds wise."

"Does it bother you that I talked with Father Dan? I know the whole religion thing is sort of problematic."

"Hold on." She disengaged herself. "I'll be right back." She found her totebag on a kitchen chair, rummaged inside, and returned to the sofa. "Remember I told you about visiting the shrine where the Virgin Mary visited a young Belgian woman? I got you a present in their gift shop." She pressed it into his hand.

Roelke gazed at the small medal.

"It represents St. Michael," she explained, in case he didn't know. "He is, I was told, the patron saint of law enforcement officers."

"Yes, he is." Roelke's voice was husky. "There's a prayer my friend Rick used to say. 'Holy Michael, the Archangel, defend us in battle. Be our safeguard against all wickedness.'" He finally met her gaze. "Thank you, Chloe. I'll carry it with me."

"I hoped you would." If St. Michael wanted to defend Roelke from danger, that was fine with her.

Roelke seemed so pleased with the gift that she wondered if now might be the time to propose after all. Before she could decide, he stood. "I have a gift for you as well."

"You do?"

Instead of fetching something, Roelke pulled Chloe to her feet. Then he got down on one knee.

Chloe felt her eyes go wide.

"Ingrid Chloe Ellefson, my gift is my heart. Will you marry me?"

Somehow she ended up on her knees too. "Yes. Yes! Of course I will marry you."

"Are you sure?"

She had to laugh. "Absolutely."

He kissed her, and hugged her, and kissed her again. "I don't have a ring. I figured you'd want to help pick it out."

Chloe wiped her cheeks. "That would be wonderful."

"And ... " He hesitated. "I don't know where we'll get married. Who will marry us. I'm trying to believe we can work all that out."

"You just keep on believing," Chloe said firmly. "And if you have doubts, well ... " She cupped his face in her hands. "I have faith enough for both of us."

*1. The Massart family farmhouse, near Rosiere, Wisconsin,
prior to its relocation and restoration.*

2. Massart House (and glimpse of barn), restored at Heritage Hill.

University of Wisconsin-Green Bay Archives, WI.BelgAmrCol.0147b.bib

3. *Massart family summer kitchen, near Rosiere,*
prior to its relocation and restoration.

Kathleen Ernst

4. *View into the oven in the Massart farm summer kitchen*
after restoration at Heritage Hill.

Scott Meeker

5. *The author at the back opening into the bake oven shed at the Massart summer kitchen.*

Heritage Hill Historical Park, R9907 a & b.
Photo by Scott Meeker.

6. *Wooden shoes with decorative carving.*

7. Skirt.

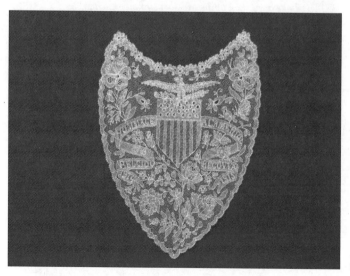

8. Lille bobbin lace in the shape of the American Allie shield, worked by Belgians to show appreciation for American support during WWI. It reads, "Hommage-Belciou-1914 A L'Ameriqu-Reconna-1915."

Heritage Hill State Historical Park, 5680.
Photo by Scott Meeker

Tribute to America, Belgium Remembers, 1914-1915.
From the collection of The Lace Museum, #2013-0412-001

9. *Valenciennes-style bobbin lace made by Belgian lacemakers to express appreciation to the Americans for their help during World War I. The American Eagle is flanked by the coats-of-arms of Belgium and the municipality of Ruysselede in West Flanders. Top: "AAN DE VEREENIGDE STATEN" (to the United States). Bottom: "1914 Hulde En Dank 1915" (Honor and Thank You).*

10. *An example of Duchesse de Bruges bobbin lace trim, circa mid-nineteenth century.*

Cliché des Amies de la Dentelle

Commission for Relief in Belgium records, Envelope AAAA, Hoover Institution Archives. Photograph produced by the Friends of Lace.

11. Lacemaker working in front of her ruined home, Belgium, World War I.

ACKNOWLEDGMENTS

Several years ago I met Beverly Wolov, lace historian and photographer, at an annual convention celebrating the traditional mystery called Malice Domestic. I couldn't have written about Belgian lace without her help. I'm also grateful to Karen Thompson, Lace Collection volunteer advocate at the Smithsonian Institution's National Museum of American History, for her tour and assistance. To learn more about the Smithsonian's collection of World War I lace, see http://americanhistory.si.edu/collections/object-groups/world-war-one-laces.

It is no small thing to write about a culture that is not my own, so I am also particularly indebted to Sandy Orsted, Treasurer of the Namur Belgian Heritage Foundation, and to historian Barb Chisholm for welcoming me and sharing their knowledge.

Warm thanks to the staff and volunteers at Heritage Hill State Historical Park, especially Liz Jolly, former Visitor Experience Coordinator; Nick Backhaus, Restoration/Maintenance Manager; and Erin Comer, Educator. Thanks also to Debbie Ashmann, Fundraising & Events Manager for the Heritage Hill Foundation. Their assistance was invaluable.

I am indebted to James K. Hayward, former Restoration Manager at Heritage Hill for sharing his knowledge about restoring the Belgian Farm. Thanks also to Alan Pape, Former Restoration Chief at Old World Wisconsin and preservation editor for *Log Home Guide* magazine; Louise Pfotenhauer, Collections Manager at the Neville Public Museum of Brown County; and Sergeant/Detective Gwen Bruckner, now of the Town of Brookfield Police Department.

For assistance with photographs, thanks to Deb Anderson, Coordinator, Archives and Area Research Center, UW Green Bay; Sarah Patton, Public Services Archivist Hoover Institution Library

& Archives, Stanford University; Jennifer Strobel, Museum Technician, Division of Home and Community Life, Smithsonian Institution National Museum of American History; and Kim Davis, The Lace Museum.

I'm grateful to my agent, Fiona Kenshole, and Sarah Binns of Transatlantic Literary. Thanks to Terri Bischoff, Amy Glaser, Nicole Nugent, and the Midnight Ink team; to Laurie Rosengren; and to Katie Mead and Robert Alexander, and Write On, Door County, for providing space to write.

Thanks to my parents and sisters for their ongoing encouragement, and to my husband and partner Scott Meeker for sharing the adventure. And finally, heartfelt thanks to all the readers who want to know what's next.

Geri Gerold © Kathleen Ernst

ABOUT THE AUTHOR

Kathleen Ernst is an award-winning author, educator, and social historian. She has published thirty-five novels and two nonfiction books. Her books for young readers include the Caroline Abbott series and *Gunpowder and Teacakes: My Journey with Felicity* for American Girl. Honors for her children's mysteries include Edgar and Agatha Award nominations. Kathleen worked as an interpreter and as curator of interpretation and collections at Old World Wisconsin, and her time at the historic site served as inspiration for the Chloe Ellefson mysteries. *The Heirloom Murders* won the Anne Powers Fiction Book Award from the Council for Wisconsin Writers, and *The Light Keeper's Legacy* won the Lovey Award for Best Traditional Mystery from Love Is Murder. Ernst served as project director/scriptwriter for several instructional television series, one of which earned her an Emmy Award. She lives in Middleton, Wisconsin. For more information, visit her online at https://www.kathleenernst.com.